THE MANX DOSSIER

THE GATHERING STORM

ALAN L. WEINSTEIN

This is a work of fiction. Names, characters, places, and incidents are products of the author's imagination or are used fictitiously and are not to be construed as real. Any resemblance to actual events, locations, organizations, or persons, living or dead, is entirely coincidental.

World Castle Publishing, LLC
Pensacola, Florida

Hardback ISBN: 9798891265240
Paperback ISBN: 9798891265257
eBook ISBN: 9798891265264
Second Edition World Castle Publishing, LLC, February 23, 2026
http://www.worldcastlepublishing.com
Prior edition ISBN: 0-595-13652-4

Licensing Notes

Cover: Cover Designs by Karen

Dedicated to:

Toby and Stephanie...whose inestimable love, patience, and support were directly responsible for the conception, construction, and completion of "The Manx Dossier."

Marlys Howard...for her unconditional friendship and for her insightful commentary on the human condition.

Dick Renckly...for always stopping by...and for caring as deeply as he did.

Jim Mathews...an everyday hero who, after his courageous and valiant battle against impossible odds, now stands with the Spartans of Thermopylae.

Epigraph

"The only courage that matters is the kind that gets you from one moment to the next." —Mignon McLaughlin

CHAPTER 1
DRUIDSVILLE

R. Treavor Mackenzie was put together like a kid's caricatured cat: round, short-limbed body attached to rounder head, seemingly without the benefit of neck; whiskered halfway between anarchist and satire; desperately in need of a haircut—a shaggy haystack of unruly, mud-clotted hair streamed like a straw-colored rat's nest out from underneath his faded El Alamein campaign hat; bulbous nose ruddy from a torrid love affair with Guinness Stout; hairy nostrils perennially inquisitive; bushy eyebrows perpetually arched in amazement at the human condition, but never more so than today.

Bedrizzled and bedraggled in sopping field-research khakis, Mackenzie squinted through raindrops on the lenses of Zeiss rubber-armored binoculars. The spectacle was about to begin.

Baldy is at it again.

Intermittent showers played absolute havoc with Mackenzie's rain-soaked arthritic knees on this eleventh morning of observation. Squishy socks had him feisty to the point of feral. His ample stomach puddled through a trough into which his girth fit tongue-in-groove. This morning, Mackenzie found a tick in his matted, full-face beard. Too long overdue for a bath, yes, with the ripeness and rot that comes with damnably damp field living, but personal hygiene took a back seat to the bonkers boyo out there.

Curtain going up!

The object of his rapt attention: the bald man at Stonehenge, on Salisbury Plain, Wiltshire. On Morning Four, Mackenzie christened the weirdo: "Mr. Pate." By Morning Six, Mackenzie knew for a surety that Mr. Pate was more than just a little crackers; the nutball was completely 'round the bend.

Mackenzie's doctoral thesis plowed brave new ground in geopolitical sociology: Stonehenge—the cynosure where power gathered and where, through interpretation of heavenly wonders, power lanced out to...and radiated through...the select few capable of first harnessing raw knowledge, then refining it, defining it and using it...thanks to their innate affinity for celestial mechanics.

Mackenzie scheduled one field trip to Stonehenge, more as a sop to duty than out of deep personal interest. But then Mr. Pate materialized one acid-rain morning, like a quirky jack springing out of a garish box, and the sociologist/PhD-to-be knew he'd latched onto a world-class kook. Boredom's back was broken, courtesy of Mr. Pate's incredibly varied floor shows.

Quite the schizoid star, our mate...this Mr. Pate.

Act I persona was Incan ruling class, praying to Inti; next, a Teton Sioux warrior, rising on tiptoe to the scherzo of boom-box amplified, eagle-bone-whistle music, the haunting notes of which were whisked away immediately by keening wind; then Mayan, worshipping Kinich Ahau; followed by Aztec high priest paying homage to Tonatiuh...not to mention ancient Egyptian, Sumerian and Persian.

Mackenzie peered out from behind an obelisk brutalized by centuries of inclement weather and present-day vandals. Today, Mr. Pate was a Mandan Indian, the chief's costume dead-on accurate, right down to handprints on clothing representing enemies killed in hand-to-hand combat.

Oh, this guy is so very good...deliciously good.

Mackenzie carefully focused his 50-300 Nikkor zoom. Four frames away from the roll's end, Mr. Pate drove a large stick into the ground while bellowing mightily from well-practiced lungs.

A real bravura performance!

Mackenzie blinked through dark-morning mist, carefully shooting the buffalo skull mounted atop an ornately carved pole.

Damn thing's freshly skinned and still bloody!

Then, zooming out to take in Mr. Pate.

Too late!

A flash of freak-show sorcery magnified by a zoom lens stabbed lancing brightness through Mackenzie's good eye. He rubbed his face, cursing as Mr. Pate vanished behind a blossoming curtain of rolling, gray-white ground smoke.

The son of a bitch actually waved!

Then Mackenzie stood alone as far as his zoom could see.

Whirl left, whirl right; ain't no Mr. Pate in sight!

Carefully rewinding now—very slowly, to prevent static-electricity marks. If the photos couldn't be shoehorned into his thesis, Mackenzie would sell them to *The Sun* or *The Star* or *The Daily Mirror*. London's tabloids were always slavering for offbeat tales, and any one of them...or all of them if he were shrewd enough...would pay handsomely.

CHAPTER 2
BOOMTOWN

Thanksgiving not being an Israeli holiday was only one reason why Avi was stamping frigid tingles out of his toes at O'Hare International Airport during this four-day traveler's nightmare. Twenty other reasons included the fact that he had eight separate, virtually impenetrable IDs and spoke 12 languages—all fluently... his best being American, which he managed without even the slightest inflection of accent.

Everything about Avi was off-the-rack medium, which made him a difficult quarry in a surging crowd and therefore an ideal *agent provocateur* for covert West Bank activity, particularly Crowd Ops. Softening in the middle from too much fast-food saturated fat and not enough isometrics, Avi walked atilt thanks to a steel pin in his femur, courtesy of the Six-Day War, and because the better part of his formative years were spent dodging the oncoming jabs of kibbutz bullies before unleashing a powerhouse left hook coming out of nowhere to inflict tremendous psychological and physical damage on unsuspecting adversaries. Through eyes the color of Caribbean shoal water, which contrasted sharply to skin burned otter brown after a lifetime of unscreened sun, Avi peered out critically and world-wise from under a broadly protruding simian brow

Underdressed in an unlined London Fog raincoat, he shivered bitterly, gritting his teeth against the pain in his thigh while hunkering further down behind a hot-air vent. Frenetic activity continued unabated on the tarmac under his unauthorized, off-limits observation post. Bundled figures blinked in the teeth of glacial wind threatening to ice up watering eyes.

This Turkey Day, Avi was Jonathan Marshall Stoddard, special liaison to the Governor's Task Force on Airport Security. The phone number on his card led to a telecommunications substation that routed calls, via TelSat, to the fourth-level basement of the Israeli Embassy's Department 43—Disinformation. But that number had never been used on Avi's behalf, so adroit was he at palavering his way out of law-enforcement challenges.

Avi's body temperature was inching up, thanks to an against-regulations gulp of schnapps and blue banter with Miriam, his personal generator of eternal youth. Carnal brainwork involving that May-December merger kept him from freezing solid to metal railings while surveilling Service Apron 119 and environs.

When in each other's hedonistic company, they communicated in Body Braille...her incredible anatomy forming a fiercely powerful electromagnet to his questing, iron hands. While apart, they ached mightily and addressed each other cryptically, keeping themselves just inside the foul line of Federal Communications Commission rules and regs.

He was Oh-India-Oh (OIO), she said, because of his manly virility, standing as it did like a sturdy cedar of Lebanon flanked by the duality of spherical potency; she was 99, which paid homage to implanted, full-breasted femininity sloping inward to the concavity of a hard, flat belly rippling with washboard abdominals—the trademark of a rated bodybuilder.

Six miles away, in an apartment never warmer than 68 degrees—because heat makes you lazy—sultry, long-haired, ravishingly gorgeous Miss Tel Aviv, 1989; second runner-up, 1990 Miss Israel competition bounced frenetically to a hard-rock, high-impact aerobics program, gasping prurient responses into her constantly shifting headset.

Chrome-black hair, the consistency of spider's silk, was pinned up in a tight French braid. Her lacquer-smooth skin was drumhead taut. Agate eyes narrowed with gulped-air exertion. A confessed endorphin junkie, Miriam gripped a 7.5-pound weight in each hand. The rewarding high she craved came only from an advanced killer-aerobics program modified to include the best of savate and black-belt taekwondo.

Pelvic-thrust gyrations agitated air molecules to microwave intensity, steaming up the apartment's windows. Avi's taste ran heavily to bare midriffs and Day-Glo colors, and so Miriam would greet him eagerly in black-leather bikini panties and a fluorescent pink, skin-tight, crop-top that Avi swore melted his earwax.

When not physically under the blankets, Oh-India-Oh and 99 operated enthusiastically under moderately deep cover. Gulf War wind-down saw antiterrorist postures relaxing worldwide, while Israel maintained round-the-clock coverage at international facilities, ever alert for terrorism directed against institutions through which Jews might pass in large numbers. Being in the country solely in an advisory capacity, and with only the tacit approval of the U.S. government, meant that work had to be done with utmost delicacy: State had been lobbying for their removal since the handshake agreement was made...with the National Security Council and the Central Intelligence Agency blocking eviction so far.

"Ninety-nine, I want you S-U-A," he rasped, now walking his beat buoyantly and liquor-warm.

"Sweaty upon arrival," she crackled back. "Yes, my darling Oh-I-Oh."

But Mr. Pate had other ideas.

The red-tint flash of a 747's ventral rotating beacon on a hard-hatted head caught Avi's eye momentarily, but chatter with Miriam took precedence over the baggage handler who was having trouble with the pedals of his propane-powered tractor, there in the shadow of TransPac Air Flight 117, the Empress of Diamond Head.

Once every 11 weeks, TransPac Air supplemented its freight-hauler revenues with money collected from a very lucrative Chicago-to-Honolulu charter. This load's "geese," dressed for the most part in polyester/rayon sports clothes accessorized by Kmart, were strapped in tight...eagerly awaiting the first leg of New Horizon's Oahu Dream Escape Package.

The great whale of an airplane was loaded to maximum takeoff weight with fuel, baggage, and 447 economy-class passengers. Because it was not a regularly scheduled, high-profile airline, TransPac reaped another bounteous dividend: the economic advantage of lower security...reduced, but still legally within the parameters lobbied for by transport/charter companies and rubber-stamped by an overworked Federal Aviation Administration.

Mr. Pate was well-versed in the Achilles' heel of TransPac's loosely woven security because Mr. Pate had been watching for a very long time.

It can be done, it will be done.
OH, YOU ARE THE EAGLE, YOU ARE THE ONE.
For if this task were easily done...
TELL ME PLEASE, WOULD IT BE FUN?
Wigs change me so much faster than dye.
YOU'RE SOMEONE ELSE IN THE BLINK OF AN EYE!

The maintenance shed's lock was easily picked by this slightly overweight man with the surgical gloves. Safe in its damp, cavernous shadows, the pot-bellied driver, who today called himself the Eagle, spun a fist-size socket wrench like a master mechanic. He swung away the top of a dummy propane fuel tank on the back of his gasoline-powered tractor and slid out two shapeless, heavy-vinyl masses. A sharp tug on each valise's handle inflated both packages plump as they hissed up like Mae Wests.

The first case contained a large portable stereo, pop-riveted to the bottom of the valise to prevent shifting. The second vinyl suitcase was lined with scrap steel to give it just the right heft. Preparations complete, the Eagle backed out carefully; it simply would not do to take a single risk now. The tractor idled roughly as he refastened the lock. Then he wheeled away briskly for the short ride past the catering trucks; moments later, he was hitched up to a string of empty baggage carts.

After hoisting his considerable bulk aboard his tractor, he hunched over the steering wheel, cursed the cold, drove upfield, and waited....

Forty-five seconds, right on cue;

THIS IS OH SO EASY TO DO.

...then he danced on the tractor's pedals and swung back downfield in time to first take up echelon position and then speeding up to get closer...now parallel to...a tractor heading for TransPac's grossed-to-the-max Empress of Diamond Head, warming up for its rendezvous with the beautiful sun.

Careful!

A very energetic wave now and...

"Yo! Late for departure," the Eagle yelled, waving his left arm up and down in broad strokes while jerking his head at the two bags on the seat beside him, jouncing to the cadence of cracks on tarmac.

"Say what?!" the other driver yelled, yanking off his ear protectors.

"Late baggage!"

"Get fucked!" the other driver spat disgustedly. "I ain't got time for that shit." Then his eyes narrowed. "They been through goddamned security?"

"Whadda you think I am, a fucking Heidi?!" the Eagle screamed, wiping splashed slush off his face. "Look, their cab blew an oil gasket coming in. Lucky to get here at all. Wouldn't have if a bus hadn't happened by."

The Eagle awkwardly dragged one bag across his lap and held it up between the racing tractors, where it swayed like a hypnotic pendulum.

"See? Security seals, bro." The Eagle kept hammering. "Look, just like regulations. You got eyes. C'mon! I'm off duty as of six minutes ago. *Slow the fuck down!"*

"Shit! Goddamn!"

"Back off on the gas, Leadfoot. This ain't fucking Indy. Don't stop. Just slow down, fer Chrissakes," the Eagle hollered. "We'll pony-express it."

"Asshole fucking airline!" the other driver raged. "Goddamn it, I hate it when it's people!" He slowed his baggage train as the Eagle handed over first one, then the second case... after which he slowed while pretending to peel away on a new heading.

So much yet remains to do.

NOW YOU MUST SEE THIS THING THROUGH.

Satisfied that both bags were riding the belt up into the airliner's cavernous cargo hold, the Eagle swung around the back of the airplane, shielded from the terminal and the random sweep of Avi's binoculars. Standing on the top of his tractor and mimicking a maintenance crewman snugging down an access panel under a fuel tank, the Eagle reached up and lovingly stroked the bottom of the wing while quietly whispering goodbye.

Circumspectly tooling off again, looking like another chilled-to-the-bone pinion in the great machinery of air-service industry, the Eagle edged his tractor carefully between two out-of-service fuel trucks, shut down, and pocketed the key for disposal later. Circuitously and very carefully, making triply sure he was not observed and not being followed, the Eagle reclaimed his windowless, black Ford cargo van from employee parking. After wolfishly gobbling a snack pack of Sunshine Hydrox cookies, he navigated carefully out of the parking lot.

It would not do to go home today. Home will be a hellish inferno, the ground zero where TransPac Flight 117 was scheduled to terminate moments after takeoff.

But wait just a moment...

YOU ALMOST FORGOT.

To leave a memento...

WHERE "X" MARKS THE SPOT.

Travel plans hastily reorganized, the Eagle reversed direction and carefully headed back the way he came. By maintaining a road speed only three miles over a most generous limit, he would arrive just in time to play pitch-and-toss.

A crackle-wrapped "Oh-I-Oh," usually followed by hot-and-dirty talk, was punctuated instead with thunderous bomb blast exploding as jarring static overload from the radio's small speaker.

Miriam?!

Rumbling rolled in from over the active runway's threshold. Steiner 7x50 autofocus binoculars instantly jammed up tight to Avi's eyes brought a painful corona of pulsating spots. *Clear, dammit!* Rapid scan and...there...an ugly yellowish-white fireball, too small and low to be the sun, now turning orange, then greasy red...birthing an airborne smear of oil smoke out from which corkscrewed a blackened, split fuselage folding up as if hinged in the middle, dark dots of falling bodies, many of them on fire like grisly shooting stars, then a scatter of shredded wings...a spreading meteor shower of component parts...all of which moments before had been ascending Boeing 747.

Sheet fire licked low cumulus at the far limit of his vision, then went black and smoky as the catastrophic wreck of a ruptured airliner plunged in glowing streamers toward unyielding ground 200 feet below.

"Miriam? Miriam?!" The rolling boom of an overhead thunderclap now fading out under pounding aerobic beat. *"Miriam! Miriam!"* Avi loud in her headphones.

The disaster's shock wave shattered plate-glass windows on both sides of the street. Miriam's chest heaved unevenly, breath catching awkwardly, aerobic rhythm a limping stagger as she tried to comprehend splinters of glass sprouting like painful cactus needles from her muscular chest, midriff, and thighs.

Shocked, still in superheated air, fear-frozen by heat and an unearthly ringing in her ears, Miriam watched shifting curtains of flaming aviation fuel ignite the roof of the brownstone across the street. Curling sheets of volatile candescence drifted toward smashed bay windows, a horrifically surreal aurora marching inexorably forward against the mottled backdrop of gray-black mackerel sky.

Eerie silence prevailed momentarily, pierced by rising, tea-kettle whistles. The brickwork facade of Miriam's apartment exploded violently in her face, imploding under the punch of a massive four-wheel landing gear. The scorched assembly whipsawed past, scything steel tubing, amputating her left arm. Tires aboil in oily fire, trailed stenchy smoke while plummeting through her tiny living room on their way to crush innocents below.

Miriam retched on the stink of burning Jet-A fuel and hydraulic fluid. Smoldering seat cushions fluttered down like twirling petals of death. Staggering backward, she was knocked flat by the lower half of a human body. The stunning impact spurred urgent scrabbling. She backstroked desperately on the floor, blood spraying from the mincemeat stump.

"Avi!"

The floor lurched twice, like an elevator car snapping its cables, then collapsed completely. Miriam, enmeshed in mangled, scorched metal, crashed through the lower apartments. Twisted and pummeled like a Cabbage Patch Kid in a cyclone, she dangled twisted and torn, hanging upside down with a broken back in a tangle of sparking electrical conduits, halfway through a ceiling two floors below.

Shocked insensate, Miriam's brain flooded the inside of her skull with an overdose of natural painkillers, mercifully smothering this physical outrage. She surrendered her earthly everything to the surging glow now geysering her skyward toward the welcome warmth of heavenly resurrection.

Avi?

Avi's radio, half-covered with drifting snow, crackled out broken static at his feet. Toward the north, the ascending, hellish beanstalk of Miriam's funeral pyre towered tall and fulminating, black smoke churning angrily as it fattened into a toadstool spreading an ebony cap over faraway billboards.

Miriam?

Kneeling at his transceiver, Avi thumbed CHAN. SEL. to SCANNER. First, a steady hiss, as if the radio itself could not fathom the enormous monstrosity of heinous deeds...then two scattered pops...then three, eight, and finally a continuous burble of static-laced calls for immediate assistance.

Sirens moaned insistently above the chatter as emergency crews from all over Chicago mobilized to begin the futile search for survivors...and to take care of the dead.

CHAPTER 3
REUNION

Several days previously, a weary and unwashed Ahmed Janoob (or Ahmed "South"), heading northeast, entered the rock-rimmed oasis of El Qouzah from the direction after which he had borrowed his surname. Ahmed Janoob's long-time friend of many seasons and several prior meetings, Tahsin Shamaal (or Tahsin "North"), entered from the direction after which he had taken his last name, after himself traveling generally southwest for many days.

"Ahlan," Tahsin had shouted joyously upon approaching the ancient well from which water would be ceremonially drawn. "Hi, and welcome."

"Ahlan beek," Ahmed yelled in happy reply. "Hi, and welcome to you."

Ahmed was 39; Tahsin was 44. Dressed in the threadbare miscellany peculiar to aimless nomads, both were burnished and wizened from too many hours traveling over land first harshly baked by an unforgiving sun, then forgotten just as quickly. Three weeks unshaven and each with the eyes of famished ospreys, either could have passed for the wandering patriarch of any anonymous group of stateless migrants.

Inclement night found them settled cross-legged on oilcloth rippling beneath frayed, red-checked canvas awning barely four shoulders wide. Each gazed idly west, with only Ahmed hoping for a break in the chilly, intermittent showers. For comfort, they drew on remarkably smooth Cuban tobacco smoldering fitfully in the bowl of a bubbling hookah; large, battered-metal cups full of thick, nearly boiling *qahwah*-flavored with cardamom helped them fight the cold; their feet drew warmth from a small campfire sizzling unevenly in defiance of dribbling rain, while wind gusted in from a squall line hanging westward like dirty, flapping laundry...its turbid clouds fighting to mask a weakling moon.

"Kayf haalak?" Ahmed asked earnestly, firmly gripping his friend's left arm. "How are you?"

"Ashaor bi-tahassun," Tahsin sighed noncommittally, his crevassed face ravaged from more than just the obvious discomforts suffered on the long journey south and west by donkey. "I'm feeling better."

But Ahmed saw the tangled lines crisscrossing Tahsin's face for what they were—deeply wrought etchings giving adamant lie to casual words—so he wasted no time in giving his friend a flat packet of 500 Percodan tablets. True, Tahsin could easily avail himself of priority access to superb medical facilities in his country of birth; however, a superabundance of spies, who together gave new meaning to the word "infestation," meant that going through any channels, black market or otherwise, would immediately red-flag the poor state of his general health, said condition having been surreptitiously confirmed during secretive visits to well-respected and very discreet specialists in the Russian Republic, England and Switzerland.

"It is good to see you once again, my old friend," Ahmed said. He slowly cranked open a tin of Norwegian sardines, the first taste of which his companion declined with effusive thanks while taking a six-high stack of saltines instead.

"Much as I take great pleasure in seeing you once more," Tahsin replied. He chewed thoughtfully for a moment, then added: "Provided, of course, that you remain circumspect in your application of that most sensitive adjective."

"Without a doubt."

"You have news?" Tahsin asked intently.

"The winds of change blow savagely across the land," Ahmed replied. "Even now, old orders tremble with awe; some are sure to fall."

"But their demise will not come soon enough to affect either of us, I am afraid, or our yet-to-be-born children," Tahsin said with profound pessimism.

"Of these things, one can never know for sure. And what have you learned of the others?"

"We know that the chance of lasting peace is now apt to slide away even more rapidly than perennially shifting Saharan sands," Tahsin said. "I have learned only that there is a plot which targets the House of Saud..."

Ahmed interrupted impatiently with a wave of resolute conviction. "Hoary information. So old, in fact, as to be ancient. As for myself, I would feel completely out of sorts if there were not an ongoing intrigue of some kind or another directed against the monarchy. Such schemes form the ever-flowing grist for many a conspirator's mill."

"Would but that this were one of those times," Tahsin said dispiritedly. He lit a cigarette, took one deep drag and then... unwilling to risk the onset of more coughing...tossed it into the fire. "No, I'm afraid this is much worse. The ambitious plan of which I speak is of sufficient magnitude to crush the whole royal family completely flat in one wet smear."

"It cannot be done," Ahmed argued. "They are too carefully protected, with some dispersed across considerable distances: three in Europe and two as far away as tightly guarded safe houses in Singapore and Sydney."

"And what you know, others know as well...in more precise detail."

"That is certainly true," Ahmed agreed.

"And now," Tahsin said, "I think we had best prepare ourselves for the arrival of visitors. Look there...to the northwest."

Ahmed squinted hard in the direction Tahsin's trembling index finger pointed. The man from the north yanked to full extension the brass tubes of a 19th-century seafarer telescope, then handed the spyglass to his younger friend.

"Wait for the next flash of lightning," Tahsin counseled. "Your people without a doubt," he said. "There is no way mine could have survived even the first, tentative leg of so distant a journey across disputed territory as unremittingly hostile as that upon which we sit."

Ahmed trained the telescope on a pair of sandy-gray command cars already almost upon him. Serrated bolts of sawtooth lightning flashed vividly like forked lacework, followed by the booming cannonade of nearby thunder. Pastel light ghosted off tense soldiers under the command of a brawny colonel packed like chiseled ironstone into mud-splattered fatigues, flak vest, and web gear. From brow up, the officer's jar-shaped head was wrapped in a brilliant, ruby-red scarf emblazoned with a green, white-winged snake—the calling card of the Israeli paratroops. To the colonel's left and right were his driver and a Druze Muslim tracker. In the rear of each vehicle, four soldiers sat back-to-back, eyes peeled for trouble. Both armed cars were heavily laden with a full complement of rocket-propelled grenades, light antitank weapons, Galil assault rifles with underslung M203 40mm grenade launchers, and FN MAG light machine guns with projection lights.

The first vehicle slid to a crisp stop 20 yards from where Ahmed and Tahsin sheltered under wind-whipped canvas. Its dazzling searchlights and 7.62mm machine guns held uncompromising beads on the pair while the second vehicle slowly circled the oasis, itching for a chance to quash dissenting opinion. The colonel dismounted and strode closer in the company of two stout paratroop senior master sergeants, all of whom casually kicked a spray of stinging, muddy pebbles at the two men huddling together for spiritual warmth.

Ahmed and Tahsin didn't meet the colonel's slitted eyes as he addressed them in Hebrew. They gave no indication of having heard, much less understood, questions barked on behalf of a security patrol with apparently nothing better to do than sieve locals through the sifter of casual field investigation in the hopes of catching a rotten fish or two.

Neither interrogatee responded to increasing bellicosity. Their inaction pulled the plug on the officer's store of patience, which drained rapidly to depletion, and he didn't ask again. Instead, a paratroop sergeant hauled Ahmed to unsteady feet. The colonel slapped the Arab hard across the right cheek while the huskier of the burly noncoms rifled the slender man's pockets for identity papers.

A moment later, the colonel was humming happily over a timeworn ID shedding mist in the beam of a krypton-bulbed flashlight. The faded photostat had been creased and unfolded so many times it would crumble if sneezed upon...held together as it was by an unripped seam here, a thread of fabric there, a spot of dried saliva in the middle. With a grunt of apparent satisfaction, the officer casually dropped the brittle paper into the campfire... where it briefly smoked white before flaring into crinkled black ash. Then, without so much as a glance at Ahmed, the officer unleashed a potent, close-range monkey punch, the impact of which knocked off the smaller man's kaffiyeh as he backpedaled clumsily.

"That is because I find the stench of your donkey-dung lifestyle so greatly offensive to my delicate sensibilities," the colonel said gruffly while his men frisked Ahmed for additional identity papers.

"My goodness! My goodness!" the colonel roared, laughing as he examined the shorter detainee's paperwork in the gleam of battery light. "Not only do I have the pleasure of holding in my hand an extremely poor forgery, these papers have expired, to boot...just as your freedom is about to."

A no-nonsense slap across the face was punctuated with: "You people really are the body lice on the backside of humanity." Then the colonel jerked his head and stepped back as his sergeants dragged Ahmed to the command car. After first taking a leg and arm each, they swung him bodily toward the tailgate like an ungainly duffle bag...and with a laughing *"E'chad! Sh'teye'eem! Sha'losh!"* threw him unceremoniously facedown into the back.

"Shukran ala diyaafatak," Ahmed managed to call out from where he lay hurt in a twisted tangle of arms and legs. "Thank

you for your hospitality."

"Haz sa'eed," Tahsin shouted back as loud as his hacking cough permitted. "Good luck."

The oasis was soon only a storm-drenched memory lost far behind chaotically zigzagging military vehicles. Ahmed slowly pulled himself up off the floor of the command car, nauseous with the knowledge he would not see Tahsin again. While massaging his chin and licking a drop of blood away from his inner lip, Ahmed glared balefully at the unconcerned back of Colonel Yossi Gavron, who this night seemed to have taken just a little bit too much enthusiastic pride in his job.

"Zvi, those papers really were expired," Gavron said casually over his shoulder, as if that fact alone were sufficient justification to deliver a hard punch to the face.

"What?!" Zvi shouted.

"What happened back there wasn't just some bullshit for your butt-buddy's benefit!" Gavron yelled, his bass-saxhorn voice rising over the egg-beater clatter of a border-patrol vehicle pushed to the limit.

And then the granite colonel, who was listed in RESTRICTED—Eyes Only dossiers as the Poultryman, snorted like an African Cape buffalo. Gavron's robust amusement complemented the only insignia worn in predawn half-light: the conceited self-assurance of a highly regarded neck-breaker, a covert-operations expert wise to the ways of all flesh, and 200 percent sure about everything.

"I'm surprised you were so sloppy!" Gavron shouted. "After all, a man in your position should take greater pains to attend to the little details."

"Next time, let's have less theatrics on the snatch." Zvi rubbed his chin while pushing his tongue gingerly against an incisor to check the firmness of its mooring in the lower gum. "You didn't have to be such a prick about it."

"And why not?!" Gavron bellowed angrily. "Last I heard, that particular piece of real estate is still part of our security zone. Look, my orders were to get you out convincingly. I was told

to make it look good, to protect your credibility should you be talking to a source of even minor importance," Gavron said, while carefully scanning the seesaw landscape of patchy grassland with night-vision binoculars that couldn't quite handle the wet weather.

Try the head of the Syrian secret police, Zvi thought, *which is why it is just as well that you are not actively interested in promotion to a higher rank.*

"And so get you out convincingly is precisely what I did," Gavron said evenly. "Mind you, I'd rather be killing those vermin as opposed to wasting my good time with this stinking step-and-fetch-it. But orders are orders, and I have done very well."

"So it would appear."

"Why you can't take your sabbaticals at the seaside, like most everyone else, is beyond me."

"Among other things."

"What?!" Gavron shouted.

"Which would save you from what you feel is all of this unnecessary running around!" Zvi yelled.

"Yes! Especially because we're in bandit country."

"Since when is a big, brave man like you worried?"

"The lives of my men are important to me, too important to risk unnecessarily in this absurd taxi duty." Gavron spat contemptuously backward, the large gob of unidentified matter narrowly missing his soaked passenger. "So tell me. What's really ailing itty-bitty Zvi?" the colonel asked, laughing condescendingly at the drowned rat of a man who looked as if he couldn't take a punch even in the best of times.

"Don't you think it's about time you told me what the hell's going on?" Zvi asked pointedly, his right elbow crooked tightly around a machine-gun post.

"As you probably know, it's way over my head," Gavron muttered, his words whipped away by bracketing thunder, howling wind, and scarf tails snip-snapping over the back of muscle-ribbed neck.

So what else is new? Zvi thought.

He grabbed for a coiled-cord handset dangling from the bulky AN/PRC-25/77 field radio Gavron held menacingly overhead. Zvi's buttocks bounced completely off, then slammed painfully back into the uncomfortably wet sheet metal of the command-car floor. The sharp edge of a loose, hex-head screw carved its painful way into the bottom of his right thigh.

"Go!" Zvi said into the transceiver.

"Big Blue Eighty-Two/four-four-seven P plus C; niner-six G," a static-wrapped voice crackled urgently. "This is not a drill."

No, Zvi thought sadly. *It wouldn't be.*

"Repeat!" he barked.

The radio did.

Damn! Would it never end?!

"Whose?" Zvi asked immediately.

"Big Daddy's."

"Where?"

"Well inside his three-mile limit."

"When?"

"It's still smoking."

"A fresh scent," Zvi mused.

"Tailor-made for a prime sniffer."

"Luckily, we've got one across the pond," Zvi said quietly.

"Youtka?"

"Who else could there possibly be?" Zvi wiped blearing rainwater from his eyes. "Get word out ASAP," he ordered. Then he switched off the field radio and watched it swing pendulously away from precarious suspension over his rain-splattered hair.

"You and I will talk more later!" Zvi shouted above the punishing din of the patrol vehicle's rickety journey.

"You think so?!" the colonel yelled back over the clamorous roar of the straining engine. "Zvi, it is rather presumptuous of you to entertain the notion that I'd be even remotely interested in hearing anything you've got to say."

"Not even an invitation to dance on the canvas?" Zvi challenged, loudly enough for the other soldiers to hear.

"With Cuban gloves?" Gavron asked.

Suddenly very interested in what his soggy passenger had offered, the paratroop colonel passed his binoculars to the tracker and crouched down next to Zvi...his broadly satisfied grin accenting wanton appetite twinkling out from green-carbide eyes set deep in a battle-scarred face.

"If you think you can take it," Zvi said coolly.

"I'm sure my appointment calendar's got room for an easy, six-round walkover."

"How about twelve?" Zvi asked for reasons not immediately fathomable. Momentarily feeling like a complete idiot, Zvi just as quickly reasoned that the match wouldn't last for more than a few rounds anyway.

"You're on!" Gavron said immediately, lest Zvi have a chance to think things through more clearly and perhaps change his mind.

"Any other news?"

"Well," Gavron said, surprisingly chipper and talkative, "you'll probably be glad to know that before picking you up, I did get word about six from Samir Arboon's group, who were intercepted four clicks west of your position. Those thugs have now taken to looting, pillaging, raping, and otherwise making life extremely difficult for the indigenous population. Anyway, we martyred them."

"Which means?" Zvi asked, gazing idly out over the tailgate at the braying donkey still struggling valiantly to keep up with the command car's jouncing journey on the goat path of muddy, tertiary road.

"Which means that today just happens to be your lucky day," Gavron said happily. "And based on your generous offer, it appears to be mine as well."

CHAPTER 4
DOGGER

For Judith Levy, the precision of professional football served up tripartite satisfaction. She found the sport joyous to behold, spiritually uplifting, and emotionally gratifying. Judith fully appreciated the suddenly intense mobilization of ponderously heavy frontline forces, the tap-dancing quarterback, the high-stepping ballet of a quickly cutting wide receiver under intense cornerback pressure, the orchestration of long passes lofted high and greedily snagged in diving catches.

And nothing could ever compare to the peculiar consistency and potent aromatics of the hot dog distending her usually lean cheeks. Mystery meat it might very well be, but the mustard, relish, onions, cheese, ketchup, chili, and air pollution combined to brew an astonishing experience with a singularly unique flavor all its own. Judith had industriously shopped each major supermarket and minor *bodega* in the greater Washington, D.C. area, and every convenience store in between, but had never come close to duplicating those preciously delicious dogs of R.F.K. Memorial Stadium.

The human wave went up, and she joined it, struggling to keep her treasured frank as evenly keeled as possible. She fell back awkwardly into her seat, the shaky pyramid of onions, relish, and chili wobbling precariously...but marginally safe from upset for the time being.

The stacked snack caved in on the next play. Second and eight inside the Other Guys' 42-yard line—it hardly mattered who was playing as long as her face was crammed full of hot dog. She leaned her shoulder toward her companion, the better to see through hedge-rowed fur hats and jumping jackets in front of her...and artfully dumped half the precious condiments onto the arm of his brown serge overcoat.

Judith smiled giddily between wolfing grunts as she gator-bit the hot dog down to a mere stump of roll. Dr. Murray Mertz, distinguished psychiatrist and father-confessor to the better part of upper-crust Washington society, couldn't help laughing at her slow, affected, bulge-eyed chewing, looking as she did like a six-year-old girl happily enjoying an outing with Daddy. He knew them to be making progress, which pleased him greatly, because soon he would pick the lock on the dungeon door behind which her deepest secrets were sequestered, and then she would be fully his.

"No question but that you're having fun," Mertz observed affably, "as will my dry cleaner before the week is out, I can assure you." He seared his throat with hot coffee then sucked in ice air to cool himself down, shivering with the chill.

"Delicious."

"Eat up, Judith. You always look so seriously underweight."

"Thanks!"

"Truer words, on my part, were never spoken."

"That is why I like to hear them."

"And more to the point, I might be able to get you the recipe...the ingredients, anyway."

"For these?! You mean... Yeah, sure," she scoffed. *"Right!"*

"No, seriously!"

Seeing Judith about to take the bait, Mertz drained his coffee cup, tossed it under his seat, then half-turned and took both her mittened hands in his, squeezing her left hand more than her right, which was his way of showing that his caring was genuine.

"This is for real, Judith. One of my patients? He owns the food concessions here. *He honestly does!"*

"You know that I would kill for it," she stated matter-of-factly, leaning forward and rubbing noses with him. "Tell me or forfeit your life right now on this very spot."

"Never in a hundred million years! Never will I ever give it to you."

"Murray, please!" she begged, lively eyes intensely suppliant. "Don't toy with me. If you have it, I must know. I simply must. Murray, you don't have to tell me what it is. Yet. Just tell me if you have it. That is all I ask."

"Sorry! Doctor/patient confidentiality," he winked, giving her an awkward hug before turning his attention back to jersey'd mayhem on the field. "They'll be going long on this one," he predicted. "Can't you feel it? The seats are a-live," he sang, "with elec-tric ten-sion. They're going to fake a screen...and then go long. Massaro will feint to Hanson and go to Reed. *Watch!"*

"And if you are wrong, I get the recipe!"

"Absolutely not!" he countered with mock indignation. "Do you think I would compromise my dignity and sell out so weighty a responsibility for so small a reward as your lucky guess concerning the next play? Has my name suddenly become Esau?"

"You would do it, I know you would, if I told you that along with the bet riding on the next play, and in exchange for the recipe, I would gladly spend three days as your love slave at your precious hideaway on Chesapeake Bay, where we would rewrite at least two chapters of the *Kama Sutra* before ravenously devouring breakfast in bed late Tuesday morning."

Dr. Mertz was hooked faster than a fly-starved trout.

"You mean you..."

"Did you hear me?"

"But I..." he blustered, taken aback and momentarily off guard.

"Did you hear what I said?"

"Yes, but..."

"Well, evidently you were not listening very closely, my good doctor. What I said was: 'If I told you.' I didn't say that we actually would."

"Tease me! I absolutely adore you for it," he said, squeezing her hands again before turning his attention back downfield.

"It is the hairy-chested male in you that I take such great pleasure in tweaking," Judith said, leaning over to huddle with Mertz. "Time-out is over," she breathed into his right ear. "Play-action pass."

"Nah! They'll go to the air and long. Massaro will fake to Reed and go to Hanson."

"You have changed your tune, Doctor Mertz."

"That's what we call hedging one's bets. Standard procedure, especially because the stakes seem to have gone up."

"Excellent choice of words."

"Watch," he urged. "And remember, you heard it here first."

Washington ran the ball up the middle for a gain of nine, with Mertz jeering mightily in disappointment.

Her hoots muffled by the last mouthful of the second hot dog, Judith licked her fingers, threw back the hood of her parka, and fluffed out an "early tousle" hairdo.

For Judith, life was too precious to waste time fussing with inconsequentials, so one pass of the towel followed by air dry would have to do. Her cosmetic half had to be on line when her real self reboarded the Adrenalin Express. Blow-drying, styling, and other fripperies of femininity were luxuries that rapaciously devoured precious minutes she was forever chary of frittering away.

Judith's face was canted higher on one side than the other, perennially inclined as if questioning every fact and circumstance laid before her by a world perpetually ablaze. Her eyes were predominantly hazel, although indirect lighting turned them into mirrors of stained glass flecked with chips of green and blue. The left corner of her mouth pulled in and back a little tighter than the right, mirroring the permanent dash of skepticism with which she toned down the optimistic bouillabaisse her bureaucratic coworkers served up without so much as a passing nod to pragmatic reality.

Judith's workday responsibilities were an unmindful 10,000 miles away, which was mistake number one and which alone should have been her first warning of trouble afoot. Whenever she repressed as deeply as today, things barreled back with cockamamie vengeance. Thinking about it, dueling with it mentally, fretting about it, agonizing over it, worrying about it all combined in the construction of a talisman mighty enough to keep personal troubles at bay. But she'd been so engrossed in feeding her face that she'd neglected to enforce that cardinal good-luck rule and so...as was inevitable when she forgot what she was supposed to remember in order to keep it away...there it was: the accursed pager insistently vibrating against her right thigh.

But not today! Judith decided defiantly. She reached down and artfully stroked the sliding kill switch that took the battery out of the circuit. *Definitely not now!* She was off duty. Everyone deserved a day off now and then. She had worked 19 weeks straight on her last case, without so much as half an afternoon to herself. *I am entitled!*

And for a moment it worked...but on higher authority and as allowed by the house rules so tightly structuring her tightly tubular life, the beeper jumped the first circuit, energized backup electronics, and nudged her again on Command/Override. From all-too-brief glimpses at long-forgotten schematics, Judith knew her pager could unmute itself if the order came from high enough up the chain of command, although her hardware had never hot-wired itself before, which fact alone substantially jacked up her worry quotient.

She groped far down in the baggy pants pocket and pulled out the small receiver. Its whining warble rose insistently, as if in raucous complaint about 20-degree wind...the nerve-grating Code Red wail so unlike the gurgling burble she was accustomed to.

"Trouble?" Mertz, ever solicitous, took his arm off Judith's shoulder and gave her the maneuvering room she needed to shield the beeper from sunlight, blanking out the display panel.

She leaned back and angled the LCD. Message: BIG BLUE 82/447 P+C; 96 G. Meaning: a Boeing 747 had been blown completely apart in midair, killing 447 passengers plus crew, and 96 people on the ground.

"Judith! What is it?! What's wrong?!" The human wave rose and fell to a Redskins' touchdown, but Mertz ignored the undulating rhythm of humanity and stared at his companion's face, which had blanched two shades whiter than evaporated milk.

"Judith?!"

"I have to go!" she said urgently.

He got half up out of his seat, but she leaned over and pushed him back.

"Not today, my good Doctor Mertz."

"A patient?"

"Isn't it always?" she said, forcing a cheesy smile that played across her face like the palsied rictus of gross insincerity. "They are forever..." she said, moving away briskly efficient while committing to nothing in particular.

"Wait," he said, snagging her sleeve and pulling insistently.

Judith tugged loose and looked around frantically. *Back and up,* she told herself, *back and up. There!* At the portal. Where she had been told they would be, just as they had practiced that one time, which had been more afterthought than serious training because the security team had nothing better to do that day...and there had been a game...and there had been the hot dogs.

"Yes, Murray. A patient."

"I'll go too," he said, hardly believing her. Mertz edged to his feet again as she turned and began politely sidestepping her way toward the aisle. "Judith, I'll get..."

"No!" she yelled, straight-arming him to a standoff, reestablishing enough control to launch a legitimately warm smile that disarmed him long enough to let her widen the gap.

She willed color into her face. Back-flash to the rainy day, the combat engineers hooked their crane's cable up to the women's latrine, then lifted the little building without mussing so much as a flake of uniform lint...and left her squatting in full view of a passing army drill team. The memory worked. An embarrassed flush crept up her face. Mertz would buy her story if it were broadcast in color. *He had to!*

"I am being...the clinic sent a car. I will be all right."

"You sure?"

"Trust me," she shouted over the "Ooooh" of the Other Guys' fumble.

"Just don't ask me to buy a bridge from you, or land," he shouted back, fur hat slipping in and out of sight between and behind a wavering forest of overcoats, sweatshirts, banners, and flags. "Because from that look on your face I can tell..."

She blew him a kiss from the aisle. *"Tell yourself that I had a wonderful time!"* she yelled, enunciating each word slowly through cupped hands. "And while I will not be back for the halftime show, there will be other games."

"And hot dogs!" he shouted back.

Judith watched him watching her. She jabbed her forefinger emphatically toward the Other Guys' sidelines. With Mertz temporarily distracted by the seething mass of stadium activity, she bolted up the stairs in giant leaps, her mind tossing up unbidden scraps of military training and a long-forgotten class on explosive weaponry.

"BLU-82/B."

The instructor was Gelfik, a short and abhorrently unpleasant pit bull of Sephardic Jew who briskly stoked his thinly veiled dislike for all of his students. They would be going out into the world as field operatives; he would be forever anchored in port. Their opportunity would never be his opportunity because he had been tarred and feathered by a whispering campaign sprouting from the long-simmering Muhradah Affair.

By then totally soured on life, Gelfik still remained the expert's expert on bangs, blasts, and booms...and so the IDF had no real choice but to keep him on...his expertise weighing the scales more heavily in favor of utility than obnoxiousness pushed the balance toward outright dismissal.

"The largest, conventional bomb in the American inventory," Gelfik barked pompously, purposely scraping his chalk on the blackboard as he diagrammed the device. "At 15,000 pounds, it is so hugely bulky that it must be delivered by C-130 transport."

"Which is why air supremacy is of such paramount importance in the application of the weapon."

"Thank you, Yoni Ginsberg, tactical expert nonpareil," Gelfik growled, bowing formally...one arm across his stomach, the other behind his back. He straightened up and looked around, hands on hips, daring anyone else to interrupt his lecture.

"And now, my esteemed Mr. Ginsberg. If I may be permitted to continue."

"But of course, Herr Professor," Yoni cracked, loudly clicking together the heels of his combat boots.

Gelfik chose to ignore the dig. "Thank you. This particular gem of explosive engineering," he went on, "is also called the Daisy Cutter or Big Blue 82."

Judith had been drifting in and out of reality all that spring morning, when the iron in Yoni's blood had clearly turned to lead in his pants. When not needling Gelfik with sotto voce interruptions, he passed Judith salacious notes, gallivanting dangerously close to the obscene-short, pungent verses abloom with impassioned erotics eliciting surprisingly intense flutterings in her loins. Judith was surprised she had retained anything of what the little wart of an instructor said about the device's construction.

"Comprised of a cast-steel case filled with 12,600 pounds of DBA-22M," Gelfik croaked.

"I love you, Judith Levy!"

"Not now. *Yoni!"* she rasped, bending his pinky back almost to breaking and removing his hand from her inner thigh. Those butterflies again!

Gelfik: "A watery mixture..."

"Darling Judith, my knees go watery thinking of your..."

"Stop it!"

"...of ammonium nitrate and aluminum powder, with polystyrene soap as a binder."

Gelfik worked a toothpick between the large gap separating his bottom-front teeth and waited patiently until he had their attention. "The Daisy Cutter," he continued, finally exasperated, "produces an explosion of a size and intensity described as 'the closest thing to a nuclear bomb.' Mine clearance? Need a helicopter landing pad? Then Big Blue is the device for you. Produces blast overpressure in excess of 1,000 pounds per square inch. Shears off trees and other obstructions at ground level."

Big Blue 82 became the Mossad code name for any device large enough to completely shatter a Boeing 747...and Dr. Mertz was forgotten by the time she reached the landing, with Mike and John falling in at her side.

"You must be freezing," she said, snugging her parka shut while eyeing their three-piece Brooks Brothers suits and Rudolph noses.

They were a study in contrasts: Mike, tall and angular, given to Grecian Formula, Rogaine and spending endless hours cruising health spas frequented by hard-bodied, female aerobic animals in their mid-twenties; John, a grandfather twice over, round and portly, bearded, totally gray, receding hairline but with enough personal dignity not to let the sides grow longer to compensate for what he was losing in the front and middle.

Both men were GS8 "floaters" who had requested this particular liaison assignment because when this percolator started brewing up, which wasn't often, things got hot enough to more than make up for lost time.

"We've seen worse," Mike said.

"Chosin Reservoir," John echoed.

"Talk cold, and you're talking Korea, 1950-1953," they chorused.

"Tell me it is more optimistic," she entreated her pager while jogging down the ramp. But the message wouldn't go away. She turned the unit off, then on again, wanting to doubt but unable to deny the accusatory blinking—BIG BLUE 82/447 P+C; 96 G. It had come across too often to be a mistake, and no one would be sick enough to joke about so grave a circumstance.

It was genuine.

They burst out through the stadium's VIP entrance. Judith momentarily lost her bearings. She looked around anxiously, then raced after Mike and John to a Cadillac stretch limousine with diplomatic plates.

John yanked open the back door. Judith dove into the car, and John slid in after her, grabbing for his handkerchief and wiping his nose as the door slammed shut. His jacket bunched out as he sat crosswise on the seat, the butt of a Glock Model 22 .40-caliber semiautomatic protruding from a Bianchi spring-loaded holster.

Mike skated around to the front passenger seat of the Cadillac, sliding on a patch of ice like a figure skater having a bad day. He grabbed at the fender to right his balance and snapped off one of the embassy flags, regarding it in shocked surprise until the angry honk of the horn woke him up. Mike dropped the pennant, scrabbled for the door, pulled it open, and threw himself into the car.

"Go!" he ordered.

Abraham's left foot was already halfway off the brake. Size-12 boot jammed the gas pedal flat. Speed-rated tires squealed in protest while generating churning puffs of rubber smoke. The limousine surged into motion before the door locks clicked down.

Mike buckled in, then slackened his shoulder belt. He half-turned, laying his arm over the top of the seat while bringing Judith up to date.

"A chartered airliner was brought down just after takeoff from O'Hare."

"Arabs?" she asked.

"That's what the phone call said," John said, lighting a cigarette.

Judith accepted an unfiltered Camel from the proffered pack. "Who put their name on it this time?" she asked wearily, having looked down this investigative road and seeing that she'd been here before...and before that...and before that, too.

"El-Fahd el-Aswad," Abraham hissed. "Bastards." He

cursed while swerving to avoid a parcel-delivery van wandering dispiritedly left to right in lazy search of a lane to call home.

"Nothing's been confirmed yet," Mike said.

"No hard evidence," John echoed.

"We know what we know," Abraham said with firm-jawed conviction.

"The White House got a message that a large terrorist bomb destroyed the airliner," Mike said. "The message was: 'Death to those who nourish the Zionist entity.'"

"The White House?" Judith asked. "Not the media?"

"No, which is a bit unusual, considering how publicity hungry and otherwise starved for attention they are. We're sitting on it for right now. Take a left at the next light, Abraham."

"Since when?"

"Just finished the alley yesterday," John offered.

"It'll cut fifteen minutes off our time," Mike said.

"Money in the bank," Abraham laughed. He grinned happily, smoothly cranking in all available power steering as their bodies leaned with forces nudging the car's suspension nearly past its design limits.

"According to the passenger manifest," Mike continued, "there were four hundred and forty-seven passengers on the plane, plus crew. They're all dead. So far, we've got ninety-six confirmed dead on the ground."

"I heard," she said.

"Already?" Mike asked with genuine respect. "We pick you up at a football game, and you're riding herd on it. I knew you people were good, but..."

"We cannot afford to be otherwise. No one has ever been keen on giving us a second chance. Name of the flight?"

"TransPac Air," John said. "Flight 117. Chicago to Honolulu."

"I will need a printout of what you have so far."

Mike handed her a small, scrolled computer sheet. She speed-read cryptic abbreviations, then folded the report into a one-inch square and shoved it deep down into her shirt pocket.

"And the body count is still preliminary?" Judith asked.

"Yeah," Mike whispered. "Though from what I've heard, there were at least two apartment buildings fully involved, so Christ only knows how many crispies will turn up by the time they're done raking through the wreckage."

"He's about the only one who will know," John said solemnly. And then he looked up and around abruptly, and said, "No offense."

"None taken," Judith said firmly.

"But only if you say two Hail..." Abraham began.

"Enough!" she said, shutting down Abraham's abrasive commentary because she was bone-dry on patience. "I speak for both of us."

Abraham glared at her in the rearview mirror but bit his lip and said nothing. Judith's barely constrained fury told him he was wise to hold his tongue. She leaned back in the seat, suddenly weary as the huge scale of the tragedy bubbled through her body, washing outward from her psychic edges before doubling back insidiously and squeezing her blue in the straitjacket of melancholy overload. The cigarette abraded her throat, and she stubbed it out impatiently.

An abrupt lane change and the blast of an upgraded horn yanked Judith upright and alert. Diplomatic plates, ambassadorial insignia, and insistent red-and-blue grille lights gave Abraham all the license he needed to drive like an unreconstructed madman with one foot in the grave.

He whipsawed through sparse traffic on East Capitol Street like a migratory weaver bird craving an accident to make his day. The limousine angled sharply south, then careened abruptly east, picking up Central Avenue and crossing into Maryland and over Interstate 95 to Enterprise Road.

One mile north of a Circle K owned by Pakistani expatriates, Abraham braked sharply, slid off the main road in a professional four-wheel drift, then fishtailed onto a tortured cow path, which he followed for another two miles at 43 on the speedo. The limousine's jerky movements showered each side of the road with huge clumps of muddy slush.

Abraham took the road's increasing degree of difficulty as a personal affront: The narrower and bumpier it got, the faster he drove…each new constriction providing him with incentive to prove manly mettle in the face of added challenge.

He pressed on recklessly through naked, slapping branches clacking against the outside of the limousine as it torpedoed through the woods. The car soared briefly airborne over a fallen tree, then bottomed out and bounced clumsily before exploding into a tiny clearing barely large enough to contain the car's swinging rear end. Abraham jammed both feet down on the brake pedal, steered like a frantic demon, and slid them to a barely controlled stop inside a musty barn.

The door slid closed on well-greased rollers. Overhead studio lights clacked on sequentially, illuminating the deep recess of the cavernous expanse. Behind the facade of country comfort was a four-level garage, three levels of which were underground. Security patrols circumnavigated the shadows, headsets and walkie-talkies alive with constant chatter.

Mike and John wasted no time exiting the limousine. They shook hands all around as Judith climbed aboard a waiting golf cart. The PFC behind the wheel saluted smartly in the limousine's general direction, unsure of who might be lying in protocol ambush in the backseat. He made a broken U-turn and spun off down the ramp to the basement with Judith hanging onto a roof rail, desperately seeking support.

Lighting got brighter the deeper they went. The golf cart stopped short on Level Four, where two hulking-brute U.S. Army Special Forces sergeants guarded the entrance to the equipment room. The first undressed her with his eyes while the second gave her credentials a time-consuming twice-over before lapsing into casual and flippantly waving her through.

In the suit-up section, Airman Dave Reynolds—aka Pumpkin Face—was already hoisting flight gear off the rack. Judith slowed only long enough to shrug impatiently into a custom-tailored G suit; Reynolds shuffled alongside in parallel urgency, tightening midsection laces as they went.

"Always a pleasure to see you, Dave, despite the gravity of the circumstances."

"You still owe me lunch, Judith."

"When this is over, I promise...and this time I mean it."

"Our difference in rank wouldn't have anything to do with it, would it?" he asked seriously.

"Do not confuse the trappings of authority with the reality of rank, Airman. And that is an order."

"Yes, sir. Ma'am!"

"In that regard, you outrank me."

"Ma'am?"

"Got to run. Thanks!"

"Shalom," he said, handing Judith a crash helmet.

"I see that you've been practicing while my back has been turned." She laughed good-naturedly and gave the airman a quick hug. "Very good, very good. *Shalom* to you, too," she replied with a grin, then turned and dashed across the concrete to the hardstand and waiting mount.

Judith ran clumsily and slightly off balance, stiffly awkward left fingers stuffing hair under a crash helmet. The special two-seat Israeli F-15, with "Fast Taxi" calligraphied on the nose, pulled at its leash like a beagle with a noseful of fox.

Stripped of all weapons and targeting electronics, the plane carried only basic avionics and just enough jet juice for a straight-in approach at the destination. Top-priority clearances made loiter-time fuel unnecessary. Reskinning with lightweight, composite material made the aircraft considerably lighter than factory specs. Capable of substantially more than 1,900 mph at 65,000 feet, the jet would have her on Chicago ground in less than 20 minutes.

Israeli ground crewmen swarmed over the jet like worker bees tending their precious queen. The plane's twin Pratt & Whitney turbines purred at high idle; the airplane strained at the chocks, the pilot impatient to be gone. Judith scrambled up the ladder, which slid back and away almost before her feet cleared it.

She dropped clumsily into the cockpit's rear seat as strong hands fastened her in, helped pull the buckles taut, and proficiently connected hoses and wires. A strong shoulder slap signaled she was as ready as she'd ever be.

"Move it!" she ordered as the canopy came down, inched forward, and locked.

"Recline and relax," was the terse reply. And then forgetting that the intercom was still on, the pilot muttered: "Look, I may not be absolutely crazy about chauffeur duty, lady, but I'm a damn good driver."

"Better than that," she shot back.

"You'll get there," the pilot continued, too engrossed in gauge-tapping to have heard her response.

"That should go without saying," she replied respectfully. "Should I expect any less from the living legend who bagged five MiG-23s in seven minutes over the Bekaa?"

"You know about that?" he asked, halfway between surprise and sudden interest, his head angling backward for a closer look at his passenger.

"It is my business to know all about you, Captain Kamyanski. I make it a point to know everything about everyone with whom I work. I requested you personally, Captain, because I am far too precious physically and way too important politically to be entrusted to just any pedal-pusher capable of toting miscellaneous metal tonnage through cloudless, unchallenging skies."

They both got a kick out of her arrogance. The last part was a lie, and they both knew it, but the pilot was clearly pleased, with his enthusiasm for the mundane mission powerfully invigorated.

"You have a musical preference? It's going to get really noisy back there in about thirty seconds, and we're not big on sound-deadening insulation."

The plane jerked abruptly, as if Kamyanski had popped the clutch on a powerful sports car. He pointed its nose at the opalescent sky at the top of the ramp.

"Concrete Blonde," she said, her throat already itchy and

dry from oxygen pumped in from onboard tanks. That cigarette had been a mistake, but it was too late for regrets now, however small and insignificant they might be.

"Coming right up."

"When was the last time you changed the air in here?"

"You should know better than to ask such a damn-fool question," Kamyanski chuckled. "The Israeli Air Force is no advocate of personal amenities."

His fingers danced over the control panel, then nudged the throttles forward. The jet rolled easily up the inclined ramp to the runway outside, turned hard right, and taxied rapidly to the end of the strip. Judith blinked away pink dots lasering through her eyes from the snowbanks plowed up high on either side of the rain-slick runway.

"Try dropping your visor. It'll work wonders."

"Thanks. Your mind reading is right on."

"Comes with the territory," he laughed.

"You been here before?"

"More times than I care to count," Kamyanski admitted.

Judith slapped down the heavy dark shield, knowing full well that darkness would work her over like a narcotic, but she was too tired to fear sleep…even though she was long overdue for another vicious excursion down the back-street abyss of time. Judith knew she had forgotten to think about it in time to prevent it. Her choice was simple: Either live with it all the time and thereby keep it at bay, or let it come unbidden at the time and place of its own choosing. Since she didn't have enough room to daily shoulder such crippling baggage, it was perhaps best to just relax and let things take their inevitable course.

Knowing it would come was knowledge; knowledge was power; maybe she would do better this time.

"Liftoff in twenty-five seconds," Kamyanski said. "Rib?"

"What?"

"R-I-B. Sorry. Talking in acronyms adds pepper to this mashed-potato run. What I meant was: Ready in back?"

"As close as I will ever be, I guess."

The intercom clicked off as Kamyanski contacted both Washington National Airport and Dulles International Airport to let them know that the man-made meteor soon to be rocketing through their jealously supervised airspace was not a UFO, so please do not contact the mass media. The U.S. military had already been briefed on the fast-mover scheduled for abrupt takeoff, near vertical departure, and quick acceleration to almost Mach 3 as it raced the sun westward. American engineers would be tracking him to see how the latest IAF modifications had expanded the F-15's performance envelope.

They made a fast rolling turn at the end of a runway wide enough to handle jets twice their size. The engines spooled up to a high-pitched roar as the F-15 fought the brakes.

"Creature comforts weigh too much and cut down on time," Kamyanski said, picking up his conversation where he had left off. "Not that you'll hear much engine noise over your rocking racket. You got a favorite track?"

"Cue up 'Dance Along the Edge.'"

"Coming at you," Kamyanski said, half to himself. "This is one pretty decent sound system, if you ask me."

She leaned back, reclining comfortably in the intensifying press of G forces pressing stomach spineward while the flight suit pushed back. The airplane accelerated and lifted sharply off the runway at a rakish angle, its landing gear and flaps winding up as Kamyanski cleaned up for supersonic flight. He banked left, twisted violently level, then the F-15 stood on its tail in full afterburner. The jet clawed madly for its comfortable niche at altitude, far above a lightning-laced T-storm heading in from Virginia.

Exhaustion crept over Judith as they bulleted west. As if out from under a soapy blanket of scopolamine, sparkling ghosts played ring-around-a-rosy on the mind's center stage. Today, she would be denied the comfort of white dreams. Already sneaking out from the malodorous compost heap of terror was the nightmare she was doomed to relive whenever time and tide were right.

Israeli Independence Day; Aqaba Gulf shore; 27 years ago; a vacation at the beach. Finally...after long months of broken promises. And then sneaking away from her parents. That was always the best part.

Judith, the ever-rebellious child of six, ran as fast as her little *pulkes* would propel her over tickling sand spurting up between her toes and spraying back from her heels. She was angling toward the boardwalk and the oh-so-pretty package no one else had yet espied...the one wrapped in yellow-and-green paper and capped with a large, eye-catching pink bow.

Didn't that young man realize he had left his pretty package behind? She would get the package. She would run after the young man, catch up to him, and tell him that he had forgotten it. Surely he had not meant to leave behind something so incredibly pretty. *No! She would not tell him!* She would reach out...and touch it...and take it for her own. *Finders, keepers; losers, weepers!*

"Youtka!" The echoing warning of her terrified father: *"YOUTKA! NO!"*

She had then been close enough to the package to walk, having momentarily forgotten her joyous enthusiasm, but the urgency of father's cry prodded Judith into a forward lurch, and once more she began to run. Her father was huffing and close behind now, coming up, she running faster, he passing her, then apparently stumbling on a beer can...*how shameful that the beach was not kept clean!*...and falling back...down on one knee...back up again...running...Judith is almost at the finish line and the prize waiting beyond.

A race with Daddy! How she loved to race with Daddy! Why couldn't they do it more often?

But Daddy was not...Daddy was...grabbing desperately at the collar of the sunsuit, yanking Judith backward, gaining purchase on her lower body...his fingernails digging into ribs and hurting so much...*Daddy!*...at once yanking his little girl sideways by the upper arms and throwing her sharply left while place-kicking the box away.

Judith was rolling away from the bright flash, sand in her

eyes, fear in her mouth, the loud BANG stunning her ears...a tug at her side...*look!*...the bloody tatters of flesh and jagged, splintered bone that used to be her left hand, hanging by tendons and veins, twisting slowly this way and that, like strips of dripping crepe paper and crushed straws.

Then wandering aimlessly in the silence of post-trauma shock, through which cut the burbling hubbub, the guttural throb of panic-stricken voices, and then the piercing agony of her mother's wail...and her father, face down near the smoking boardwalk, unmoving—"Daddy? *Daddy!"*—the back of his shirt ripped raggedly red...ocher, clotted sand under him.

"DADDY!"

Judith jerked desperately awake, madly fighting the restraints, thrashing furiously against the harness like a mental patient in full seizure, gagging on her heartache, grabbing frantically for the long-gone left hand, too late to save it...*it was always too late to save it!* Awake and gasping in the oppressively narrow confines of the cockpit, gulping at life as machinery force-fed lungs with precious air, awash in the stink of rancid sweat, a mere slip of shuddering human flotsam bashed senseless by roiling seas of recurring dread.

Nine years she spent in therapy, nine years of intensive counseling before she came to accept the fact that it was not her selfishness that had cost her father his life...*that it had not been her fault!* But rational emollients were powerless against the demon dream. Daylight answers never slaughter black irrationality, constantly fighting for audience from its dank lair under the peeling corners of the conscious mind.

"Hey!" Kamyanski shouted. *"You okay back there?!"* His head moved from side to side, helmet banging into the canopy as he tried unsuccessfully to glance rearward at Judith—shrunken, shriveled, and shaking in the backseat.

"I screamed, didn't I?" she asked through raggedly stifled wheezes. *The Dream was always so real!*

"We'll be down in three minutes," Kamyanski said brusquely, as he threw the F-15 into a sharp right bank.

Approach plates memorized, Kamyanski turned off the chatter to better concentrate on the task at hand, taking time only to scold Judith about her listening habits in general and that day's musical selection in particular.

CHAPTER 5

ROADRUNNER

Cold and slick battleship weather was definitely putting clamp-down squeezers on pudgy Mr. B′ Bearing...

Game name?

NO MATTER!

...whose defenses against imminent death crumbled in direct proportion to the clattering hammer of freezing rain pelting his black Ford cargo van.

With the day tougher than the Chicago Bears′ front four, this climactic eight ball should have presented no real astonishment; Mr. B′ Bearing anticipated the unexpected and carefully structured his world to prepare for the unforeseen. But after an unremitting week of *Sturm und Drain,* organic-energy depletion was more massive than originally calculated in yards-long charts, graphs, and complex, convoluted equations...the most recent of which, up until a week ago, had filled a classroom′s width of physicists′ blackboards in an abandoned elementary school 11 blocks southwest of the old stockyards.

The slush-stained van was parked meticulously; gray-smear lane lines were as far away from the right-side 60-series, raised-letter tires as they were from the left, that peewee perfection having been seen to on six previous dry runs...precision being Mr. B′ Bearing′s king, exactitude his god. The vehicle shed icy sheet rain far enough away from the restaurant′s steamed-up, double-door entrance so as not to be too obviously apparent to doughnut-dunking state troopers ducking in for a well-deserved break from inclement-weather cruising...yet in close enough proximity to blend with other vehicular comings and goings.

Thanksgiving's oppressively worrisome predicament centered on higher-than-anticipated voltaic depletion. Galvanic skin response was horribly skewed by infernal weather, the gusty deluge outside a natural conductor extracting way too much current. Mr. B' Bearing was now seriously weakened to the point of being barely able to ease his considerable bulk out of the driver's seat. Gasping for breath, he twisted uncomfortably under the tremendous effort it took to make doubly sure all interior triggering mechanisms were unarmed.

Frightfully exhausted by miniscule effort, the fragility of personal specifics conspired to scare the living hell out of Mr. B' Bearing. Fear opened perspiration's floodgates...

WHOA! SPIGOT DOWN THAT ACCURSED...

...reversed?

...CONDUCTION!

...even though he knew it was fatally foolish to be bathed in free-flowing sweat, considering the already low barometric pressure of an ice-storm day.

A pressure suit would block-valve it; pump it up, pump it up, pump it up! I'll have to...

NO TIME NOW! CONCENTRATE!

Mr. B' Bearing's body was a 5' 9" pulsar radiating life's most precious AC/DC energy. Ammeters unwound in crazy, counterclockwise retreat...unspooling like the altimeters of ground-bound jets, resistance falling, internal ohmmeters going...

WRONG WAY! WRONG WAY! WRONG WAY!

Damn the weather!

NO! DAM THOSE EMOTIONAL OUTBURSTS NOW DISCHARGING YOUR SAP!

Slowly deflating in the driver's seat, it took Herculean efforts to wiggle the wallet free of the jeans' rain-soaked back pocket. Mr. B' Bearing pulled out a recently purchased Nevada driver's license and stared hard at the picture.

Eyes closed; less leakage that way...

YOU SHOULD HAVE THOUGHT OF THAT FIRST!

Next time, never to be so weak;
Given name is what I seek.
THE NAME ON THE DOCUMENT?
Remembering...

...was agony: psychic nakedness in bone-chilling, breeze-thatched room. Cheat with a peak and then...

Discovery!

GOOD AFTERNOON, RICHARD!

Middle initial? L? Was it L? What was it? What was it?

WUZZA-WUZZA! WUZZA-WUZZA!

L?

JAMIE!

For one's first true love;
Or the lack thereof...

JAMIE! JAMIE! JAMIE!

What can I find to remind me of...?

Eyes closed.

LAWRENCE!

Eyes open...

Goody-goody...

SERVE UP SOME GUMDROPS TO THE DUMB DITZ!

Hunched over the steering wheel, shivering and vacant-headed at this worry-laden crossroad, prayed-for enlightenment's arrival pending; identity-festooned with barbed grappling hooks—still buried deep in Stygian darkness; defying all attempts at excavation; his chief spring...

On wind-up manual...?

UNTRUSTWORTHY!

...and not nearly as powerful. The reserve motive agent almost fully untensioned as Richard the L-Man choked, proximately scared witless.

But not quite!

WHY WASTE TIME?

Knowledge be thy power...

WHICH YOU LOSE EVEN NOW!

Jefferson sucked in deep gulps of wet air while running

figures on the added loss of amps-volts-watts...clanging awareness heralding minor miracle: the remembrance of long-blocked surname.

Without trying?

THERE'S ALWAYS A COST! IT'S WHAT YOU HAVE LOST!

His spring-jumping singularity catapulted first by compressed-coiled iron's bounding leap, then somersaulting in whirligig fan dance, jerkily erratic like a free-tailed bat on haphazard, bug-eating patrol: sideslip, stall, wingover-and...

Flutterings...

...friendly, not a bloodsucker....

Bela! Bela! Bela!

JAMIE! JAMIE! JAMIE!

...the last name having popped up like a pasteboard flash card pushed erect by grease-stained hydraulics, almost effortlessly...unless he were too sickly weak to know for sure.

It took far too much preciously charged plasma to calculate how much energy was used up solely in trying to remember, even before nub recollection shone illumined for in-mind display, so Jefferson uncupped fear-clasped hands and launched that robin redbreast...sent it flying free.

POSITIVE?

...meant less than total depletion...therefore pleasing...

Yes, 'twas good!

...therefore favorable. Yet all told, this was before the drain fully registered.

Heavier wire gauges...

LEAD TO FRIGHTFUL RAGES.

Bad boy!

Preteen Jefferson's fingers caught between closing Dutch-door panels...him and rusty hinges screeching like African parrots...there again materializing the musty pantry itself.

Beaten/going in;
Beaten/coming out;
The switch flew fast

And cracked my grout.

And now with precious neuroelectricity hissing moistly airborne from scraped-bottom reservoirs, Jefferson tumbled to the fact that it was critical he go...

Back-back!

NOW!

Immediately!

IF NOT SOONER!

Rushing the try...

IT WORSENS YET! BAD BOY! BAD BOY!

...he had to go backward, in itself a terribly awesome struggle...

Perhaps fatal...

IF TIME RUNS OUT!

They want me dead...

MISERLY SECONDS!

The Take-All-Jefferson-Has struggle found him twisting painfully between front bucket seats and scrabble-crawling into the bowels of an unlit van.

Wall to wall and edge to edge was the slick-scale skin of cargo bay's inner liner: multicolored, Arabic-emblazoned posters trumpeting the impending triumph of the Palestine Liberation Organization over the Zionist entity; Arafat in battle dress addressing a rapt United Nations' General Assembly; Walid Masyaf acknowledging cheering throngs flanking his flag-waving, Damascus motorcade; Gadhafi blessing marching rows of determined guerrillas; Abul al-Abbas thumbing his nose at the western world after making good his escape from rollover Italians following the Achille Lauro Affair; fedayeen rallying commando squads; AK-47s and Soviet APCs redundant.

With ohmic resistance practically nil, Jefferson ignored the decorations whose curling bottoms popped free one at a time from duct-tape anchors to snap-clatter up like *"Scared ya!"* window shades. Of sole importance were flicker-glow discharges of precious potential, soon to be memorialized as wastefully frittered kinetics.

Memory's dying fluorescence flickered coolly as amoebic phosphors gobbling broken islands of consciousness, all pulsing like ebbing picture-tube glowworms wriggling in trashed TVs. Things...concepts...a sign touting ENTENMANN'S in glittering letters pinwheeling end over crushed-foil end...swirling, barber-pole pyrotechnics fed by grid emissions crackling all around Jefferson in wasteful disarray. Fragments at first, then...

The accident...

NO!

...barrages of jangled discordance at first insinuating, then trying unsuccessfully to body-block their way completely back in, full ingress prevented by nearly parched accumulators: Leyden jars, NiCads, wet cells and alkalines…all insufficiently powered up to run in-head projections of assorted multiple-choice pasts.

Scarlet tanager, my absolute favorite shoulder-percher...but why is it....

JAMIE'S DRESS, ABLAZE IN FIRE'S FINERY!

I did not strike the match!

YOU HELD IT HEMWISE, LICKING CRINOLINE!

No!

SEE JAMIE TURN AS SHE BURNS, YON PYROTECHNIC PIROUETTE...

Turn back...

TO BEATINGS!

Where has Uncle Joey gone?

DOO-DAH! DOO DAH!

Fragments skeet-balled haphazardly through retrenching backstops of collapsing psyche...curlicue edges promising only The Pit. Images passing so quickly that Jefferson had no clue as to what had whistled through in the first place. The posters were...

Secondary?

FOCUS!

His internal meters dutifully monitored talc-dusted cerebral cortex shorting out against itself while digesting its own nuclear marrow in impetuous drive toward hunger-slake. Cohesion dripped out of eyes, ears, nose, every hole, every pore.

He'd forgotten again; even remembering to shunt the unimportant stuff swilled energy like a manic wino swigging rotgut.

Tentacled pipes busily vacuumed up every last dreg of energy from rickety reality. Not a flow now; too tapped out for gushers; this next demanded darkness. With eyes shut, Jefferson-tight, fear was a grim-lipped specter playing his rib cage like a devilish accordion.

Danger Land looming...

RIGHT LANE MUST EXIT!

So seriously hollow as to have almost neglected the basics, Jefferson jiggled in wild apprehension, fretful of booking passage on God's winged spirit ante-transformation, lest he become...

Incredibly shrunken...

PISSED AWAY IN WORTHLESS VANISHMENT!

Groping blindly for the unmatched cloaker of Silly Putty, its worth proved by 111 carefully controlled experiments...finding it and nearly fumbling it away, now opening it...stretch-snapping elasticity into five unequal pieces: one for each ear—twist and jam them in; one for each nostril; repeat the drill...then agitated oral oxygenation into...

GULP, GULP, GULP!

One/Two/Three/Four/Five/Six/Hold-On-Lucky-Seven

STOP!

...deep, lung-bursting breath, stretching in pain...

TO 11-NOW!

...and press-flattening the last long strip across tightly compressed lips fronting pristine-white, reconstructed teeth. Patched and plugged, Jefferson's spinal-tap clock began its inexorable countdown, a lifespan previously calculated as...

Three minutes?

PLACE YOUR BETS!

Fewer?

STOP THE LEAKAGE!

Leakage stopped, sir!

I AM NOT A SIR! I AM A SERGEANT. I EARN MY PAY!

Spinning around on a rebuilt right kneecap like a frenetic

break dancer, Jefferson punished himself further by forcing third-time confirmation that the cab/van crawl-door was indeed locked. The...

RICKETY-TIK-TIK!/RICKETY-TIK-TIK!/RICKETY-TIK-TIK!

...inside his chest, more badminton birdie than heart, dipping like a novelty drinking duck; pawl and ratchet clicking off waning moments marking the distance between present and final ecstasy's onrushing arrival. Latched inside the safe cocoon at last...

I'm sure! I'm sure!

ARE YOU?

...the right wall's arming panel displaying unseen CODE GREEN status on all area-denial devices...his eyes shut tight and working only by feelies.

Yes, of course, they're on "Safe."

ARE THEY?

Jefferson yanked off latex pinky shields worn on pampered, tender-soft, baby-smooth fingers...rarely removed rubber covering ensuring ultra-tender touch pads sensitive enough to feel even the fractional warmth emitted by pinpoint LEDs.

Most assuredly...

The proper bulbs are glowing warm like pinhead boils.

NEVER IN SEQUENCE; REMEMBER THE SERIES; THREE AND SEVEN...

Are bogus, of course!

PRESS DOWN...TO BLOW TOWN!

Blood pounded in his ears as miscalculation nudged him toward...

A new reality?

IN TRUTH? FATALITY!

Jefferson splashed William's 'Lectric Shave into trembling hands...

TOO SLOW!

...then frantically shook the bottle over his head and feverishly worked the liquid in, panic suddenly an eerie, mystic goo all around...hypoxia as the freight elevator slowly pushing him groggily aloft.

Air?

YOU MUSTN'T!

With time running out, he slapped the fluid onto his cranium as lungs peeped with patient protest. While polite though insistent...

TWO-MINUTE WARNING!

...alveoli geared up for their *"Feed Me!"* scream, Jefferson plugged his carefully maintained Norelco into the well-dusted outlet on the bottom of the arming panel.

Click-on!

Z...Z...Z...Z...Z...Z...Z...Z...SHALL BE YOUR FINAL SNORE!

His methodology was achingly precise—11 circles clockwise; 11 circles counterclockwise-until...

Finally?

HURRY!

...each quadrant was cleanly depilated in a queer spectrum of blotchy reds—ruby, scarlet, maroon, rust, strawberry, salmon, rose, pink—from too much rotational enthusiasm in some places, lightly over scars still healing in others, no spot could remain uncleaned lest disaster ensue.

Jefferson swatted away the intrusion of multicolored Ferris wheels spinning crazily in his head, each tilting axially before ripping free to skim waterward like fishing lures over rippling rings of star-bright ocean...next forming binary systems with neon rainbows scything sun-dappled seas.

Breathe?

NO!

Stacked-left echelons of soap-bubble UFOs orbited inside corners of scrunched-tight eyes. Silly-Putty'd closed. Consciousness slipping, fearful to gasp, there rumbled...

I am become Jefferson!

THY HEAD ALONE SHALL NOT SUFFICE!

I am become Jefferson!

THOU SHALL BECOME A CORPSE ON ICE!

Jefferson anxiously ripped off stone-washed coveralls in a spray of Unique Boutique buttons. He peeled off the shirt next, then yanked down boxer shorts and cast them away with socks... stripped totally naked and working feverishly now. Shaver tossed aside, eye protection snapped on, then...

CLICK!

...overhead tanning tubes blinking bluish...

All on?

OF COURSE ALL ON!

Course-a-lon!

JAMIE'S WAITING!

The putty ripped off, he was grateful for life-giving breath guzzled greedily in the mellow-purple van-back, misted air tasting primo now that he could suck in great lungsful. No more worry about reverse conduction as the van's muggy atmosphere absorbed the last of this day's extorted, splintered vitals, corkscrewing crazily outward toward an eternity only narrowly avoided.

Jefferson gurgled like a well-fed baby, lushly comfortable in the flow of beaming ultraviolet rays bathing his earthly entirety...right down to rigidly outspread fingers and toes, and perhaps a Nair bath later this evening. Waxing simply takes up too much precious time.

Turning stomach-down so as to better launder all epidermal surfaces directly, the whole of his physical body functioned as an energy-absorbing panel, each pore a solar cell of God's incredible design. Eleven minutes later, Jefferson flipped himself over and sat up to funnel intellect-restoring radiance more directly into bald pate, thereby ensuring efficient tank-up of ever-hungry, slow-running brain...which was now clicking over faster now, thank you very much.

Direct sunlight was pump without peer, but Jefferson fully understood that all one could really do was make do, especially in dirty, unforgiving winter. He unputtied his ears and nose, then ungoggled to better imbibe visual gusto...teasing himself with a taste of true power's incredible potency. Measured doses taken in cautiously through unprotected eyes were natural highs hitting him stronger than jolts of pure cocaine to the brain.

Eyes closed again as magenta cotton-candy spun amiably across the ear-to-ear Cinemascope screen unfurling inside his head. Images taking tentative form as diaphanous puff quickly hardened into a parody of filmed A-bomb destruction run in reverse. Firming up as swirls turned concrete solids was the accident...prefaced as always by the stink of hot slag assaulting nostrils as ears stereoed the steel-mill thunder of prime-time recollection.

I'll live through this as I lived through that.

BACK ON TRACK WITH A TIP OF YOUR HAT.

Jefferson was buoyed by the compliment. Life ran smoothly as a timing chain in an oil bath when he was able to work with Head Man, instead of being flogged by that worship-worthy presence.

Now listen while I play the old story.

WHEN THE SUN REROSE IN ALL HIS GLORY.

Jefferson never moved an inch either way without agreement affirmed thrice.

I'm ready if you are, I say to the voice.

I'M HERE FOR THE RIDE, SO THERE'S REALLY NO CHOICE.

Southeast Georgia summer. Air too uncomfortably thick for normal respiration dripped foundry fallout while painting every worry in the world on Jefferson's sopping back...and he wished desperately for a renegotiated birthright rooted deep in aridity. Shrouding it all was the purgatorial reek of raw steel in the making, real men doing rugged work in the closest thing to Dante's Inferno, topside of Hades itself.

Everyone from the seashore to Savannah was bone-weary of the tease. Native American drums beat for precipitation. Sticky-damp unfortunates cast about eagerly for every rain-making charm imaginable, while conscripting all manner of old wives' tales into immediate and fervent use. Jefferson himself had sacrificed three female opossums in a backwoods sacrifice peppered with Cajun/voodoo undertones.

And still, Mother Nature demurred.

While silently praying along with the humidified multitude for surcease from overbearing dankness, Jefferson and the maintenance crew he ably captained were about to casually happen by Furnace #5 of the ex-Star Steel Enterprises' minimill, recently become part of the Southeast Division of Coastal Steel Corporation, and what a lube job that had been.

The snapping up of Star Steel's physical assets for pocket change and a handful of Coastal preferred stock—a deal that Wall Street said gave new meaning to the term "garage sale"—had been an incredible steal for reasons later painfully obvious while digging out from high-casualty disaster. Yanked away from criminal mismanagement and just inches away from the near-bottomless pit of Chapter 11, steelworks' maintenance had been absent for months, turned years. Corner-cutting and cost shaving? To bank higher profits? It made good enough boardroom sense, but the only thing showing up in real-world P&Ls was fancy, not fact.

Corporate records later revealed doctoring that had transformed a marginally truthful reality into high-tech fiction fully worthy of a Pulitzer Prize for corporate lies. Specifically:

—Furnace #5 had been in nonstop operation for 48 months straight, not the 24 attested to by company maintenance logs.

—Furnace #5's firebrick had been substandard to begin with, and long overdue for general repair, if not outright replacement.

Lawsuits filed later on behalf of maimed and crippled survivors cited additional irregularities, including but not limited to:

—Skip cars carrying too much high-grade coke with their loads of ore and limestone.

—Faulty valving bottoming out the pressure of water used to cool the furnace.

—The temperature of the air coming in from the giant

stoves jumped 750 degrees higher than poorly maintained *tuyeres* were designed to handle.

—The increase showing up later, one horribly burned survivor testified, while sight-sick jury members averted their eyes, as a small up/down arc on a rusted gauge, the movement of which set off a siren...

—Whose brief whoop-whoop was just as quickly silenced by rotted wiring smoking to a quick meltdown under the sudden influx of electricity.

Shift change coming on; feet don't fail Jefferson coming off. He congratulated himself on passing up the latest "opportunity" advanced by rapacious management, who evidently thought this hardworking son of a hardworking man was dumber than a box of rocks. Jefferson casually booted aside his chance to sweat off another dozen or so ounces in pursuit of the elusive goal of "making things right."

Not for Jefferson.

No siree!

Six more minutes of energy absorption, and perhaps he would be able to fill in the face of the pneumatic woman with whom he stopped to chat. That foot-dragging face-to-face with Tits-A-Plenty, who was now treading inky water just beyond the reach of memory's ever-eager grasp, personified Lady Luck's blessing. Dame Fortune held Jefferson in check, while no doubt snickering over his vain attempt to spark a liaison with the Georgia Industrial Commission's most ogled safety inspector, a full-breasted divorcee with whom Jefferson had cemented more than just a nodding acquaintance.

He hardly cared about that now; what really mattered was that Fate casually punched the final time cards of 43 men and women in the immediate vicinity of Furnace #5, all of whom died instantly in the blast, bringing late-afternoon sunrise to waterfall day. Yellow/white sphericals afforded Jefferson his amazing chance to see firsthand how truly brilliant Old Sol was when His Royal Skyness deigned to come down and play.

Details of the aftermath filled 35 three-ring, evidentiary

binders. It took investigators six weeks to shovel up 43 sets of "mostly complete" fire-charred bones for unceremonious dumping into industrial-strength, black-vinyl body bags. For Jefferson, it was in and out of county operating rooms to repair skull fissures punched open by molten steel...breaks initially patched over by doubtful paramedics who'd written off the near-dead man with the half-crushed head. "Beats The Odds With Bashed Brain," tabloids screamed.

Hail spatter on the van roof brought him back to plum-purple present day. The automatic timer *clicked,* turning off all eight parallel tanning lamps as one. Refreshed, revitalized, and with brainpower potently resurgent, Jefferson opened the sliding door to the van's cab, smiling boyishly up at the rain-smeared windshield. Broken skies mottled with rays of random sunlight and light-gray cirrocumulus bode well for the upcoming journey west.

With body and warmly recharged head comfortably toasty to the touch, he was at last able to ponder other pressing projects lined up like interstate telephone poles between here and now... and his final coming due.

"But first things first," Jefferson murmured good-naturedly.

He fastidiously spread two pounds of desiccant around the van's inside perimeter to combat moisture always driven in through small leaks that no amount of caulking could ever fully seal. Then he carefully crouch-dressed completely in black, energy-absorbing clothes: thermal underwear; snugly zippered cotton jumpsuit; waterproof hiking boots laced tightly over woolen socks; black-silk scarf knotted at the throat; light pancake makeup on his face and the back of his neck to seal pores against draining; hands sheathed in kid-leather gloves; bald pate fully protected by black-felt porkpie hat.

Finally satisfied, Jefferson carefully removed the propaganda posters adorning the van's inside walls, then banded and stacked them neatly for planned drop-off near State Road 224, outside of Kellogg, Iowa—population around 700, plus or minus.

Now that will get them wondering why...
THEIR 747 DROPPED OUT OF THE SKY.

CHAPTER 6
AFTERMATH

On Thanksgiving morning, the six-square-block Hawes/ Rodriguez Project still veritably glistened as the Hope Diamond in the tiara of North America's finest urban reclamation effort on the plats. Making the most of sweat equity, far-sighted planning, and Lotto dollars, the project scribed Chicago's inviolable line against the rapidly spreading cancer of urban blight. In the process, the city had taken back the land.

Corner-anchored by mid-rise apartment buildings, the project highlighted affordable residential brownstones. French-curve greenbelt landscaping softened the impact of vandal-resistant concrete and steel; playground equipment doubled as modern art; genetically engineered, pollution-resistant trees dotted rolling grounds.

Exemplifying the cutting edge in metropolitan resurrection, Hawes/Rodriguez had pried itself free of the deadly grip of drug dealers, gun-slinging gangs, and crack-addicted prostitutes, all of whom had been unceremoniously drop-kicked into permanent exile. The prestigious *Urban Planning Magazine* extolled Hawes/ Rodriguez as a model hope for city revitalization worldwide.

But Thanksgiving afternoon was daubed somber, as if from a palette of 18 percent neutral-density gray and a runny spray paint of powdered cinders and dirty slush. Visible only in snatches through drifting draperies of snow flurries parting randomly before closing up almost immediately, Hawes/ Rodriguez had been warped into a napalmed, post-apocalypse battleground reeling after a turf war executed by rampaging robots: ruined brownstones smashed to gravel over whole families killed instantly during turkey dinner; powdered brickwork whorling smoke after being pounded flat as if under the feet of angry, fire-breathing giants.

Monolithic smog rose like a gravestone 10 stories high by four blocks square, casting a funereal omnipresence over utter devastation. Denuded parkland evoked foggy English moor scarred raw as if from peat-bog fires only just extinguished by fast-moving squall lines...with far-off skeletal steel spiking hauntingly up through distant mist.

Serpentine clouds mixed fitfully with tapering tendrils of grayish-white smoke. A black column of rain-spackled vapor rose from a small brush fire left to burn itself out. Police and MedEvac helicopters buzzed like confused cicadas through Jet A-laced haze. Red rotating beacons went slick pink; green marker lights faded to pale, washed-out emerald. Rescue workers poked and prodded the fume-wrapped remains of the tangled 747 tail section, hopeful of finding strapped-in survivors but despairing that anyone had come through the searing holocaust alive.

From the harrowed edges of recently extinguished inferno, Judith could absorb only segmental fractions of frightful vista; her eyes stopped at each compass point to take in what she could before gagging took over and eyelids locked shut in hopes of making breathing easier. The cruel leveling, as if by bulldozers run amok, was almost total: Smoking ruins could have passed for a firebombed Dresden or Tokyo after a nocturnal visit by vengeful, incendiary-sowing B-29s.

Judith's diplomatic ID squirted her past the uniforms, sternly keeping gawkers and potential looters at bay on the safe side of the already-crowded cordon. She carefully avoided hot-spot craters, crackling spews of black smoke. Jagged strips of ripped aluminum twinkled in scattered light like haphazard streamers of cast-off tinsel. White smoke wafted in confused spirals, first fighting the shifting wind, then dispersing in horizontal acquiescence.

She steeled herself while skirting what little remained of passengers and crew. Nature breathed angry wind at snapping yellow sheets, aggrievedly determined not to let this atrocity remain under baleful wraps. Judith knew it was far too soon for all wrenched-off limbs to have been flagged. Invariably, hands having suffered violent separation from murdered owners splashed her with cataractous anxiety; it was that particular human detritus to which she studiously gave as wide a berth as possible.

Three FAA investigators, one from O'Hare and two from downtown, prospected wreckage in search of the aircraft's black boxes, whose locating beacons had gone unaccountably mute. One sidelong glance was all Judith rated as she carefully trod scorched earth between the uneven goalposts of sheared-off trees. Thickly moist air cloaking lungs' insides made breathing a full-time job...carrying as it did jet-fuel residue commingling with the sickly sweet odor of cooked human flesh.

"You're new." That from a florid examiner nodding curtly at credentials flipped open for his incurious inspection. "You telling me I got State sniffing around this one?" Judith dodged the question, concentrating instead on shark eyes that stayed insolently full while scoping her lengthwise with cold, unmasked distaste. "Cavanaugh, John C. FAA."

"Judith Levy."

He eyed her crookedly, taking manifest care to keep their handshake brief, obviously uncomfortable at having had to touch her at all. And judging by the way Cavanaugh's fat lips puffed out when their hands parted, Judith knew him to be greatly relieved when the brief contact was finally broken.

"Mind your manners, Ms. Levy," he cautioned. "Whatever you do, don't step on anything."

"I have done this drill before," Judith replied, her slit-eyed aloofness at least 20 degrees colder than Cavanaugh's frigid politeness.

"Sure you have, Ms. Levy, but they're all different, and this one is no exception."

"Mind if I walk along with you?"

"Free country."

"First thoughts?"

"No time was wasted bringing her down," he said laconically.

And no words were wasted in describing the deed.

Cavanaugh stopped his attentive, slow-footed shuffle and used a gold fountain pen to gently tent a sieved raincoat half-cloaking a decapitated corpse jammed between a sliding pond's stainless-steel steps. Then the inspector pulled an aged meerschaum out of his trench-coat pocket, tamped a fresh load of North Country Glen into the bowl, and flared a stick match.

"Should you be doing that?" Judith asked.

"Now would you be asking from the standpoint of the crash or my personal health?"

"Maybe both, maybe not."

"For the most part, what's burnable's already gone to ash. Besides, this helps keep the stink of death out of my nose, which means I can do a better job for you and your...masters."

Judith broke away from the staring contest, gambling that deference would loosen his tongue.

"First thoughts, Ms. Levy?" Cavanaugh's cheeks went shallow as he drew deeply on his pipe. His perfectly launched string of six, almost-interlinked smoke rings broke up quickly in the rain. "For starters, they could have waited until TransPac 117 was well out over the Pacific; the technology for that is yesterday's news. Bulbs planted these days can lie dormant through multiple takeoffs and landings, if need be, before blooming lethally. At the very least, they could have waited until the plane was at cruising altitude westbound. For damn sure, it would have been harder to piece things together then." Cavanaugh glanced around, checked wind direction, and jotted a few shorthand notes as overworked stretcher-bearers carried another one away. He puffed up a smoke screen while taking in the sight of leveled houses. "The sons of bitches went for a low-level, overland kill," he continued. "This one was engineered to ensure a maximum number of dead on the ground, and for damn sure it looks as if the evil bastards got their wish."

"Suspects?"

"Now you're way out of bounds, Ms. Levy."

Cavanaugh's roll-away eyes went blank at Judith's crossed-arm shiver. Too ungenerous to take her any deeper into his confidence, Cavanaugh immediately resumed his tack of studiously pretending she was vanished vapor, but his unsubtle presentation of broad back didn't deter her from tagging along on the preliminary fact-finding tour. Then Cavanaugh abruptly dropped to one knee, using a corner of the clipboard to gingerly lift a burned section of landing-gear door still sizzling like bacon on a griddle. Two grasped hands came visible underneath a bent-back corner of ragged-edged metal.

A little boy's left? His mother's right?

Judith whirled away while raising mental defenses against the scaly demon forever clawing for egress from the rusty cage in which it was only temporarily incarcerated. And then her ears were tweaked by a wind-borne snatch of gossip about a strange artifact blown totally into a charred-black body. Moments later, she was hunched over in the windbreak formed by two men standing like ice-rimmed astral spirits trailing wisps of patchy ground fog.

"That was one I saw 'em cart downtown right away," Big Amos said, taking Judith immediately into his confidence. He leaned a ruggedly square chin casually on the tip of a long wooden staff while standing astride a wreckage-plowed picnic mound like a black Joshua gazing out over a war-ravaged promised land. Big Amos pulled off an olive drab cowboy hat and wiped rainwater off his brow with the sleeve of a camouflage poncho. "Huge goddamn thing it was, too, Miss."

"No kidding," Tiny Mike said. The smaller man glanced around furtively, then pulled a paper-bagged fifth of Cutty Sark out from the inside hip pocket of a jungle-green raincoat. He took three deep gulps before offering the bottle to Judith. She declined with a nonjudgmental headshake. "It's for the cold," Tiny Mike apologized. "I been cold ever since the Nam."

"It is close to freezing today," Judith offered.

"Don't make no difference to me. Winter or summer, it's always the same." Tiny Mike's haunted eyes carried the look of a pile-driven gnome who'd seen far more than he could catalog... or cared to remember. "My body temperature's always been a coupla degrees below normal since I took one in the gut," he murmured. "I was in country..."

"Way, way in country," Big Amos interrupted with obvious respect. "So far in country that he was out of it, if you're hearing what I'm saying."

"No kidding," Tiny Mike said bleakly, tar-black BB eyes aglint with the desperate need to keep secrets still. "Senior scout observer with a long-range patrol team of the 151st Ranger Infantry." Tiny Mike broke off in midthought; then he shuddered and fell silent.

"Talking helps," Big Amos said.

"Only sometimes," Tiny Mike spat gruffly.

Big Amos waited until he was sure Tiny Mike was finished. While the smaller man chugged his way through half the fifth of whiskey, Big Amos piped in proudly: "Got mine with the 101st Airborne Division at Hill 937, Ap Bia Mountain, about a klick and a half in from Laos. You mighta heard about it. Press called it Hamburger Hill."

Judith shook her head.

"Even made a movie out of it," Tiny Mike said.

"Weren't like no goddamned movie," Big Amos huffed angrily. "I tell you, lotsa grunts didn't get up when the ChiCom chatterguns went mute. Wasn't no Hollywood extras with phony guts decorating the landscape, for damn sure. Those KIAs were for fucking real, man."

"No kidding," Tiny Mike offered.

"Yeah, no kidding is fucking right," Big Amos chimed in morosely.

Judith nudged the conversation back on track. "I heard you mention a cross."

"Yep-indeedy," Big Amos said, his face brightening again. "My caseworker, she's taking Comparative Religion at that there new, downtown city university. I'll have to ask her about it. It had like a head on it, for Christ's sake. I ain't never seen the Lord Jesus with that big a noggin. Damndest thing, it was. Couldn't see all of it, but I saw enough of it to know the damn thing was a cross. A cross with a big goddamned head on it."

"No kidding," Tiny Mike mumbled, hitting on the bottle again before turning aside and blowing his nose toward the ground.

"Yeah, no kidding for damn sure," Big Amos said, beckoning for a brown-bag swig. He gulped down a strong double shot, then pulled out a half-crushed pack of generic cigarettes, shook out one for each of them, cupped his large hands around Judith's, and bent down toward her match. "My case worker," Big Amos said softly, his face wreathed in glowing cigarette smoke and fog, "she'll know what it was. Anyway," he boomed, straightening up, "they hustled that crucifix outta here pretty damn quick, along with the crusty critter it was sticking into, which was one for the Dental Records boys, I might add, although, as far as I could tell, all its teeth were gone, too. So they'll have a helluva job filling out a toe tag on that one, not that it had any toes left to take the wire anyway."

"No kidding," Tiny Mike said.

"Yeah, no kidding is one hundred percent correct. That once-was got more VIP treatment dead than it ever got alive, if you ask me. Mighta been on the plane tourist, but it sure as hell got transferred out of here first fucking class."

"Transferred where?" Judith asked.

"Downtown," Big Amos replied. "Me and Tiny Mike, we heard a coupla suits yakking up a storm about it. Medical Examiner's office, if I'm guessing right, and with a police escort like you'd think they were carrying what was left of His Honor the Mayor himself."

And then from behind she heard: "And right now you're thinking they might have found out who John Hancocked this one."

Judith whirled, her ever-ready left hand a poised gutrammer angling upward for solar-plexus thrust.

"Consistent, too. You're still jumpy as a fall whitetail."

That voice!

"Reflexes. Michael!"

Business first. Damn it to hell...business first!

The fog blew aside. She saw him dressed in a weathered, Western-style, smoke-leather greatcoat tucked back behind hands thrust far down into linty pockets. A washed-out flannel shirt fit tightly into lightweight jeans laundered almost into oblivion. Cowboy boots that never tasted polish put him head and shoulders above every other man in Judith's life. Michael's black hair was combed straight back into a ponytail, the style more befitting Armani clothes than faded Plains outfit, which looked as if it had been laboriously hand-sewn for his lanky, well-muscled frame.

Dark, usually shrouded raven-breast eyes set back deep over high, sheer-angle cheekbones today gleamed with the lavish appreciation he beamed at no other woman.

"We were about to compare notes," he said, trying vainly for serious.

"A crucifix?"

"Well, you're ballpark. Not bad for having been on site... what?" He squinted up at the sun, which had just broken through clouds adamantly fighting its nervy trespass. "All of nineteen and a half minutes, by my reckoning."

"And you managed to stay away that long?"

"It's almost as much a pleasure watching you from afar as it is to be within touching distance. A cross, huh? Well, you are good."

"That is why they sent me. What is your excuse?"

"Just happened to be in town for the Field Museum's exhibition of Native American art. Other than that, it's the same old/same old."

"You are in on this?" she asked hopefully.

"More on you than on this, but I can extend."

"Babysitting again?"

"Officially, yes. Remember, I've had some practice. But unofficially...?"

The unspoken hung between them like a pregnant cloud, bulge-bellied with rain but chary of giving.

"So I'm your tabby again," he said, resignedly appreciative for any mote of captivating presence on which he could feast.

"Since when do I rate chaperoning?"

"Since word went out to keep you and your mischief-makers in line. This has to be done strictly by the numbers, completely by the book. Apex is royally pissed off, and he wants it done right."

The President of the United States!

"And you are privy to that?"

"High enough up the chain of command to merit my personal copy of *The Wall Street Journal.* No comment other than that, Ms. Mossad."

"Well, it is no secret how your people reward their marginally competent," Judith cracked. "And now I see that Native Americans have gotten to ride on that particular wagon."

"Better than attacking them," Michael laughed. "Actually, you're seeing the Peter Principle at work. Tell you the truth, I'm convinced they matched us both on skin color. Seeing as we're both children of the olive, we can hold hands without running afoul of racists."

"It would never work. Peas in a pod, we are not. Besides, you wear your hair too long for my taste, Michael. How your people let you..."

"A minor concession they make to Comanches. They don't quite trust us not to come back and scalp them in the dark. So they let my kind slide on the grooming regulations. Of course, I can always claim religious exemption."

"You should have been a lawyer, Michael."

"Stop 'shoulding' on me."

"You know," she said seriously. "I never fully thanked you for Uncompahgre Plateau."

Chilly, body-punching gusts of heavy Lake Michigan

weather wind-sailed her back to the biting breath of vicious Colorado winter. Seven years ago. Still a virgin in counterterrorism. She displayed more enthusiasm than brains while tracking two Black September killers northeast to Escalante Forks, carelessly leaving her back perilously exposed.

If not for Michael...

Mossad, had it cared to, might still be looking for her perfectly preserved body, buried somewhere deep in Colorado high country...deep-freeze intact save for a skull cracked apart and brain scrambled to omelet by a jacketed bullet. Only later did she learn that the Palestinians had been deliberately sloppy, in hopes of drawing her in...and she'd been too pridefully blind to see it.

The Syrian shooter on their team was hanging way back in the timberline high on her left, and she had obliged the opposition by placing herself directly in the crosshairs of their night-sight-equipped sniping rifle. The bullet split her right earring before thunking through tree bark and underbrush. Twenty-two slow-motion seconds seemed to pass after the shock of the near miss before she heard the *craack* of a faraway high-powered rifle. Only much later, while nursing a potent double Chivas in the plastic comfort of High View Lodge's great room, was her equilibrium fully savaged by the realization of how dangerously close it had been.

Right-hand fingers seemed to squeeze moisture from the water-beaded glass. Left hand's fingers, as always, were extended straight out and awkward. A shadowy flicker hinted at company. Someone seemed to have notched down the jukebox's country/western wail of true love gone sour. So silent had been his approach that she became fully cognizant of his presence only when the cocktail waitress hurried over to take his order: club soda, dash of grenadine, twist of lime.

Eyes darker than the south side of midnight picked up twinkling flecks of tarnished light. He seemed to bore-sight her brain, augering intently through to the attic of her psyche like an alien probing for weak spots in emotional bulwarks. She pegged him as a heavyweight and instantly raised inside shields. His Kirlian read: "DANGER ALL THE WAY." She tensed involuntarily as he gingerly pulled back his lapel with his left thumb and forefinger.

"As you can probably tell," he said, "I'm a righty."

"How would I know?"

"Statistically, most people are," he replied nonchalantly, very carefully, and awkwardly reaching into his shirt pocket with two left-hand fingers.

"You don't strike me as 'most people.'"

"Point well taken."

She relaxed only slightly as he slowly withdrew his identification, transferred it to his right hand, flipped it open, and introduced himself.

"Michael Running Horse."

"You always enter like a ninja?" she asked evenly, taking his ID for a closer look.

"My people taught 'em everything they know. The world's first and most famous cross-cultural exchange. And you're...?"

"Kayla will do for now."

"A lovely name, Kayla."

"Something you are sure to remember."

"Bank on it," he said firmly.

She squinted in the squirrelly light, then held up the photo ID for closer examination, taking time to carefully compare face to credentialed image. His eyes were as striking and fiercely intense under plastic as they were across the booth, alive and drilling through bar smoke like bluish-white arc lights. The picture was more hologram than snapshot. It set her teeth on edge.

Catching movement across the room, Judith shook her head almost imperceptibly.

"That would be your backup," Michael noted. "Fatso behind the bar. And let's not forget the hostess, ball-busting calves on that one...and the dishwasher who gets weak in the knees at the sight of a sweaty college halfback. You know, it just might be time to call Orkin down on this here nest of pests."

"Special Investigations Division," she read, ignoring his comments while sizing him up. "Bureau of Indian Affairs, Department of the Interior. Personally, I think you are dialing the wrong number."

"It's a big country, with plenty of interior. Lots of things come my way. Let's say people like yourself. Sometimes out for a nighttime walk in the woods."

She closed his card case and tapped it thoughtfully on her glass. An ice-cube pyramid collapsed. She handed back his ID, deciding it was time to go eye-to-eye. "Are you investigating stolen artifacts?"

"Actually, this discovery comes from a present-day dig...and much more interesting than ancient history," he said, pocketing his paperwork. "About nine-thirty this evening. Some forty minutes before you showed up here. Close to twelve miles back in the hills."

Shivers played xylophone on her vertebrae. A large rifle cartridge suddenly appeared in his hands, where moments before a moist swizzle stick twirled. He rolled the cartridge back and forth between pianist's fingers, stopping it with a well-manicured forefinger before setting it in motion with a concealed pinky.

"Got this little jewel from a recently deceased. Coincidentally, he didn't have a lick of ID on him, not even a label in his Jockeys. But he was snuggling a Dragunov SVD sniper rifle, which around these parts is a mighty unique calling card; 7.62mm, but I guess you're up on your calibers."

He looked up and snared her eyes.

As a man interested in a woman? As an interrogator, interested in an answer?

TAKE NO CHANCES! GIVE NOTHING AWAY!

"Russian gun," he continued, staring halfway through her. "Not your garden-variety hunting weapon. Not the hour for it, either. No, this guy's prey is...I mean, was...the only kind that runs both day and night. No matter; he's sleeping under a snowdrift now. And you? How're you doing?"

He reached out before she could draw back, took her chin

roughly in his palm, and carefully examined both sides of her face.

"None the worse for wear, Ms. Mossad, in spite of that nasty tumble you took tonight. Care to share some details?"

She pulled free and shook her head angrily, eyes narrowing. "I have nothing to say."

"Did you nail the other two you were pursuing?"

"Other two?"

"Figured as much." Michael glanced around the room, nodding amiably at the swag-bellied bartender staring their way while wiping the same spot of oak-plank bar over and over. Then he locked eyes with her. "I don't suppose you have any ID either."

"Nothing I would care to show you right now, unless this is official business."

"It would be if I thought for a minute that you were running stolen Indian artifacts." Michael grinned broadly. "You know, I think I'm beginning to like you, in spite of myself."

Her icy return smile was merely a social nicety. Then she looked down at the metal object he had slid across the table to clink up against her cocktail glass. A six-inch lock of thick black hair was braided carefully and knotted around a platinum ankh. The loose ends, at first limp and flat, curled suddenly in the room's warmth as if coming alive again.

"El-Fahd el-Aswad," he said, watching for a reaction. "Isn't that what you people call Black Leopard?"

She looked at him sharply, her eyes flat.

"Yeah, I thought so," he said. "Never figured to come across them...or you...this far west. Out here we call 'em bubonics, 'cause that's how they're spreading: like a goddamned plague. You people ever gonna kiss and make up?"

"You want it in twenty-five words or less?" she shot back.

She reached out to touch the precious-metal talisman. Her fingers trembled as they brushed the strands of black hair.

"Twentieth-century good taste precludes my giving you the whole scalp. Not enough time to properly dry and cure it."

She snorted out two puffs of nervous laughter before

coming close to breaking down completely. Then she reached up to touch the place where her cheek still throbbed after having been sliced open by a fragment of an earring. When she regained enough composure to look up, he was gone. He had left the ankh, the bullet, and his business card, on which was written: "Breakfast tomorrow. Six a.m."

If not for Michael...

She saw him several times in the hectic weeks that followed before the Palestinians slipped through the dragnet and got clean away. Their compressed courtship consisted mainly of dinners ranging from the ridiculous to the sublime, during which he proposed marriage 18 times. The moment she found herself hesitating before saying no, she excused herself to make a phone call to the Israeli Consulate in Los Angeles. Less than 12 minutes later, her request for transfer home had been granted, and return transportation arranged.

Over the intervening seesaw years, he tried valiantly to keep in touch. Most times, his beautifully poetic letters lay unopened for weeks, but she thought of him more often than she admitted to anyone except the image in her dressing-table mirror.

Judith gradually came aware of gloomy, mournfully hooting vespers of missed chances. Her tortured heart twisted through agonizing metamorphosis into a melancholy pincushion jabbed unmercifully by the stinging needles of extinct opportunity. Only gradually did senses pierce the past, waking Judith slowly to insistent pressure exerted by Michael's strongly capable hands.

"*Hey!* Come on back here," he ordered. "*Right now!*"

"Okay. I am okay." Wobbly and still vaguely unsure of herself, she added: "Been getting a little drifty in my old age is all."

"Speaking of *bevakasha...*"

"*Toda raba,* you mean."

"Whatever. That thanks you keep promising? Fitting reward would be that which you steadfastly refuse to do, although for the life of me, I can't understand why. We both know that I could make you happy, given half a chance."

"That is not your job."

"Job? Oh, for Christ's sake.... *Lighten up!*"

"Big 'oops' for you; wrong deity."

Ignoring her interruption, he said: "I'd consider it an honor and a pleasure, although not necessarily in that order."

"I must work on making myself happy."

"So, at least let me have a hand in it. Look, there can be no question in your mind but that we're genetically matched to produce beautiful children. Furthermore, I solemnly promise to honor every long-term commitment which that entails."

"You are still the emotional bush-beater."

"While you're still one for the direct approach."

"Sabras are built that way."

"And speaking of built..."

"Michael..."

"Will you marry me?" His arms slid off her shoulders and danced lightly down her back before settling onto her hips as he pulled her close. "Mmmmm. Better than I remembered...tighter than I recalled."

"And now you are taking liberties, of all things."

"When have you known me not to take whatever I could get away with?"

"There is that about you."

"Which you love."

"Possibly."

"All right. So how direct do I have to be? Do you want me to get down on one knee?"

"I don't want you to do anything," Judith snapped impatiently, bringing her forearms down sharply over his elbows and breaking free, adamantly steadfast in her refusal to hobble through another episode of "Levy and Crutch" while sorting out the prevailing angst enshrouding her mental affairs. "This is not the time. This is not the place. I have a job to do."

"And when the job is over?"

"This one might go on for some time."

"Only if you want it to."

"Michael, I was never very good at divining answers. Whatever the price is in weeks or months, I shall pay it."

"Well, I'm nothing if not patient. I'll be nosing along your trail like a bayou hound in hot pursuit of whatever got its nostrils twitching in the first place."

"And so now you have gone to the dogs?"

"You do tend to arouse the animal in me."

Judith's smile was at last genuine. "Okay, so we shall continue this discussion at a more appropriate juncture. Yes?"

"End of discussion?"

"For now."

"Are you lying about later?"

"Concerning that, Michael, you will just have to take your chances."

"There's always another time."

"That is right, Michael," she replied, sounding no more convincing than she truly knew herself to be.

"All right, Judith, a bargain is a bargain. Now on to the command performance awaiting us downtown."

They bandied polite, weather-related chitchat on the way to the medical examiner's office. Michael's high-end shifts got them up well past 60 in a scatter of seconds. A police cruiser with all lights blazing came on briefly in hot pursuit, but fell away from the sports car's back bumper after Michael radioed Dispatch, and the cops confirmed his story with a license-plate check of their own.

The partial carcass of blackened flesh and splintered bone waiting patiently in the ME's middle-basement examining room was initially thought to be a seat cushion melted over a flattened control-system pushrod. Compressed into burned crumble, the remains looked more like a charred clump of Joshua tree covered with blackened, congealed rubber than anything even faintly resembling a human being.

Traces of bone showed through here and there – a fragment of broken rib in the chunk's middle, a femur split lengthwise below-both bits of skeleton…sooty gray in contrast to the mass of burnt cork from out of which they poked. Both arms were gone at the elbows; the legs blown off above the knees. There was little distinguishing the head from a roughened bowling ball burned to blisters in a blast furnace. The face approximated an incinerated lunar landscape with craters for eyeholes above a jagged, gaping gash of toothless, lobster-red mouth from which the lips had been crudely sliced away.

"You said you recovered an ankh."

"Yes, ma'am, and it be laying there in that tray beside you, to your right." Assistant Coroner Dean Strover hovered uncomfortably close to Judith's back, his breath a wheezy intrusion wreaking complete havoc with her concentration. "Weird as all hell, if you ask me. FBI's on their way over; agent in charge is probably upstairs hitting the garage elevator's down button even as we speak."

Michael glanced at the huge ankh leaning half out of a dented stainless-steel tray next to the dead meat. "There's practically no blast damage on it, considering what it went through," Michael observed.

"Well, it got shoved down in there pretty goddamned deep," Strover said. He stuck his thumbs into suit vest pockets, the better to hold his jacket open in a proud display of a solid midsection toughened by more than its share of abdominal crunches and rope-climbing in the L position. Judith ignored the childish thrust of the torso, having decided at first meeting that the boyish assistant medical examiner with the pug-nosed, pumpernickel face was not as devilishly sexual as his body language indicated he thought himself to be. "Driven in vaginally," Strover said, "as far as the round part of the head. Can you figure? Chicago PD is investigating the possibility that the cross was pushed in afterward."

"Thrust all the way up through the body?" Michael asked. "You can hardly tell this thing is human remains."

"All I said was it's a possibility being checked. You said you wanted to know what I know, and now you do," Strover said, his barnacled crust of voice rough enough to take on 36-

grit sandpaper and come out the winner. "Maybe it was done that way, maybe not," he rasped coldly. "Believe me, you don't know the half of all the strange goings-on we get to pick through when a jumbo trenches Mother Earth," Strover remarked, endeavoring to convey the authority attendant with knowing precisely what happened during each split second of TransPac 117's dismemberment.

"Been through a lot of these, huh?"

"I've done my share, Miss."

"I see."

"No," Strover said thoughtfully, "I really don't think you do, but I'll lay it out for you anyway. There are lots of ritualistic weirdos hanging out around that part of town, in spite of all that urban renewal. Keep in mind that some street people you never get rid of. They figure it was their turf before, and it's their land now...to this very day. To their way of thinking, a change in topography don't mean squat. The steam tunnels under Hawes/ Rodriguez are infested with them, despite our best efforts to flush them out. I oughta know. I met some of them."

"So have I," Judith said.

"Savages if you ask me," Strover remarked.

"If your 'possibility' is correct, ghouls would be more like it."

"I hear you, Mike."

Clearly bereft of anything concrete to offer in the way of hard, investigative facts, Strover nevertheless probed incessantly. His forward lean perched him almost plumb-square over Judith's left shoulder, whiskers of Vandyke chin practically grazing her coat. Strover's wintergreen breath constituted an ongoing affront to a sense of smell already brutalized by huge amounts of disinfectant chemicals liberally slopped over the white-tiled examining room.

"Look, I really could do with a little privacy here," Judith said finally. "Do you mind?"

"No, ma'am," Strover said, taking two steps backward while refusing complete ejection. "I most certainly do not.

That is definitely not a problem for me." He moved away only slightly while leaning forward to snare fragments of whispered conversation.

"If we need you..."

"Ma'am, believe me when I say that I fully understand your feelings."

"Hardly likely."

The corners of Strover's mouth flicked up into a marginally civil smile, but cave-ice eyes told Judith he wouldn't piss on her if she were on fire. "In truth, ma'am, I have been ordered by my superior, Chief Medical Examiner Willie Tomlinson, to extend you every possible courtesy, as well as to provide you with any and every assistance you may find necessary."

"We're perfectly capable..."

"Order be orders, Mike."

And with that, Strover refused to budge any further than an annoying, clasped-hand hover at the edge of earshot.

Judith and Michael did their best to ignore him as their heads met over blackened crowbait that only a few hours ago had been a 27-year-old woman just entering her fifth month of pregnancy.

"El-Fahd el-Aswad, Michael."

"Absolutely no doubt in your mind?"

"None whatsoever. They have been planning a barbarity like this for years. But they are tight; we have had absolutely no luck cracking into them. I assume you heard about the phone call to Washington."

"Yeah. On the way over to the crash site. No name ID, though."

"That is not unheard of."

"But not exactly par for their course either."

"The ankh ties it for me," Judith said evenly, fending off even the hint of devil's advocate deterrence. And then she spun around to bare teeth at Strover, whose moist breath gave away his position as being well within biting distance of the exposed nape of his neck. "Goddamnit, you son of a bitch! Enough of your bullshit already! *Back the fuck off!"*

"Look, lady, I don't got to take that kinda crap from..."

Michael interposed himself immediately. "Wrong, *compadre.* You do!" He jabbed a rigid forefinger into Strover's chest, just under his heart. "So either I see your back flat up against that wall there," Michael barked, his thrusting finger driving the assistant ME into awkward reverse, "or you're gonna be Frenching it while I pat you down. Your next fashion accessory? Steel bracelets. Next destination? The holding tank at the Federal Building, while I press charges against you for obstructing my goddamned investigation."

Strover's face flared close to boiling, but only briefly. His mouth clamped shut as he swallowed, fighting words threatening to run riot. Fists clenching, he temporarily turned down the heat by taking two overly theatrical steps back. But the retreat was less than momentary, and even before attention was fully turned elsewhere, Strover was inching his way back.

Michael and Judith finally gave up on the pest and eyeballed the ankh in the basin. She fished deep in the right front pocket of her jeans, finally managing to draw out a full-function Swiss Army knife.

"I see that you're packing," Michael observed.

"As usual. This is definitely the most worthwhile piece of hardware ever devised by man."

And then she fumbled while pulling out the magnifying glass, almost dropping the knife in the process.

"Give it here," Michael offered. "Let me help you with that."

"I do not need your help! I am not a goddamned basket case! I am perfectly capable of doing it myself!" The magnifying glass jerked out slowly while Judith popped the brake chute on the runaway violence of her hairspring temper. Four deep breaths opened the door to temporary respite...and what had sprung up like a vicious Cape Horn storm vanished quickly as exasperation's wind sagged out of her sails.

"Ouch," he complained.

"Michael, I am really sorry. I didn't mean for that to come out the way it did."

"I understand."

"Oh, the hell you do!" she snapped irritably. "Look, just don't patronize me. All right?" Judith's anger geysered up again, heated as it was by the Bunsen burner of an uncharacteristically mercurial bent. Then, as if hoisting herself hand over hand away from a dangerously foul pit, she pulled clear of the volcanic crevasse of steaming temperament that promised only superheated explosion. "No one understands," she sighed, slowly enunciating each word with a full exhalation of breath. "Nobody has; nobody does; nobody will. No one except me."

The Mossad woman slammed the knife down on the examining table, then made good use of her teeth as she clumsily pulled on surgical gloves. Strover took a juvenile giant step forward at the sound of snapping latex.

"Get lost," she hissed over her shoulder, and Strover flinched away momentarily.

Judith picked up the knife and jammed it awkwardly into her left palm, then sharply bent the prosthetic thumb down over the handle to hold the tool in place. She picked up the ankh and examined it carefully, turning it slowly from side to side before uttering a mild expletive that stoked up simmering frustration.

"Michael, pull down the overhead light. There is something," she said, too consumed to care about Strover's intrusion back into hearing range.

Michael adjusted the light fixture, then pulled on his surgical gloves. Judith handed over the ankh and the knife. The transfer was made left hand to left hand with the knife, right hand to right hand with the ankh.

"Look there," she said, pulling off her gloves and tossing them into a receptacle under the autopsy table. "On the base. The letters 'AR' in serif type. I make them out to be six-point Times Roman."

"Looks like your old friends have definitely gone big time."

"Or their nest mates."

"What?"

"The 'AR' is new. Abu R? I have not seen that before."

"Father of?" Michael asked.

"Father of whatever the R stands for."

"Could be a jeweler's mark."

"It isn't," she said wearily. "That would be too easy. Goddamn them. They are like hydras. Now even the splinters have splinters," she said disgustedly, her fury clearly evident as Michael slid the ankh back into its semifinal resting place.

A brief but intense commotion at the door lassoed their attention. Perfectly matched glares on the faces of two equally livid FBI field agents marching over in high dudgeon told Michael that he and Judith were officially *persona non grata.* Nothing more would be learned from the baked lump of human matter, so he spun Judith around and fast-walked her toward the double-doored exit, giving one of the passing federal agents as good a shoulder block as he got.

"You folks happen to find anything else of interest besides that cross?" Strover queried from his vantage point just over their shoulders.

The press was jockeying noisily for position just outside the examining room's opaque doors as FBI Forensics set up shop over what was left of Passenger Jane Doe, Seat 27-B. Inside the fragile partition separating sanity from incipient fracas, Chief Coroner Willie Tomlinson checked his appearance in a medical-cabinet mirror, tremendously concerned about the squareness of his tie, the lie of his collar, the general cut of his jib...and an unfortunate gravy stain on the left lapel of charcoal-gray, double-breasted suit.

Ignoring his casual *"Adios,"* Michael and Judith walked brusquely past him, opened the door, and backed out toward the unruly mob of recently arrived, news-hungry reporters. Michael's main concern lay in keeping his and Judith's faces away from clicking cameras and, by extension, exposure in the Chicago media.

"You'd be wise to keep your lips welded tightly shut on this," Michael said. "Those G's are madder than a matched pair of bee-stung grizzlies. They won't appreciate your leaking all over this one."

"You got it, buddy. Sure thing," Strover offered. Tomlinson paid them no heed, fussing as he was with Alfalfa hair that refused anchoring until finally smacked down with a generous gob of saliva. "You're credentialed enough to give me federal orders, Mikey. There's absolutely nothing wrong with my hearing."

"No doubt this good city's widows and orphans are clawing for a place in line to buy into that one," Judith hissed.

Strover shot her a look of 90-proof malice. The press's salvoed questions bracketed them all, but the clamor immediately fell to a low rumble. The barrage of whipped words was mercifully brief. "Forget them," said the leader of the pack. "They're nothings."

"And grateful for it," Michael whispered to Judith.

They forced their discourteous, head-down way through the crowd, brushing off protests of *"Hey!"* and *"Geez, buddy! Watch it!"* Momentarily safe on the far side of the jostle, Michael turned to watch Tomlinson and Strover step into the limelight. Tomlinson rammed his right elbow sharply into Strover's unprotected rib cage, sending the assistant ME stumbling ungracefully off camera.

"I lip-read," Judith said, giggling as she reported on the terse monologue delivered 25 feet away. "Tomlinson just carved a huge chunk out of Strover's ass. Told him: 'Next time, don't go making jerk-off promises you can't keep. You do absolutely no deals with anyone until you check with me first, boy, else you'll be swabbing basins from now until the proverbial doomsday, you miserable son-of-a-goddamned...' Okay, Strover has been cauterized. Now Tomlinson is lathering up the lions in waiting."

The hard authority lines in the ME's pushed-in face went cream-cheese soft as he prepared his informational canapé for serving under the glaring camcorder lights. "Now, boys," he said. "Now, boys! And girls. Excuse me, Ms. Parker-Jenkins, and please accept all apologies due to you for my gender-based oversight. But if all of you will just... *Please don't crowd!* Please." Tomlinson's mouth compressed itself rigidly flat until the crowd quieted down and took a clearly visible, collective step back. "Much better. That's so much better. Now I want you to understand that there's plenty here for all of you. More than enough for everyone. You people on a deadline? Kinda thought you were. You always are."

"Stop blowing smoke, for Christ's sake!" Parker-Jenkins shouted.

"Knock off the worldly wise bullshit!"

"The election's not until next year!"

"Kill the goddamned wind machine!"

Tomlinson fended off Michael's angry stare with a venomous "up yours" wink. "People's right to know!" he shouted over the newspeople's bobbing heads. And then he played to the press like a prize trombonist strutting his stuff in Alexander's Ragtime Band. "Now I really don't know how much I can comment to you on this..."

"Oh yes, you for damn sure do," Parker-Jenkins rasped, holding her seal-fur hat almost on straight while thrusting a microphone wildly at Tomlinson with her free hand.

"...but you might be interested to learn who I think's behind this here heinous act of indiscriminate bombing."

Michael started muscling his way back through the crowd, but the fact-famished reporters had already closed ranks, and cleaving the pack of snapping news hounds was an impossible dream. Seeing Michael safely blocked, Medical Examiner Willie Tomlinson turned his full attention to a taunting, impatient audience.

"I assume you have this on high authority, Willie?" CNN asked.

"The highest," Tomlinson said.

"And where have we heard that before?" *Chicago Sun-Times* wanted to know.

"Let's just call it a highly placed source," Tomlinson said.

"Very close to the investigation, I might add."

"Bastard!" Michael fumed. He again tried powering his way through, but Judith wrenched him back forcefully, struggling vigorously before finally turning him around. She thrust rigid left fingers hard and deep into his right armpit, making him grunt with pain, then yanked his wrist and dragged him bodily and off-balance toward the elevators.

"Happens more times than I'd care to admit," she told a motorcycle policeman who had no idea what she was talking about. Michael finally shrugged her off, glaring over his shoulder at Tomlinson as the cotton-ball politician chummed the roiled waters of a hastily convened news conference. "Calm your *kishkes,* Michael. We have already lost this one."

Ninety minutes later, over waterfront clams Casino and shrimp *fra diavolo* at Guido's Dock Side, they brought each other up to date on personal comings and goings while tenuously building eye contact like sheepish first-daters hoping for lover status by midnight. Amorous chatter continued through dessert, stopping only when their cheerfully bubbling isolation was burst by Barry the waiter, whose overly enthusiastic coffee-pouring sent steaming brown liquid splashing onto a red-checked tablecloth already bearing the ghosts of considerable battle damage inflicted by sauces, gravies, alcoholic beverages, and soft drinks gone awry.

"*Ooooh!* Excuse me. I am truly sorry, Miss."

"No harm done."

"Did I get your sleeve?" Barry asked, dabbing helpfully at her blouse with a white overarm towel dripping from its dip into a nearby pitcher of water. "Damn! I did, didn't I? *Oh, for God's sake!"* Barry put the coffee carafe on the table, carefully steadying it with both hands before pulling out his billfold. "I insist on paying the cleaning bill. *Just, please!* Don't say anything to the boss. This is my job we're talking about here."

"No damage done, waiter."

"You sure?" Barry asked, desperately wanting to believe Judith...tremendously relieved at her pleasantly graceful smile.

"Seriously," Michael said. "Put your wallet away."

"Thanks, mister. *No kidding!* My boss? *Whooo!* Believe me, tonight he is definitely in no mood for any grief, gripes, or objections. Guido is taking no prisoners, if you understand my meaning. He doesn't even want to hear a grievance about the weather. Feelings are running pretty high back in the kitchen. Been here through three years of premed, and this is the first time it's ever been this ugly."

"Feelings?"

"Yes, Miss, about what happened. Maybe it's news to you folks, too. I just heard about it on the radio, so I really hope that you'll forgive me for being just a bit upset. It's about that airliner. The radio said that some fatheads brought it down."

"Who?"

"Fathead Oswalds? Something like that. It made absolutely no sense to me. Mean anything to you? My FM got directional fade, so I didn't hear enough to figure it all out. Anyway, I was just coming on duty, so I didn't catch it completely. We're shorthanded as it is. Our number-one cook? He had family on that plane. Damn tragedy; damnable shame."

"El-Fahd el-Aswad, maybe?" Judith prompted. "Do you think that is what you heard?"

"Yeah!" Barry gasped, his magnetic grin drawing chuckles from them both. *"You got it!* That's who the radio said did it."

"Do you remember hearing anything else?"

"Nope," Barry replied, spinning away from the table to get them each a complimentary pie à la mode. "And thanks again about that other business."

Judith stared at Michael over steepled fingers opening and closing metronomically, her even disposition frayed to the point of frazzle. Industrial-strength anger and general disgust with the Americans' appalling lack of security made short work of already-eroded patience. "Your boyfriends," she said sternly. "Strover and Tomlinson."

"We expected it."

"That still does not excuse it."

"Looks as if the 'AR' didn't make the news," Michael said hopefully.

"Not yet, anyway."

CHAPTER 7

BLACK LEOPARD

The ramshackle, weather-scarred barn 23 miles east of Deir al Balah was laced heavily with layered odors of dried salt, tannic acid, pressed dates, and slaughtered lamb. Each nuance of the pastiche of rain-dampened scents was warmly comforting to Abu Alam, or Father of Pain, as he called himself this evening. A grandfatherly and once-gentle man, Alam, following the burial of two cousins and both parents after the Irgun blasted its way through Deir Yassin, stayed hidden by day and traveled only at night, never using the same name, disguise, or facility for more than eight consecutive hours.

Trading handily on a reputation yielding incremental increases in stature and glory from each successfully completed operation, Alam never wanted for a convenient, albeit temporary headquarters from which to command his anti-Zionist crusade. Deir el Balah and its environs had been under his close personal scrutiny for the past day and a half. His enemies, he knew, would have set up a counteroperation by now, if there were to be one.

Alam had watched all afternoon, long after the departure of the minions who had delivered the prisoners first to the tearoom behind which the unfortunates spent much of their last afternoon on Earth and then to the hardscrabble farm from which final transfer north to heaven or south to hell would take place. Alam had canvassed the town carefully through the drippy haze of late day.

During an earlier, ill-considered test to see how deeply imbued the land was with the legend of his personal creation, the proprietor of the languid town's only greengrocer paled at the whispered words and the secret sign drawn on a dusty, rough-hewn tabletop.

"Truly, the lion of Judah is no match for Black Leopard," the shopkeeper murmured with utmost respect and courtesy, his voice quavering with fear as he pressed upon his "guest" a thick bankroll of large-denomination Egyptian pounds. Alam responded only with a barely noticeable nod of thanks that kept face pointed downward and cowled features hidden from close scrutiny. The suddenly obsequious retailer might have collapsed had he but known how highly placed Alam was in the organization. On the other hand, however, he might have sold the old man out to the next passing Israeli patrol in exchange for a small purse of gold. One never really knew for sure.

So many times had his identity changed, through papers purchased, stolen, or fabricated, and by virtue of intricately constructed lies expertly peddled, that Alam had no clear-cut memory of either his given or family name. Immediately after this night's business was concluded, he would substantially change his physical appearance. So adroit was Alam at metamorphosis that he was known to some of his followers as the Chameleon, though none dared call him that to his face.

Successfully functioning in earnest over the past 13 years, Alam's superbly tuned orchestration of swirling veils, diaphanous curtains and carefully honed methodology had borne fruit in the form of 3,600 acres of forest destroyed by arson-caused fires; 5,000 cases of export oranges dumped because of injected cyanide found in random lots; car bombs with a kill rate consistently in the middle teens; machine-gun/hand grenade attacks on buses and knife attacks on unarmed civilians, each with a commendable number of fatalities; the disabling of three oceangoing freighters, and the near sinking of a 75,000-ton American container ship in the Gulf of Suez.

Alam's perniciously effective group was organized in concentric hermetic cells based loosely on Mushashi's Seven Rings. Girdling the shadowy center of their leader's veritable black hole of identity were seven separate and distinct circles, each one carrying up to nine "planetary systems" of 12 core members each. Around each core member whirled two servile, expendable inductees, or "moons." Each system of 36 was in a different stage of terrorist development, with the more advanced groups operating farthest from Alam, and occasionally independently of his control. His International Section was poised to strike at any moment.

All of his battle-tested men had proved their intrinsic worth in any number of missions, from covert insertions to massed, coordinated attacks causing considerable consternation on the part of both Christian militiamen and the pro-Israeli South Lebanon Army. Alam came away from long-range observations with considerable pride of accomplishment, despite the fact that news accounts of such successes rarely surfaced in the foreign media, hamstrung as it was by Israeli censorship.

He was laying the groundwork for an operation that, when successfully completed, would gain him express, equal-footing entree to the Council of the Most Venerated. Having served his own cause too long to be content with coming up through someone else's ranks, Alam himself would decide when he would sit on the dynasty's highest and most consecrated mount. The moment would soon arrive when all of the Most Venerated would greet him effusively as a brother rather than a standoffish, unwashed stepson, as the rumors reported this free-thinking revolutionary was now regarded.

After again making doubly sure that he was unobserved and that the occupants of the farmhouse had taken their leave as strictly instructed, Alam entered the stable and drew shut the battered door. He carefully examined the broken-down building's foul-smelling insides. In the far, left-rear corner, past manure-speckled stalls and illuminated only by the anemically flickering flame of a dim kerosene lamp, a blindfolded man and woman hung suspended from chains like human stars, stretched to the limit of their limbs as if shackled for drawing and quartering. Alam decided that he would henceforth think of them as Otto and Marina.

While attempting to pass himself off as a German bureaucrat with a Czech traveling companion, Otto...some 39 hours earlier...made the unfortunate mistake of asking a single, red-flag question only peripherally related to a minor operation undertaken six months previously by Alam's so-far impenetrable paramilitary combat teams. That unfortunate indiscretion resulted in the couple's spending the last day and a half hungry and parched during incessant transfer from place to place before finally winding up just outside Deir el Balah, where nobody would have cared about the captives' fate even if their presence had been known.

After examining the inside perimeter once more to ensure himself complete privacy, Alam, ever cautious by nature, checked his reflection in a shard of broken glass. His dark, disposable contacts were in place. The zero-prescription lenses, a Taurus PT-92 9mm semiautomatic pistol, and a battered flashlight were Alam's only concessions to modernity while on the road during his unending, peripatetic travels through the Occupied Territories.

The eyes being true windows of the soul, unavoidable pupil movement could always be depended on to expose one's true leanings at the worst possible time...unless care was taken to neutralize that one aspect of human physiology which could not be controlled, no matter how honest, straightforward, or truthful one pretended to be. The lenses ensured that Alam's eyes would remain impenetrably black. So skillfully were they fitted that, even upon close examination, any contraction in the eye proper was impossible to detect.

In the absolute worst-case scenario, Alam was, of course, fully prepared to sacrifice both his life and the lives of those in his immediate vicinity through activation of a slice of C4 explosive surgically embedded in his right thigh. The personal mine could be detonated simply by pressing in on both ends of the implant at the same time, a mere finger length apart, thereby sparing him both the inconvenience and pain of prolonged question-and-answer sessions.

It was Otto who perked up first at the sound of Alam's sliding sandals. The fact that the East Germans' visibly swollen tongue made speaking difficult was a fortuitous footnote to Alam's situation...moist tongues being that much harder to cater to properly.

"Ana atshaan jidan," Otto croaked, tilting his head back in a vain attempt to see out from underneath the black cloth tightly wrapped around his upper face. "I'm very thirsty."

"Tuhib tashrab shay?" Alam asked. "Would you like a drink?"

"Koobaayat maay lou samaht," Marina said, turning her head as if targeting her captor's voice. "A glass of water, please."

"Hal tatakalam ingleezee?" Alam inquired. "Do you speak English?"

"*Aywa.* I mean...yes."

"Excellent! I do so like to practice mine."

Alam cut off their blindfolds and sized up his prisoners. Weight and general corpulence being determining factors in how much pain a body could safely tolerate, Alam was glad to see that Otto, who appeared to be three-fourths through his forties, weighed in at about 85 kilos. The East German seemed well kept, though his heavily bruised face was still puffy and purplish-yellow from the harsh beating he had taken while unsuccessfully resisting capture.

After confirming Otto's eyes as safety intact, Alam turned his attention to Marina, whom he estimated to be around 37 years old. Marina had the face of a softly rounded Dutch milkmaid, complete with blonde, page-boy bangs done in slightly uneven, Iron Curtain-style, with the requisite amount of split ends. Alam decided she might have even been considered very pretty once, in a hefty, bovine sort of way.

"Truly, your garments smell extremely bad," Alam said softly, standing before them in hands-on-hips judgment. "We shall be providing you with new clothes immediately preceding repatriation, which, I suspect, is scheduled to take place anytime now. Your respective governments, after all, have put up quite the diplomatic stink. This has gone all the way up to the ambassadorial level, if you can believe that." Alam shook his head slowly as if unable to fully appreciate what the fuss was about. "And all of that for a simple, most unfortunate case of mistaken identity."

Marina smiled faintly, displaying dental work far surpassing Eastern European standards. Otto, however, remained skeptical of his captor's intentions.

"So, Fortuna has indeed smiled down upon you," Alam continued. "But be that as it may, I cannot unchain you so that you may change, else you might attempt escape. And who knows? You might be very successful at it, which would serve only to cost me my life. And that, you may rest assured, is a bargain I have no intention of striking...your freedom for my existence." Alam's laughter shook a chuckle loose from Otto. "Therefore, I will cut away your garments. As I do this, please use every measure of your internal discipline to make sure that you remain absolutely still." Alam's glistening commando knife rasped out of its self-sharpening sheath. He smiled broadly at Marina, but got only a confused, lopsided grin in return. "It would be most unfortunate, not to mention painful," Alam whispered disarmingly, "were I to cut into your flesh by mistake."

Then fully savoring the charade, and with the deftness of a supremely skilled surgeon slicing away skin for eventual transplant, Alam divested Otto and Marina of their garments, carefully and patiently working knife tip along seams so as to preserve the apparel for resewing and later use, all the while silently admiring the rounded fullness of Marina's upthrust breasts, standing firm and proud after having been freed from the confinement of sweat-stained undergarments.

Alam kicked the khaki material away from his suspended captives. "You will understand if I gag you now," he said apologetically, secretly troubled that this crucial detail had not been seen to originally. "I cannot take the chance that the roughness of the final journey will cause you to cry out...with unfortunate results for those whose crime was only to expedite transportation."

Slowly waking up to what was coming but too dehydrated to scream, Otto shook his head violently. The contagion of raw fear quickly infected Marina. Alam instantly dammed her outburst with a hard-rubber doorstop thrust into her mouth, which cut short her garbled cry, and he facilitated full silencing with a strip of crusted rag. It simply would not do to have desperate shouts for help attract double agents who might be passing by on a random prowl.

After double-checking the security of facial bindings, Abu Alam took from his breast pocket a small plastic vial containing the deadly Middle Eastern buthid scorpion. The wiggler flicked its tail in frenzied anticipation as Alam drew it out with a long pair of tweezers and held it up for Otto's nose-close inspection. Using a second pair of tweezers and a swatch of cotton, Alam milked as much as he could of the scorpion's highly poisonous venom. Next, he approached Otto and slowly waved the flailing arachnid back and forth in front of the German's mesmerized, fear-crossed eyes. And then with a swiftly corkscrewing motion, Alam drove the scorpion's tail directly into Otto's left eye...a practiced wrist flick ensuring that the stinger penetrated directly through the center of the pupil and well in toward the middle of the eyeball itself.

Otto went immediately rigid, then fought mightily against the clanking leashes of inflexible, linked restraints. Neck ligaments stood out in bold relief. Unable to scream, Otto jerked like an epileptic marionette, lashing violently, disjointed against the rusty chains, his body flapping like a schooner's unsecured foresail snapping in hurricane winds. Agonized, dying-fish flops continued spasmodically without letup for five minutes and 17 seconds on Alam's ancient Bulova, after which Otto spiraled into unconsciousness and sagged limply in the chains. With blasé amusement, Alam regarded the mounded excrement above which the German's bowels had voided themselves.

After tossing away the scorpion and pocketing the tweezers, Alam used his commando knife to carve an inverted ankh in Otto's chest...just deep enough to bleed the German ritually, as if for a ceremony only the progenitor of el-Fahd el-Aswad fully understood. Then, after cleanly slicing off Otto's ears, Alam turned his casual attention to Marina, whose brown eyes were dark, pinpoint dots swimming starkly vulnerable against the wide white backdrops of unfathomable terror.

Alam took a moment to explain himself patiently, as would a father quietly addressing his only daughter about a matter of grave concern.

"You must understand that I am not proceeding thusly for the sake of extracting information. There is absolutely nothing that I wish to learn from you. I merely intend to ensure that your passing from this life to the next is accomplished slowly and with great pain. There is nothing inside your head that is of any interest to me. Your only purpose here is to die. So for now you shall remain gagged, as there is no need for you to bargain in order to extend what little remains of your squandered life."

Alam took from his sash a small linoleum knife honed well beyond razor sharpness. As Marina looked down in stomach-churning horror, he quickly incised a large "X" deep into her lower belly, halfway between navel and pubic bone, then stepped smartly away from geysering blood. White-hot pain mule-kicked Marina wildly toward unconsciousness. Alam paused only long enough to slip on a leather glove bristling with thumbtacks mounted point outward. He slapped Marina viciously awake so that he would not be deprived of an audience for his work.

Alam redid the cut to make sure the "X" was deep enough. Then, using rusty, slip-joint pliers, he ripped down the triangular flap of skin at the base of the "X." From under his robe, he pulled out a jar of maggots and flipped off the cap. Still holding the flap of skin away from Marina's belly, he shook the larvae into the gash, then used paper tape to crudely close the wound. After stepping back in critical appreciation of his handiwork, Alam left the barn and washed his bloody hands in an adjacent horse trough. Then he sat down and undid his rucksack, from which he unpacked a few meager provisions, finally settling in for a quiet evening meal of day-old humus and slightly soggy taboolah.... after which he napped under the wood pile for an hour and a half.

Upon reentering the barn, rested and refreshed at 9:35 p.m., Alam immediately gave a low-key snort of profound disappointment. Despite his initial precautions, not enough of the scorpion's venom had been milked; far too much of the deadly poison had scorched Otto's innards, quickly frying most of the German's nervous system before slowly and cruelly sautéing the better part of his gray matter. An unfeeling Otto was muttering to himself in a confused babble of Romanian, Pashto, Spanish, Haitian Creole, Bellacoola, and four Sino-Tibetan dialects...his reedy, high-pitched voice rising and falling erratically like a clown's slide whistle. The eye that had taken the sting was pus-filled and swollen up to the size of a rotten, brownish-red tomato.

Alam drove an awl roughly through Otto's right eardrum, just deep enough to cause an excruciating jolt of pain but not deep enough to invade the brain itself. The East German's head bobbed up to regard Abu Alam curiously. With both feeling and reason erased, the dying man didn't blink as Alam's linoleum knife sliced through his right eye, nor did the chains jiggle even slightly as Alam cut out the German's tongue.

Turning his attention again to Marina, Alam cut away her gag, removed the doorstop that had been bitten halfway through, and then woke his prisoner by jabbing his awl deeply into her left thigh. Marina's feverish eyes opened slowly to regard Alam casually, as if she were light-years distant in an indistinct, soft-focus valley swept cloudy with wrappings of raindrop haze...a gauzy land where pain was a casual abstract of little concern to either giver or recipient.

Alam wrenched her face, rudely left. Marina's eyes widened only briefly while glimpsing her companion's mangled head hanging limply down, blood still dripping from facial lacerations. And then her eyes closed halfway in response to the dull, throbbing ache of cuts suffered earlier and the insistent gnawing of ever-hungry maggots, which for the past few hours had been eating her up slowly from the inside out.

"You work for Israeli intelligence, do you not?"

"Haadha jeenan," she barely managed to whisper. "That's crazy."

Yes, Alam thought, *falling victim to absurdity was always a clear-and-present danger, although I am still astride the proverbial fence in that regard.*

Were Marina only Otto's arm piece, Alam reasoned, the German certainly would not have apprised her of all the facts regarding the ill-fated journey's dead-ending here. *Either she is speaking the truth, or I have not yet drilled far enough through her fictions to mine the mother lode of fact.*

He pondered both possibilities while smashing Marina's nose flat with a balled fist before forcing his pliers past her lips and brutally yanking out four front teeth in rapid succession—twist/pluck, twist/pluck, twist/pluck, twist/pluck; dodge the bloody gusher. Then Alam repeated the question.

"Kuluh waahid..." Marina drooled almost inaudibly.

"Speak English!" he hissed impatiently.

"Two languages will ensure that even a miserably filthy pig such as yourself fully understands," Marina said softly. Getting each word out cost her dearly in terms of physical stamina. She tried to vomit but found herself lacking the strength even for that. "I want to make sure you get the message." Marina clamped her eyes tightly shut as if marshaling thoughts, and then skewered Alam with her piercing gaze. "I said, 'It doesn't make any difference.' You are going to kill me anyway. And if you torture me long enough, you will get me to agree to whatever you want me to agree to. How stupid you are. How truly deep your ignorance runs. That is why you always lose."

Alam brought up his knife.

"Haaza hadeeyah lak minee," Marina whispered finally. "This is a present to you from me." And then expending her last reserves of physical strength, Marina hawked up a mouthful of bloody phlegm and spat it directly into Alam's face. *"Ala kul haal, sa-nadfa lakum,"* she croaked through cracked lips. "Whatever

happens, we shall pay you."

Marina's last words told Alam everything he felt he needed to know. With polished determination, he slid the blade of his commando knife between the ribs under her left breast. The point unerringly found her heart, its last beat an unnervingly violent quiver felt all the way through to the handle of the tempered-steel killing tool. Alam held Marina's chin up until the light of defiance turned opaque in her eyes, then let her head fall forward as her body swayed in the chains. Into her corpse he scribed, in cursive Arabic, specific instructions on how both bodies were to be returned piecemeal to the office building with the extra basements on Tel Aviv's Rehov Shaul Hamelech.

Two hours later, encamped just over 60 yards from the northeast road, Abu Alam had no trouble picking up a black Saab 9000's headlights or the throaty burble of a well-tuned, turbocharged engine. Long-standing arrangements permitted contact on any one of 16 possible routes, the Israelis never having shown the inclination to cover even half that number. The convertible in his field of view lurched fitfully every few moments, its taillights flashing like locator beacons as the driver tapped on the brake pedal to transmit a coded message. Alam knew it to be important, else such a potent machine would not have been risked in flagrant violation of the long-standing curfew.

Clear skies' full moon permitted superb visibility for 24 flat miles in every direction. The vehicle would continue its pattern for precisely two minutes and 15 seconds, unless Alam signaled back. Still, he waited until the last possible moment so as to convince himself beyond all doubt that the recognition signal's seventh permutation was correct, based as it was on Cassiopeia's position relative to Venus ascending.

The recognition signal thus confirmed, Alam beamed a three-second countersign at the driver's windshield. The car immediately skidded to a crooked stop. Alam left his flashlight on its weakest setting, the driver having been previously warned to keep the convertible's top down, his eyes on the distant light and his hands in plain sight on the top of the steering wheel.

Alam circled the car cautiously, approaching slowly from the right rear. His double-action automatic was ready for firing as he yanked open the door and slid halfway across the front seat.

The messenger's face was flushed with crazed excitement. Beaded sweat glistened like semiprecious stones in dim dashboard lights. In direct violation of procedures, the driver turned immediately to Alam.

"Ya akhee!" the contact blurted. "My brother!"

The gaping bore of Abu Alam's heavy automatic instantly nosed up, aimed, ready to blast out the better part of the man's chest. Alam's mouth was grim as his finger tightened on the trigger.

"Intazir!" the driver gasped, clearly seeing in the darkness of Alam's emotionless eyes Death's pale horse galloping his way madly. *"Wait!"* he pleaded.

With the trigger moving incrementally closer to tripping the firing pin, the driver cried out desperately, his knuckles white on the steering wheel, arms vibratory with fear.

"Anta zaboon muhim jidan!" he screamed.

"Yes! I am a very important customer," Alam snapped angrily, easing the pressure on the trigger only slightly while wondering whether abject stupidity was reason enough to kill the fool. However, the appropriate verbal recognition signal had been given, and so Alam decided to forgo the practice lectures on the importance of strict, unwavering adherence to established procedure. Instead, he asked: "Now what is so important that you have so incompetently risked this excellent machine as well as your miserable life to tell me?"

"Your plan for the Americans. Over the radio, it has been reported as an unqualified success."

Plan?

Even while looking directly into Alam's eyes, the driver could discern nothing of the surprise Alam would have displayed instantly were it not for the special contact lenses shielding his eyes from the driver's direct stare of awed respect.

"You have achieved a tremendous victory, oh my brother.

The airliner was blown up completely, as was foretold. There are many, many dead." Despite Alam's urging patience, the driver's body jiggled like spastic Jell-O as he rattled off the few details available. "You have thrust the Arab dagger directly through the heart of their security. BBC reported five hundred and forty-three killed," he gulped.

Despite his long-standing policy of swiftly curtailing any overt display of pleasure, a toothy, self-satisfied smile slowly brightened Alam's flushed face as his whole physical being warmed to the richly rewarding blessing just bestowed upon him.

A boon almost completely beyond imagining. God is indeed great.

Which of his squads had accomplished this soul-stirring victory would be determined later...with suitable rewards dispensed, of course. Most important was the fact that what was delivered unto him was a tremendous success upon which he would capitalize in his own way, in his own time.

"I can well understand your pleasure," the driver said with adoring reverence.

"The Council of the Most Venerated will have no other choice but to grant me special audience now," sAlam whispered, before slipping out of the car as a moon-washed specter vanishing quickly in the night.

CHAPTER 8

COLORADO TUMBLEWEED

The motorcycle jacket Richard Lawrence Jefferson wore while casually motoring westward in the conservative right lane—no hurry-bug he—garnered vast slews of gutter superlatives, having caught the appreciative eyes of Harley-mounted bikers thundering past in an intimidating stream of rolling thunder and glistening chrome. The most stirring accolade was echoed by two leather-clad Lesbians demonstrating vociferous, clenched-fist approval while rumbling by.

More than mere studs festooning a jacket, the tightly packed mass of glistening squares attracting so much outlaw-biker attention was inch-square solar cells whose wires extended through leather and lining to form a comforting metallic skin against his naked upper torso. K-Y Jelly applied before the dawn of each day's journey facilitated absorption of solar/electric energy directly through the thirsty sponge of skin.

Full-blast heating was easily bested by teeth-chatter, 60-mph wind roaring in through the open driver's side window. Icicle airflow pushed the chill factor down to 14 degrees, but Jefferson still had a commendably good angle on the 3:35 p.m. sun in boiling-red, west-southwest descent. And he was making the most of it...contentedly amping up while enjoying the wonderful solace of mental quietude, however temporary so sublime a state of grace might be.

The usually raucously loud Head Man was understandably quiet, having more important things with which to occupy Himself, which boded Jefferson well because carping criticism by Constant Companion was fraught with incalculable danger.

Head Man was resolutely capable of inflicting terribly lacerating damage whenever His merciless anger was fully aroused. Right now, however, He was too busy guzzling photoelectricity to have anything to say.

Jefferson's habitually malicious psychological judge, jury, and hair-trigger executioner dined with gusto...fed via a specially modified ceiling. The van's sunroof was precisely that: Skillfully engineered into the cab's top was an articulated, solar-energy collecting panel, any side of which could raise 20 inches, thus enabling Jefferson's recharger to track the sun accurately from any angle...no matter where roads led.

Inside the cab, minimally resistant wires coiled down from the panel's lower left-hand corner. The thin conductors ran through the button atop a Chicago Cubs baseball cap, their leads jammed hard into holes drilled into the edge of a circumferential metal band sewn into the hat's rim. There they were carefully fastened—epoxy to rubber coating—to ensure that the low-resistance transmission lines stayed in place without interfering with Mission One: unhindered conduction of the sun's revitalizing power directly through the skull's superior temporal ridges to where it could wrap arc-nets frontally over forebrain and do the most good.

For corporeal nourishment, Jefferson needed only Sunshine Hydrox cookies...

Heavenly matter in disguise.

KEEPS ON THE LIGHT BEHIND THE EYES.

...Power-Up high-protein drink and yellow multivitamins, which he gobbled thrice daily like a kid overdosing on M&Ms. The only downside to freezing interstate wind and mostly liquid diet was the need to make frequent pit stops, this time at the tree-shrouded Byron R. White Rest Area. Minimal facilities consisted of two ill-tended bathrooms and six wind-blasted ramadas overlooking a forbidding, cone-shaped gorge dead-ending in a boulder-strewn box canyon.

Although empty when Jefferson pulled in, the rest area had attracted one other vehicle by the time he flushed and washed. A white GMC Sierra pickup nuzzling the left side of his van was parked to within an inch of the driver's side door. Its grille ornamentation was two beefy locals lounging against the front bumper.

When Jefferson sauntered out of the restroom, snugging down the bottom of his jacket and zipping up against the first tentative flurries of incoming snow, the road pirates had already marked this overweight "tourist" as criminally easy pickings.

"Nice jacket," Number One said, theatrically evaluating the garment's Liberace glow and likely fit.

He was a rough-hewn cask of a man with hairy staves in desperate need of planing. Both his red-flannel work shirt and stained overalls were strained to their absolute limits with densely muscled girth, branding him a dangerous dude capable of more than holding his own in bare-knuckle bar fights.

Jefferson evaluated the roughneck's chaw-stained teeth, bog-brown eyes, and acromegalic hands, obviously used to the heavy work of wildcatting when not breaking heads considerably less dense than his own. The rowdy's blonde hair had been cut as if by a nervous, unskilled haircutter using a pot for a pattern, and wasting no time, shearing unevenly all the way around before bolting for the nearest exit.

Obviously, he's of Swedish stock...

AND CLEARLY BUILT SOLID AS A ROCK.

Jefferson flashed his warmest, down-home country grin and anted up with: "Bet your grade-school name was Tunnan. That's Swedish for 'barrel,' ain't it?"

Tunnan immediately puffed up like a walking blowfish, his strained shirt telling Jefferson the shot had landed very close to home.

"Not a bad jacket...for a faggot," Number Two said.

Tunnan's muddy-eyed companion was only slightly less burly than his buddy, with a red-veined face coming from too much cheap whiskey, a diet heavily laden with saturated fats, and apparently limitless indolence. Chapped, nicotine-stained lips pulled back over yellow teeth to spotlight infected gums where two long-gone incisors once stood. The label Trough Licker garnered Head Man's instantly shouted hoots of riotous approval.

"I hear tell faggots got good taste," Tunnan said. "Proof's right here, a-fore my eyes."

"You a faggot?" Trough Licker inquired. He blew a noisy, stop-motion kiss at Jefferson. "Sure looks to me like you'd suck a dick."

"Be more than willing, be downright eager, if'n you ask me," Tunnan said.

"Tell you somethin' about the looks-a that fat frame," Trough Licker muttered conspiratorially, crossing meaty arms over pumped-out chest. "Lungs big enough to keep that tub-a lard movin' gotta be strong enough to suck a grapefruit right on up through radiator hose."

"Sure enough," Tunnan replied. "I figger that be the case. Mebbe I'll let you go if'n you suck my dick," he told Jefferson, while hooking his thumbs around the frayed straps of overalls. "And then again, mebbe not."

Deciding the two posturing bulls had hooved ground long enough, Jefferson broke up the banter with: "You no-account road rash got something on yer minds 'sides jawin' in the wind? 'Cause if'n you don't, I'd sure as hell appreciate yer moving that there hunka junk whut's blockin' my entrance. And then we can all mosey on down the road."

"Jus' like that?!" Tunnan asked in exaggerated disbelief.

"Jus' like fucking that," Jefferson averred, "unless you got somethin' meaningful on yer mind."

The no-nonsense, hardball delivery snapped Trough Licker's resolve like a week-old wishbone. Bald uncertainty flared in the Coloradan's eyes, which flickered uneasily while broadcasting stark discomfort in the face of Jefferson's unnerving calm. Two-to-one odds didn't faze the prey's conviction, which set Trough Licker's upperworks to as much thinking as he could handle without blowing a fuse.

He carefully scrutinized Johnson in last-gasp daylight.

Substantive sass came only once previously, followed by trouble flaring like fierce, high-country wildfire. Not that he and Tun... Mike...hadn't been able to handle the situation, but the fallout kept them from partying all weekend and cost three teeth besides. Still, in all, not a bad investment when you consider the payoff was $2,500 cash money, a solid-gold Rolex, and four grams of space-trip crack.

Trough Licker was betting on a repeat of that previous oddity, if only because Mr. Spangles yonder didn't sound very much like he'd be inclined to just strip down to his skivvies without at least a burp of protest. But what gave him pause was that so much verbal valor was coupled with so interesting a garment, all of which was quickly turning Fat Boy too uncomfortably peculiar for Trough Licker's liking.

Right now, he wonders if I'm quite the type.

HEAD MAN TO HOST MAN, "THAT'S TROUGH LICKER'S HYPE."

"You boys got names?" Jefferson asked mildly.

"What's it to you?" Tunnan asked, thunderous voice blaring menace as he hitched up his overalls and swaggered forward.

"Because if'n any ass-kickin' gets to bein' done," Jefferson said, freely giving ground while sarcastically mimicking Trough Licker's accent, "I'd sure like to know the names-a those involved."

"Fer what?"

"Fer police reports," Jefferson said. "My dear mama, she always told me to get the name right. Yer mamas ever say anything more'n 'oink'?"

As Head Man had accurately predicted, Trough Licker broke first.

"Hey Mike, I don't know about..."

"*'Hey Mike?!' Hey, you shut the fuck up!*" Tunnan shouted, stiff-arming Trough Licker sideways. "Just do like you was told." And then to Jefferson: "You got a name 'sides 'Shit Fer Brains'?"

Jefferson glanced at the fifth of whisky poking half out of Tunnan's overalls.

"Jack Beam, boys. Jim Beam's fraternal twin. I'll answer to either name, but it's Mr. Beam to dirtbags like yerselves."

Tunnan yanked out his 80-proof fortification, drained it in two drippy-lip gulps, then threw the empty pint bottle down like a glass gauntlet. The shatter of dull, fused-quartz fragments sprayed the tips of Jefferson's heavy boots.

"I'da thought littering be against the law 'round these parts," Jim/Jack Beam said.

Game name?

THE SAME!

Head Man took an immediate liking to the pop-up alias, promising complete and cooperative silence if Jefferson stayed so labeled. With enough driver's license blanks in the back of the van to duly certify half of Idaho, the name Head Man pined for so hungrily could be easily imprinted, though such cuteness would be dangerously provocative.

"Funny, just ain't yer middle name," Tunnan said. "Asshole'd be more like it."

"No, really," Beam replied amiably. "I'm the heir to all-a that there fame and fortune, so you two puss buckets got yer sights fixed on a rich mark standing right here a-fore ya. But if'n it's just the jacket you want," he continued, shrugging out of it to stand shirtless before them. "Hell, then just come on over here and take it from me. No muss, boys, and definitely no fuss."

"Christ-oh-mighty!" Tunnan exclaimed, slapping his knee in bulge-eyed mirth. "You got fucking teats!"

Vigorously forceful laughter firmed up Trough Licker, whose posture and resolve stiffened as he surveyed Jefferson's torso for vulnerable target areas. Kidneys were his favorite. A vicious punch-up was all well and good, but when you left someone pissing blood for a week...well, that was calling card aplenty. So with push now definitely coming to shove, Trough Licker figured that he'd circumnavigate the gut while Mike sledgehammered the face. *Piece of fucking cake,* he thought.

"You a woe-man, is what you are," Tunnan chortled.

"Gonna punish that pot belly-a yours," Trough Licker

promised, rhythmically slamming clenched right fist into open left palm.

"Jacket's yours," Beam said emphatically. "Hell, I don't mind. Plenty more where this one come from." Then, looking directly at Tunnan, he said: "Plenty of fat, old steers like you ta skin for leather."

Which was all it took to double-clutch potential into kinetic, and set the road show in motion.

They came toward Beam in a classically first-grade attack pattern: Tunnan straightforward; Trough Licker circling in from the right. Beam was holding his jacket by the collar and toward his left front. The metalwork inside caught the dying embers of late-afternoon light, its silverfish inner lining glinting reddish-orange in frigid Colorado air.

Frontal first...

HE'S THE WORST!

Beam casually whirled the jacket to the right in the style of a sober-minded matador. Head Man in skull back's sun-baked bleachers shouted: *"Ole!"* as the brightly spangled garment wrapped completely around Trough Licker's face like a barber's hot towel. Then Beam high-stepped into an acrobatic roundhouse kick that slammed the hob-nailed bottom of motorcycle boot punch-press hard into the left side of Tunnan's head...shattering his jawbone into pebble-size fragments as the bottom half of his face unhinged with a sick crunch reminiscent of fist-cracked walnuts.

And then the thickset Swede was *mano-a-mano* combat casualty number one, down sideways in hard-packed dirt and bleeding heavily from between broken teeth...brain concussed, breathing raggedly uneven.

Having swatted off the jacket, Trough Licker glanced in horrified awe at his fellow buccaneer. One quick look told him the odds of seeing another sunrise were suddenly reduced by half. His lower lip quiver mirrored a crystal understanding of clear and present danger, and he broke frantically for the pickup truck's door.

And almost made it, too.

Trough Licker had a handle in hand as Beam, displaying lightning speed belied by his considerable bulk, came up nightmarishly fast, set his feet, and methodically went to work. He drove six powerfully repetitive, callused-knuckled punches deep into Trench Licker's middle back. Bone-breaking hammering splintered the right half of Trough Licker's rib cage. Then Beam took one step back, aimed carefully, and put all 217 pounds into a final blow whose ground zero was the top rear of the pelvic cradle. Trough Licker screamed at impact, then slumped into broken-backed deformity, his body slowly deflating into half-loop grotesquerie. One lung sluggishly pumped blood-bubbled breath through gapped teeth and out past wind-chapped lips.

And then it was Beam's turn to hyperventilate raggedly. There was a witness inside the truck: a girl of about 25, regarding him incuriously through defocused eyes.

"Git out th' truck," Beam ordered huskily, keeping his accent right in the neighborhood. The girl scrambled out fast, then turned and stopped like a fear-frozen fawn caught in a poacher's night lights. Her locked-tight head relaxed only enough to aimlessly scan Beam from bald pate to boots, as if seeing him for the first time.

She wore a bleached-out western shirt over which flapped a brown-fringed vest...the kind of overpriced, pseudo-buckskin that Rockies convenience stores foisted on bused-in tourists. Her nose was artfully bobbed, indicating money leafing out of whatever family tree had borne her as fruit. She stood stiffly to one side, playing with long brown hair cut unevenly over her forehead and straight down to midback. The girl's becalmed, Dresden-doll face was proof positive that neither care nor alarm counted for much in her flitter-light world.

Beam's hip braced the driver's side door open against rising wind. Raising Trough Licker's mass was a gut-buster, the derricking made more difficult by twisted hips moving at bizarrely disjointed angles to a clay-cold upper body.

Bending industriously to his work, Beam planted his left

shoulder in Trough Licker's buttocks, then grunted, sweated, and finally shoved hard enough to force the dying paraplegic halfway across the truck's foul-smelling, sheep-skinned bench seat. Then Beam walked over to where Tunnan lay barely conscious in the wintry dirt. A light beard of freshly fallen snow had just mellowed the Swede's darkly bruised and broken face when two cranium-cracking stomps delivered powerfully to the temple stopped the moaning for good.

Beam shook his precious life jacket free of dirt and pebbles. Considerable scratch damage at the shoulders would be repaired later. After using a spotless handkerchief to dust undamaged solar cells to a glistening shine, he slipped back into his sunsuit. And then, with dexterity almost equal to his first loading job, considering the extra weight involved, he hoisted Tunnan's corpse, slung it spine-down over his shoulder in a reversed fireman's carry, staggered backward momentarily under massive deadweight imbalance, then lunged awkwardly forward around the front of the pickup truck and dumped the body into the bed.

Still breathing heavily, Beam glanced at trees shielding the rest stop from the highway, breezily thankful that current events had not been interrupted by drive-bys with bladders full to bursting.

After wiping his hands in the dirt and clapping the dust away, Beam came around to the driver's side, rolled down the window, and slammed the door. Then he leaned in from the custom-chrome running board and started the fuel-injected engine.

But then there still remains the girl...

SHALL SHE FLY DOWNWARD IN A WHIRL?

He looked up again to where she stood totem-pole still, and slowly shook his head in bewilderment.

Beam backed up the idling truck until it was 30 yards from the wooden guard rail separating the flat parking area from the rocky gorge behind. He thrust the gearshift up into Park, skidding the truck to a locked-tranny stop. After wiping down the places he'd touched, Beam leaned in through the window, jammed the gas pedal down with a jack handle, and used his wrists to yank the automatic transmission out of "P."

Knobby, all-terrain tires bit aggressively into gravel. Swerved acceleration hurled Beam off the running board as the GMC surged ahead. Rutted ground aimed the racing vehicle toward the girl, who nonchalantly watched its roaring approach as if front-row center at a 3-D movie.

"MOVE!" Beam shouted...and the girl did...but only just barely and not vigorously enough to have ensured salvation had not the charging pickup already glanced off the heavy-rock base of a water fountain and abruptly changed course. Angling hard right at high RPMs, the vehicle smashed through a weathered redwood guard rail to hang momentarily suspended in a spray of toothpick wood. Then gravity exerted its merciless influence, and the truck nose-dived toward disaster.

The girl watched only marginally interested as the four-wheel coffin plunged down the ravine to crash into a massive boulder at Box Canyon's bottom. The tremendous impact punched the engine hard back and halfway through the accordioned passenger compartment. And then the stalled truck rolled slowly backward to jiggling, flat-tired rest...smoking, dusty, and quiet.

Beam came up to where the girl stood on the lip of craggy precipice...her toes high-dive even with the edge...and looked down over sloping shoulders to the contorted, bear-bait bodies far below. Then Beam reevaluated the girl's tapered back... touristy buckskin...painted-on 501 jeans sheathing apricot-smooth buttocks. Gingerly sidestepping until directly behind her, he again checked for witnesses and was grateful for having seen none. Nose close to fragrant hair, Beam knew one quick shove would suffice. First impact would snap her neck around through 270 degrees long before her cartwheeled body caromed off the 90-foot mark of rock-ridged, straight-down fall.

Hands waist high, he heard: *All this would take would be one tiny push...*

BUT OH WHAT A PITY TO LOSE SUCH A TUSH!

Head Man's rationale bade him wait...and so instead

of launching the girl into her next incarnation, Beam roughly grabbed her upper arms, yanking her away from the gust-kissed ledge.

"There was no fire," she stated matter-of-factly.

Two hundred feet below, a marauding wolf sniffed tentatively at Trough Licker's corpse, then bit savagely halfway through the dead man's neck. The famished animal's fangs clicked and snapped fragile vertebrae as it thrust its hungry snout deep into blood-red meat.

"You seen too many movies," Beam replied, as the rest of the ravenous pack gathered below.

"What am I going to do for a ride?" the girl asked herself, still only marginally mindful of Beam's presence. "That there was my ride."

"Where you headed?"

She turned and looked up as if seeing Beam for the first time.

"Oh. Hullo. Didn't see you standing there."

"Where are you going?" Beam asked, patiently trying to measure the size of the gaps in her loosely woven mental mesh.

"West...where all things good and gracious come together joyously to merge spiritually at that well-trodden crossroads of time and space."

Whatever she smoked sure as hell wasn't store-bought, Beam reflected, while Head Man joyously sang a song of sixpence, a pocket full of rye.

"Did you have any kind of knapsack or travel bag?" Beam asked. "Anything like that?"

"Why would I?"

"For your stuff. Clothes and things. Whatever women usually carry."

"Nope. Weren't carrying nuthin'," she replied, gazing out beyond snow-capped peaks of northern mountains toward discordant, gray-zone beachheads where jingle-jangle dimensions clashed openly with five-sense reality.

Frost-wind gusts shiver-shook Beam, but the lightly clad

girl was oblivious to the weather. At first, wondering if anything made an impression, Beam decided that nothing much did.

"Just the clothes on your back?"

"I always travel light, Mister."

"You can ride along with me."

"Why not," she said, her words more statement than question.

As they got into the van, she flicked her eyes on and then just as quickly off the smashed guard rail.

"Someone ought to fix that there broken fence," she said casually. "A body could come to grievous harm 'cause of it." And then she went back to watching things only she could see... saying nothing more during the nine minutes it took Beam to get comfortably settled with headgear properly situated. The girl blinked once at the wired Chicago Cubs baseball cap Beam carefully adjusted, and then she turned to look out the windshield.

"How old're you?" Beam asked, paying strict attention to the speedometer needle's winding up past 57 during the transition from bumpy, cold-patched access lane to empty interstate.

"As old as yesterday. As young as tomorrow. What's your name?"

"Jack Beam."

"Naah," she said, genuinely amused for the five seconds it took that thought to sprout wings and fly south. "It can't be. You don't look like a Jack Beam to me."

"What would a Jack Beam look like?"

"First off, he'd be carrying a long, knobby staff, with a sharp point on one end. Like an abo digging stick."

"Abo?"

"Aborigine."

"Oh."

"For making all the holes he pours seeds into for the apple trees. I know who Jack Beam is," she said proudly, nodding twice with deep conviction. "He's that apple-seed guy. Sure enough, that's who he is."

Beam smiled amiably. Comfortably content in the

interstate's right lane, he dialed in a new angle on the roof's solar collector to more accurately focus on ebbing sunlight's canted, crimson rays jabbing irregularly through pine needles on the highway's southeast side.

"What else?" he asked.

"Huh?"

"Jack Beam. What else would he look like?"

"Well, he'd have white hair and a long white beard. And he'd be wearing a coonskin cap hung heavily all around with sprigs of fresh hollyhock and chicory. And he'd be old and gruff, and hairy as a bear. But you're none of those things," she said. "I can see that right off."

"What would you like my name to be?"

"I would like to call you Solomon," she said, eyes smokily vacant while looking him over carefully, as if seeing him for the first time. "You seem to be very wise. In fact, I'm sure you are."

"May I please call you Jamie?" he asked politely in a timid, straight-ahead stare, hands tightly gripping the steering wheel, fearful she might say no, hoping and praying that she wouldn't.

"I've been called worse," she said indifferently.

Beam immediately iced up at "Jamie's" lackadaisical acceptance of so highly prized an expression of personal calling, but her plaintive voice just as quickly vised his heart into yielding, even to the point of redirecting jealously guarded energy so as to broadcast genuine sympathy her way.

And then he went back to paying careful attention to precision driving and keeping at least three mph under the speed limit. The sun was a dying, iron-red winker between tree limbs, waving eerily in the teeth of western ice wind...and Head Man, uncharacteristically patient thus far, would soon be lobbying loudly for sustenance.

GIMME MORE FOOD. GIMME MORE FOOD.

Yes, it is time. I know your mood.

Getting stopped by the highway patrol this late would be the height of damn-fool stupidity.

De Beque kept its promise of GAS-FOOD-LODGING.

One mile off the interstate and four miles outside of town, Beam drove carefully into a rundown rent-a-cabin operation. After making sure the cottage numbers went up high enough to suit his taste, he backed up to the office, gave Jamie two tens, and told her to buy whatever looked halfway edible in the adobe-block general store. Standing lonely sentry across the parking lot was the broken-window hollowness of what peeling paint and rusty-hinged, *cree-akk* metal advertised as once having been Stiv's 24-Hour Garage, and Towing. Other than that, they were alone.

The displaced Pawnee behind the office counter looked up only long enough to curse the blast of icy wind Beam let in. Then he repositioned the sawed-off, double-barreled scattergun on his lap and tried to doze off again as Beam politely requested Cabin Number 11.

"Any one you want, Mongo, twenty bucks cash," the Pawnee muttered, no paperwork necessary.

Jamie still wasn't back when Beam drove over to Cabin Number 11, brought his one special suitcase around front, and reached underneath the dashboard to arm the van's unique alarm system: an ignition-keyed timer coupled to a powerful, arc-shaped bomb centered under both front seats. Whoever stole the van would have between five and 12 miles worth of Grand Theft-Auto career, depending on how fast they were going when Siamese claymore mines shredded them into blast-dried strips of beef jerky.

After casually checking for interested observers and seeing none, Beam locked himself inside the weather-roughened log cabin. He immediately pulled down the single window's tattered shade, patched two holes in its middle, then used duct tape to seal it tightly to its frame. The bathroom had an overhead vent instead of a window—no blocking needed there—so he placed his large case carefully in the recess of the dust-ball closet and quickly set up shop.

By the time Jamie shuffled lethargically over to Number 11, climbed the sagging steps, and knocked halfheartedly, her dinner of Hostess Fruit Pie had been washed down with half a 12-ounce

Mountain Dew. The door opened only body-width wide as Beam took her soda while drawing her into kingly purple light, all of which Jamie accepted comfortably unpuzzled, as if such visual cocooning were so second nature as to render comment moot.

Sixteen ultraviolet tanning lamps, four to a wall, gave the room an ectoplasmic glow. They were fed off one thick snake of junction-boxed, heavy-duty extension cable. If Jamie noticed Beam's nakedness as he put her half-finished soda on the fruit-crate night table, she paid no heed.

"Put these on right away," he said somberly, urging Jamie to wear thick-lensed goggles for safeguarding virginal eyes and preventing them from being overwhelmed by the room's freely flickering, grape-light forces.

It would not pay to have you power up too soon. Unfortunate crisping might ensue.

MATCH SCRATCH IS HEAVY ON THY BROW!

Not now, not now, not now, not now!

"It warms me," Jamie said. "I like it very much. It's otherworldly. Thank you for accepting me into your universe. Are you from Alpha-Centauri?"

"Please tell me all about your day," Beam said sincerely, close to resting assured that Jamie had no more than a featherweight grasp on reality.

"I can still taste the cherries from my Hostess Fruit Pie. Behind that..."

"Behind?"

"Before."

"Before that?"

"You have no hair at all. May I touch your smoothness?" she asked, reaching up toward the bald head without waiting for permission.

"Please do," he said, taking her hands gently in his but guiding curious fingers to his electrolysis-denuded face, because Head Man would not permit so much as a single skylight pore to be filmed over by even the slightest trace of a nonbeliever's skin oil.

After blessing each cheek with gentle, front-to-back circles, Jamie got naked. Beam's eyes and hands were drawn magnetically to bounteously full, passion-warmed breasts...and the high, impertinently swollen nipples urging him to take further liberties. His fingers danced lightly along taut flanks, gently tracing the flaring swell of rounded hips, then circling Jamie's waist and drawing her close. Whirlpools of boiling disturbance radiated directly between their midsections, further fattening the swelling heaviness already rising eagerly.

"I would like to become one with you in all your glory," Jamie said earnestly.

"Yes. It would please me greatly if you would."

"What's your name?"

"Jack Beam."

"Jack. I like that name. Jack is a very nice name."

"Do I look like a Jack Beam to you?"

"You are everyman's Jack Beam...and so therefore you are mine as well. Yes, Jack Beam, I do accept what you, in godlike majesty, so generously offered...and so do I cleave willingly unto thee."

"What's your name?"

"Whatever you would like it to be."

"I would like to call you Jamie, if that's all right with you."

"I've been called worse," she said indifferently.

Coming conversationally full circle, her poignant whisper again strummed chords of chronic despair. But this time, Beam was unwounded by nonchalance because he knew that Jamie was totally and unselfishly giving all that she had.

And when Beam pulled up their goggles to look straight through to the back of Jamie's benign head, he confirmed the total lack of conscious presence. Utter vacuity was no act: Her mind held little more than the present tense; her past extended no further back than 10 minutes max.

Such assurance heartily gladdened him, meaning as it did that he would be spared the operational necessity of choking life's precious breath from harmless hedge sparrow...that it would be wholly safe to let her live...that Jamie's memories would vanish faster than weed smoke in a gale.

"Which bed would you like?" he asked.

"Whichever bed you're in. I like to snuggle. Would you like to lay with me?"

Her hands roamed the soft skin of his upper body. She pressed curious fingertips inward and, in probing deeply, felt the coiled strength of ropy muscles. And then she reached lower to fill both hands full of growing hardness...as sweetly innocent ministrations brought his throbbing maleness more openly and potently awake.

"Which bed would you like...?"

"Jack," he reminded gently, the lump again blocking his throat, uncharacteristic sadness threatening to run riot, Head Man weeping openly for them both.

"Which bed would you like, Jack?"

"Whichever bed you're in, Jamie," he sighed. "Whichever bed you're in."

Jack Beam and Jamie Roadie didn't so much make love as meld in a politely antiseptic union, as if such a connection were proper, just, and expected at this juncture of circumstance. What surprised him most was Jamie's bed-shaking, megavolt orgasm, as if she were a young woman who...in drawing energy in equal measure from him and from the room's amethyst aurora...was experiencing loin-lashingly cosmic climax for the very first time.

Which...considering her porous state of mind...was exactly what she was.

Head Man grudgingly allowed Beam five hours of dreamless sleep before bugling him awake in chilly darkness. Preparation for departure began with electrically melting enough wax in the bathroom basin to paint the head and upper body. Dry time was 20 minutes. After pulling off the wax and steam-showering to further open his pores, Beam jellied up, gently roused Jamie, and they were rolling southwest at sunrise. At 8:35 a.m., fully powered up thanks to a fantastic angle on Day Star, Beam checked in with Jamie again, confirmed that she didn't remember more than what happened four minutes previously, and again made her acquaintance during breakfast.

While sopping up the last smears of congealing yolk from a four-egg, double-bacon meal, Jamie didn't realize that the name Beam bounced off her after the waitress took their order was not the same one used the night before, and that the one given after paying the check was another name still. Her moppet eyes broadcast a total absence of recollective thought, and Beam knew that such a complete lack of retentive logic meant headwinds would scour critical memories from nonresistant brains before she was five minutes gone.

Beam and Jamie separated in Los Angeles, just outside the grimy washroom of a U-Pump-It at Atlantic Boulevard and U.S. 5. He watched her saunter off without looking back, left thumb side-hooked in the direction she was walking. Within 40 seconds, a golf-capped driver was buckling Jamie into the right seat of a red Miata while taking easily seen liberties with the hard thighs that only hours ago were squeezing omnipotent vitality from Beam's thrusting groin.

And just that quickly, Jamie vanished, whizzing off to nowhere in particular, interested only in widening the distance from where she had been...while narrowing the gap between here and now, and wherever else she might be bound.

Lonely is as lonely does...

THINK OF "TO BE"; NOT WHAT WAS.

After losing her in traffic, Beam carefully stowed the glittering motorcycle jacket behind his seat and donned a black windbreaker. Then he accessed the freeway and drove at a moderately enthusiastic speed down to the Broadway and Pico Boulevard Post Office to claim his package from General Delivery.

The Hispanic clerk did the paperwork with painstaking precision bordering on outright nuisance, even to the point of photocopying the Minnesota driver's license that would be ashes within the hour. In exchange for the right ID and a dash of obeisance, Beam took possession of a Canadian-postmarked box containing a locker key wrapped in a communiqué extending both profuse thanks and abundant assurances that his prearranged instructions had been carried out to the letter.

Back inside his van, Beam ate the rice-paper note and barbecued the box. He finished off his Sunshine Hydrox cookies and the last high-protein drink on his way down to the bus depot bracketed by Main Street and Maple, 6th Street and 7th. From Locker 111, he retrieved a black-leather, zip-around Kmart suitcase containing $500,000 in untraceable $50 bills. The payment was a deposit for his next "service"—an atrocity of his own choosing—the only requirement being a body count commensurate with money paid.

TransPac 117, after all, had only been Richard Lawrence Jefferson Transitioning Jack Beam's coolly indifferent demonstration of what a man of his obvious expertise could do.

Late afternoon's falling barometer of incoming El Nino storm had already siphoned his energy level down through bottom green and alarmingly deep into high yellow. So after loading the suitcase into the van, Beam opted for additional protection: a black-felt head cap serving as additional insulation between skin and wig to forestall as much power loss as possible.

The giant Traax Parcel Service facility, recently opened four blocks from the bus station, was a beehive of activity. But as frenetically busy as things were from loading docks to lobby, what with the Christmas mailing season clearly looming on the event horizon, the high-hemmed TPS Human Resources officer still had plenty of time to spend with this decorated Desert Storm veteran earnestly seeking employment.

While reflecting on the vivid masculinity inherent in a conversation so politely sprinkled with "ma'am," perhaps to mask passionate strength smoldering below, Carla DeMas-Wade assured candidly direct Mike Moran, formerly USMC—honorably discharged—that there would be no trouble at all securing him a job in Maintenance, seeing as he eagerly embraced the prospect of working nights. And, most important of all, he could certainly look forward to eventual consideration for promotion to delivery driver, seeing as how he had a New York chauffeur's license, and getting California credentials would present no trouble at all.

"All of which suits me just fine," Moran said engagingly. "When I landed in the battalion's motor pool, it was like coming home again. For as long as I can remember, I always loved taking things apart and putting them back together. You know. Fixing things."

"Innate skill?"

"I kinda grew into it, you might say."

"How so?" DeMas-Wade asked, grateful for the childhood-development change of pace. "Out here, everything's genetics... from acrobatics to water skiing."

"When I was a kid," Moran replied enthusiastically, "I used to take apart those friction-motor toys...the kind fastened together with slots and tabs. Probably way before your time."

"Thank you," DeMas-Wade said demurely.

"My aunts said: 'You always want to see where the feet come from.'"

"And did you?"

"Yeah," Moran answered shyly. "And then I buttoned them back up, all nice and neat."

"Probably be worth a small fortune today."

"Sure are," Moran noted. "When you can find them."

After several more minutes of desultory chitchat terminating in a handshake that communicated more from her than he wanted to capitalize on, Moran took his leave, reclaimed his van from Visitors' Parking, and drove off to where previously arranged housing waited only for key's insertion in dead-bolt lock.

His requirements were boilerplate simple. The neighborhood didn't have to be particularly savory; neither could it be a cesspool of urban decay. Lower-middle class would do; blue collar was even better. His domicile was large and anonymous, nestling comfortably under the queen-palm cover of urban obscurity...where people still took "No" for an answer, where steel-shuttered doors and windows deterred the inquisitive and where case-hardened, high-security locks kept out the uninvited.

There was, after all, still quite a lot of work to do.

CHAPTER 9

MERRY CHRISTMAS...

Slayzak and Blade, toasted nightly by Traax Parcel Service's dispatchers, were the radio call signs of two macho gear-jamming Teamsters, aka the Testosterone Twins; aka Sidewinder and Stork; aka Flamingo and Fooge.

Slayzak: six-foot-three, give or take; the meditational vibes of an aspiring Dalai Lama pupil coveting The Master's throne; harbor-seal smile; trim-waisted decathlete's physique perfectly packaged in he-man spandex; motto: "Focus, my brother. 'Tis all in your focus"; ponytail tucked up tightly under bent-brim N.Y. Mets baseball cap; continually fending off barbs critical of his team's poor standing in the National League East.

Blade: five-foot-nine, plus or minus; perpetually cranky, as if craved naps skipped his hammock without bestowing "snoozoids"; ratcatcher scowl; pear-bellied from too many brewskis; motto: *"Bartender, another long-neck down here pronto!"*; up from Maintenance with a Chicago Cubs baseball cap covering bald-pate bubbles of volatile mind-set...but his hair was said to have been lost to chemo so LA staffers cut him mucho slack.

Lunatic, pants-afire driving styles swirled equal thirds of high-pitched hazard, "Heaven help 'em" and *"Jeeeez-us!"* No merge was too tough, no rush hour too hairy, no lane change unmanageable, no hairpin turn beyond the robotic perfection of Zen-inspired artistry. Though their unique brand of squeal-rubber rodding pushed reality to damn near fatality, each man's proficiency bordered on supernatural: Neither had so much as "buffed" fender wax during frenetic, hombre-a-hombre competition to garner accolades attendant with becoming *numero uno* driver of North America's third-largest package-delivery firm.

Featherweight headsets were worn with the casual nonchalance of "Dare ya!" jet jockeys on combat air patrol guarding against marauding MiGs. Shift-work pastime was laced with spouted road-surface factoids cloaked in arcane, zippity-zoom lingo. The more obscure the phrasing, the more each relished the report. Slayzak and Blade were duplicate incarnations of tank-busting A-10 pilots diving vertically through Force 10 gales to pound depleted-uranium cannon fire dead center into enemy armor caught naked in "No Trespassing" areas.

Dwindling Christmas-shopping hours found Blade overrevving north on San Pedro, angling out of Little Tokyo with 20/20 gunsight vision riveted on 1st Street crossing and the final lay of egg-drop day: a foreign-deposit "bankola" for an international-exchange house located between City Hall East and City Hall South, across from law enforcement's Parker Center administration building.

One would think you couldn't get more secure than locating money-changing ops within spitting distance of the po-leece, Blade ruminated, finger-flicking a clutchless shift from second to third, *because who'd try robbing a bank with the Little Boy Blues only a hopscotch away?* But the bear-trap location hadn't fazed one transient bean-brain, the TPS ace recalled. And predictably, poor Mr. Heister had been swarmed by a blanketing constabulary's collar-hungry crew the minute he bolted from the bank building's lobby.

"Yo! Slayzak! Where you be? Talk to me!" feisty Blade radioed sullenly, careening wildly around a nearly rear-ended taxi. "Blade to Slayzak..." Damned S.O.B.? "Yo, my man. *Hey!* We still on for liberation's libation?" A wage-docking TPS reprimand for using a beer's brand name on eavesdropped airwaves constituted sufficient warning for the ornery Blade, who quickly switched to a multisyllabic generic. "I ain't hearin' you, man! *Come to Poppa or my friendship stoppa!*"

"Back in yo' face, Blade. This be Slayzak. What ya doin'?"

"Last droppa the day."

"Gonna make it pay?"

"For sure. You be rhymin'?"

"Like Simon," Slayzak shot back.

"Where ya be?" Blade inquired idly.

"Three-point-five long etudes westa Raucous Caucus."

"You be comin' in mighty clear for all that convention center concrete 'n' steel twixt 'n' 'tween us."

"Must be primo atmospherics suckin' fastball bounces offa Daddy Discus," Slayzak crackled back, a reference to city-girdling microwave towers relaying TPS chatter. "You in the thickets?" he asked, which was shorthand gab for massed shoppers and downtown office workers.

"Like the ram of Abraham."

"'Nuf said?"

"Nope-de-dope," Blade chuckled, warming to the patter. "Shift change cumma-through Blue U," he disclosed, telling Slayzak that extra uniformed officers were leathering pavement. "Plus halfa city government bringing down day's curtain early on this eve of blessed birth."

But Slayzak didn't require Blade's sectoring, because the man with the killer-prefix name was leaning on a lamppost well northeast of counterfeit coordinates. Golf-putt range ensured crisp communication. Even as he watched, broadcasting phased into direct line of sight...

Now here comes the Cutter...

...SANS ALL BROADCAST FLUTTER...

...with reception crystal clear as the walkie-talkie antenna drifted in a lazy, sweep-track traverse of the parcel van's compass course.

Bebopping Blade's ivory/green truck passed six yards close, turning right off of 1st and onto Main between the city-hall annexes. Slayzak nodded amiably at reinforced concrete and steel rising like double-strength backstops between him and Blade. Stout, earthquake-proof walls would provide vertical tamping... and engorge the savage *jinni*, whose impatient battering on the lamp lid signaled imminent exit.

Got plenty of buffer...

...SINCE BUILDINGS GOT TOUGHER.

Cornered-and-gone Blade was square-pin tacked like a glass-cased butterfly. Amplifying repeater boxes duct-taped behind street signs and under "Recycle CA" cans pegged the doomed Blade inside bull's-eye rectangulation.

"Yo! Blade!" Slayzak radioed into his handheld unit, as any undercover narc might. "You locked 'n' chocked?"

"Radial rubbers kissin' tar in Loading Zone Mayor," Blade chuckled into his headset, "and dollyin' up these canvas tonners now."

The third grunt coming over Slayzak's transceiver was Blade lifting weighty Coin Bag Number 3 atop two already stacked on a wheeled conveyance. And so from behind his well-shielded vantage point, Slayzak thumb-spun his walkie-talkie's squelch. The radio wailed high-frequency garble as flaring wraparound fuse cord broiled electronic internals to extinction.

In the chilly Traax Parcel Service truck, interlinked events sequenced in microseconds quickly...and the fast-talking Blade never knew what hit him.

Vaporized at the core of a four-stick, gelatin-dynamite burst, he instantly dissolved into boiling moisture. Bone-flecked crimson haze splotched the parcel van's interior. Walls bulged ominously. Fracture cracks webbed sheet metal. Rivets popped. Jagged panels curled down like rose petals opening in time-lapse bloom. Metal money slashed sideways in murderous dispersion.

Then Hell's incinerating inferno was fully unleashed as fireball incandescence touched off 16 floor-mounted charges of putty-boxed HMX high explosive, pyro-powdered aluminum, and zinc dust.

TPS truck #22612 disintegrated with a sonic-boom craack, spawning a monstrous roar. Saw-toothed sections guillotined laterally, cleaving pedestrians' body parts. Pebbly, white-hot shrapnel shotgunned ill-fated passersby. Incendiary debris amputated limbs. Hashed-human carnage extended 300 yards beyond the spindly quiver of the gutted vehicle's blackened frame. Billowing monsoon clouds of noxious brown smoke obscured the knifed-open sidewalk.

The ejected roof second-staged at 125 feet up, mortaring meteors on random, 30-degree trajectories. Time-fused globes' eruption shattered dual-pane windows. Molten orbs gouged brickwork. Axing, star-shaped brass decapitated sixth-floor onlookers.

The half-melted drive shaft and charred rear end corkscrewed earthward in oil-fire plummet, pulverizing a hophead boutique 12 blocks from the sulfur-stench pit around which 24 people were atomized into traceless disappearance. Eighty-nine knocked-flat unfortunates died almost as quickly. Others' final reward dallied only slightly longer. Tallying the casualties would take weeks.

After double-timing three floors down into a public parking garage, Slayzak morphed spiritually into Ball Peen...the newly hatched identity already madly spinning fiber-optic networks for channeling the skittery impulses of a rigidly dedicated mind.

Death's coldly calculating hammerhead swung open the rear doors of his windowless black Ford cargo van. The dank-cement corner was siphoning psychic energy dangerously fast. That contingency had been meticulously planned for, however, and the van's sunlamp dome light held off fringe nibbling's prelude to the massive, pulled-plug drainage threatened by subsurface passage.

The bomber dove inside and rolled face up, making sure the blue-glow recharger stayed lit as the clamshell doors' cushioned slam cocooned him safely inside. But Baby Sun's rays were only marginally adequate; miniscule efforts were sapping more than remained in nearly exhausted bioelectrical storage. So Ball Peen twisted violently, frantically gobbled one-half bottle of yellow multivitamins, and chugged a liter of Power-Up high-protein drink.

Eleven minutes later, Ball Peen sat up cross-legged and ripped off elevator shoes, plasticized clothes, physique-slimming corset, ponytailed wig, and N.Y. Mets baseball cap. An innocuous jumpsuit slid on just as quickly. Next were donned accoutrements best suited for the command performance of street-side serenade.

Following ascension and reemergence, Ball Peen bobbed through the pandemonium of moan-spiked massacre. The tattered exodus sine-waved outward. Zigzag streams of panic-stricken wounded wandered aimlessly in chaotic confusion. Deafened and bleeding survivors...some legless, others cradling severed arms like swaddled infants...milled around shell-shocked, numb in the stinking-fume holocaust of butcher-blast graveyard.

While aerobicising his lungs on a westward amble toward decimated LAPD officers lending woefully inadequate aid, Ball Peen's eye caught a pay phone. He angled toward it, stopped short, and reslung his strap-supported instrument. The bomber flipped idly through J's listings...trying desperately to fathom the compulsion for continued searching even while being reined away by the equally pressing need to solo a concert for those beyond music's aural reach.

CHAPTER 10

FATAHLAND

Along with much lip-biting thought, Mordechai Z. had invested the better part of 48 fly-ridden hours trying to target his most vexatious botheration: the sand fleas bedeviling him for these past eight days in the field; the scorpions persistently trying to crawl into his boots, up his sleeves and down his pants, or the sensual *National Geographic* photographer in Bazooby jacket, safari shorts and Tony Lama alligator boots—"Tootsy" he called her—who'd ignited his hormonal burner and was most directly responsible for the simmering, unfulfilled aches throbbing incessantly in his loins.

For a little over a week, Mordechai's tight group of flinty, hard-boiled ruffians had been drifting nomadically northeast-southwest-and back, along a line of position nine miles above the northern edge of Israel's self-proclaimed security zone in southern Lebanon...and were now encamped just outside the flyspeck village of al-Bazna, well within spitting distance of the Sidon-to-Tyre Road.

There were 10 animals in Mordechai's band: Esther, whose apparently obese pregnancy covered a fiberglass reservoir of hand grenades and extra clips of ammunition, plus Ignatz and David, young paratroopers in their mid-twenties specifically chosen for their knife-fighting skills, but now casually tending the four sheep, two goats, and one donkey on interest-bearing loan from Kibbutz Ein Gev.

Early on during the reconnaissance, Mordechai had checked in with Colonel H., using a burst encoder that compressed his outgoing messages into "threeps" of barely audible whistles, each only a fraction of a second long. Bounced off an Israel Defense

Industries Skibbler satellite in low orbit, the signals flicked to a suburb of Tel Aviv, where they were decoded and then replied to in mere moments.

"*NatGeo* has photographers all over the Middle East. It's easier to monitor milkweed in a tropical storm than it is to nail down the location of each of their full-time staffers," Colonel H. replied coldly. "And listen to what I got from a junior editor, who, let me tell you, was definitely on the muscle for one reason or another. Maybe bad news on his AIDS test. The little prick said, 'After all, there ain't a goddamn pay phone on every goddamn corner of every goddamn famine-stricken village in the goddamn Middle East, or isn't the goddamn high-and-mighty Undersecretary of Lebanese Cultural Affairs able to realize that, *goddammit?!*'"

"Your English is a lot better than his."

"I was certainly hoping you'd notice," Colonel H. said, genuinely pleased.

"So maybe they were on deadline, which might account for their rudeness," Mordechai offered hopefully.

The disembodied disgust of Colonel H. was not easily turned aside. "American arrogance takes second seat to no one's, as far as I am concerned, and you can quote me on that. Without using my name, of course. Anyway, for you, Mordechai, she is strictly hands off."

Tootsy had every right to be there, Colonel H. said, but her presence nettled Mordechai...and it sure as hell had gotten under Esther's skin faster than a bad case of Taj eczema.

"Think of her meddling presence as a bonus. This will give you a much-needed chance to show how good you are at what you profess to be doing out there in that glorious, sun-speckled countryside," Colonel H. joked. "If she finds out who you *really* are, you're fired," he laughed. "I'll see to that much, I guarantee you."

"Or dead?"

"Firing's worse," Colonel H. said. "Believe me. At least dead, you might be a hero. Maybe. I'll say Kaddish for you, though it is unlikely anyone else will. But a fired bureaucrat? Ha-ha. Dear Mordechai, we have enough deadwood stacked up in our ministries to feed all the Franklin stoves in North America for a decade of Antarctic winters. And you can quote me on that."

"Without using your name, of course," Mordechai replied wryly.

"Now you're talking."

Colonel H. added only that an infiltration of unknown size might be on the agenda of the Palestine National Salvation Front, the coalition of three Damascus-based factions: Fatah-Uprising, Saiqa, and the Popular Front for the Liberation of Palestine—General Command. Fighters from one of those groups would be smuggling a member of Hamas, possibly posing as a Druze peddler, through the Occupied Zone, then into northern Israel and, later still, farther south into the teeming underworld of the occupied West Bank.

"So they're all working together now, those scum?" Mordechai asked.

"Apparently, they've rejoined Arafat. Looks like they're giving up their long campaign to topple his leadership. For a while, anyway. But that's who you want. Hamas," Colonel H. said. "Let me spell it for you."

"The Islamic Resistance Movement. Believe me, spelling it really isn't necessary."

"H-A-M-A-S," Colonel H. chuckled.

"Surely you can do better?" Mordechai said, trying to elicit more information without wheedling, which would have been unseemly.

"Be thankful for what you get...and be grateful for this acid test of your courageous resourcefulness," Colonel H. replied tartly. "This Hamas operative? The one we want? He was exiled during the last deportation. Now he'll be coming back...we think with a clue to the identity of those behind the bombing of the American jetliner."

"I remember that one," Mordechai said.

"Good for you; it is best that we do not forget. Five hundred and forty-three Americans. None of us, thankfully."

"Some Jews, though."

"But theirs," Colonel H. reminded him quickly. "Not ours. So we're interested, but not incensed, if you catch my drift."

"I do."

"Remember, too, that the Americans are our friends, in spite of all this West Bank arm-twisting, so don't fuck this up."

"What makes you think I'm going to fuck this up?" Mordechai asked, struggling to keep his temper under control.

"Because you fucked up the last one is why, and your track record is right now pointing my rather large nose down a path I would prefer not to tread. There's a limit to how much string-pulling even one as well-connected as I can do. By the way, have you given any thought to sheltering? You'll at least get a promotion...and a bigger pension."

"Thank you, Colonel, but no. Coming back inside is not currently on my agenda."

"We'll talk more about that later, I'm sure. Just keep your options open," Colonel H. said.

"I always do."

"Never more so than today, my friend."

"Each day is its own singular priority," Mordechai replied.

"Then we understand each other. *Good!* Now here is your mission."

Mordechai listened patiently. Part 1: Extract the infiltrator from his shepherds. Kill the others, if necessary, which it probably wouldn't be because nine times out of 10, surprise sent the Arabs scrabbling away like panicked spiders in full retreat, although the more radical ones were tending to stick around longer than usual, especially if the numbers were on their side, which Colonel H. strongly indicated might very well be the case this time. Part 2: Get the Hamas swine to headquarters undamaged.

"It will be your ass and those of your unborn children, believe me, if he winds up missing so much as a fingernail," Mordechai was told.

"What about backup?"

"Backup?!" Colonel H. asked incredulously. *"You ask me about backup?!"*

"From a purely academic point of view, you understand."

"Mordechai, the West Bank is right now a Cajun cauldron of boiling Tabasco. What can I tell you? This is what I can tell you. I can get you a hot-response team...if you would like...." the last said teasingly, as if intimating that Mordechai wasn't soldier enough to handle a simple extraction by himself.

"Not for now."

"You sure?"

"Yes, sir."

"What about air?"

"No," Mordechai said, not willing to seem too cautious, knowing full well that lack of balls would wreck his career faster than outright failure.

"Good," Colonel H. said. "They'll be at altitude about nine klicks east, anyway, just in case. Don't be shy about ringing them up. Now don't bother me again unless you have something," Colonel H. ordered, breaking contact with a louder-than-usual CLICK.

To make matters more confusing from the standpoint of operational clarity, Tootsy was coming back again and showing every indication of closing the distance considerably.

"As-salaam alaykum!" he called out.

"Alaykum as-salaam!" Tootsy replied, courteously and circumspectly approaching Mordechai at his campsite. Gritted teeth kept him from laughing at her clumsy curtsy.

Here we go again.

He licked his lips very perceptibly, extending a bit of tongue, hoping for a reaction and grimacing when nothing materialized. The striped canvas tent behind him snapped in the sea breeze, trying futilely to expunge the stink of dung-heap human misery infesting the Red Crescent refugee camp to the south.

It was a mammoth struggle to bring his mind back to Tootsy and his tent. He wanted her inside. He wanted to be inside her. *A little Chivas, perhaps. A little hashish, maybe. A tight, 28-year-old clench, for damn sure.*

In response to Mordechai's hand gestures, Tootsy hunkered down on the other side of anemic fire while gargling up phrases of grammatically perfect Berlitz Arabic. He, in turn, sighed behind the singsong slang of a marginally educated Bedouin right now interested only in sampling the exotics of Western lovemaking. Out of the corner of his eye, Mordechai saw Esther glaring rudely at him. He turned his stooped back slightly so the shrike with whom he shared his lodgings could not intrude on his frank appraisal of Tootsy, who was plunked down comfortably on the other side of white-ashed coals and scrap wood.

Pallid light eking through stunted trees cast her eyes as a soupy, indeterminate color. Tootsy's blonde hair was black at the roots, split at its ends, and bake-oven dry. Splintered fingernails and rough hands hinted at work considerably more laborious than pressing a shutter release. The etched patina of hard face had Mordechai convinced that shellac formed the base of her makeup.

Tootsy's nose had been put back together a shade off-center, as if someone had walked her into a door—or worse. The scuff patterns on her boots told him she was a lefty who dragged her opposite foot. He carefully examined her legs without seeming to. And there it was...on her right calf...the barely noticeable pucker of a long-healed gunshot wound.

Mordechai offered her a piece of sizzling lamb on a stick, burned blacker than the coals that crisped it. She politely declined, while also passing on the nonalcoholic arrack he gulped deeply between bites of light lunch.

He wiped heat-cracked lips on ill-fitting gabardine sleeves while Tootsy brought up her Leica M6. Another bite, another drink, and it was time for Mordechai to upshift and hasten this show on down the road to what he sincerely hoped would be a hasty and favorable conclusion.

"Picture? Okay, okay? *Yes, okay!* My English not good. Learn from cards."

"A damn sight better than my Arabic, that's for sure," she said, relieved to be at last conversing in her precious English, however fragmented it might prove to be. "Cards, you say?"

"Bees-bowl," he grinned, showing her cosmetically blackened gums and yellowed front teeth. "I show you, yes? You like? You buy? Many good things I sell," he said, moving to get up and hoping she'd take the hint and make good her departure.

"Oh, base-ball. Baseball," she said, stretching out her legs to settle herself in more comfortably. "Actually, your English is very good."

"Smoke?" he asked her, rocking on his haunches while reaching forward with a half-crushed pack of Marlboros.

She shook her head.

"Very good," he urged. "Yes! You take! American!"

"No, but thank you very much anyway."

Mordechai shielded his eyes from the peekaboo sun while scanning the festering town scooped out of onshore gravel below. Esther caught the signal immediately. She tied up the sheep and waddled forward to take up her position. The truck would be along any minute, and Mordechai wanted Tootsy back over the arid hillocks to where her Range Rover baked in the kiln of oppressive heat.

"Very dangerous you be here, lady. There is trouble here many, many times," he said, forcing his attention up from the swell of Tootsy's hips, past her wasp waist, higher than that glorious Mount Rushmore of chest…to her eyes, which now viscerally perturbed him. The word "trouble" narrowed them to where they flickered with the dangerous unpredictability of a rabid weasel.

"Palestinians, lady. Israelis." Mordechai hawked up a large gob of sandy phlegm, then paused to spit...clearly demonstrating where his sentiments lay. "Always shooting."

Tootsy sucked in her breath, stomach flattening under field jacket, breasts rising and thrusting toward him, pushed up and out by athletic lungs expanding almost to overcapacity. Mordechai pulled his eyes loose from her riveting stare and gazed out over the rubble-strewn landscape. Arrack gourd to his lips, he drank deeply again...hoping that even a nonalcoholic beverage, if swilled in sufficient quantity, would deaden the foreboding spreading like a chilly contagion through his chest and thighs.

Brief meditation complete, Tootsy exhaled slowly. Looking around carefully as if having to take time to remember where she was and what she was about, Tootsy picked up a black-bodied Leica R6 and motor-drove her way through a roll of Kodak Tri-X. She shot him almost too professionally, both eyes open and pausing only to reload the R6 before going to work with an R5.

He squinted past a black rangefinder camera dangling between her robust thighs. Mistaking the object of his attention, she offered him the Leica for a closer look. He grasped it crudely, his thumb pressing firmly into the lens and rubbing in a fat, lamb-gravy smudge while scraping his fingernail sharply over the lens's unfiltered glass.

"Lee-kaah," he said, trying for excitement while wondering who she really was and how best to dump her...looking up into her eyes and hoping for a reaction...disappointed and unsettled at having found none.

"Lie-kuh," she said, eyes suddenly widening as she obviously humored him. "Leica."

"Yes! Lie-kuh," he answered, sweat running down his socks, knowing full well that she was not what she purported to be and...much worse...realizing she knew that he knew.

"You take picture, I take picture, yes? Then you go? Okay, okay? Unsafe for you here. Much trouble."

That reaction again: midriff tightening, breasts rising, chest filling with air, oxygenating for action, and Esther too far away, her back to him now.

Damn!

"I'll stay," Tootsy said, eyeing him carefully.

The knowledge that she was on to his little game convinced Mordechai that Colonel H. would make good on this threat of banishment to the far reaches of the Agriculture Ministry. That is, if he didn't come home in a body bag.

"Trouble is what my magazine pays me to capture," Tootsy laughed, her words abruptly polysyllabic, their tone briskly conversational, her phrases no longer spaced out as they had been when she thought herself to be in the company of a near-savage who might be uncomfortable with her native tongue.

Tootsy tried for a lighter mood, psychically telegraphing Mordechai that she was not the enemy, disappointed that he seemed bound and determined not to pick up on it. "I noticed you and your family wandering back and forth. Do you barter?"

"Bar-terr? Who is bar-terr?" he asked, trying to keep the ball at least moderately in play.

"Trade," Tootsy said, now thoroughly enjoying this bantam slice of human comedy, potently puffed up with the success of having successfully snatched the adversarial high ground. "For food? Goods? Gifts?" her tone saying: I can keep this crap up for as long as you want.

"Yes-yes! Lebanese soldiers come back. Long time gone. Back now. Good for business. You go now!" Mordechai hissed, getting up, then yanking Tootsy abruptly to her feet and physically dragging her away from his encampment because the donkey's neck bell was ringing in signal of more in the air than sand, grit, and uneven farts of foul-smelling desert wind.

Mordechai could see the transport's dust devils dancing on the cracked macadam of the Sidon to-Tyre Road. The once-a-day produce truck had been under surveillance for the past seven months. Mordechai's group had seen the truck on the perfect schedule for the past eight days now, but today the truck was riding suspiciously low while carrying what at first glance appeared to be the same amount of cargo.

"You go now," Mordechai said, roughly ushering Tootsy over the rubble of shell-blasted rocks, turning her violently around and forcing her to take giant strides as he propelled her down the slope.

Mordechai long-stepped briskly away from the clearing while patting the small of his back for the bulky comfort of the double-clipped submachine gun snugged there. The truck had stopped—*ALL WRONG!* David drove the donkey forward with smacks of cypress fronds delivered smartly to the animal's ass, preparing to do business – *NO!*

The truck shouldn't have stopped. *It had never stopped before!*

"Hafez!" Mordechai screamed, breaking into a loping run, then long-jumping desperately over gravel-filled foxholes in hardscrabble land. But the warning came too late to save David's life. A burst of AK-47 fire caught him high across the top third of his chest, the slugs shredding both lungs and heart, killing him instantly.

The donkey took off running, bleating in alarm as it disappeared into the wavering imagery of the wadi's water mirage. Mordechai lunged forward, Tootsy forgotten as he yanked out his Glilon SAR, cocked it, and broke madly for the only position with a modicum of cover, a low rut not deep enough to protect his fragile forehead from an energetic sneeze, let alone from the mobile firepower ejecting itself from the truck's flatbed.

Exploding out in a cascading shower of rotten fruit was a Toyota pickup with a tripod-mounted 12.7mm DShKM machine gun. The driver cranked his steering wheel hard left as the gunner sprayed lead over the small truck's battered cab. Fedayeen swarmed out of the back of the fruit truck like rampaging fire ants.

The bastards are coming over in force!

The little pickup bounced over rough terrain, most of its shots going wild until a burst shredded the tent as the gunner lowered his muzzle, desperately trying to peer through reeking dust and find the range of Mordechai's unprotected vantage point.

His meager forces scattered and reduced by a vital 25 percent, Mordechai popped up only long enough to fire a tellingly accurate burst from his short assault rifle. The fruit truck's windows were instantly hammered into fragments by the staccato hail of 5.56mm bullets. Shattered glass and rising tendrils of smoke stood as mute testimony to two dead on the front seat.

Mordechai's beleaguered eyes reflexively counted heads in the horde of Saiqa guerrillas now streaming from the rear of the modified troop carrier. Then the Toyota was back again, skewing wildly through rubble-strewn desert as the gunner peppered anything vertical with bursts of heavy-caliber fire.

Bullets splanged around Mordechai's feverish hand signals. Ignatz waved back happily, glad at last to be back in the topsy-turvy swirl of close-quarters combat. He feinted left and casually unleashed a burst at two guerrillas. They stumbled backward, diagonal lines of death stitched across torsos, jellied blood and pureed body parts spraying out their backs. Ignatz gleefully gut-shot another one at point-blank range, pausing only long enough to jam an outrageously long cigar into the corner of his mouth and light up with his faithful Ronson.

"Huey's inbound," Ignatz called out through huge gouts of cigar smoke. "And Dewey and Louie," he laughed, while Mordechai belched on acidic fear, seriously doubting that the whirlies would get there in time to save their slinged asses.

The nearby impact of 12.7mm bullets refocused Mordechai's attention. The Toyota careened around sharply, jouncing wildly up and down like a bumper car bucking over massive speed bumps...its front soaring three feet off the ground, then juddering down while rear tires kicked up dirt like a mechanical mule.

Hammering lead shattered a tree trunk to Mordechai's right. He threw himself awkwardly left as slashing squares of bark opened up a nasty gash in his face. Esther was half-hidden in gun smoke, heaving hand grenades like a major-league pitcher gone berserk, but the driver maneuvered superbly, and the grenades burst harmlessly behind the truck.

"Incoming!" Ignatz yelled joyously, hooting like a drunken cowboy shooting up a frontier town, strutting brazenly upright as if daring the bursting shells to call in the bet he'd taken on his immortality.

The rest of his words were lost in explosions walking all over them. A nearby *whoomph* lifted Mordechai up in a geyser of sand and sent him spinning in a half-dazed roll that ended in gonging impact with rusted oil drums.

Katyushas now. What the hell is next?

Stunned, semiconscious, and coughing out sand and blood from two shattered teeth, he rolled over onto his stomach, looking up just in time to hear the angry buzz of an overrevving Toyota engine as the vehicle bore down on him from scarcely 100 feet away. The machine gun's barrel banged ineffectually into the top of the truck's cab, the gunner lividly frustrated by his inability to lower the weapon sufficiently to target Mordechai directly, but the left-front all-terrain tire would soon crush his skull like an overripe pomegranate, making the point moot anyway.

With his head scant moments from flattening, Mordechai half-jerked in surprise as Tony Lama boots bracketed each ear. Disappearing into an orange cloud of pain-generated smog were the long legs after which he had lusted only moments ago.

Crouched down icily, businesslike in a combat shooter's stance, Tootsy faced down the rampaging Toyota with studied composure...totally unmindful of the AK-47 waggling out the passenger-side window and angrily spitting hot 7.62mm lead in her general direction. She leveled a Behlert-customized Browning Hi-Power, held her breath, and squeezed. Six 9mm slugs barked out of the pistol and impacted in a tight, 1-3/8" group. The express loads pulverized the windshield, turned the driver's face into a mess of bloodied meat, and splashed his cerebrum out through the truck's back window.

The Toyota roared on momentarily, then reared up on its left side. Engine screaming, the Toyota bounced down rattling and gimballing four ways before curving away in a frenzied semicircle, its rear wheels spewing twin scythes of eye-stinging sand and rocks directly into Tootsy's face.

She recoiled from the debris as the truck hit an axle-busting boulder. The impact launched the machine-gunner abruptly skyward past the edge of a cactus grove. As he cartwheeled like a cheap, tinplate ornament in a wild-west shooting gallery, Tootsy shot him twice through the heart.

The Toyota caromed back on its tailgate. Then, as if tired

beyond measure, it sagged over onto its left side, its engine chuffing twice before wheezing into silence. The stink of leaking gasoline hung heavy in Mordechai's nostrils...the *whup-whup-whup* of choppers finally breaking through the silence roaring in his ears.

Tootsy ambled slowly toward the truck, bouncing cat-like on the balls of her feet. She quickly mounted the right-side running board and looked down into the dazed passenger's fear-glazed eyes. His left hand scrabbled ineffectually at a bloodied shaft of scrap steel driven side to side through both kidneys.

Tootsy bent into the window. She stroked the guerrilla's close-cropped hair, pushing it up slightly over the right side of his head. A tic twitched in his cheek as he tried to smile up at what he misread as humane ministrations.

"Kayf tashaor?" she asked solicitously. "How are you feeling?"

He barely managed to gasp: "Touja; it hurts..." before Tootsy leaned down to kiss his cheek, pushed his head gently forward, then straightened up and calmly shot him once behind the right ear.

The single echoing gunshot unnerved Mordechai more than the artillery rockets, which up until a moment ago had bracketed their position with frightening, preordained precision. As he struggled to his feet, he wondered which side had been more successful in setting up the other.

Two recently arrived AH-1S Cobra gunships wasted no time working over the produce truck as Tootsy walked back to where hot-response medics field-dressed Mordechai's wounds. The helicopters' chin-mounted 20mm cannons diced and riced the truck's cargo into a cornucopia of leaping fruit salad, which was then stir-fried in the smoke-wreathed fireballs of detonating air-to-ground missiles.

Reinforcements rappelled down from a Sikorsky CH-53. Paratroopers from the rapid-deployment unit quickly set up a defensive perimeter and rounded up three surviving guerrillas. Mordechai shrugged off the corpsman and stomped over to where

Tootsy stood defiantly, pistol butt gripped in both hands, barrel pointing downward, eyes wide with the twisted lust of dark-side perversion, now eliciting from Mordechai equal measures of revulsion and pity...and dour dejection for having seen the same, repulsive look in Ignatz's eyes.

I will never countenance murder.

"Oh, gimme a break," she sneered. "For Chrissakes, he was run through with a rusted pipe. The doctor hasn't been born who could have saved that pig. He was as good as dead anyway. So actually I did him a favor. Sent him to Allah right off. Express ticket. No pain; no waiting around."

Mordechai blinked dully while rubbing the stiffness out of the back of his neck.

There it was again.

What had he said aloud? What went off inside his head? What was real? What was not? Colonel H. was right; Mordechai's time was up. He was right now neck-deep in another fuckup. The people who pulled Colonel H.'s strings rarely tolerated two-time losers; a triple was out of the question. And even if he weren't forcibly retired, no one would volunteer to go out on a mission with him. Word was already making the rounds over military radio. If he hadn't been so enamored of that bimbo, David might have been warned in time...might be alive right now....

Tootsy!

"Who are you?" he rasped.

"To judge? *Fuck off!*" she snarled.

Tootsy's wolverine eyes augered into him, but he stared her down. Feeling like a square peg inside the tightening round hole of curious professional soldiers, she suddenly shied away from the vulnerability of total exposure, trying instead for a weak smile.

"Answer my question! Who the fuck are you?!" Mordechai yelled, jamming his palm squarely into the center of Tootsy's chest and jostling her sharply, only dimly aware of the throbbing ache from shrapnel in his left shoulder.

Tootsy cross-blocked his next straight-arm shove, her

eyes blankly opaque and clearly unreadable as she tossed off a crooked grin, not yet fully back from the blood-lust excursion she had just sucked up greedily, even now quietly savoring every delicious twitter of adrenaline aftereffect. Her intense tightening and breathing caught Mordechai's eye. And then she shook her head, immediately clearing the baggage of the past few minutes while simultaneously gearing up to go on the offensive.

"Don't bother to thank me for saving your life," she snapped.

"What? *That?!*" Mordechai laughed in spite of his anger. "Shit like that happens all the time."

"Sorry, but I'm not buying into that macho crap. If it weren't for me..."

"I was just getting ready to roll out of the way."

"Sure you were," she said, coolly ejecting the magazine of her Browning and inserting a fresh load.

Her proficient movements reawakened Mordechai's thinking.

"I asked you a question," he said evenly, incensed that she had successfully railroaded him, aggravated at the nonchalance with which she sipped achievement, exhausted from the jackass fencing, at once remembering where he was and wondering what the hell she was *really* doing there.

"So you did, so you did," Tootsy laughed, offering nothing more in the way of reply. Her nostrils flared while sucking in great lungfuls of the essence of exploding Toyota. "Regular unleaded," she opined. "Premium's a touch more piquant."

"What?"

"And your English suddenly shows substantial improvement."

"The heat of battle. Happens every time."

"Yeah, right. Kelley Murphy, CIA. Or Tootsy to you," she said, obviously tired of the game as she shoved her pistol into the Galco "Miami Classic" shoulder rig under her Bazooby jacket. "And I'm looking for an Arab with no left ear."

"So am I," he said, secretly furious over his ignorance

about the ear detail and wondering how the goddamned CIA came to know more about what was going on in his own backyard than IDF Intelligence did. Or that IDF Intelligence *told him* they did. Did mistrust run that deep? He trolled for an explanation—surely it was just an oversight—but Tootsy was clammed up too tight to pry open.

Ignatz was laughing and joking with the special-forces team, oversize cigar wagging like a baton of extraordinary manhood, his free arm tight around Esther's waist. Esther's hip pressed meaningfully into his, the fingers of her left hand tickling his shirtless back. *Ignatz is definitely moving up in the world,* Mordechai thought morosely. Esther looked his way spitefully over the top of her nose and mouthed: *"Fuck you!"* The two soldiers who saw it looked at Mordechai and laughed.

"Let's go," he said wearily. "They're laying out the bodies over there."

Tootsy followed him over to where the casualties were now lined up neatly...11 Arabs on one side, a single Israeli on the other...kept separate and apart, especially in death, lest the corpse of one nationality infect the other. And who knew how many had gotten away.

"Already the flies have dined," Mordechai said. "They're the only ones who benefit from this bullshit." Then he snarled at a corporal in rapid-fire Hebrew. The soldier blinked under the roar of Mordechai's crudely arrogant tirade before leading them to a man laying face down in the wadi...a man missing an ear from a battle long forgotten and with both legs blown off in the firefight just concluded.

"We're still checking the general area, but this is all he had on him," the soldier said, viciously sidearming a white orb directly at Mordechai's injured shoulder.

Tootsy's hand lashed out and snagged the object in midflight, her fingers clamping over it like a bear trap as she reamed the soldier's ass in perfect Hebrew. The corporal blushed deeply. Tootsy hissed a sharp order. The soldier snapped stiffly to attention, saluted Mordechai with grudging respect, and turned away smartly. Tootsy's next shouted command sent the soldier double-timing over to his buddies, who guffawed heartily at his obvious discomfort.

"Where the hell did you learn that language?" Mordechai asked in awed amazement.

"I did some time on the Haifa docks. What the hell is this?" Tootsy asked, turning her hand over, uncurling her fingers, and rolling the sphere around in her palm.

"Looks to me like a white billiard ball," Mordechai said.

"A cue ball, you mean."

CHAPTER 11

FLATFISH

Judith battled taut-tendon tenaciously against sluggish levitation... fighting locked-joint desperately to reverse the spiraling, updraft journey from the cozily cloaking depths of near-coma sleep. Like a scuba diver seduced by nitrogen narcosis, the Mossad woman's mulish subconscious kept neural circuit breakers "OFF" in hopes of satisfying the craving for addictive immersion in the womb-cling contentment of even-keeled peace.

Consciousness trickled in IV-drip slowly. Judith stretched languidly in the curled-toe afterglow of soulful fusing. Fluttering aftershocks still rippled outward from pivot-point nucleus.

The recent, frenzied clash had reduced aggressively vital players to flaccidly swirling rag dolls ripped nearly limbless by yank-apart vortices gusting impassioned desire. Omnipotent spiritual conjunction unleashed violently twisting whirlwinds of killer-hurricane strength...which in turn sparked fire-stalk lightning and quaking upheaval.

The Chicago Hilton's shadowed-suite bedroom was slat-sliced vertically by blue-fluorescent flickers of cable-TV imagery...the volume loud enough only for close-range hearing. Azure beams front-lit Michael hip-wrapped in a crookedly slung, green bath towel...his cell phone clamped tight to his right ear. Sitting-room furniture was dyed by glimmering, chalk-wave slivers of wide-screen hucksters. Judith could barely make out the female-voice lead-in to the program's return from quarter-hour commercial break.

"And now back to our NBC News special presentation of 'The Bombers Among Us.'"

She swung svelte legs over the bed's rumpled edge,

wriggled into a knee-length "Lake Shore Madness" T-shirt and fired up a Marlboro while straining to hear the anchorman's description of "connections now believed to exist between the downing of TransPac Flight 117, the Traax Parcel Service truck bombed in Los Angeles and a terrorist alliance which informed sources report is 'afterburner active' in the United States of America."

Judith took a sip of warm Coke, drew deeply on the 100mm cigarette, exhaled wearily, and launched herself erect and into a barefoot saunter toward the roost's threshold. She slouched cross-armed against the doorjamb, 20 feet behind Michael's rapt conversation. His broad-shouldered presence kettle-drummed a clamorous din of discordant interpersonal rhythms: candy-cane past; scrambled present; inclement future.

Judith pushed sullenly off the door frame and made a silent-stride entry...slipping quietly across the thickly carpeted sitting room, sliding into a black-leather recliner and stubbing out her cigarette. Quiet time was spent in careful observation of Michael punching in another number and listening half-heartedly to barely audible reporting buttressed by file footage on TransPac and L.A.

"From what is known specifically of these incidents," the newscaster said, "and from details provided by authorities close to each case..."

Stinking leakers, you mean!

"...bombings are quite often, though not invariably, signatured...that is, signed by those who perpetrate attacks they call 'direct actions.'"

Welcome to Terrorism 101.

"In the TransPac bombing, the signature was an ankh found at the crash site, reportedly the symbol of the shadowy el-Fahd el-Aswad, or Black Leopard, a tightly knit group operating predominantly in the Israeli-occupied West Bank and Gaza Strip, though now, apparently, having extended its reach considerably."

Duh-uh, no kidding!

"In the L.A. truck bombing, investigators found Deutsche

mark coins, which informed sources tell us indicate involvement by the National Socialist Common Action Group, or ANS, whose cells are based in Germany and who reportedly have recently forged links to the Middle East."

Oh!...My!...Gosh!

"These two characteristics...and certain other similarities between the two attacks...are fueling increasing speculation about premeditated cooperation between the German group ANS and el-Fahd el-Aswad, although the motive for such a combined enterprise remains a mystery at this point in time."

How about random killing, pure and simple?

"And while authorities have so far declined to comment officially, our investigative-reporting unit is pursuing strong leads indicating that this second group...the German ANS...has indeed joined with Black Leopard to carry out chaotic acts of terror against American citizens on this country's home shores, with TransPac and Los Angeles only the curtain raiser and Act I respectively of more murder to follow."

You betcha!

"These collaborative operations are said to be financed from Middle East coffers, whose moneymen dispense funds under the auspices of either Iranian or Libyan intelligence, with hard-currency payments funneled through European Union banking institutions. Speaking through their ambassadors to the United Nations, both Libya and Iran strongly deny any link to these terrorist attacks."

No doubt they would!

"All of which puts our current national situation on a par with those regularly encountered in the war-torn Middle East," the anchorman said, his pudgy-jowled bombast awash with dime-store melodramatics.

"As if you know diddly-squat about what is going on over there," Judith spat disgustedly.

"Didn't hear you get up," Michael said, abruptly terminating his hand-held conversation and tossing the cell phone onto six cities' worth of daily newspapers spilling off a smoked-glass coffee table.

"Hard to sleep through all the goddamned blather," Judith lied.

"Resentful of the analogy?"

"Damned right. Yonder gent probably has been no closer to my neighborhood than lusting after a belly dancer during a businessman's-special lunch at some trendy Lebanese cafe."

Michael watched the newscaster say, "As was described in news reports of the day, the TPS device was a frightful antipersonnel weapon giving new meaning to the word 'nasty.'"

"You should spend six weeks walking my beat," the bomber-tracker groused.

"Pipe down and listen," Michael ordered.

"Why?" Judith asked snidely. "Because I might learn something from Dunderhead?"

"It has been known to happen. By the way, what's the genus and species of the bug up your ass? Get up on the wrong side of bed?"

"There is no right side," she complained, "unless you are in it."

"Thank you for what I think was a compliment."

"Consider yourself blessed," Judith sighed over chewy disappointment. "I have not been that generous since the last blue moon."

"Lucky me."

"For now, just jack up the volume. There will be time enough for counting blessings later."

Michael circled behind Judith's chair, leaned down, and nibbled her left ear. She reached up stiff-fingered and pulled him cheek-rub close. The two silently watched split-screen TransPac and L.A. recap: cratered perimeter of TransPac debris field; jet-fuel smoke; ambulances; tiny, wind-whipped flags marking mangled corpses' locations; stretcher-bearers; minicam crews jockeying for position; first responders scattering helter-skelter during secondary and tertiary explosions at the TPS scene; firefighters held back; the sundered hulk of a fire-blackened panel truck.

The horrid catalog was twist-tied neatly by a montaged, freeze-frame segue into the mournful skirl of bagpipes' haunting melodies. Played by a chunky passerby during final cleanup in California, the chilling music was said to be "one humanitarian's way of reaching out in some small measure to ease the bereavement of those who lost loved ones," reported a jack-a-dandy clotheshorse who chirped like a canary.

Leave it to some California fruitcake, Michael mused.

Judith's beeper suddenly screamed raucously for attention, the nerve-grating squeal of automatically unmuting Code Red shriek scaring her nearly witless. Michael lowered the TV's sound to 3 in response to Judith's cursing lunge toward the pursed communication device he had monkeyed with when late afternoon slid into evening.

Audacious bastard, she fumed silently.

"And now for the information update promised earlier," the anchorman intoned solemnly. "Highly placed sources have confirmed that a dual-cassette radio bomb was responsible for the destruction of TransPac Flight 117, the Empress of Diamond Head, several weeks ago."

Michael scooped up his ringing phone, clicked on, listened for a moment, and muttered, "Yeah, just got wind of it. Dundee? Right after, we grab some road food. Later." Then he commandeered Judith's attention with: "Throw on some clothes. We've just been granted a special audience."

Orders, she seethed. *Always with the orders. First, I get: 'Pipe down and listen.'*

DON'T FORGET: "THROW ON SOME CLOTHES."

"With who?" she asked crossly.

"The Pope of Explosive Dope."

"Where?"

"Ringside seats at an encore performance of 'All the King's Horses and All the King's Men.'"

And gamester answers, to boot.

"Can you tell me straight, or must I enlist Berlitz for translation services?"

"A visit to the Humpty-Dumpty shatter of the Empress of Diamond Head," Michael said, clenched fist ready to fend off trouble afoot.

"Why did you fiddle around with my beeper?" Judith asked heatedly.

"With all the jet-lag commuting you've been doing, I figured you needed the rest."

You figured?

HE FIGURED!

Go figure.

WELL HE SURE AS HELL DID!

"That is a decision you are not to make for me," Judith rasped furiously, leapfrogging over simmer and swooping directly into full boil.

"I think you're overreacting..."

"To your running my life?!" she shouted angrily.

"What the hell ever gave you that idea?"

"You tell me when I can speak..."

"I never..."

"Don't interrupt!"

"Give me...

"You screw around with my pager! You tell me to pipe down! You order me to get dressed!"

"Shut the hell up in there!" an adjoining-suite guest shouted between pounding fists' rolling-thunder thumping through surprisingly thin walls. "This is a respectable establishment!"

"UP! YOURS!" Judith screamed.

"What was so important that the damn thing turned itself on?" Michael asked nonchalantly.

Halfway to the bedroom, Judith turned and rudely pitched the pager at Michael, who caught the case bouncing off his stomach.

"See for yourself," she huffed.

"I can't," he laughed after finger-working the unit's "Commo" button. "It's in Hebrew."

"I am surprised so small a detail would stop a bigshot like

you."

Building 23 of the Iroquois Industrial Park, Dundee, Illinois, was half mausoleum, half National Transportation Safety Board/ Federal Bureau of Investigation field laboratory, given over to the meticulous reconstruction and continuing autopsy of TransPac Flight 117. Peaked, roof-high snowdrifts gave the gray, rectangular structure the look of a half-buried bunker at Battle of the Bulge Ardennes. Government four-wheel-drive vehicles bristling with whip antennae iced up in haphazard disarray, in a parking lot, days overdue for salting and snowplowing.

Even before the Quonset door slammed fully closed behind them, murder victims' agony buffeted Michael like a pummeling Force 10 gale. The wail of roasted infants formed the first assaultive wave; those whose spirits had not yet been dissipated by life's struggles always screamed the loudest from the Other Side, followed by teens, young adults, middle-agers, and on up to twilighters, all shrieking in incandescent agony... giving croaked voice to fathomless pain.

Judith heard none of this, but flooding the four corners of Michael's skull...hosing down his punished cerebrum...was a tsunami of human anguish, a chorusing barbecue suffering the first hellish moments of physical incineration, before nerve endings were burned mercifully dead under shriveling, blackening skin... victims' gagging as their nostrils filled with the stink of their own cremation, while retching and choking on flames cooking their throats and boiling their vital fluids.

Falling to his knees...

"Michael?!"

...the pain, a cacophony of palpable, physical torment... scrabbling desperately in the deep recesses of a greatcoat. Then finding it, fingers closing gratefully around the small leather pouch, yanking it up and out while fumbling with the ceremonial drawstring and thankfully jamming two fingertips into soothing comfort.

Fragments of animal hide, pieces of dried bird skin,

miniature ceremonial pipes, bits of aged herbs, flakes of tobacco...a host of secret curatives handed down through generations...his panacea for thunderous invasions fighting efforts at eviction... now mercifully being beaten down to a dull ache outside his ears, pressing in from outside of his head, out of him finally though at great physical cost...exorcised...driven farther away, out there now, muscled out behind rapidly rising spiritual dikes, leaving behind the inevitable residue: a forehead glistening with the drench of pain-induced sweat.

"Help me up," he coughed, bones quivering uselessly like wind chimes in a typhoon.

The *vibrato* tremors finally faded to random shivers. He blinked under purple-tinged arc lighting, bathing the interior in harsh, alien brightness. Needles of light drilled into the backs of his eyes.

"The voices," Judith said.

"Strongest...they've ever...been."

"You okay?" she asked doubtfully.

"I...will be...soon," he whispered, weak and embarrassed, defiantly shrugging her supportive arm off his waist, rocking unsteadily, and berating himself for his curtness.

Still clenching the precious medicine pouch right-fist tight to solidify his strength, Michael blinked dully...focusing on distant, white-coated technicians swarming over the airplane's carcass in close imitation of industrious termites tending their beloved queen.

The bomb-ravaged cadaver sagged sadly limp, like an underinflated pool toy. Webwork cables hanging from latticework-girdered ceiling cradled crinkled sections of fuselage. The cockpit leaned left over incomplete wings; the tail section tilted awkwardly right. Massive burn damage disfigured the aircraft's middle—a melted, sooty concavity running two-thirds of the 747's length, roped together with black licorice twists of sooty longerons, bulkheads, and rods. Damaged engines lay crooked on oil-stained woodworks.

Drafts played along the birdcage wiring, holding the

swaying structure together. The aircraft's battered corpse shifted restlessly, its creaking metal incessantly rebuking human attendants for their abject failure to prevent this horror.

I deserved better than this, the dead airplane reproached Michael, but the medicine bag squeezed hard to forehead's center drove the intrusion away.

Judith impatiently twined anxious fingers through wind-tousled hair. She pulled a handful tight, tried vainly for a ponytail, then let brown strands fall free while heavily exhaling profound exasperation.

"Are you back?" she asked pointedly.

"Five hundred and forty-three," he said softly, succored by the buffalo-skin pouch osmosing strength into his body from its nestling place close to his heart.

"Men. Women. Children," Judith added.

"Random chance," Michael shuddered, crossing arms over his coat-wrapped chest, fighting to stave off a recurrence of the chills unleashed by the screaming of the dead. "Orchestrated by Grandma Fate...in all her fluky...wonder."

"Which would put current circumstances considerably at odds with your little pouch of beliefs," the Mossad woman noted dryly. She opened her peacoat and fluffed out her scarf, feeling sleep-fogged, terminally itchy, and in desperate need of a two-hour, near-scalding shower.

"Like yourself," Michael said, "I'm somewhat assimilated... at least philosophically though not completely spiritually."

"So to you it is the tenuousness of earthly reality: time runs out; numbers are up; tickets are punched; the vagaries of circumstance, that sort of thing."

"At least in part."

"Or another stab at The Final Solution," she said grimly.

"Which is why you're here."

"Michael," she replied patiently, "seventy-nine of those men, women, and children were members in good standing of Highland Park's Temple Beth Shalom. Were they murdered because they were Jews? I want to know why they were put in that furnace. This is more than philosophical nebulosity. I take it very personally."

"I'm wasting time is what you mean. *Gutierrez!*" Michael roared. Gutierrez! Gutierrez! resonated back.

"Hey! Shit for brains!" Michael yelled again, echoing syllables jumbling in cross-purpose conflict with another. *"Front and goddamn center NOW!"* he bellowed. *"Where the hell are you? Welcoming committee...Fall! In! GUTIERREZ!"*

Half a football field away, Carl Gutierrez jerked up like a prairie dog on high alert. Eyeball inspection of the horizontal stabilizer immediately forgotten, he quickly semaphored an excited hello.

Gutierrez was shirtless under the white-silk, double-breasted Courreges Homme suit serving as his lab outfit, the pant cuffs of which were rubber-banded around ankles and stuffed into tan Converse Hi-Tops. His face was a cafe au lait oval of multinational bloodlines. A once-intrusive Roman nose had long ago been fashionably restructured into a cosmetically acceptable nasal work of art. Eyes the color of mood-ring stones, tending toward slate the higher his emotional charge rose, were set unusually forward over a smooth drop-off to slightly underfed, male-model cheeks—a subtle hint of facial incurvation being *de rigueur* for the social nuclei Gutierrez orbited. Brunswick-black hair was cut short on the side, Hollywood-long in the back, the top in stylish lockstep with next month's *Gentlemen's Quarterly.*

Magnifying glass vanishing into hip pocket, he swung pristine athletic shoes over ladder's hand rails, sliding navy-style to the cement floor while bowing legs out expertly to keep silk pants safe from soiling metalwork. Then Gutierrez grabbed two Commonwealth Edison hard hats and was on his theatrical way.

Marching through intermeshing circles of harsh white light, Gutierrez strutted like an energetic drum major, back ramrod straight while glancing smartly left then right...nodding slightly while in imperious stride as if acknowledging roaring adoration from fan-packed parade stands. Whirligig hands and arms flailed chest high, then down in measured, constant motion.

He skidded to an abrupt halt 36 inches away from recently arrived visitors, marking time to march music only he could hear and tossing them each a hard hat.

"Put those on right now." *Hut! Hut!* "Right this minute," Gutierrez snapped officiously. "House rules." *Halt, one, two!*

Then, standing arms akimbo, Gutierrez eyed Michael critically up and down before grinning broadly and abruptly lunging forward to envelop his blood brother in a huge embrace. Kisses impacted noisily wet on Michael's cheeks.

"Carl Gutierrez," Michael gasped, struggling free of the smothering bear hug. "May I present Judith..."

Gutierrez was on her in an instant. Gassed half-insensate by offensively orchid cologne, Judith squirmed uncomfortably under Gutierrez's soggy, lingering liplocks. Roughly jerked back at arm's length for critical examination, she dangled tiptoe high and turned side to side while held aloft in the vise-like grip of strong, wire-clamp fingers.

"And a cheek-kisser? *You betcha!* You're uncomfortable, are you not? My apologies, if you like. Genealogy is a half-hearted hobby of mine...that is, when I'm not working twenty-hour days trying to figure out why some airplanes land hale, hearty, wholesome and, most importantly, intact, while others come down in dribs and drabs.

"Michael, you must tell me true. No lies, perish the thought. Oh, I do hate liars. *Liars and quiche!* The hand-in-glove banes of the civilized world as we know it. Now would this be... could this be, perhaps...the new Mrs. Michael Running Horse? Judith Running Horse. Now that's got quite a stylish ring to it. Well, dear boy? *Am I in the strike zone?!* Quickly, now. *Si o no?"*

"Wrong," Michael said, obviously stalling for time.

"The new Mrs. Running Horse?" Judith asked. "It would be nice of you to bring me up to speed on the old one."

"He means my mother," Michael laughed. "Old Injun trick."

"Sure. And I am The Little Mermaid," she retorted while clipping a palm-sized tape recorder onto Peacoat's lapel.

Gutierrez whipped off magenta-tinted granny glasses and flicked them shut, hooking them over the lip of his jacket's side pocket. After honking a noseful of mucus into a dainty lace handkerchief, he folded the fine fabric carefully, though distastefully, and pushed it far down into an out-of-the-way back pocket. Then he retrieved his glasses and squinted at Judith and Michael until his vision cleared.

"*Yuckity-yuck!* Children, I already feel like I'm sitting in slush. Contrary to popular belief, snot does not stay warm on your person. There is nothing on God's green earth worse than a winter allergy. I can't handle road salt, of all things, and now with having to visit Chicago because of this...this situation. Boogers the size of a Chrysler New Yorker. People think I have a cold, which means I haven't been invited to a single party all week. *Can you imagine?!* "

"Carl," Michael said patiently. "You said you had something for me."

"And I do. Yes, I most certainly do. Now then," Gutierrez chuckled proudly, boyishly relishing his newfound celebrity, "the Microscope Militia has already dicked my newly hatched theory on this, and they came away grinning like sailors on a booze-and-babes liberty."

"NTSB and FBI too?"

"Yep. So what you'll get is sloppy seconds. Yes? *Good!* Anyway, if the feds know, it won't be long before the 'highly placed source' of the day is quoted all over the AM/FM airwaves, and the evening news to boot. Probably was already."

Gutierrez speed-walked them back to the wreck, where he snagged a soggy Lite-Bite burrito off a snack table wobbling uncertainly in the slipstream of frenetic passing. He bent at the waist and came up chewing.

Michael dodged scraps of overdone green chiles as Gutierrez waggled snacks' remains toward the fire-charred fuselage's right side. Just behind the cockpit, buckled rips slashed randomly ragged around the massive acne of gaping holes and the dried pus of melted windows.

"More burn here than bang, going from port to starboard," Gutierrez mumbled through his food, waving his arms in expansive arcs encompassing the whole of the grisly tableau. "The fuselage was torched by a fireball working its way in from the left side...over the wing...and then out on the right side, again...over the wing.

"A blast that blowtorched in from the outside?" Michael asked.

"Definitely. The Empress of Diamond Head wasn't blown open from the inside out. A fireball from a proximity-fused SAM might mimic some of the initial burn damage we found, but hauling around tracked SA-series missiles would be obvious even to Chicago's finest."

Michael jerked his thumb upward. "Hand-held, maybe? Javelin, Blowpipe, Stinger?"

"Nope."

"Grail, Gremlin, SA-16? Anything like that?"

"Negative, Michael. Nothing shoulder-launched. The engines didn't explode inward from their tailpipes. March around to the back, if you please."

Gutierrez cha-cha'd an imaginary partner past the airplane's tail, then merengue'd under a left wing supported by trestles and jacks. He grabbed Judith's hand while wriggling carefully past twisting shards of torn aluminum, then pointed upward through thin piano wire vaguely tracing the shape of what used to be the jumbo jet's wing but was now mostly empty space with half a dozen mocked-up components.

"Blast's point of origin?" Gutierrez paused to dab his right eye with a fresh lace handkerchief. "Here...under the left wing's main fuel cell...blowing it up and out through the top of the wing. Minus the wing, the plane lost all lift on this side and fell off to port, into the fireball..."

"Which burned through the fuselage from left to right over the wing, like you said."

"And immediately turned half the passengers to toast," Gutierrez finished. He dropped Judith's hand, sneezed violently, then blew his nose mightily. "Total meltdown from the root out," he sniffed. "Half the wing went molten, coming down as a sunshower of raindrop metal. Then, as near as we can figure, the tanks on the right side blew."

"Which is why there's practically nothing left of the middle of the plane," Michael said.

"Precisely."

"Definitely not your usual pattern," Judith observed, her back-pocketed hands safely out of Gutierrez's germ-ridden reach.

"No indeed," Gutierrez whispered. "Take Lockerbie, for example. A clear case of can-opening birthing fatal structural failure. Decompression spread debris crosscounty. Of course, Pan Am 103 was coming down from about 35,000 feet, so you got over eight hundred square miles of scatter. But Lockerbie was inside/out, the antithesis of what happened here. This was definitely outside/in."

"Positive?"

"Absolutely, Michael. And the envelope is laid out for viewing, if you'll just step this way."

"Already?!" Judith asked.

"Trouble is, it's a ghost wrapper."

"A what?"

"Totally spurious, Michael. Unquestionably ersatz. Clearly a sham. Downright bogus."

"Another anomaly."

"Precisely, Ms. Spade," Gutierrez chortled proudly. "In two minutes, you will have graduated to Holmes; in four minutes, you'll be giving this lecture. That's how much I like you already."

"Can we please get on with this?" Michael asked.

"Stop whining! I simply loathe it." Gutierrez snorted imperiously, then moved out at a quick-march pace to the other side of a hangar-sized building, and index-carded boombox parts carefully laid out under a sheet of plastic on a six-foot-long redwood picnic table.

"Okay," Gutierrez said seriously. "If your goal is to bring down a jumbo using a personal stereo full of Semtex H...*CHOOT!"*

"Gesundheit!"

"Thanks...you won't find much wrapper, as you can well imagine. The blast fuses case and components into a gibberish that takes months to decipher, even with our best metal detectors and state-of-the-art sniffer boxes nosing around for trace elements. Oh, we'll eventually find enough to show there was a bomb in a CD player to begin with, but it's no overnight job. We found this puppy right away. In unusually big chunks. One quarter of the case; one speaker undamaged; the other one burned, but easily identifiable; equalizer controls intact; a cassette still able to carry a tune."

"So you are talking two bombs," Judith said.

"More like one and one-sixteenth, my quick-study friend. One in with the baggage, but in no way, shape, or form strong enough to bring the plane down, else this Panasonic would have been vapor."

"So this guy wants us to think..."

"Not a woman?" Gutierrez harrumphed pompously, while grinning like an affected circus clown. "Not maybe you," he lectured sternly, "who has probably forgotten more about explosive mayhem than I shall ever learn?"

"The perp," she laughed. "Back on track? Remember?"

"*Right! Right! Right!* And focused, too. Knows what she wants, I'll wager. I like that in a gal."

"For chrissakes!" Michael huffed. *"Get on with it!"*

"Temper, Michael. *Okay! Okay! Okay!* This perp is cute to the max. Most desirous of us getting the word out, through the usual...persistently annoying...leaks that dog our investigations like camp followers trailing invading armies."

"Carl!"

"You verified that special-report anchorpersons are right now quoting unnamed sources as saying that a bomb hidden in a cassette-player/radio was what did the deed," Gutierrez continued, frowning while daintily poking circuitry with a well-manicured finger. "Couple this latest rumor with the stooge of a coroner who dangled the ankh early on. Palestinians worldwide get another nail hammered into their collective coffin. Anyone for a convenient scapegoat?"

"What?"

"Believe me," Michael muttered. "He's getting there. It's coming."

"Thank you," Gutierrez sniffed self-importantly. "Now then. Even one as erudite as myself has to pause for breath every so often. Your turn, Michael. Refresh my memory. The name, if you please, of that radical Palestinian splinter group that broke from Walid Masyaf because it felt the Popular Front for the Liberation of Palestine-General Command wasn't tough enough on the Jews."

"El-Fahd el-Aswad," Judith said. "Black Leopard."

"Based on the ankh and this, yes. The name's right, but the act's wrong. Wasn't them," Gutierrez said simply.

"But they claimed..."

"Credit. *Of course!* And why wouldn't they? This kind of atrocity makes their stock soar on the Arab street. Syria, Libya, and Iran can't bankroll the black cats fast enough."

"You are absolutely sure it was not them?"

"No question about it, dear Judith."

"But it could have been someone in their employ. Their hired gun. Oil money can buy a lot of expertise in any market: Europe, Asia, the Middle East."

"Maybe," Gutierrez said, not sounding entirely convinced. "I will agree that your Semitic brethren have wet dreams about this kind of operation, but if I were you, I'd be gunning for suspects with roots below the equator. South America. Maybe a drug connection. Before going global, TransPac hauled in freight from Laos, as an offshoot of Air America. More often than not, heroin was on the unwritten manifest."

"Warlords financing their personal armies," Judith said.

"And their eventual retirement," Gutierrez noted. "Glenn Frey summed it up best: 'The lure of easy money has a very strong appeal.' Could be that TransPac was moving Colombian dream dust and got sticky fingers. Maybe this was payback."

"Why South America?" Judith asked.

"I'll get to that in a minute," Gutierrez declared, waving a disciplinary finger. "Remember what I said about rushing?"

"Conviction quotient?" Michael wanted to know.

"One hundred and twenty-five percent," Gutierrez replied, his voice daring a challenge.

"That's a needle-bender, Carl."

"Right off the top of my scale. It doesn't get any stronger than that."

"And you back it up..."

"With pleasure, my dear Judith, with pleasure."

Gutierrez unfolded a fresh lace handkerchief, thunderously evacuated his blockaded nose, buried the second handkerchief where he parked the last one, then continued the seminar.

"The radio bomb was a teaser. An appetizer. The one in the luggage? Wouldn't have sunk a fair-sized rowboat. A radio bomb is how Black Leopard would do it, yes, but like I said, we'd be weeks—more likely months—finding parts. The one with the baggage went off like a big firecracker. It alone wouldn't have punched out enough tweak to let the pilot know he had a situation. These pieces here? Way too big to have been at the core of an explosion as massive as what devastated this aircraft."

"The idea being to spread receiver parts around..." Judith said.

"So that we chase imaginary baddies," Michael interrupted.

"While the perp has free run and rein," Gutierrez concluded. "Attention is askance."

"But there wasn't enough here to totally destroy the carrier," Judith said.

"Right. Because the doer wasn't serious about misdirecting attention; he was merely having sport with us, knowing in advance that some half-wit would leak misleading information to a vulturine press. It's his way of playing Chinese checkers with himself."

"Charming," Michael said.

"Which is why you're gonna positively eat up the CAD

display on my Cray. Let's go."

They double-timed across the hangar to a pasteboard cubicle knee-deep in computer cabling and cartons of high-tech test equipment. Gutierrez plopped down on his stool and smoothly pretzeled himself into the lotus position. He stiff-armed the table, did a 360 turn, jabbed his computer's ON switch on his way around, then spun himself twice again.

"Master at work," Gutierrez said. "Don't keep the master waiting. You'll have to excuse the paltry accommodations. Those folders are all we're budgeted for. Chaired down comfortably? Good. Now slide forward and check this out.

"I've established...to the satisfaction of the federal government to which we pay excessive taxes...that there wasn't enough bang in that valise to burst a decent set of eardrums, let alone punch through monocoque. Allow me to present Exhibit A, otherwise known as the burbot that brought down the whale."

Gutierrez's fingers raced over the clattering keyboard. Mouse strokes fine-tuned a yellowish, three-dimensional rectangle floating slowly clockwise on the screen. Gutierrez levitated the six-sided box while data printed upward from the screen's bottom.

"Michael and Judith, meet Flatfish...the latest in limpet technology and reputedly the star performer of the Medillin cartel. In a perverse sort of way, you've got to admire the brains behind this barnacle. Eleven months ago, cocaine cowboys used one to bring down an Avianca flight out of Bogota. It was just a cargo flight, only four killed, so the murders didn't rate a peep's worth of stateside coverage. It was said to have been a warning to the Colombian government."

"Or maybe a dress rehearsal for TransPac 117."

"You're getting ahead of me again, Michael."

"It's what I do best."

"Remember that I do not suffer interruptions lightly. Okay, Flatfish is tailor-made to exactly match the length and width of your target's average inspection panel. We're still guessing about its depth. All of this is theoretical, mind you, based on reconstruction of the last one, which, I might add, is the only other one we've come across so far. The TransPac device could have been smaller. It's still too early to know much of anything for sure."

"So you have not found parts from this one yet?" Judith asked.

"Nothing solid, except we just came across traces of magnesium and phosphorus where there shouldn't have been any. Ergo, my call to you."

"And the crosshatch pattern?" Michael asked.

"That represents an aluminum sheet on the bottom of the device. Reflectivity makes it look like part of the plane itself. My guess is that if you yank it off after initial attachment, it'll blow immediately, taking out you, the plane, and whoever happens to be wandering around vacuuming carpets inside. But that's only my educated guess because, like I said, we've determined only one prior use. We're not positive about this one, but it's my best conjecture...and the feds agree...that we're looking at a picture of what probably did the TransPac job."

"Nasty fucker," Judith said.

"It gets worse. The damn thing's got a grip like a lamprey. Slap one of these babies on an F-16, and you won't shake it loose no matter how fast you go, or how many positive or negative Gs you're pulling."

"Impossible!" Judith scoffed.

"Wish it were, woman, wish it were."

"Jesus!" Michael whispered.

"And Joseph. And Mary," Gutierrez said crisply. "Five Skovde-designed, superconductive electromagnets-one in each corner and one in the middle hold it in place. Cooled by liquid oxygen in modified CO_2 cartridges, the electromagnets are powered by a single nine-volt lithium through a new, step-up transformer design based on the old Ruhmkorff coil. The device sets up a field strong enough to reach through an airliner's aluminum skin. It'll hold snug if placed within 75 feet of compatible metal. Any alloy with fifteen percent iron content will do."

"Helluva reach," Judith said.

"We're talking some real extension here," Gutierrez replied.

"It looks so..."

"Innocuous? Easy to overlook?" Gutierrez interrupted. "It is well camouflaged, looking as it does like just another piece of sheet metal. Except this carries a small, devastating shaped charge. And because shaped charges concentrate their punch, you don't need much explosive. I estimate he used about thirty grams here. Just over an ounce. Granted, that doesn't sound like much, but it was actually twice what he needed, considering position and direction, to make the wing go completely tatters on us."

"So we're eyeballing a pocket-watch claymore."

"That's one way of stating the case. Most likely placed just before takeoff," Gutierrez said, "when everyone's gotten lazy. Let's face it, airline security is an inversely proportional affair, getting progressively weaker the closer you get to the central target-the winged beastie itself."

"What about the trigger?" Judith asked.

"Miniaturized genius. Detonation is by the venturi principle," Gutierrez said. He stopped Flatfish's rotation and enlarged the front end.

"That penny-size front hole there is where the air gets sucked in before venting out the back. Wait; I'll make it bigger."

Four mouse strokes and two key taps inflated the image, the graphic quickly ballooning up to fill 40 square inches of screen.

"Entry air spins a little generator wheel. The wheel has spring-loaded brushes you can adjust by tightening or loosening set screws. Wait a sec. An exploded view, if you'll pardon the pun, will make this easier."

Three clicks later, the point of Gutierrez's No. 2 pencil tocked on the computer screen.

"The cylinders in each corner and in the center are the

electromagnets. Okay, the red square is the explosive; the blue square is the lithium. They're at opposite corners. It's got one small board for a brain, with a logic circuit that's state-of-the-art. Flatfish factors in weather conditions, particularly outside air temperature, to make minor compression adjustments on the generator-wheel spindle bearings, thus assuring uniform performance in any climate."

"The green square?" Michael asked.

"The way it's wired, we think that's the jerk alert...to trigger the device if you try to pry it loose after arming and mounting, or mounting and arming...whichever comes first. So far, no one's gotten close enough to one of these buttfuckers to find out.

"Turn those two small set screws—there and there—and you can make the generator wheel spin freely...or more slowly. It's infinitely variable. You can set it anywhere from taxi speed—which would be suicidal, considering that a fart might set it off—on up to 1,500 miles per hour.

"When airspeed gets high enough, air going through this inlet port spins the generator wheel fast enough to generate enough voltage to goose that orange microswitch there...which closes this amber contact here and shunts the lithium's power to that black dot: a detonator the size of a pinhead LED, which you now see flashing on and off. The bomb releases its grip on the wing and—*BLANG!*—it goes critical one nanosecond later."

"All that out of a little metal box," Michael said respectfully.

"We finally determined that the Avianca bomb casing was magnesium and..."

"Phosphorus," Judith said evenly.

"Right. A phosphorus inner liner that burned like a bandit. Terribly hard to reconstruct. But the trace elements we just came across here got me thinking about the Avianca...and then about TransPac 117 blowing up from the outside in."

Gutierrez spun around to face them, slid the No. 2 pencil over his ear, leaned back, and twiddled his thumbs.

"Michael," he said over the top of magenta-tinted lenses, "we are talking some very serious shit here. These days, baggage is bombarded with enough x-rays to make it glow in the dark." Gutierrez hooked fingers under the lapels of his suit jacket and pushed forward. "These two radiation badges I'm wearing? They're no joke. These days, folks are beaming roentgens around like Buck Rodgers on a hate trip."

"So the problem has moved away from curbside check-in, no-parking zones, and baggage handling," Judith said.

"Right," Gutierrez replied, taking a desperate moment to blow his nose violently in the vain hope of emptying it once and for all. "This cancer has long jumped way inside. It's pole-vaulted from suitcases to the field itself, where, let's face it, security is a loosely woven joke because the bombers are already on the tarmac and no one, to my knowledge, is checking for false-bottom lunch boxes."

"So our perp placed this..."

"Don't interrupt me when I'm holding forth! Yes, Michael, our perp placed this device under the wing, between the root and the Number Two engine, which touched off a brimful 747 tank. So he created the civilian version of an FAE..."

"Fuel-air explosive..."

"Thank you, Judith, resulting in a respectable shock wave. People under the plane think they're looking up at a palm-sized nuke. Scares the hell out of nearby witnesses before flame-roasting them. Ground casualties quadruple because you don't have to depend on secondary sources for ignition. The fuel is guaranteed to be burning when it sprays the neighborhood."

"I still can't believe the radio was..."

"Only an artful dodge, Michael. Made to look initially like el-Fahd el-Aswad, but only because the bomber was half-heartedly yanking our chain. It was like he was going to play this game with us at first, then lost interest and went off in another direction."

"Maybe he had something else on his mind," Michael said.

"Like the L.A. truck bombing," Judith replied.

"Back in the days of alarm clocks, copper wiring, and dynamite," Gutierrez continued, "the more complex the device, the more failure-prone it was. More parts, more problems. Logical, right? But not anymore. This whole design...even if you take just the weather-adjustable spindle bearings on the generator-wheel axle...is incredibly complex, conceptually, but amazingly reliable, mechanically."

"Solid state. Miniaturized..."

"Ring any bells, Judith?"

"No," she said quickly.

"So you know where I'm coming from." Gutierrez took off his glasses, laid them in his lap, and thumb-rubbed watering eyes while sniffing mightily. "It took us over a year before we were eighty-five percent sure about Bogota. TransPac was finessed beyond Arab technology, even though it did carry their signature. Not only that, but Bogota was C4 plastic. But it was C8e that brought this TransPac down."

"Odorless," Judith said. "Undetectable."

"A next-generation plastic explosive, intensely concentrated and especially formulated for military use, " Michael said. "It makes Semtex H look like a damp squib."

"Exactly."

"I was not aware that C8e had left the country," Judith said.

"It hasn't in bulk, as far as we know," Gutierrez replied. "It's too new. Only one firm has the formula. They haven't been licensed for full production yet, and we know they're not geared up for mass manufacturing."

Gutierrez crossed his arms over his stomach, bent over as if in deep thought, then walked his stool forward and looked up at them owlishly.

"But get this, Michael. Cratering Technologies lost a pouch-load about eleven months ago. Now that wasn't a story Uncle Sam wanted leaked. The idiots at Cratering sent it to Traax Parcel Service."

"The truck people?!" Judith asked.

"Yep."

"Christ!"

"Can you believe it? Turning C8e over to anyone except a heavily armed military courier? Anyway, the stuff got lost in the cracks of the TPS cargo-handling facility outside of Los Angeles. 'So some slipped through the cracks,' Cratering's chief asshole said. 'It was just one point five kilos.' So I told the jerkoff that's more than enough to turn seventy-six percent of downtown San Diego into dust and send it drifting back across the Pacific to Mainland China...without any debris touching the water.

"We did a spectro-chem workup on fragments from where we think Flatfish was attached, followed by neutron activation analysis testing. This stuff wasn't even pure; it was cut with modeling clay. That's how deadly C8e is. Very little does an awful lot of damage."

"But it hasn't gone overseas?" Michael asked.

"I'm thinking that it's too new to have made the diplomatic carryall."

"Too bad they are still sacrosanct in your country," Judith said smugly.

"But I've saved the best for last."

"You always do," Michael said.

"Step right this way, please. My curtain call, if you will," Gutierrez said as he put the Cray to sleep.

Back at the tarnished hulk, Gutierrez scampered up a ladder like a banana-bound monkey. He reached into a burned-black section of the airliner cabin over the right wing. The wreck jittered like a twitchy marionette as Gutierrez crawled halfway inside.

"You're going to absolutely adore this," Gutierrez shouted, his words echoing sepulchrally inside the gutted fuselage.

Michael handily snagged the tossed offering—an unburned toupee—as Gutierrez scooted back down the ladder.

"My guess is, you're holding the perp's trademark, Michael. Odd for that hairpiece to come through completely intact when everything else nearby was turned to charcoal. Especially since there were no bodies within a country mile of where we found that."

"What about wind drift?"

"That rug was too heavily weighted for anything but straight-down descent."

"With?"

"A lead liner no one in their right mind would wear."

"Not that this guy is."

"I hear you."

"Were the seats burning when they hit the ground?" Judith asked.

"They were totally involved...and there were localized fires all over the place. A veritable mine field of hot spots. But that? Not a hair was singed. I'll bet three steak dinners that that's your real signature," Gutierrez said. "Placed after the crash. Not a trace of scalp oil on it. It's never been worn. Our perp knew exactly where the Empress was coming down. That asshole was right there at ringside."

"Definitely not Black Leopard."

"Not by the looks of that particular piece of evidence. Based on that exhibit, Michael, they're completely exonerated."

"As the actual mechanics, yes," Judith insisted, unwilling to let go. "But not as the brains and the bankers."

"You do have a point there," Gutierrez admitted.

"They could have hired someone to do the job," Michael added. "A person or persons with the freedom of movement Black Leopard couldn't achieve themselves."

"Yeah, I suppose so," Gutierrez agreed. "And believe me, if that's the case, this wouldn't be the first time a double sig tickled our fancy. They're bound to sprout when you're dealing with prideful bastards."

"So that is how it will read for now," Judith said.

"You sound disappointed?"

"It is going to make things harder, Carl."

"So said the feds," Gutierrez said seriously. "Now snuggle up. This place is under very sensitive, very directional sound surveillance. So come close while Uncle Carl tells you this." The air-crash expert lowered his voice and drew them near with shoulder-draped arms. "Folks, I've been doing twenty-hour days with sleepless nights since The Day Of, and I overhear gossip aplenty. The feds don't know jackshit about where to even start looking. Our alphabet soup of government agencies is wheel-spinning, Michael. This is a brand-new ball game. Anuses are puckering from sea to shining sea."

"The constipation factor always sky-highs on airliner bombings."

"Never this badly, Michael. Whoever's pushing buttons and whoever's paying the freight, the team we're playing footsie with is definitely not sloppy. I've already networked with the boys on that L.A. truck bombing. For that, you can thank an HMX/incendiary composite seasoned with C8e. There's more, but the suits are sitting on it, hoping something will hatch."

"Figures," Judith said morosely.

"Children, we've been finding only what we're supposed to find: tidbits from technology on the leading edge of mass murder. We're not dancing with dunces, and that fact alone has the G-Men very, very worried. They're peeing pickles on this one."

Gutierrez straightened up, hands thrust deep into jacket pockets, lips evenly set, slate eyes flatly humorless. "Defuse this situation fast...or a lot more people are going to get blown away."

CHAPTER 12
PARIS GREEN

The lazily pendular motions and gut-jarring air-pocket drops of Swissair Flight 614, Berne-Antwerp-Brussels-Paris, were churning stomachs hard enough to turn milk into butter. Zvi snugged his seat belt tighter while gazing through his Perspex reflection and deep into dirty, gray cotton billows knifed endlessly by fluttering wings. His thoughts were turbulent, his eyes uncharacteristically moist.

He was on Day Four of the religious pilgrimage, repeated each winter. But all the regularity in the universe couldn't make this terribly bitter pill any easier to swallow, wouldn't lighten the load of hurtful burden, didn't make the protective callous any stronger...or the pain any less real.

Visiting Nanny's and Poppy's graves was impossible because such interment of remains did not exist in the conventional sense of the word. And so this payment of profound respect would have to do.

His grandparents' lives were derailed fatally in 1942. After being shipped via boxcar through increasingly dismal and diseased stations of detention, both were gassed in Auschwitz. Only the timely and pious intervention of Righteous Gentiles saved Zvi's parents from a similar fate, but escape had been a close-run thing and not without considerable psychological cost.

To Zvi's way of thinking, long-gone relatives drifted aloft still, as confluent spirits holding high-level summit wherever the four winds blew. Once a year, he recited Kaddish softly and with dedicated reverence...addressing his prayers to an innocuous stone marker on fallow, weed-choked ground where home stood before deportation and Nazi bulldozing...five miles outside

Epernay, a stone's throw from the Marne.

"Ladies and gentlemen, this is your captain speaking. We are beginning our descent into Paris. At this time, we request that you please fasten your seat belts and make sure that your tray tables and seat backs are in the upright position. The temperature in Paris is 68 degrees...."

Probing indelicately toward Mother Earth, the airplane plunged abruptly out of grimy-gray overcast and fishtailed clumsily toward wind-buffeted touchdown. Zvi's sympathies lay fully and unequivocally with worry-bead-wielding passengers. If the plane crashed and blew apart during a stormy, bare-minimums approach, it would be others—not Zvi—leaving loved ones behind. Only the inconsequentials of a rigidly ascetic personal life waited back home.

Zvi's older brother, a tank gunner in the elite 7th Armored Brigade, burned to death when his Centurion MBT brewed up in the Golan Heights during the Yom Kippur War's battle in the Valley of Tears. One week after the burial, Zvi's father turned sex with his secretary from a part-time avocation to a full-time career pursuit. No extramarital slouch herself, his mother soon embraced Scientology and a man half her age, then headed for Southern California without leaving a forwarding address. On leave from the Sayeret Matkal, the elite reconnaissance-commando arm of the IDF general staff, Zvi came home to find the wreckage of a nuclear family strewn skimble-skamble, with no single fragment worth even the miniscule effort involved in kneeling down to pick it up.

But though warfare had skinned much from him, armed conflict also pumped salvation into his blindered life. During mandatory military service, Zvi had demonstrated an almost supernatural affinity for outmaneuvering the region's best war strategists, both on and off the battlefield. And so after mustering out, his weather vane pointed toward intelligence work. Recruited by the Mossad, he immediately waded chest deep into the ongoing quicksand of no-quarter struggle between the Jewish state and its Arab neighbors.

And at long last, having finally grown bone-weary of looking over his shoulder for he knew not what, Zvi borrowed a page from his mother and never looked backward again.

Tires chirped as the jet bounced once, shuddered, then came down for good. Spoilers popped up. Nosewheels kissed the runway as both engines roared in dual crescendo with the application of maximum reverse thrust. Zvi slid up against his seat belt as the aircraft slowed sharply on a wet runway. Cabin tension evaporated in a collective sigh of relief...and it was only then that Zvi realized he had been holding his breath.

The transit bus was packed, humidly full of chipper travelers ecstatic over safe return both to terra firma and their native soil. Once inside the terminal proper, Zvi slipped sideways through clustered knots of passengers thronging home to wives and lovers. After shepherding a medium-sized suitcase through customs, he negotiated passport control under Belgian papers.

A rented, Irish-green Jaguar idled patiently at curbside, its V12 engine burbling throatily potent in neutral. Zvi undertipped the attendant to hasten his departure, then slid behind the wheel. For several overanalytical moments, he watched rain sheeting the windshield. After shrugging at nothing in particular, Zvi turned on the wipers, put the car in gear, and aimed for central Paris.

Forty minutes later, Zvi was comfortably registered at Hotel Georges Braque, whose eight regally proud stories stood imposing sentry where *Blvd. de Courcelles* and *Blvd. Malesherbes* intersected in a mist-streaked view of bare-tree Monceau Park.

The hotel staff knew him well from previous visits. Most importantly, they understood that the boundary separating doting from smothering was a line never crossed. And while the bill was always substantially heavier than what his expense account could safely shoulder, Zvi had no trouble making up the difference out-of-pocket when calculating final reconciliation in the unelaborate though starkly masculine comfort of his bachelor apartment in West Jerusalem.

Suitably refreshed after a 45-minute nap, cold shower, and blade shave, Zvi was quietly relishing with small bites and thoughtful chewing a late dinner of *vichyssoise Falaise, escargot, cotelette de porc frais Courbevoie,* and fresh-baked bread. The meal was washed down, surprisingly enough, with a rather cheeky claret of unusually dubious ancestry, whose clear lack of breeding was hardly in keeping with the usually high standards of the hotel's discriminating sommelier.

From the moment he sat down with his back to the heavily draped wall and accepted the courteously proffered wine list, Zvi kept his expansive surroundings under casual but prudently careful watch. The newly redecorated *salle à manger* added a nicely brocaded touch to white-linen, fine-china dining, while playing host to only two other "guests," if that they were: a loving couple feeding each other generous helpings of raw oysters, *Cendre d'Aizy* and *Sauvignon blanc,* while taking no pains to hide their exaggerated desire for a fireworks evening.

Feet flat on French soil always guaranteed itchy discomfort, but what really pulled pleasure's plug on desert and deep-roasted coffee was the apologetic appearance of the courteous, white-gloved bell captain...who placed at Zvi's right elbow a folded-up message for *Monsieur* Anston, and departed quickly.

No one other than Rhonda at the head office had been apprised of his destination. On the other hand, Maurice had not achieved his hard-won rung on life's ladder by letting even the smallest minnow swim through his finely woven and diligently tended net. And Zvi thought of himself as no less than Catfish class—slimy and spiny, and definitely a force to be reckoned with.

He carefully unfolded the ragged-edged stationery and read: "Contact *Mademoiselle* Serif, Lome Transshipping, Ltd.—Marseilles, soonest upon arrival re: incoming shipment of novelties."

That the name was new did not surprise Zvi. He wondered only if this were a genuine call to hounds.

Zvi rubbed his thumb hard over the ink, which immediately warmed to his touch. Epidermal oils moistened the words just enough to liquefy them before the writing vanished, leaving neither blur on paper nor residue on skin. And then the small square of vellum warmed uncomfortably to the touch. Caught by surprise, Zvi barely got the note into the ashtray before it was consumed by smokeless, methanol-based flames that left a residue of gray, talcose ash.

Zvi semaphored his waiter, signed for dinner, put on his overcoat in the lobby, and nodded "Good Evening" on his way past the concierge's desk. Once outside, his hand gesture okayed the doorman's offer to whistle up a cab. Taking the hotel's front steps sideways two at a time, Zvi turned his collar up against foggy drizzle while resisting the Holmesian impulse to insist on a taxi from further down the line of seven.

The doorman bade him *"Bonne nuit!"* and closed the car door as Zvi leaned over the front seat and said, *"Gare St. Lazare, s'il vous plait."*

"Oui," the driver replied, immediately tipping his hand by paying too much attention to his inside rearview mirror and not nearly enough to what was going on outside the cab.

Amateur night, Zvi thought.

At the intersection of *Ave. de Villiers* and *Blvd. des Batignolles,* Zvi scattered a handful of franc notes onto the front seat and jumped ship. Bolting through the left-rear door demanded artistic weaving through an angry, life-threatening racket of crunching sheet metal, impatient beep-beeps, and cursing, fist-waving drivers.

But rain was his ally, and Zvi made the best of it.

So far, his moves were clumsily unprofessional and of little use if the second tail had been far enough behind the first to casually pick him up. *But it's still early in the chase,* Zvi thought, while hastening through *Chez Monique's* front door, sliding past the sputtering *maitre d'* and striding boldly kitchenward to sample the chef's deliciously fragrant *potage à la tete de veau* before exiting in the U-shaped loading area behind and running wildly down the shadowed alley.

It wasn't until Zvi finished doglegging west-south-west that the hairs on the back of his neck finally lay flat. He doubled back into paired, triple-pomme reversals before descending to make contact from a subterranean news kiosk. The rapidity and clarity of connection confirmed that the number reached was a local exchange. It was *Mademoiselle* "Serif" herself who answered immediately.

"Your posters for the Metro, *Monsieur.* They have arrived."

Metro = underground = covert activity. Zvi's senses ratcheted up a notch closer to full alert.

"Of the several batches that I ordered, *Mademoiselle,* which have come in?"

"Apparently, the African jungle cats," *Mademoiselle* Serif said. "As far as I can tell by looking at this invoice, which seems to be incomplete."

Jungle cats—genus: leopard; species: el-Fahd el-Aswad, aka Black Leopard. Incomplete, though. No way of telling for sure. Maybe yes; maybe no.

"Monsieur?"

"Oui."

"If you would be so kind as to follow the usual payment procedures, we will gladly and most expeditiously ship them to your warehouse."

"But of course."

"Permit me to confirm your location, then. Is *Monsieur's* firm still located at the same address in *Ton Marmert* Industrial Park?"

Montmartre.

"Oui."

"Merci, monsieur. We appreciate the rapidity of your call."

"De rien," Zvi replied, hanging up as Mademoiselle Serif did the same.

Zvi emerged to intermittent showers, thankfully breaking up to the west. He taxied to where *Blvd. de Rochechouart* met *Place Pigalle.* Waiting comfortably tipped back under the rain-swollen, red-and-white awning of Cafe Lisieux was the chief of operations—GIGN.

The antiterrorist expert looked like a devil's walking

stick in night battle-dress uniform, dark beret, and loosely belted woodland raincoat. Maurice was dry-bark, prickly, and backwoods coarse. Flint-spark eyes projected the shrewd intensity that had served him so well during his highly decorated military career, most recently as regimental commander of mechanized infantry in the 9e Division *D'Infantrie Marine* of France's *Force D'Action Rapide.*

Zvi's customary Pernod awaited; Maurice was already one-third through his.

"You slipped several of my best," the Frenchman said respectfully.

"I counted only three."

"Now I feel much better. Thank you."

"Think nothing of it."

"Did you make the woman?"

"No."

"Good! I was hoping that you wouldn't. I have high hopes for her..."

"Professionally or personally?"

"Sacre bleu!" Maurice gasped in flustered amazement, as if thoughts of seducing female operatives-in-training never crossed his mind. "Professional, of course. What kind of a man do you take me for?"

"I won't answer that."

"Merci beaucoup!"

"You're quite welcome."

"Anyway, I am quite glad to learn that she did not disappoint me tonight."

"Not yet, anyway," Zvi joked.

"Still the mouthy upstart."

"You would not be comfortable with anything less."

"And surprisingly agile. Which alone rates a tip of my figurative *chapeau,"* the Frenchman said, half-turning to give Zvi a lazy salute.

Maurice took a last sip of his drink while Zvi pushed his away.

"So tell me honestly," Maurice said, leaning his chair forward and down on all four feet. "Are you in France on business? I hope your answer to that question shall be no. Pleasure? Ah, that would make my heart swell with pride."

"As well as other parts. But first, tell me. Are the Visions of Vosges still blonde, buxom, and willing?"

"Even better," Maurice said brightly. He pushed away his half-finished drink and chuckled softly. "You and I are penciled into their date book for tomorrow night. Stunning Sonja for you; curvy Katrina for me. We can have a hot time, the two of us." And then Maurice grew serious again. "But first, you must be absolutely truthful with me. Duty demands no less than my absolute insistence upon it."

"I am here on a matter of deeply personal veneration."

"Yes, of course," Maurice said briskly. "I had forgotten that this is the time of year for that other business."

Zvi looked away abruptly, visibly shaken as he slid a cigarette out of Maurice's pack, lit up, and drew the smoke deep into his lungs.

"Please don't get me wrong," Maurice said hastily, gripping Zvi's right forearm hard enough to infuse the Israeli with heartfelt empathy. "You must understand that I meant absolutely no disrespect. However, it is also my business to learn everything there is to know about people with whom I walk the high wire."

"As I said. Strictly personal. Nothing more."

"Now, as a matter of honor, I shall need your word on that."

"You have it...as long as I am not required to present my case in writing."

"Of course not, but you must understand where I am coming from."

"I do. And tonight's target?"

"Come. Let us stretch our legs," Maurice said, only slightly less aggrieved. "What with this rain and advancing age, surely you know how it is."

"Not really."

"Zvi, I am warning you...."

The French counterterrorist chief stood up in stages, his wrists, elbows, and knees cracking in quick succession as Zvi reached for his wallet.

"Careful!" Maurice chided good-naturedly. "You must warn me before you do that again."

"Purely reflex."

"On both our parts. But your money buys nothing as long as you are in France under my personal care," Maurice said, dropping a 50-franc note on the table.

"Don't you mean 'observation'?"

"Let's not quibble over words, you and I."

As they walked west under stars winking white in velveteen night, Maurice held off speaking until passers-by thinned out and no one was within earshot.

"The villa is located on substantial, tree-studded acreage seven miles south of Nimes. The woods are heavily patrolled by guards armed both with automatic weapons and the most vicious animals we have yet encountered: rottweilers force-fed steak tartare, white horseradish, and Benzedrine, which makes them as vicious as they are unpredictable."

Zvi fought off a shiver.

"The dogs' vocal cords have been cut," Maurice continued. "They have been trained to go for the groin first, then for the throat. We call them land sharks. Very nasty."

"To say the least. Who has center stage tonight?"

"The Palestine Action Front in Occupied Territories."

"They're minor players."

"They used to be. But after two political assassinations in Ankara and one just ninety minutes ago in Lisbon, they have shown themselves to be up-and-comers worthy of at least a modicum of surveillance. Our Basque cell-breaker tipped us off to PAFOT's peripheral involvement, which led, of course, to other party animals. Further investigation revealed there may be a tie-in to the running dogs in whom you have expressed interest.

Tomorrow we shall invite the Italians in, but I wanted you to be first up at bat."

"What's the package?"

"On the surface, nothing more than a whorehouse pandering to the upper crust...foreign and domestic diplomats most likely...plus the usual mix of satyrs and sops produced so copiously by my own National Assembly. Of course, that in and of itself would not be so bad," Maurice shrugged. "Above all, one must remember that the affairs of the heart..."

"Or the loins..."

"...are usually far removed from GIGN purview. So if that were their complete MO, rather than only topside cover, we would have gone our separate ways, and you and I would not be discussing this affair. But apparently, this is a money-processing infrastructure of considerable magnitude. For example, they do not count their cash; they just pack it into tractor-trailers and simply weigh the van box."

Zvi's respectful, low-key whistle was lost to the rustle of a raincoat as Maurice glanced at his Swiss-made, tritium military wristwatch. He signaled the turbocharged BMW 750 sedan trailing them at a discreet distance. The powerful car sped up briefly, then squished to a near-silent halt as Maurice opened the door and hustled Zvi inside. As if making a gangster getaway, the driver pulled briskly away from the curb before the rear door closed completely.

The BMW sped past the Israeli's hotel, then hooked around *Place des Ternes* before heading south behind the *Arc de Triomphe* to pick up *Ave. Foch* and a fast route out of town. Zvi slipped out of his overcoat and suit jacket and rolled up his sleeves. Maurice took off his raincoat, then reached into the ice chest between the jump seats facing them and pulled out and popped open two cans of Jolt Cola.

Zvi blew crushed ice off the top of the can and quickly knocked back three long gulps of caffeine-charged soft drink. "The owner?" he asked.

"So far as we know, and believe me, we know plenty,"

Maurice said, belching on carbonation as if it punctuated the point, "Monsieur Vauban is totally above reproach in this matter."

"So far as..."

"Oui. The pansy is on his way to Paris by motorcade and will soon be heading for the United States for an extended stay. At least I hope it will be, although many of France's upper-crust fops and assorted dandies will no doubt be heard squalling their raucous disappointment from one end of *La Belle France* to the other."

"And yet you say he is not infected."

"Not as far as we can ascertain. But his staff? Ah, that is another matter entirely."

Maurice leaned back stiffly as the car sprinted through the night. Street lights grew more widely spaced as suburbs gave way to country roads. The Frenchman opened a package of anise gum, unwrapped three sticks, and stuffed them into his mouth.

"Zvi, you know the old saying about the cat's absence infusing the mice with moxie enough to do business. At any rate, my higher-ups knew intuitively that it would be profoundly embarrassing for the present head of state to have this raid conducted while the host occupied the premises...just in case something goes wrong."

"I'm surprised you would even accede to such a possibility."

"Only in your presence, Zvi."

"Security at the villa?"

"What we call state of the art is older than last month's news to them," Maurice reflected somberly. "Intermixed with the armed guards is a forest full of first-rate, cupcake-size cripplers dreamed up by the best area-denial minds money can buy: Jumping Jak bounding-fragmentation antipersonnel mines; IR trip mechanisms; thermal sensors; stealth-technology plastics emitting barely enough leakage for us to get a fix on. Every time we catalog one of their toys, they come up with another, even more deadly modification. Not that we can't leapfrog them, of course, but they are pesky little devils. Thank goodness I have under my command men who view this as a challenge and not as a chore."

"I see that there is no moon tonight."

"And I am pleased to see that you have kept up with your astronomy," Maurice said approvingly. "Now I bid you sit back and enjoy my hospitality."

"I am looking forward to it," Zvi said.

Bereted guards carefully checked Maurice's face against his ID before coming to attention, saluting crisply and waving the BMW through the gates of the GIGN antiterrorist commando base southwest of Paris. On the puddle-spotted helipad, ground crewmen radioed "Go!" status to the pilot of a black Aerospatiale AS 332M Super Puma helicopter. Maurice's car slid to a sideways stop precisely over its mark as the chopper's twin Turbomeca Makila 1A1 turboshafts powered up to high whine. The craft was light on its wheels as Zvi and Maurice clambered aboard. Before they were fully strapped in, the aircraft jumped up, hovered momentarily as if gathering its wits, then roared away nose-low over darkened countryside, hugging the ground as it hustled its strategic planner to a top-secret military staging area WNW of Arles.

Landing was willow-wisp light on recently cleared woodland lit by generator-powered arc lights. Maurice and Zvi ran to the first of four Chobham-armored AMX-10P infantry fighting vehicles whose muffled engines idled patiently in the chilly darkness. GIGN troopers made last-minute adjustments to their web gear, checked their equipment, and climbed back aboard the tracked vehicles.

Zvi slipped on P.A.C.A. body armor and night-fighting helmet, then checked his H&K MP5 SD 9mm submachine gun. Maurice helped his friend aboard the lead APC as the other three formed up behind in line-astern formation. Then the convoy lurched and then moved out at 60 kilometers per hour. Twenty minutes later, the strike force slowed to inch-ahead crawl before stopping 700 yards down from Villa Vauban's main gate, which lay hidden between two hillocks around a 60-degree bend in the road.

"Walk in or taxi?" Maurice asked, clearly hoping for the latter. "After all, it would be a damn shame to ruin such a splendidly tailored pair of trousers."

"Not a problem," Zvi replied cheerfully. "I have a superb haberdasher in Berne." Then he got up, checked his weapon, and moved toward the vehicle's rear hatches.

"*Bon.* Then we shall stroll in together," Maurice sighed. "And you will most definitely need these," he said, handing Zvi a thick codpiece and a throat guard, both made of Kevlar 129 covered by black, rip-stop fabric. "Strap those on tight and make sure you stay whole, *mon ami.* Sonja must not be disappointed."

"Perish the thought," Zvi replied with a lopsided grin.

The GIGN chief issued final instructions to the lead officer, then stepped back smartly as the convoy moved out again at high speed and vanished around the mist-wrapped bend. Their disappearance was almost immediately punctuated by the pom-pom drumroll of diversionary 20mm cannon fire fracturing the country-night quiet.

The villa's black, cast-iron gate blew away in fluttering strips of curlicue metal. Heat-fused bars glowed cherry-red then hissed to black as they whizzed away through the moist tangle of fog-wreathed underbrush. Sappers blew a 10-meter section of cement-block wall into a billowing cloud of gray dust. From all sides ahead came confused, ineffectual pops of misdirected small-arms fire. Skyward and beyond, air-dropped commandos landed on the roof of the main house and, in murderously brief hand-to-hand combat, quickly neutralized outmatched defenders.

Immediately after smash-through, the AMX-10Ps fanned out from line astern to battle formation. They clanked brusquely overland through bocage aglitter with the twinkle of exploding, man-killing devices ranging from Shaitan castrater mines to flechette-firing canisters. Night-sight 7.62mm machine guns fatally targeted defenders foolish enough to pop up near the meandering, cobblestone road winding through tall firs to the palatial residence. Bullets splanged harmlessly off APC treads. A pair of LAW 66mm rockets, fired high and wide, blasted to matchwood five closely packed trees on the far side of the relentlessly advancing machines.

And then swirling ground fog ahead swallowed up the mechanized infantry vehicles as Maurice and Zvi began their shoulder-to-shoulder walk...to face the demon dogs that fell upon them immediately.

Having already beheaded its dead handler, the first rottweiler attacked savagely before the interlopers were 50 feet past the blast-wrecked gate. A bare whisper of onrushing air was their only warning as a heavily muscled animal torso catapulted through a V-shaped break in waist-high, fern-laced grass.

Zvi's spin/shoot hip-level firing was dead-on accurate. His buzzsaw burst caught the frothing, four-legged killer in mid-jump, chopping the dog's hindquarters cleanly away from the front half of the arcing body. Still targeting Maurice, the disemboweled remains soared through a near-perfect trajectory. Its aim was off only slightly, the bare-fanged snout clamped down hard enough to crack teeth on the body armor protecting the Frenchman's left shoulder.

Maurice's submachine gun broke into a snarling voice. Its authoritative stutter accented the vertical stitching of hot slugs opening up an armed guard from crotch to throat. The burst of lead punched the dead man hard into a tree trunk. As the corpse slid down to a sitting position and fell forward, it was immediately set upon by ferocious rottweilers fighting wildly over the kill like starving wolves.

"Back to back now!" Maurice screamed. *"Quickly!"*

Spine to spine in the nick of time, Zvi and Maurice loosed a withering hail of circumferential gunfire at drug-crazed dogs charging at them from all around their intensely focused world. Kicked-up dirt bisected the road. Alerted to mortal danger above, Zvi quickly calculated the trajectory. Muzzle flash confirmed a treed sniper. One deadly accurate burst blew the bad guy downward, minus right arm and shoulder...but alive enough to shriek horribly as snapping jaws of death voraciously ripped into him.

Then almost as quickly as it had started, the heavy-caliber firing stopped, and eerie silence draped the villa's gardens like a dense quilt of heavy-wool insulation. Still back to back, and with the unblinking wariness of hooded cobras, the two soldiers of remarkably good fortune emerged from the smoking carnage of deadly woods. Zvi kept his eyes riveted to the back door as the two men walked over to the four-story, red-brick mansion surrounded by GIGN forces.

Having climbed blast-scorched Italian marble to the first fountain-flanked landing, the APCs grumbled menacingly on the terrace, their high-intensity searchlights bathing the 44-room main house in garish, purple-fringed light. Sporadic bursts of gunfire erupted behind and between auxiliary buildings.

Maurice double-timed up the front steps to the inlaid-brass doorway where eight ravishing women in various stages of undress were being ushered out under the quietly appreciative eyes of a GIGN sergeant and three equally grateful troopers. The women, all in their early twenties and still decked out in bikini underwear and underwired, cleavage-enhancing bras, broadcast hot-tempered multilingual indignation at having been so unceremoniously rousted.

Snobbishly disdainful of the uniformed men pressing in around them, the women squawked like angry geese all the way down the steps to join 16 white-uniform servants, nine maids, five chauffeurs, and four chefs clucking nervously in military transport trucks idling patiently on the expansive sweep of immaculately tended driveway.

Maurice and Zvi strode through the remarkably undamaged entryway and eyeballed the vast sweep of the eight-chandelier grand foyer. A single shard of shattered Dordrecht crystal crunched in loud surprise as a heavy combat boot ground the glass into deep-pile, Japanese-red carpeting. The Frenchman's manner was curt, his voice decidedly surly as he looked down and scowled.

"I will definitely have a talk with them about that."

"Still, in all, a remarkably neat strike," Zvi consoled. "Better, perhaps, than even my people could have done."

"Without a doubt, *mon ami,* but even this much is too much," Maurice said with genuine disappointment. He looked up and down the main hallway. "And without even a stiff to show for it."

"Over there," Zvi noted dryly. "On the stairs."

The deeply tanned body on the winding, purple-velvet stairway leading to the upper levels had taken three in the chest. Its white-silk dinner jacket was wetly red. A Tokarev semiautomatic pistol lay two steps down from where the corpse had voided bladder and bowels.

"Apparently, not even one of your own bullets," Zvi said approvingly.

"You have no way of knowing just how much better that makes me feel."

Maurice acknowledged all-clear waves from troopers on the four landings above, then tugged attentively at the tactical two-way radio clipped to his left shoulder.

"Downstairs," he told Zvi. "The loan office awaits."

After passing through two dining rooms connected by a six-stove kitchen, it was 75 steps down to the wine cellar. A cobwebbed wall at the far end was pushed aside. A chevron cross-section of Haley & Weller Dartcord strip explosive had worked like a laser-powered cookie cutter to cleanly excise the stainless-steel door's locking mechanism. Behind the forced-open portal lay a 3,500-square-foot data center and cash depository. Tanks of liquid nitrogen cooled a two-deep bank of high-speed supercomputers. The machines silently processed financial-transaction information as antiterrorist commandos lined up 12 bodies for inspection.

In contrast to the untouched rooms above, the banking center bore the battle scars of an intense firefight...most of the damage having been inflicted by the recently deceased. Blue vapor fogged recessed fluorescent lighting. The acrid smell of gun smoke hung heavy in the treated air. Electrical smoke curled from a blasted circuit-breaker box. A shotgunned Pepsi machine spewed fizzling fluids while pumping out change in random, jingling intervals like a whacked-out one-armed bandit.

Maurice slowly toured the computer center, nodding respectfully at the immense cash-storage area behind. He booted aside a portable compact-disc player. Like a startled baboon, the unit screeched out two stanzas of garbled martial music. Then it clicked into fast-forward, spat sparks, and crackled into silence.

"Banking," he told Zvi. "Definitely not a shooters' nest. Still, in all, not a bad night's work."

Maurice used the muzzle of his submachine gun to flip open a thick paymaster's ledger...hard copy for only a small fraction of the transactions being transmitted electronically via mil-spec. modems to financial institutions all over Western Europe. His gloved finger slowly turned pages until a precisely lettered entry halfway down one of the page's eight columns caught his eye and stopped his inspection.

"Democratic Front for the Liberation of Palestine," Maurice read. "Force 17 out of Jordan. Recruitment Committee 77. Committee 88. Islamic Jihad." He turned a few more pages. "Codes. Passwords. Special clearances. Bank names. Deposit-box numbers. Contents."

The Frenchman shouldered his weapon and tucked the ledger under his left arm, then stepped aside as a sergeant, dogged by a diligent, note-taking corporal, swept papers, logs, and computer hard drives into the hungry maw of his fifth olive-drab evidence box.

"And who knows what else," Zvi said.

"Maybe the evil bastards you're after as well. Whatever the case, this will make for some damn interesting, late-night reading."

"What about the owner of the villa?" Zvi asked hopefully. "With an operation of this size..."

"He surely must have known? That's what you're thinking, is it not? Maybe...but I would tend toward probably not," Maurice said. "Let's go topside. You will perhaps get a better perspective when we review tonight's events from outside of this pesthole."

The Frenchman was silent until they reached the pin-drop quiet of a vine-covered band shell 500 meters west of the villa's 10-car garage. Back in the topiary shrubs, Maurice shook two cigarettes out of a fresh pack and bent down to the wind-whipped flame of Zvi's lucky-charm Zippo lighter.

"As grand a scale as this may seem to you," Maurice exhaled, "*Monsieur* Vauban, the owner, claims honest title to five other villas larger than this in France alone. Additionally, he enjoys extensive holdings in England, Switzerland, Venezuela, and Brazil, most of which make what you see before you more *pissoir* than palace. Wealth, like so much else, is a matter of relativity. So I would tend toward this being mouse-play with the cat in absentia. I honestly believe that he has too much at risk for it to be otherwise."

"I sincerely appreciate your having me along tonight."

"Think nothing of it, *mon ami*. For too many years, your trips to Paris have been wallpapered with anxiety, then painted over with the repressed tears of considerable regret."

"I mourn only as much as the next man," Zvi said, but Maurice was not convinced.

"Zvi, about the past, we can do nothing...you and I... except permit it to gorge upon our innards until we become merely drained-dry husks of men. But only if we so choose, Zvi, only if we let that happen! However, as far as tomorrow goes?" Maurice brightened visibly. Hearty back-slapping succeeded in finally jarring loose a smile from Zvi. "About our short-term future, I had hoped that perhaps tonight's close-quarters combat would lighten your mood, as well as whet your appetite for the pleasures of the flesh."

"Which it has, my friend."

"Then we have reached a pleasantly amicable settlement. Now let us avail ourselves of the distaff companionship I spoke of earlier. Paris today is even more decadent than you might remember. And I am just the man to show you the latest pitfalls."

"I appreciate the offer, Maurice. But there is that other matter."

"Which can wait."

"Well, I suppose..."

"You suppose?! Suppose nothing, Zvi. Supposition is the food of fakirs and fools, and thank God we are neither. There is a time for love, and that time is now!"

The last departing APC swung around to claim them. Maurice sat pensively cross-legged and lit a second cigarette from the glowing butt of the first. With the ledger wedged safely tight under his right boot, the Frenchman was silent until the tracked vehicle completed its bone-crunching journey over the extensive litter of human and canine body parts and had passed through the blast-shattered front gate. And then he told Zvi: "Don't concern yourself about Monsieur Vauban. Arrangements will definitely be made to question him extensively at some point following his return from those wide-ranging travels. But in this case, and with so many political connections..." Maurice shrugged philosophically. "You must understand, *mon ami,* that it may take some time to invite *Monsieur* to the forum appropriate for official interrogation."

"But unofficially?"

Maurice grinned wickedly, took a last drag of a cigarette, and athletically flicked it away.

"Unofficially, he has been under my watchful eye ever since the first red flags were raised by our Basque brothers in Spain."

CHAPTER 13
WITCHES' BREW

Goldilocks's head reverberated melodically with the joyfully rhythmical magic of symphony-orchestra rhapsodies. Concertos flocked in roost-circling flutter, like homing pigeons spiraling down to coo-flap landing.

After accessing the B-Q-E southbound, he exited short of the Brooklyn Battery Tunnel. Journey's next maneuver was 25 minutes of aimlessly angular cruise past shuttered second-hand stores and gaily lit *bodegas*...checking intently for trailers before heading toward a dockside workshop long ago contracted for, though only recently stocked and secured, in northeast Gowanus Bay.

Triple-edge wipers intermittently swished away ice rain's random spatter. The van's heater blew all the Saharan scorch it had, keeping the driver's body temperature hovering just below a breakout of the sweats...the flash point where perspiration's moisture would facilitate teeth-chatter cold's siphoning of sinew-bonding protons and electromotive bindings through that most dreaded osmosis of all: the ruinous nightmare of reverse conduction.

As a desperate countermeasure in tug-of-war combat against marrow-ache weather's oppressive fickleness, Goldilocks—who in acknowledgment of upcoming evolvement had lately taken to referring to himself as Mr. Egg—sucked on and spewed out silver 1.5-volt button batteries stacked in tubular dispensers spiking up vertically from a Styrofoam block safety-belted into the passenger seat. Every 11 minutes, another fat, clear-plastic straw was tipped onto and around his tongue. The metal disks rolling between cheek and gums were sucked voraciously to discharge during two blocks' worth of roundabout travel, then stream-spritzed onto the van's right-side floor.

Head Man piped in with:

NIGHT IS SO MATERNAL, HOW IT CLOAKS US LIKE A WOMB...

To which Mr. Egg replied:

Though when we visit N-Y-C, we'll make their night go BOOM.

Five hundred feet from the sanctuary, Mr. Egg's Ford sidled up to the curb as he flipped up the lid of a seat-separating console.

Alarm board's lights are all shiny and green.

SYSTEM'S INTACT AND ALL ENTRANCES CLEAN.

Behind the ridiculous masquerade of laughably ineffective aluminum tape, which in this case was legitimately phony and only for low-rent appearance's sake, Mr. Egg's antipenetration network depended first on bin-shaped meshwork grates bay-windowed outward to keep rodents, cats, and dogs two feet distant from blacked-out, spyproof glass. Next line of defense was an electrified Zapster grate capable of incinerating even the borough's largest, sewer-infesting bug. Third buffer was an interlinked network of gray-light sensors coupled to UHF beepers with a transstate range. Invisible to the naked eye, pin-thick beams would snag crazed crooks and feverish junkies seeking any score available for financing their next taste of Thai Street White.

But nothing showed.

NO, NOTHING GLOWED.

Then let's proceed.

WE'VE ALL WE NEED.

Mr. Egg put the van back in gear and approached his armored lair at 15 on the speedo while swinging open the electronics forward. As two reinforced-steel panels clanked sideways, he gunned the van's engine, shot forward, turned sharply left, and screeched to a stomped-brakes halt. The Ford's tonnage on the parking spot's weigh scale abruptly reversed the door motor direction, and the screw-drive barrier clanged shut...

bolt-locking automatically with the hideaway's solo resident safely out of sight.

Upon exiting the van, Mr. Egg stripped himself bare, flung off his hairpiece, and flicked on suspended overheads. Individual fixtures merged into a seamless sunlamp ceiling; tubes' serial pop-ons turned the 10,000-square-foot shop warmly lavender.

Eleven deep-breathing minutes later, and with the scent of L.A. carnage still ambrosially thick in his nostrils, Mr. Egg felt recharged enough for blood-warming calisthenics. Instead, the buck-naked bomber positioned an unloading ramp and dollied six stoves from the cargo van to the hardwood floor, slashing and tossing aside cardboard casings as he went. All cookers were connected in 27 minutes, squatting on insulated, nonskid mats four-corner grounded against static-electrical discharge.

Following brief, blue-flare tests of burner function, Mr. Egg pushed into 30-square-foot working areas…the castered-trusswork structures snaking with glasswork utensils linking Bunsen burner attachments, Pyrex beakers, lab-grade tubing, NASA-specs gaskets, pipettes, and calibrated centigrade thermometers. Each special apparatus was production-engineered to facilitate preparation of heinous recipes for fueling the next step of ongoing metamorphosis.

Stoves prepped and physical plant plumbed, Mr. Egg ever-so-gently rolled over and carefully positioned rubber-tired, six-foot-high cabinets whose wooden shelving supported red-lettered containers. Then, working with a clipboard and fuchsia grease pencil, Mr. Egg double-checked previously examined inventory.

Workstation One: pure mercury, nitric acid, ethyl alcohol, distilled water, filtration material, washing solution, and litmus paper...for the preparation of mercury fulminate.

Workstation Two: ammonium nitrate, potassium nitrate, ammonium oxalate, sulfur flour, charcoal, and a polycarbonate scale...for the preparation of Ammonium Nitrate Compound Number 61.

Workstation Three: sulfuric acid, nitric acid, distilled

water, ice-bath hardware, toluene, extraction equipment, and washing solution...for the preparation of TNT.

Workstation Four: dimethyllaniline, sulfuric acid, nitric acid, ice-bath hardware, filtration material, distilled water, sodium bicarbonate, washing solution, and litmus paper...for the preparation of tetryl.

Workstation Five: phenol, sulfuric acid, distilled water, nitric acid, extraction equipment, filtration material, washing solution, and litmus paper...for the preparation of picric acid.

Workstation Six: regular coffee, decaffeinated coffee, regular tea, herbal tea, cocoa, chicken broth, and beef bouillon... for the preparation of chill-deflecting beverages.

Sheet-steel, temperature-controlled alcoves sheltered backup supplies. Bunker-sequestered, nonreactive canisters held elements for the dangerously unstable combinations of ammonium nitrate and powdered aluminum; ammonium perchlorate and asphaltum; potassium nitrate and charcoal; guanidine nitrate and powdered antimony; potassium chlorate and red phosphorus; potassium permanganate and powdered sugar, and barium chlorate, plus paraffin wax.

Mr. Egg preened, puffed-chest proud...hands on hips in near gloat over mix-and-match apothecary's ingredients for disaster in the making. But before serious brewmaster's work could begin, physical tank-up was mandatory...because tingly rejuvenation delivered by overhead beams in no way stifled persistent grumblings demanding immediate satisfaction. So Mr. Egg candlelight-dined on a camp-table spread of Sunshine Hydrox cookies, Power-Up high-protein drink, and the day's ninth helping of yellow multivitamins, which he gobbled like a kid overdosing on gumdrops.

After a hearty burp, he oiled up with a zinc-chromium sunscreen of his own alchemical creation. Skin-darkening rays were totally blocked; permitted unhindered passage were raw nucleons required to revitalize brainworks for the extremely hazardous cookery looming ahead.

Mr. Egg set the tanning bed's timer for one half hour, then

reclined comfortably—arms outstretched, fingers spread, making sure to turn every few minutes so as to guarantee uniform, comfy-cozy amping up under magenta shimmer. Occasionally teasing himself with ungoggled looks at Day Star's "second best," he restricted full-vision exposure because the upcoming roast-and-toast demanded undrugged 20/20 vision.

Fully hot-wired 30 minutes later, Mr. Egg padded naked to a drafting table, and unrolled and thumbtacked to a corkboard a minutely detailed rendering of masterwork in progress. Thumb-jabbed clicker lilac-lit the insulated alcove where his *piece de resistance* was undergoing reassembly. Mr. Egg walked over to tape-measure three large recesses on the chassis' right side, which together ran one third of the frame's flank. Body panels lay accurately positioned around the vehicle's steelwork. Each saddle-mount pan awaited shaped-charge stuffing with TNT, which over the next several days would be formulated then melted at 82 degrees for smooth pouring and spatulate molding... the calipered curvature of which would ensure maximally lethal blast.

While thumbing professorially through thick, three-ring binders of voluminous, loose-leaf notes, Mr. Egg grunted affirmatively during slow circumnavigation of murderous undertaking, stooping occasionally for close-in peeks as would a sculptor scrutinizing every chisel mark of a marble creation destined for eternal display in Anytown's Museum of Modern Art.

Rectangular cutouts?

[X] Gray primer ready to receive napalm equivalents.

Neatly bundled, color-coded detonator wires?

[X] Carefully lashed up in holding-cavity corners.

Bracketing the firebombs?

[X] Canvas-bagged, smoke-screen charges.

10 stress-tested vats for hydrogen cyanide gas?

[X] Instead, alternating between naphtha and benzene.

After taking time out to ladle, measure, and set aside each workstation's soon-to-simmer ingredients, the scratch-build bomber donned neatly pressed ceremonial whites...and—to Head Man's chirping approval—strutted onto center stage for his virtuoso performance as fiendish chef extraordinaire.

CHAPTER 14

BON VOYAGE

Judith stared pensively through the speeding taxi's insect-spotted windshield and right-side window. Backseat sights and sounds smoked quickly toward dispersion before vanishing traceless from overworked, exhausted memory. Midmorning strollers on Ben Yehuda snapped past like calico garments blown sideways on a backyard clothesline. Smears of brilliant, primary colors stretched into horizontal blur and were just that quickly gone.

Home again, home again, jiggidy-jig.

The eastbound F-15 air-taxi ride had been jostlingly uncomfortable, and she'd vomited enthusiastically when avgas fumes seeped into her mask during air-to-air refueling. Catnaps snatched between teeth-rattling bouts of clear-air turbulence were thankfully specterless but nowhere near restful. And though The Dream seemed on a temporary though much appreciated hiatus, tossing and turning restlessly in a confining G-suit and harness...while breathing piped-in air...left her cranky-irritable. The bottom line was a 32-hour headache, bucking and kicking worse than wild horses in a crazed stampede.

Summary recall wasn't unusual, considering that she hadn't been on assignment when TransPac 117 went down... only on well-deserved vacation...and unluckily caught the case through geographical fluke. Professional courtesy and interagency cooperation kept her close to that investigation and facilitated tap-in to subsequent Q&A surrounding the Los Angeles truck bombing.

Such fact-finding involvement made eminent sense; what irked Judith was time squandered in nonsensically premature debriefings. As usual, they expected miraculously intuitive results; unfortunately, her hat held no rabbits.

Go figure, she thought, bracing herself as best she could while the cab driver transformed a simple Wednesday drive into kamikaze commuting spiced with lead-footed drag racing.

And then there was Gleizer, he of the levitating desk, sometimes located in the Foreign Ministry but more often elsewhere as convenient. Gleizer ranked high enough to merit status-report updates on any assignment, long distance or local...a privilege he often abused while appropriating investigative plums from other people's pies.

With Zvi "fryin' taters" in Lebanon, interlevel insulation was poof...so Judith would have to nurse and burp the enigma that insiders called the Butcher.

Gleizer's nickname came not from prowess at dismemberment but because his only generally known civilian work experience predating bemedaled military service and ballistic rise in Israeli intelligence had been in his immigrant family's butcher shop. That enterprise had grown as meteorically as the city over which it held dietary sway: Ashdod was now home to eight GLEIZER: THE MEAT MAVEN markets.

He ran tight, well-wired missions. All of his operations were neatly mitered and greased-pole slick. As the "spanner" in charge of Tactical Projects, his agenda was mostly foreign, though he dabbled freely in domestics. "Inside jobs" usually meshed with Shin Bet stratagems, but more often conflicted with the General Security Service's game plans. After the dust settled, however, official complaints were rarely voiced and never filed.

Gleizer reported to the head of the Mossad, although he was rumored to have the ear of the PM director general, and the prime minister as well. He soldiered on untroubled and unhampered, either by interagency jealousy or bureaucratic disturbance. Results were what counted, and his tally stood at: GOOD GUYS—CLASSIFIED; OTHER SIDE—ZILCH.

The cab's screeching, curb-bumping stop nearly launched the Mossad woman over the front seat. She paid the fare with absentminded indifference, crossed the courtyard almost at a run, and walked briskly into the expansive, ultramodern lobby of the 35-story Shalom Tower. A recently emptied elevator car stood ready for service, and she rode up alone.

The doors bing-bonged open on 30. Thick-pile carpet compressing softly underfoot kept the hallway silent to the point of haunted indifference. Suite 3025 was a temporary setup six doors down on the right. Judith rapped twice on the blank, frosted-glass window...and entered in advance of invitation.

Freshly painted, egg-white walls still smelled of recently applied fire retardant. Recessed fluorescent lighting was indirect and subdued. A bottled-water dispenser stood lone sentry in the northwest corner, around which were scattered an armful of wall studs, three boxes of ceiling tiles, a drop cloth, and two tubs of finishing nails.

Cocoa-brown, east window vertical blinds were pulled back, revealing Jerusalem almost visible in the pastel distance. But having felt Gleizer's deeply reaming eyes since the split second of entry, and not truly comfortable with high-altitude sightseeing, Judith ignored the panoramic view and sat down stiffly attentive in the straight-back metal folding chair fronting the lone, centrally located desk.

A brief, mug-shot glance convinced Judith her wisest move was saying nothing while counting the neatly regimented holes in the sound-deadening, acoustic-tile ceiling.

Gleizer's face looked as if it had been cold-chiseled from Mendenhall Glacier sheet ice: Under a one-day growth of beard, gray/white vertical planes tapered to a hard-cut, cleft chin; the nose was a perfect triangle; ears lay flat against the sides of his head.

The intelligence officer was dressed in a short-sleeve, white polo shirt, tan poly/wool belted slacks, and black tennis sneakers. His sun-bleached Stetson was tilted only slightly up from T-squared horizontal, which was about as informal as an iceman like Gleizer ever got. Dark, gold-rimmed aviator glasses hid eyes that operatives swore were the color of baked brick, though no one Judith knew had ever seen them up close and personal.

There were three phones on the temporary desk, angled diagonally across the blank blotter in a bend-sinister pattern. Gleizer was on the green one in the middle and in no hurry to terminate his conversation. Pierce-point stare didn't waver during brusquely choppy chatter, a tactic Judith had been told was the Mossad executive's inimitable way of extending disadvantage.

During a break in Gleizer's conversation, Judith interjected, "You asked to see me, Mr. Deputy Minister," at which point he hung up without even a curtly formal goodbye. Judith guessed that no one had been on the other end of the line during all the time she'd been given the five-over.

"Avraham Ya'rok said I might be interested in talking to you," Gleizer finally said.

"Avraham?"

"Yes."

"He's back inside?"

"Strictly probationary, and solely as an aide to me."

"Yes?" she said, hoping that Gleizer would shade in some detail on what little she knew about her recall, and especially on where Avraham fit into the rapidly changing picture.

"You know him," Gleizer stated flatly, more as a factual assessment than as a question needing an answer.

"He was jettisoned after the sky fell in on Lakam, our Bureau of Scientific Liaison," Judith said. Further embellishment wasn't necessary; Gleizer's files already contained everything noteworthy about her and Avraham.

"You have an excellent memory."

"Which was nourished by voluminous media coverage," Judith replied, mentally reviewing stories on how the technological-espionage unit had foxworked in the Defense Ministry. The special section, tightly umbilical to Israel Military Industries, was scattered to the four winds in exile after certain "unorthodox" practices came to light. Several very promising careers were abruptly derailed; one rock-climbing accident was said to have been a hushed-up suicide, although whispers of foul play still circulated in high-echelon hallways. "As I recall, Lakam was an A-to-Z universe unto itself, specializing in the covert acquisition of scientific know-how...everything from aerospace breakthroughs to the combat-laser engineering of friendly nations."

"Friendly nations?" Gleizer sneered. "We have no true friends. We have only ourselves."

"Plus the assassination business that got unfortunately out of hand."

"Both the Marrakech and Nicosia proceedings were well warranted."

"As were Salah Bseiso in Rabat and Atef Khalaf in Bizerte. As payback for Munich, yes."

"Then what is the problem?"

"I was talking about the special undercover units operating in the West Bank and Gaza."

Gleizer's tight-lipped grimace told Judith that while he might not comment directly on statements concerning unmentionables, mental notes were taken just the same.

"You have this way about you, most specifically in tracking bombers like no one else ever in our service."

"Thank you, Mr. Deputy Minister," Judith replied formally. Gleizer, after all, was not hard of hearing...and it would be ill-advised insolence to press further into territory he had no desire to explore.

"Uri would do fine," Gleizer said, waving his hands as if shooing away pesky flies. "This 'Mr. Deputy Minister' business. It sounds too vaguely Soviet. We are socialist but..."

"Not communist?"

"Perish the thought."

It was anyone's guess how long Gleizer would waltz around the crux. A report, however scanty, would be dutifully filed on what precious little was up for grabs on TransPac 117, all neatly cross-referenced to Los Angeles. Carl Gutierrez's "technicals" on both incidents were probably already in Gleizer's computer, thanks to hotline networking. Other than that, Judith could sprinkle in little more than name, rank, and serial number.

The red, bottom phone belled out four short, staccato rings. Gleizer picked up the receiver and said, "Talk. Yes. Okay, hold on." Then he clamped his hand over the mouthpiece, holding it directly behind his head at arm's length.

"Did you come up with anything on the airliner bombing that will give us something to go on? Did you get anything from your investigation?"

"No, sir."

"Not Uri?"

"No, sir."

"How about the truck bombing?"

"Nothing more than what the media has reported so far."

"And the coins that were found?"

"One-deutsche-mark coins, mint-marked 1950. Indicative of National Socialist Common Action Group—ANS—involvement."

"Only 'indicative'? You sound doubtful."

"I am skeptical because the ANS is too financially prostrate to have pulled off such an operation. I find it hard to believe they were the doers."

"Not even with someone's help?"

"Specifically?"

"Japanese Red Army? Italian Red Brigades? Spanish International Revolutionary Action Groups? Provisional Wing of the Irish Republican Army, considering the bagpiper? French National Liberation Front?"

"I cannot answer definitely concerning any of them."

"So far, we're satisfied with what has come out on L.A."

"That does not surprise me."

"ANS, on a copartnership basis," Gleizer affirmed.

"With who?!"

"It doesn't take all that much know-how to plant explosives."

And there it was, rearing its ugly head again: ha-Konseptzia—"the Concept"—that dangerous prepossession of becoming intellectually enamored of circumstances that clashed openly with pragmatic reality. *It was precisely such chained-brain, robotistic thinking that cost us so heavily in the Yom Kippur War: The Arabs could not/would not do this; the Arabs would not/could not do that. But they did, and we wound up paying a heavy price. Blind adherence to "the Concept" cost us plenty. The only saving grace here is that someone else is picking up the tab on current events.*

"Except the truck bomb was a multistage package of considerable complexity," Judith noted.

"As was the TransPac device."

"Yes, sir."

"So you believe the media reports about TransPac?"

"Yes, sir," she said evenly, "until I am given good reason to doubt them."

"Still the Arabs as the perps?"

"As far as we know." *Gutierrez's suppositions notwithstanding, I have nothing concrete to go on.*

"El-Fahd el-Aswad?" he asked.

"Guilty until proven innocent."

"As the motive force?"

"Yes, sir."

"With a freelancer as the actual mechanic?"

"Apparently so, sir."

"It seems as if the Americans are all of a sudden having trouble with bombings."

"Not really."

"Yes?"

"Bombers have long been fixtures in the American landscape. Only this time, the number of casualties is higher."

"Substantially higher."

"Yes, sir."

"However, up until now, most bombings were rooted in their internal politics and organized crime as opposed to international terrorism with overseas roots."

"Yes, sir."

"Why do you suppose the Americans have lost their

immunity?"

"Maybe because it is their turn."

"Yet activity such as the TransPac business would serve only to stir up anti-Arab sentiment."

"Perpetrators of such deeds swear allegiance only to their own cause. They revel in blame. What happens generally in the Arab world means nothing to them. They care only about the body count."

"Unless we get dragged into it, and then everyone and their mothers-in-law suddenly become militantly concerned about everything."

"Yes, sir."

"Hmmm," Gleizer murmured. Then he brought the phone back close to his face, listened for a moment, then muttered, "Billiard balls, you say?"

Judith's mind drifted rudderless as Gleizer's side of the conversation switched erratically between Hebrew, Yiddish, High German, and Arabic. As the Mossad officer gazed lazily up at the ceiling, Judith was glad that his eyes were finally off her; the inattention subtracted at least 10 degrees from the room's cloying temperature.

But when Gleizer's face shifted slightly in apparent conjunction with sunglasses scanning blank walls, Judith realized that perhaps only his head was moving while his eyes remained locked attentively straight. Red, flushing discomfort immediately ratcheted up her body heat.

While cradling the phone between neck and shoulder, Gleizer carefully cracked each knuckle of callused hands. As if noticing Judith's presence for the first time, he pointed to the phone, then shrugged and mimed: *What next?*

"I should care about billiard balls!" Gleizer snapped rhetorically, and Judith knew that the statement wasn't solely for her benefit; if Gleizer thought the words were at all important, he'd be talking in tongues. "Yes, I did tell you to contact me. And they're all white, you say? Yes, you're 100 percent correct. It is not your job to evaluate. Evaluation is my job. And you have

done yours. Thank you." Then he brusquely slammed down the phone and told Judith, "Now it's a donkey cart smuggling white billiard balls in Gaza. The second one so far. This load heading into Abasan."

"Cue balls?" she asked.

"Yes, whatever. Cue balls. Right."

"Maybe they will be used as stones in the eternal intifada," Judith offered.

"Stones? Why, come to think of it, I hadn't considered that."

"Well, you were only just now apprised of a second dot to connect to the first," Judith said diplomatically.

"As a matter of fact, I would say that you're dead on target. But it would be...projectiles! Don't you mean projectiles?" Gleizer abruptly leaned forward, elbows on the desk. "After all," Gleizer continued, "a stone would be but a stone; however, a projectile could be anything else. Like, perhaps, a billiard ball, for example."

"But of course."

"So 'projectile' would be a better word?"

"Is this a test?"

"Of course not."

"Then yes, I would agree."

"And if it were a test?"

"My answer would not change."

"So you concur."

"I do."

"Okay, so we are agreed. On 'projectile,' that is. We entertain the concept of 'projectile' instead of 'stone.'"

"I would say so."

"Definitely?"

"Most assuredly," Judith said. Playing "stupe ball" with Gleizer came easy because, as course captain, he was entitled to sail off on whatever tangent he wished.

"That will be all. Report back to me if you catch a scent of anything else. Oh, and take the rest of the week off."

Four days?! she raged silently. *I am due at least a dozen.* But all she said was: "Thank you, Mr. Deputy Minister."

"Don't thank me," Gleizer said gruffly, as if the "away time" were coming out of his personal budget. "You earned it."

Judith pushed up and off the metal chair, politely taking her leave. Gleizer watched stone-cold silent, mistrusting her motives and intentions. In the comfortably cool corridor, with a shielding suite door between them, a backward glance showed Gleizer either engaged in thoughtful, head-down pacing or just roving restlessly while waiting for Judith to get downstairs.

The elevator took its own sweet time coming. Judith jabbed the UP button as well. A northbound would do nicely; the faster she could get away from Gleizer's temporary headquarters, the better. Antipathy of 30 would stick around awhile, no matter who next set up shop in bare-bones 3025. For her, it would be Gleizer, and the rancid aftertaste such meaningless interviews invariably left behind. *Elevator, elevator, come to Youtka!*

Grocery shopping mandated an A-1 priority. Judith's pantry housed only moldy bread, bouillon cubes, and hot cocoa mix; her refrigerator boasted minimal victuals: long-expired cottage cheese; one tin of peaches; a doggie bag of leftover Mongolian beef-likely rock-hard by now-and a half-finished liter of Chianti that was probably more vinegar than wine.

The elevator doors opened, finally, and Judith stepped forward...into Avraham Ya'rok coming out.

Well over six feet tall in a white, button-down shirt, a navy blazer, gray slacks, and loafers sans socks, Avraham towered over Judith by at least a head and shoulders, though he was surprisingly light on his feet for a hundred-kilo "hulker." His head was shaped like an inverted pear: beneath brown, crew-cut hair, Avraham's face was full halfway down before narrowing to sunken cheeks stretched tautly gaunt by circumstance as opposed to diet. Fierce independence flaring in black-olive eyes broadcast readiness to reclaim his due. Atonement having been made for past sins of commission, he was primed to move on.

Judith raised her hands to brake forward motion. Avraham

enveloped them up in his, raised them lipward for a palm kiss, then pulled Judith forward into a hug politely returned. But she quickly withdrew from the sociable, old-friend squeeze because Avraham was prologue...and ancient history was best left unexhumed.

"Coming or going?" Judith asked sharply, wanting immediate exit from the corridor and Gleizer's still-felt stare.

Avraham looked past her, nodded a brief acknowledgment to Gleizer's "Okay," then pulled Judith into the elevator. "Boss man can wait. So it's down with you." As the doors closed, Avraham jabbed the buttons lit for every other floor. "The better to provide us time for reacquaintance," he explained.

"Gleizer said you were behind my getting yo-yoed back in," Judith remarked, slouching, crossed-arm tired against the car's back wall as floor-marker lights blinked in downward track of progress.

"You overestimate me," Avraham replied with a toothy grin.

"Did you encourage Gleizer to pull me in?" Judith asked, as 26 came and went.

"I'm flattered you think I swing a heavy enough bat for that."

"You could have put a bug in his head."

"Gleizer's ear canals are blocked by tightly woven screens. Nothing gets in unless he opens the hatch."

"Even so..." Judith began, while waiting for the elevator doors to cycle on 24.

"I honestly know nothing more than commissary gossip: that you are tracker enough to make the Druze green with envy. Of course, Gleizer would want to talk to you, irrespective of whatever input I might have."

Judith said nothing while they stopped and started on 20.

"Fourteen hard cores," Avraham said, "and then the dean of disaster himself."

"Please, enough of my resume," Judith said, cutting him off before embellishment led to specifics...especially the name of which everyone was so proud, the one still swinging her around like an underweight schnauzer leashed to the hand of a sadistically abusive owner.

"Gleizer probably thought it advantageous to talk to the best."

"Why the big push to solve this one? It is not even our case."

"Everyone wants the blueprint on how TransPac 117 was finessed, the better to tighten security worldwide. If they can get to a plane in the United States, they can get to an aircraft anywhere. Besides, did you ever know us not to play for advantage when one could be had? Gleizer wants his fingers on the heartbeat of this investigation."

"He has other sources."

"Not a bloodhound like you."

"Is there a point to all this flattery?"

"Actually, there is." Avraham waited until her eyes locked on his. "I am the one who needs you."

Judith flashed a look of cold fury.

"It's not that," he said hastily, palms rising quickly as if to ward off physical assault.

"It better not be," she warned.

Avraham pushed EMERGENCY STOP, and the elevator car sighed to a halt. A multilingual, mechanical voice encouraged them to use the control panel's telephone to apprise Security of their immediate needs.

"That will set off alarms downstairs," Judith said.

"I need only a moment."

"Get us moving again. Remember what my dossier says about claustrophobia."

"You would never have gotten this far had that been the case," Avraham said, but he put the car back in motion anyway.

"Out with it."

"I have been less than idle during my time in the outhouse." And then, as if pausing for effect, Avraham said, "I have managed to develop a source on the TransPac affair."

"Why tell me?" she asked, impatiently checking the Colibri on her right wrist. "As I told you before, this is not our case. It crossed my path only because of cartographic convenience. And I learned nothing."

"But you are on it."

"Only vaguely, in a manner of speaking."

"Perhaps that is enough."

"For?"

"For what I have in mind."

"Take it to Gleizer directly. There is also Zvi. What better way to get you back into everyone's good graces?"

"Because I need corroboration, which only you can provide."

"Do I know this person?"

"Not unless you spent the last six months in Amman, and had known what questions to ask."

"Then how can I corroborate anything more than the time of day?" Judith asked, again glancing impatiently at her watch.

"You have this way about you. You know what answers don't hold water. You know when to press and when to pass. And as you are a woman, my source will be less jumpy and not as apt to bolt. You know as well as I do that if I serve up bogus bagels, my opportunity for reassignment to anything more than errand boy will evaporate faster than a snowball in the Sinai. This second chance will be my only chance. I showed bad judgment before; I dare not show it again."

"Truer words were never spoken."

Fourth floor gone. Almost there!

"You must understand, Judith. That other business wasn't my fault."

"What did your group do?"

Avraham smiled crookedly and looked away, embarrassed. "A better question would have been: 'What didn't we do?'"

"I see."

"No, you don't," he said, looking at Judith again. "Not really."

"So educate me."

"Look, I was sucked into it."

Not so surprising an assessment, she thought. Everyone found guilty by circumstance remains untarnished in their own heart. "You are not the first unfortunate to claim railroading. But knowing certain facts as I do, it is safe to say you were undone by grossly piggish ambition, all of which stemmed from your general lack of scruples and abject failure to play fair ball."

"Can't we let the past lie dormant for a moment? This lead is very important to me. If my source pans out, I am out of the back room and into the boardroom."

"Who is it?"

The elevator stopped on one. Judith brushed past the security guard's questions and crossed the lobby with Avraham in loping pursuit. She was glad for the traffic noise outside the building. As they headed for the taxi stand, she told him, "Okay. We are one-on-one now. Just you and me, and this street has no ears."

"In a minute."

"No! Right now, because I am flush out of patience!" Judith stopped walking, pushed up the sleeves of her windbreaker, and looked around in futile calculation of how far afield she'd have to travel for a hot dog worth its bun. "Have you got a cigarette?"

"I thought you quit."

"I did. But it is an on-again, off-again kind of thing. These days, mostly off."

"Judith, the liar hasn't been born who could pass your litmus test. Will you help me on this one? Please? I can't get in any deeper before taking this guy's temperature, and you're the only one I can trust. There's absolutely no one else I can turn to."

"Honestly?"

"No, actually crass and self-serving. The bottom line is that I'm tired of being Gleizer's errand boy."

"That is understandable."

"So you can see why I want back in. All the way in. Like the old days, before I got mixed up with Lakam."

"All right," she said finally, anxious to be gone. "When?"

"Tonight. It's all been arranged."

"Your place?"

"Too risky."

"Then where?"

"It's been set up."

"In advance of my agreement?"

"I have to see this through one way or another. With you or without you, it's something I have to do...whether I do it alone and it bites my ass off or whether you come with me to see if this guy's got only sand in his saddlebags."

"All right, all right! What time?"

"Pick you up at eight?"

"No. Better I should meet you."

"Eight p.m., then. The Cafe Lazy Eight."

"On Dizengoff."

"I'm glad you remember."

Judith looked Avraham hard in the eye. "And that is all either of us should remember. Do you understand?"

"Yes."

"Good. This is a favor for an old friend," she said coldly. "Nothing more."

"I understand, Judith."

"Just make sure that you do."

And then she marched angrily to the taxi stand, got into a cab, and without looking back gave the address of the little market two blocks away from her one-bedroom apartment on Dam Hamakabim. As the cabbie crunched gears at the starting gate of an energetic, racetrack journey, Judith fished pencil and paper out of her handbag and started working up a preliminary shopping list, the first item of which was: American cigarettes, any type.

The Cafe Lazy Eight on Dizengoff just south of Jabotinsky was a raucously impersonal, two-story current event that had already been closed down twice for liquor-law violations. Now ranking in bales of hard currency under its fifth new-management team in half as many years, the club lately tended toward metallic rock heavy with the nasal twang of plaster-cracking, highly amplified guitar.

Ceiling-mounted, multicolored strobes lasered the free-form, hardwood dance floor, turning shimmying figures into glowworms and fireflies of alien contour. Fashionably *outre* trendsetters streamed like harvester ants up and down two staircases leading to a horseshoe-shaped dining balcony. The upper level was decorated with this week's kitsch of neon-rimmed James Dean posters and set pieces from the movie "Giant."

Judith shouldered through swirling dancers while brushing off hand-grasping invitations to bump and grind in wild convulsions. She spied standing room next to the bar's pickup station and beelined there in time to order a double vodka martini from the overworked bartender who mistook her for a waitress. Halfway through the cocktail, Avraham glided up inch-close behind her, sweating heavily enough to have come right from a dance-floor workout.

"Okay," he gasped between hurried gulps of smoky nightclub air. "Curtain-up in about twenty minutes. I told him you're a photojournalist with *Black Star.*"

"Does your source have a name?"

"Eyad."

"Eyad who?"

"Eyad I-Don't-Know!" Avraham rasped. "Look, it's not as if he's listed in the telephone directory. But he's a talker, so he'll bite hard on the chance for media exposure."

"He won't live long enough to see his face in print if he spills bilge to the wrong people."

"So he's a paramilitary hanger-on with a streak of fatalism. What can I tell you?"

"To begin with, how about: 'Here's your camera'?"

"I told him you wouldn't bring one to a nighttime chat until you're convinced he's legit. Are you ready? You look ready. Talk to me." Avraham was suddenly an anxious pitching machine, lobbing fastball questions. "Are you okay with this? Are you in? I know, I know. I'm nervous," he sputtered, "and with good reason. There's a lot riding on this. For me, anyway. You've never been caught in this kind of three-way squeeze..."

"At least I never put myself there."

"...Gleizer; Zvi; the only service worth writing home about," Avraham whispered. "You've always been their golden girl."

His last two words set her teeth on edge, but she kept quiet for the sake of bygone days while Avraham rambled on.

"Remember—nothing fancy," he said. "I want your reading on his character. And just that. But real relaxed."

"You do not have to tell me how to do the job," she said, while chewing thoughtfully on an olive.

"Casual and offhand. Don't come on too strong and for God's sake, don't try to bust him."

"I am only the spray paint. You will not find 'takedown' listed anywhere in my job description."

"That's not what they said after Frankfurt."

The mention of Germany rattled Judith's bones. She polished off her drink in hopes of stilling the shivers, then massaged her ears in defense against the pounding, hard-rock beat.

"How did you find out about Frankfurt?"

"I was out of work, Judith; I wasn't out of touch."

"What does this Eyad know about TransPac 117?" she asked, eager to change the subject.

"Nothing."

"What?!" Judith leaned to Avraham and jabbed her right forefinger angrily into his chest. "You told me..."

"I told you that I had a source and that I wanted you along for a legitimacy test because you're damn near clairvoyant when it comes to smoking out skunks. If he's 24-karat, I'll work him, milk him, and he'll lead me through to paydirt. I'll even credit you in the write-up."

"Your generosity is overwhelming."

"I'm not one to forget friends when payback comes due. Are you ready?"

"Sure," she sighed. "Start your show-and-tell."

"What have you been drinking?" Avraham asked, suddenly alarmed.

"Nothing I cannot handle."

"Okay. None of my business. Sorry! Are you carrying?"

"You said I was a photojournalist, not a *pistolera.*"

"I have to know. In case they pat you down."

"Your friends better keep their hands off me. If your vouching is not good enough, the deal is off."

"They won't go for that."

"Good night then," Judith said, and started moving away from the bar.

"All right, all right," Avraham hissed testily as he grabbed her right hand. "We'll play it your way. Let's go."

"Where?" Judith asked, twisting her fingers free from Avraham's possessive grasp.

"To the meeting."

"But you said..."

"That we'd meet here, you and I, and we did. Okay? But my source wouldn't dare come this far north. He's an Aquarius."

"The water bearer."

"Right. And more comfortable at seaside. Come on."

It was a 12-minute cab ride to the marina at the end of Ben Gurion Boulevard. At the west end of the open-air square and mall of Kikar Atarim was the subterranean Frantic Antics Club, out of which thumped bass-heavy rock music whose seismic vibrations were strong enough to shake souvenirs in storefronts 100 yards away.

They stepped carefully over a passed-out drunk on their two-flight descent. The hairy, bear-faced bouncer energetically waved them in like oysters to the walrus. Frantic Antics' L-shaped inside was a fog-laced light show wafting curtain-like over chain-heavy leather freaks packed in tighter than canned anchovies and smelling three times worse.

Avraham plunged athletically into the melee masquerading as modern dancing and started clearing a path to the bar. Even with his mouth only inches from Judith's ear, shouting was the only way to communicate over the pounding clamor banged out by berserk musicians holding forth behind chain-link fencing protecting them from rowdy, foot-stomping fans.

"WOULD YOU LIKE ANOTHER DRINK?!"

"WHAT?!"

"I SAID..."WOULD YOU LIKE A DRINK?!'"

"NO!"

Judith's spine started itching as if under the onslaught of full-blown hives. Avraham's left hand tightened around her biceps as they plowed through human hostility pecking at them like Hitchcock's killer birds come to life.

"WHERE'S THIS MEETING?!" she yelled.

"OUTSIDE THE MEN'S ROOM!"

"CHARMING!"

"FIGURED YOU'D LIKE IT!" Avraham shouted, bulldozing his way forward while hauling a foot-dragging Judith after him. And then they burst free of the grinding crush of sweaty dancers. Fetid air, dope fumes, and stale cigarette smoke wafted like angry cumulus at the back of the club.

Frantic Antics' rear end was shaped like a garishly decorated tuning fork, and more Paris sewer system than Middle East beach funk. Segregated men's room and ladies' room lay at darkened ends of opposite arms, U-branching off a main corridor poorly lit by naked, low-wattage bulbs. Gaudy biker posters hung crookedly on paving-stone tunnel walls wet with salty condensation and smelling of pier moss. Judith held back as Avraham urged her to the left.

"You told me the men's room."

"That's right."

"You're on the wrong side!"

"No, Judith," Avraham whispered oozily, as if heavy work were finally done and he were gladly free of oppressive weight. "You're the one who's on the wrong side."

Avraham quick-stepped behind her, his left fist balling up her blue blouse collar. The muzzle of a Browning BDM semiautomatic jabbed quickly and emphatically between Judith's shoulder blades, then rapidly withdrew as Avraham shoved her rudely forward.

"Keep moving!" he hissed.

"You bastard! You sold out!"

"Not quite. I didn't sell out; I was pushed out...plucked clean by others with hands dirtier than mine. I was the one who got sold out. There's a big difference. After you're drop-kicked into that kind of cesspool, all bets are off."

Judith's sense of smell just then rang a welcome bell. Finally dead-tired of smoke-stink, her nose weeded through odored interference to telegraph Avraham's ongoing fidelity to Canoe...the cologne she once insisted he wear. "Never too much," she remembered counseling him. "Never let them smell you coming." And he had been such an apt pupil...learning all those early courtship lessons very well.

Good boy, Judith thought...because all during their progressively intensifying relationship, with Avraham so eager to please, Judith automatically filed for future reference just how far from her former lover the unique, perfumed aura extended. Smell x intensity expressed as a percentage of 100 = range...and Avraham, keenly desirous of writing *finis* to tonight's dirty work, was now too close for his own good but exquisitely placed for hers.

Judith pirouetted like a prima ballerina while slashing around with her right hand. The Browning spat lead with a deafening roar. Its 9mm slug caromed off cracked concrete and then zinged upward through a false ceiling bristling with rat traps and roach bait.

Judith blinked away blinding, muzzle-flash fireworks. Avraham cursed and backed off, his pistol leveling as sweetly perfumed air gushed like sachet cirrus through the just-opened ladies' room. Bustling, choreographed intrusion misdirected wavering focus. *Rearward!* Judith half-turned, distracted. *Three women! Reinforcements!* Then whirling back to confront Threat One—the gun and Avraham—*GONE!*

The tallest coke-freak transvestite behind did the needle work with a matador's finesse, the syringe tip going in sharply, painfully, just millimeters off Judith's spine. The intrusive metal sting immediately flowered into radiantly starred explosions of expanding numbness as brutally injected TDC animal tranquilizer blew out sequential banks of Judith's abruptly overloaded neural connections.

"Why, darlings," the first addict cooed, as its runny-nosed companions caught and held Judith in drooling suspension inches from the chipped-stonework floor. "It looks as if this poor dear has had one drink too many."

Inside Judith's silently screaming head, *WAAH... WAAAH...WAAAAH* gibberish droned like discordant 78 rpm records played at 33-1/3. With her brain jumping like popping corn on a sizzling hot plate, Judith pitched forward into a scatter-limbed, free-fall plunge through choking darkness.

CHAPTER 15
HANDIWORK

Nauseous...

DON'T VOMIT!

Upchuck...?

YOU PUKE, YOU DIE!

Judith's fluttering eyelids cracked open only millimetrically, as much because of the Herculean effort required as because it was safer to play dead until cogitation revved up to the point where first-grade math wasn't tougher than advanced calculus. Slit-lid peeks showed two guards' feet beyond the drip-stain arc of a massive pillar-pipe around which she was half-looped. Her faithful Colibri wristwatch had dutifully tracked the passage of 20 hours.

A harsh, neck-circling canvas gag was knotted intrusively behind her front teeth. Incremental movement revealed the particulars of bondage: fastened like a fatted calf at a Jaycee rodeo; wrists and ankles cuffed to their mates; body snuggling the chilly iron shaft; thickly rusted iron chain crescent-mooned around the far side of condensate-wet conduit, and knotted hands to feet.

The Mossad woman ran multiplication tables behind feigned sleep until her brain cleared enough to permit focusing on a hard-backed intruder exploring her mouth. The lack of long extension thankfully ruled out scorpion. Carapace, sharply digging mandibles, and six legs excluded the spider. The unwelcome visitor's antennae probed her swollen, dry tongue as if testing the meaty main course of an upcoming meal.

The insect was a squiggle away from triggering the gag reflex. Since throw-up would mean choking to death on aspirated vomitus, all Judith could do was eat the damned pest before it started serious chow-down on her...and hope for the best.

So when Mr. Bug appeared halfway finished with his patient circumnavigation of oral wonderland, Judith guided herself slowly through a carefully restructured recollection of the best meal ever consumed: upstate New York...Liberty, New York...Corey's Restaurant...veal parmigiana worthy of high treason.

Slowly now!

There waltzed the white-aproned waiter, S-turning balletically through densely packed tables...flourishingly positioning the thickly cheesed Italian repast.

Side order of steaming, secret-sauce spaghetti...almost ready!

NEARLY SMELLING IT...

Wafting garlic aplenty...

PREPARING TO TASTE IT...

Buttery-hot Italian bread...

LIPS BRUSH MILK-FED VEAL...

Yes!

REMEMBER FULLY NOW!

Magic cataracts thundered mighty fluid gushers, the water-starved prisoner furiously swallowed flash-flood saliva, and the critter was swept tumbling south easier than expected... wave-thrashed and spiraling down her esophagus with only a feebly protesting backstroke wriggle.

Then, as if incensed at having been callously hoodwinked, salivary-gland taps quickly screwed spitefully shut with nary a follow-up dribble, and Judith's mouth was dust-bowl arid again... but at least some protein was heading down to where it might do some good during troubled times ahead.

Both guards leapt to ramrod attention as the dank holding cell's heavy-oak door creaked partly open on rusted hinges screeching like needled chimps. Judith's eyes widened to the loudly rattling chains as warders got word that: "Abu Salak is waiting. Stomp the Mossad bitch awake if she's not already conscious."

Salak. S-a-l-a-k.

NO READING.

License having been given, each militiaman kicked Judith enthusiastically to confirm her presence in the land of the living. The belligerent gunmen wore the mixed-bag medley favored by veteran Lebanese street fighters: running shoes; faded jeans; sweatshirts; American web gear, and slung Kalashnikov AKM assault rifles...except these two were full-face wrapped in lampblack *ghutrahs*. Only sullen, ebony eyes showed through the headcloths' oblong openings.

The first came up behind Judith, wrapped breast-squeezing arms round front and hoisted...while his partner untangled and cast aside the iron chain linking wrists and ankles, and slightly loosened the dirty gag. With both legs sleepy-limb tingly, Judith stood knee-locked rigid in hopes of reducing liberties taken under the guise of holding her up.

"Under whose banner do you fight?" she asked in raspy, cotton-mouthed Arabic.

Sardonic laughter was their only reply.

"Nice merchandise," Front Boy judged. And apparently satisfied by lower-abdominal tension resisting hard-prodding fingers, he reported: "Strong loins. This bitch would deliver you many robust sons."

"How many times do you figure she'll take the rod?" Back Boy asked, grinding his crotch hard into Judith's immediately clenched buttocks.

"That would depend on how many hours you would allot me."

"Two, perhaps three."

"Could I possibly buy an extra?"

"If the price were right."

"Name it," Front Boy said.

"The still-beating heart of your firstborn."

"Consider it pledged. So bastardized a union would produce only mongrel offspring."

"So what then would be your tally?" Back Boy asked.

"I could easily give her five," his comrade judged with

an offhand shrug. "Maybe six, depending on how much tracer traffic scarred the night sky."

Cheap-thrill bump-and-grind continued unabated while Back Boy held Judith awkwardly arched in an intimate full nelson. Front Boy unbuttoned her blouse and poked questing, pumice-rough fingers between and all around her breasts and brassiere in a groping search for edged weaponry. Then he knelt, yanked up her skirt, and patiently long-stroked his exploratory way up and down rigidly tensioned legs.

Judith wriggled in a gagged protest of total denuding as her panties dropped faster than a grand piano off snapped crane cable...and Front Boy punched her hard in the stomach.

"Stand still!" he ordered.

"Hey! Easy does it," Back Boy complained. "The damned cunt just broke wind."

"Lucky you!" Front Boy shouted, forcing Judith's upper thighs apart for a crudely lingering vaginal search...after which attention wandered ticklingly rearward, where harsh, hiked-up anal violation dragged on interminably to the accompaniment of lewd snickering. Then privates were finally re-covered as wet fingers were wiped in Judith's sea-salted hair.

"We've snagged ourselves a plump one," Front Boy observed. "Tube-tight, too."

"I think we ought to get a piece. Don't you?"

"There's always something left over, providing you've got hard goods to barter."

"Hard goods are the one thing I got plenty of," Back Boy giggled, once more driving his crotch-bulge into hostage rear end.

"Nablus Billy will surely open her up a bit," Back Boy predicted.

The degrading body search completed, Front Boy opened the cell door wide enough for Back Boy to shove Judith out, then Front Boy yanked his captive leftward through pallid, bare-dirt corridors.

With her normally loping stride restricted to a yank-clank

12-inch shuffle, Judith small-stepped awkwardly, uncomfortable to the jangling cadence of ankle restraints marking inchworm progress. Four cells down the lamp-lit, right-angled passageway, the trio halted before a thick dungeon door.

While escorts awaited a response to knob-fisted pounding, Judith looked down, bewildered at her prosthetic left hand. The artificial member looked oddly real in cold propane light, its lone incongruity being four of five fingers sharing exactly matched diameters.

Only a critically close examination under near laboratory conditions revealed slightly dissimilar skin tone where the fake hand's plasticized surface met human flesh—a wide copper bracelet hid the wrist-circling fault line—but there was only so much modern science could do. After starting out with perfect equivalence, four-season weathering increased the disparity between real and surreal. But rather than opting for annual reskinning, Judith delayed fixing until the contrast between God's work and lab work was blatantly obvious. Routine maintenance simply dredged up too many bad memories.

Daydream reverie was rudely interrupted by Front Boy's slap to the back of the head, coupled with Back Boy's bruising kidney punch, both inducements forcing a stumbling lurch into the tropically moist interrogation room.

"I look forward to meeting you again," Judith mumbled over her shoulder with a boldly flirtatious wink.

"I don't think so!" Back Boy spat angrily.

"Let's wait and see," Front Boy hissed menacingly as he unslung his assault rifle, cocked the weapon, and pulled his back-stepping compatriot away.

The obese, foul-breath jailer hauling in fresh human catch looked more caricatured *bandito* than bully-beef Lebanese toady, so Judith christened him Garcia...while rating the blimpish Levanter for what he really was: every lost woman's scared-spitless nightmare come horrifically true.

"Enter," her interrogator said pleasantly, turning on a tape recorder, half-rising from his wheeled desk chair, and beckoning enthusiastically, as if inviting a duchess in for patrician high tea. "I trust that you are ready for the Levy Endgame."

Judith shrugged noncommittally as the thick-lipped, orangutan of a turnkey sat her down hard on a three-legged cast-iron stool. Cut through the bare-metal seat was a jagged, pie-slice opening through which male prisoners' testicles dangled nervously shrunken in chill-shriveled anticipation of the torturer's "special attention."

Fat Garcia slowly unwrapped the gag, his thick, grime-speckled fingers testing the resilience of lips, tongue, and gums... as if evaluating a thoroughbred's auction value. After "uh-humphing" phlegmy satisfaction, he turned away quickly and then spun back, holding a chipped glass to Judith's cracked-cork lips. She thirstily guzzled tepid tan water tasting strongly of purification chemicals, grateful for the swiftly gulped liquid's opening of parched mouth and throat. Immediate purposes having been served, the leering Garcia was curtly dismissed and ordered to lock the cell door on his way out.

While Judith waited for conversational cards to be shuffled and dealt, her eyes locked tight to the cruelly handsome features of Nidal Shafik, looking quite the underground power player in crisp camouflage fatigues and fully open black headcloth casually draped around his neck and over his shoulders.

And so now, as always...

IT COMES DOWN TO ONE-ON-ONE HORSE-TRADING.

Judith immediately knew that the mayor of Hebron, with his impeccably barbered hair, scimitar-curve nose, and black-grape eyes, was a man farther out of his league than he was physically removed from his election district. "It is always in their underestimation of our intelligence that their downfall will be found," Zvi once told her. On the face of it, indisputable proof of a superior officer's caustic evaluation lay in the fact that Shafik had "burned his cover," sacrificing anonymity in favor of confrontation in the tiny, nearly airless room.

But to Shafik's game plan, such unmasking matters little if I am to be killed...so I can safely assume that I am to be murdered, no matter what bargains he may offer or protestations he may make to the contrary. More to the point, Shafik is a cold-rolled link in the chain of events resulting in a well-managed extraction and passage through nearly airtight security to touchdown at an unknown destination. So perhaps, dear Zvi, the problem lies not so much in their underestimation of our intelligence as it lies in our underestimation of theirs.

The next 25 or so minutes of swapsy-barter chitchat would come easily, courtesy of Shafik's superlative, well-documented grasp of English. Arabic was more a second language than a first, thanks to upbringing in Attleboro, Massachusetts, and higher education at Yale University, from which the Palestinian graduated magna cum laude, clutching a master's degree in political science. Shafik's dossier noted that he thrived on compliments concerning his grasp of what was often thought to be a late-learned tongue.

"Having seen my face, you know that I cannot let you live," Shafik intoned gravely, his opening bid the notion that termination was his decision alone.

"We both know there is more to it than that. Identification in and of itself should not trouble you. For years, we suspected..."

"Oh I doubt that highly!" Shafik exclaimed, robustly derisive amusement rippling north and south along his muscular, middleweight frame. "Had there been even the vaguest idea, your Shin Bet would have plunged me headfirst into the brackish cistern of years-long administrative detention."

"Why was I brought there?" she sighed.

"It is I who will be asking the questions," Shafik replied matter-of-factly.

The question naturally posed would be why someone so highly placed in a so-far impenetrable, clandestine network would risk entrapment by casting aside camouflage to oversee a lowly tracking officer's liquidation.

Why has my rank in the slaughter game suddenly been notched up high enough to where Shafik's handlers take notice? I am not a front-line operative...

IN THE TRUE SENSE OF THE WORDS...

So why then would...?

THINK!

Death could be Forever's bunk mate...only once was I this close to greasing...confirmation coming only long after the fact...seven years ago...closer to eight by now...an anniversary for marking with celebration?... Colorado...if not for Michael...No!

NOT!...NOW!...THINK!

Still on tap were Shafik's sayonara sayings...from yet another killer invariably become voluble with intended victim and obfuscating real-life issues with lame explanations in the hope that the soon-dead would understand and forgive the assassin for his heinous crime.

"We really had no choice, you see," Shafik offered. "You are best known to us for the unrivaled talent that has been quite the nettlesome botheration over the past five, maybe six years."

"Which is?"

"You are the Mossad's best bomber-tracker. 'Eerily perfect' is the term insiders use to describe your extraordinary prowess."

"That information is hardly front-page news," she whispered hoarsely.

"You caught the world-renowned German bomber."

Judith coughed to cover quavering caused by runaway creepie-crawlies raveling crazily outward from her frost-sheathed spine. *Do not speak his name aloud, and chills will not rack my body!* "Notorious would be a more apt description. Infamous, perhaps."

"To you, maybe; however, he is more than godhead to us. And we do not want you catching this one."

"'We'?"

"El-Fahd el-Aswad," Shafik said, his flaring lady-killer grin showcasing wide, white teeth. The mayor's well-manicured thumb jerked casually over his left shoulder...yanking Judith's eyes toward the three-square-meter battle flag spiked to the hard-clay wall behind the camp table and swivel chair.

"Black Leopard."

"Of course," Shafik replied coolly. "You would liquidate

the man we are so looking forward to working with. What is this? You are surprised?"

"Only because you ended a sentence with a preposition," Judith lied, the taunt creating a momentary opportunity to pigeonhole Shafik's critically important admission for reworking ASAP.

"We know, through a mole in your mother's garden, that there is a kill-on-sight order out on this most honorable son of the jihad."

"Said rodent being Avraham Ya'rok, my travel agent for this tour into hell."

"Names...are unimportant," Shafik said, the time-delay brush-off telling hint that the interrogator knew nothing of *pisher.*

Which stood to reason.

SUCH HEAVY-CALIBER INFORMATION WOULD LIKELY BE SHIELDED BY METER-THICK WALLS OF TIERED COMPARTMENTALIZATION.

And knowing counterintelligence as a two-way street, Judith fed the tape recorder and the counterpart's warlords with: "Surely you know that Ya'rok is a triple agent."

"Of course, he is a triple agent!" Shafik scolded in skillful recovery. "And why am I not surprised that you have just now denounced him as such? Simply because you expect me to believe that everyone we turn nowadays plays three-way games," Shafik lectured.

The Mossad woman blocked out rambling rhetoric while silently reviewing the exactitude of English-proud Shafik's precise sentence structure.

The man we are so looking forward to working with. Future-oriented. Shafik had not said: The man we are working with. Could the bomber then be a wild card...with Shafik's controllers anxious to cement a hardcore deal with the doer?

Downside, there'd be no tracking the bomber through turned PLO contacts, watched safe houses, and infiltrated embassies allied with anti-Israel factions.

In the service of...but not taking orders directly from...PLO parent or any of that unholy umbrella organization's myriad splinter groups? Carl Gutierrez: TransPac could have been rigged by a freelance mechanic on an oil-money payroll. No network of support...skillful enough to knock down an airliner...working solely by solitary wits?

"Would you care to learn how we managed your extraction?" Shafik asked, clearly more intent on providing particulars than Judith was desirous of hearing them.

"All that matters is that I am treading slimy water in this stinking cesspool," she muttered. "Particulars are hardly worth mentioning."

"Perhaps you would care to barter responses for something tangible...something I am convinced would be most assuredly more to your liking."

"Which would be?"

"Mercifully quick death, if your answers jibe with current reality, and if you tell me all that I want to know. But if you won't help me...."

"Surely you could not have believed I would," Judith chided, surveying the claustrophobic room as if sizing up wet-clay walls for bookcases and bric-a-brac.

"I had hoped," Shafik shrugged. "If only to make things easier for you."

"Thank you for so kindly considering the easement of my situation," Judith replied acidly.

"All right then, enough of this stupid, delaying game."

"All of which has been your doing alone."

"You have made your choice of your own free will; now I shall make mine. I can promise that initially you shall be taken at least seven times in each of your three major orifices," Shafik vowed solemnly. "Perhaps more, perhaps less...depending upon your stamina and the virility of those who will abuse you. My grossly corpulent jailer friend..."

Who is where, goddammit?!

"...is a very impatient man, relentless in his enthusiastic quest to satisfy myriad sexual appetites. You understand, of course, that shouts for help would be totally wasted effort on your part."

"So I had guessed by the decayed-flesh odor of this polluted, underground catch-place."

"No sound that you might possibly make will likely penetrate meter-thick dungeon walls."

And who would care if it did? "May I have another drink of water?"

"Who is your controller?"

"I have no answer for that."

"Therefore, I have no water for you."

"You ask so much for so little."

"From my perspective, potable liquid would appear to be a most precious commodity. Under the circumstances, I don't think you are being overcharged."

"I suppose it is all relative."

"Even Einstein would agree."

"Screaming would be of no avail, then."

"A waste of breath and time," Shafik said, yawning with ho-hum detachment. "Are you disappointed? No doubt you would have expected more from someone of my considerable charm and breeding," Shafik said with a polite chuckle, "but then first and foremost, I am a politician."

"Most assuredly."

"So you really should have known that I would not act in contravention to my own self-interest."

"And yet one of such obvious social station would be expected to at least keep his promise."

"How so?" Shafik inquired sincerely.

"Regarding the swiftness of my demise."

"Ah, but that was only in case you agreed to cooperate," the mayor noted wryly, "which you did not."

"But after providing the information you sought, what guarantee would I have that you would keep your word?"

"Indeed," Shafik sighed. "In the end, this whole rotten business does, in fact, boil down to trust."

"Which neither of us has for the other."

At that, the mayor reached underneath the rough-hewn table and pulled up a policeman's nightstick, the skull-crusher pommel of which he slammed with measured emphasis into the grooved and pitted tabletop, as if seeking to rein in the wandering attention of clearly bored students.

"Allow me to introduce the latest addition to your social circle," Shafik rasped, all cordiality drained from his voice. "We call him Nablus Billy, and believe me, he is guaranteed to get your goat. Pay close attention to the embedded nails. See how carefully they are driven through the first thirty-five centimeters of hardwood shaft. Each surgically honed tip protrudes exactly one millimeter on the club side opposite the nail head. My niece devised this dandy tool six weeks after she was picked up outside the Balata Refugee Camp, then gang-raped by three members of your national police for the...'crime'...of going to the aid of demonstrators."

"I am familiar with the riot about which you speak," Judith interrupted angrily. "They were not demonstrators. *They were homicidal maniacs!* Six Palestinians were killed, their heads bashed in by lead pipes wielded by thugs on your side."

"Or your agents wearing our colors," Shafik countered.

"Since you were so capably ravaging your own, why should we have bothered?"

"Because no pot in the worldwide theater of operations ever escapes your meddlesome stirring."

"Regarding your niece and this...alleged...sexual assault, we never received even an inkling's worth of detail on it. Furthermore, no charges of rape were ever filed with..."

"What good would that have done?!"

"More than you might think!"

"She was knocked down windless by rubber bullets," Shafik said, suddenly flipped-switch calm, "then picked up and beaten, raped, and left to die with broken arms in a roach-infested drainage ditch two miles outside of Haifa."

"No such attack ever took place," Judith retorted, iron-jawed and defiant.

"And how did you come to be so all-fired sure?" Shafik asked snidely.

"Because I make it my personal business to follow up on such reports and to ensure that severe countermeasures are taken against the guilty."

"Next, you'll expect me to believe that you and I are on the same side."

"Certain offenses are never tolerated."

"Apparently, my niece's case escaped your all-seeing eyes."

"Highly unlikely."

"My, but you are insufferably arrogant."

"While you would be much better off indicting PLO extremists, instead of targeting the usual, convenient scapegoat."

"Rabid dogs are treated with more compassion than she was that night," Shafik droned. "During touch-and-go recovery, she maintained marginally buoyant sanity by designing in her head the device I hold here. She lives in the hope of one day being privileged to use Nablus Billy on her assailants."

"Look to your own backyard, instead of to my side's noncombatants shot, rocketed, and stabbed by terrorist vermin too numerous to count."

"In the Middle East, everyone is a combatant."

"Such an overly broad classification would surely include your niece!"

"Unlike yourself, I distinguish between casualties of war and war crimes."

"Not so your handlers," Judith scoffed. "You know as well as I that the claws of Black Leopard are smeared crimson with the blood of dead Palestinians hanging in trees all over the West Bank."

"Collaborators!"

"Innocents!"

"So, at one time, was my niece," the Shafik crooned, "who knew full well that it would be counterproductive to inflict too much damage too soon. And so it's...IN!" the mayor raged, surging anger behind his upwardly angled thrust, "then twist every so slightly...and OUT! IN! OUT! IN! OUT! YES?! I see that now you are perhaps beginning to understand."

Only that you really need no excuse...and that we are doomed to remain at loggerheads forever.

Shafik stroked the club, closely examined brown-flaked, nail-point blood, then used Nablus Billy to bang random, tabletop holes. The Mossad woman's stoop-shouldered slump ignited flaring pleasure in her adversary's darkly sedate eyes, which was just as well, thinking as Judith was about...

Matters more closely at hand...

WRIST MANACLES; LEG IRONS. IT WOULD NOT DO TO BE SEEN BUNNY-HOPPING DOWN THE HALL.

And the portal. Having been secured from outside, said door must be unlocked before...

GAMBITS METAMORPHOSE FROM THOUGHTS TO ACTION.

"Your new paramour will soon be summoned," Shafik announced.

"I can hardly wait," Judith mumbled while concentrating hard on the specifics of rudimentary basics.

Getting back home will be job enough; however, success there cannot possibly be anticipated until short-term victory has been won here, which means that my first priority is achieving release from restraints.

"I will now grant you a few moments to make your peace with your God," Shafik proclaimed with pompous self-importance. "I urge you to make the best possible use of your limited time."

"Thank you."

"My pleasure."

Finally fully weary of his one-sided game, Shafik pressed the table rim's call button. Eighty-three Colibri nik-niks later... after closing the heavy door slowly and respectfully, lest haste be misinterpreted as rudeness, depriving him of a desperately desired gift...Garcia stood drooling patiently and nodding rhythmically at instructions accompanying his craved reward.

"Use her wisely and well," Shafik told the jailer, "then dispose of the meat as you see fit."

The keys to handcuffs and leg irons at last close by on Garcia's hand-tooled leather belt. With the interview over and nothing more to be learned, the Mossad woman made ready to raise the destructive game's stakes to their lethal limit.

Judith pressed together her thumbs' fleshy bases. There came a silent click under artificial skin. She looked down in quick verification of the left thumbnail's single blink, the bright-light pulse slightly more ruby than the polish decorating the other left-hand fingers.

Confirmation of time to rock and roll.

Her crooked grimace reflecting nervous anticipation of looming unpleasantness, Judith quickly lifted both manacled hands 90 degrees to the upper body...edge of left braced in the cup of right...outstretched, shared-diameter fingers parallel-aimed directly at the nakedly exposed face of Nidal Shafik, who in the expiring milliseconds of his earthly life suddenly tumbled to the realization of rogue events gone completely and fatally wrong.

The Arab's eyes went glassy-wide as Judith jabbed her right thumb into her left palm. A sharp crack traced the flight path of a modified 5.45mm Russian short round exploding out from Judith's prosthetic forefinger to punch point-blank through Shafik's vulnerable forehead, just above his arched eyebrows. The mayor's neck snapped back broken, his castered chair drifting in reverse as the pinwheeling bullet punched out the back half of his head to spray blood, brains, and bone-dripping particulate matter across the bottom-right corner of the punctured Black Leopard flag.

Each 5.45mm's hollow tip and rearward center of gravity ensured the bending of the steel-core nose immediately upon entry...after which the deformed slug's tumbling passage guaranteed infliction of wounds much larger than so small a caliber would otherwise suggest. And so with three cartridges still in inventory—middle finger, ring finger, and pinky—Judith whirled abruptly toward the fear-frozen jailer and gave him two in the belly as gut-shot vengeance for brutality inflicted so callously upon others.

The first bullet fractured Garcia's hipbone, then angled vertically and tore bottom-to-top through food-filled stomach before coming to rest just under his diaphragm, where the deformed chunk of lead burned like a brazier of blazing lava rock. The second shot lacerated the lower intestine and ripped the common iliac artery before whirling upward over the pelvis to smash the spine.

Garcia immediately crashed hard to the floor over crumpled, nonfunctioning legs...striving mightily to hold his chest upraised on locked elbows and flat palms...already sweating heavily from excruciating pain putting insides to the torch. The jailer managed only hollow wheezes of choking gulps as blood seeped through soiled uniform pants to pool between gone-dead legs.

Judith's nose puckered in full retreat from the overwhelming stench of body fluids commingling with excrement. She stared somberly at the corpse of Nidal Shafik, sorry that intelligence could not be extracted into a distillate before brain-spray-drenched earthworks. Then she hobbled over to Garcia, relieved him of his key ring, undid handcuffs and leg irons, and staggered backward onto the stool while assessing personal damage.

Left-hand fingertips resembled blackly bubbled cheese melt. Shredded, smoking strips of charcoaled sheathing hung drip-frozen from insensate fingers. The Mossad woman pulled hard on burned, drag-stretch rubber...becoming increasingly frantic the longer sooty, plastic skin resisted before snapping free of oxidized metalwork.

Scorched polystyrene composite's nauseating smell sickened Judith terribly, finally doubling her over into gut-wrenching, acrid-bile heaves while she physically waved off Yad Vashem's Holocaust imagery of...

...DACHAU...

...BUCHENWALD...

..."The air was sickly sweet..."

...TREBLINKA...

Germany?

NOT FRANKFURT!

...wheezing through violent, jackknifing spasms...until some semblance of respiration finally replaced hackly retching and her wind came slowly back.

Nine gaping-mouth breaths finally unfogged Judith's head. She wiped her mouth, face, and brow on the damp skirt's hem, checked her normalizing pulse, and felt around for cigarettes that weren't there. Then she pushed off the stool and trudged unsteadily over to retrieve the mayoral sidearm—a rare, fully automatic Stechkin 9mm pistol. Regrettably, the weapon's unique wooden holster would stay clipped to Shafik's waist. Too much deadweight, Judith thought...avoiding death-stare eyes while shoving the Stechkin into the skirt's left-side waistband, butt forward for cross-body draw. Then she picked up Nablus Billy.

Garcia's faltering elbows shook violently in their failing attempts to hold the upper body erect as Judith unholstered the fat jailer's PA63 9mm semiautomatic pistol and placed it butt-first in the skirt's right-side waistband. Then the Mossad woman knelt, grabbed the dying man's chin, jerked his head up, and force-fed him the full, nail-studded shaft of the torture device. Grunting with the bend-over pressure it took, she made Garcia swallow Nablus Billy whole.

His upper body alive enough to rebel against the awful pain of hobnailed intrusion, Garcia's eyes widened with the gagging triggered by executioner's body-weight downthrust... she huffing scarlet with the clumsy pushing needed to overcome constricted gullet's resistance to oversize rod. After 12 inches of choking, nail-scrape invasion, the rotund jailer's chest heaved once...and he died.

"Payback," Judith murmured, "you...miserable...son of a... bitch."

And down payment on what? she stood up, wondering. *New hunt's opening act? Once more on the trail of yet another psychotic bomber?*

YES!

No! There are too many violent weeds, and I am not chopper enough to trim them all. Why me?!

BECAUSE OF A DEEPLY PERSONAL LOSS IN A TERRORIST BOMBING.

Israeli Independence Day...Aqaba Gulf shore...The Dream...

NOT!...NOW!

...father and left hand both. It was more than any child should be asked to pay!

SO WHO ASKED?!

Judith shivered like a dog shaking water, and drag-baggage considerations sloughed off. She bypassed the still-running tape recorder...

Two abduction teams tracking Ya'rok's spoor are better than one.

SHAFIK'S DEATH BOLSTERS THE ACCUSATION.

...and retrieved both men's IDs; Mossad could always use legitimate paperwork.

After racking each gun's slide, she tucked cocked pistols back into her skirt and wrapped the tarnished artificial hand in the rag gag removed...

...two lives-lifetimes?-ago?

NOT!...NOW!...THINK!

And so she did...carefully pulling the stout-oak door open a crack, holding her breath while listening, then slowly inching her head out for a detailed, east-west look. Spectral corridor's yeasty, gunpowder-pungent air was fragrantly interwoven with energizing bazaar-spice aromas...in markedly sharp contrast to the blood-slick stink permeating the room behind.

The Mossad tracking officer eased out, watchfully careful and quietly closed the heavy door. Airflow was left to right, so she moved in the direction of the draft, hugging the wall Stechkin-ready while nosing her way upward from subterranean killing ground.

Getting home was Judith's singular priority...and that would be no walk in the park.

CHAPTER 16

SMALL CHANGE

Zvi nibbled apathetically at 11 a.m. lunch's tuna salad in pita bread, slightly ill at ease on an evergreen-shaded bench downwind from a Shin Bet-run refreshment kiosk on Rothschild Boulevard. The crisp clarity of December morning's 53-degree weather steam-cleaned his brain of the previous night's alcoholic overindulgence. Fresh breezes blew out dust balls and 86-proof aftertaste, while complexioning him winter-ruddy and loosening sniffle spigots.

The intelligence officer spot-scanned the street from park-bench slouch: legs stretched out in denim jeans, hiking shoes crossed at the ankles, mind-grilling concepts on the barbecue spit revolving slowly over the always-glowing coals of shrewd intellect. Zvi drifted back to pondering Avraham Ya'rok's despicably vile treason and what that betrayal almost cost the Mossad man personally. Then there was the high-stakes horse race described in Judith's debriefing report, a write-up so coldly analytical that it bordered on snide. The Other Side was apparently chumming terror-bloodied shoals to lure in the murderous shark and pay whatever it took to cement a hard-core, long-term deal for exclusive employment...with the free world trying to cap the homicidal freelancer before the elusive son of a bitch stepped forward to personally claim his already-earned niche in the Guinness Book of World Records.

At least then we'd have him, Zvi reckoned. But as for now, insufficient data precluded preparation of even the most basic deadfall trap...with the doer clearly having shown himself in league with at least three clearly defined groups—Arabs, and most recently a German-Irish bastards' brew, depending on who autographed the explosions blooming like olive groves in springtime.

And then the Mossad officer got the wake-up call, tugging him halfway up and borderline alert in response to a portable phone's summons...the trilling chirr-reep/chirr-reep warble gusting through morning's shade-tree relaxation.

Zvi withdrew the flip-phone from his outside jacket pocket and unfolded the compact communications device. Scrambler circuitry automatically engaged at switch-on; nothing traveled "clear" these days, especially when dime-store scanner electronics were fully capable of tapping into portable-phone transmissions. And the way the wind kept shifting, the Shin Bet junior operative a few yards away could likely hear Mossad's end of the conversation even without leaning too obviously over the serving counter's edge.

After checking the battery level, Zvi held the phone up to right ear, leaned left, and opened the bidding with a soft, *"Boker tov."*

"And good morning to you, too," grunted David Blumberg at "off-campus" Laboratory 14, as joyless an individual as Zvi had stumbled across in his long years of undercover work.

"And to what do I owe the honor of this call?"

"The coins found at the L.A. bombing," Blumberg stated flatly, pausing long enough for Zvi to silently debate if the research man's voice ever rose even one quarter note above wooden monotone.

Probably not, Zvi figured as he replied: "Deutsche-mark coins. All minted in 1950. Battle symbol of the National Socialist Common Action Group, the ANS."

"Them. Right."

"So what prize have I won?"

"Perhaps a trip to the Golden State."

"As long as I have you on the phone, would you be good enough to handle my flight arrangements?"

"I hear you are still of the opinion that ANS blew the package truck."

Zvi's twitching nostrils flared at the uncharacteristically upbeat lilt in Blumberg's voice, swirling as it was with the tangy aromatics of dangled bait. But for the Mossad officer, it was just too pretty a morning to rise immediately to the hook, however tempting the tidbit, and so he said, "Yep. Working like Bobbsey Twins with the Provisional Wing of the Irish Republican Army."

"Motive?"

"Motives. Plural. The 1950 mint mark commemorates the birth year of Heinrich Biermann, recently deceased chief and war minister of the ANS; the bombing balances the books for his death under the guns of GSG 9."

"Shot dead during the German raid on the terrorists' regional headquarters. According to the pathologist's report, Biermann's torso stopped enough lead to make five kilos of sinkers," Blumberg noted.

"That's the official history."

"Caught half a dozen nines in the noggin, too."

"Spare me the grislies."

"And the Irishmen?"

"Yeah." Judith's report had contained a sketchy notation of a bagpiper and a dirge.

"How would the Provos benefit from so unholy an alliance?"

"What're we playing here? Twenty Questions?"

"Could be," Blumberg crackled back.

"Credit for future help, when they need staff and support in Europe, specifically every December when IRA poppies start blossoming in Great Britain around Christmastime."

"Which isn't so great anymore."

"England, then."

"Much better."

"One subversive hand washes the other."

"Okay, so then why the bombing in California?" Blumberg challenged openly-Clue Two that something more potent than decaf was brewing in the coffeemaker, Hint One having been principal-to-principal contact, as opposed to message routing through Secretarial.

But Zvi willingly labored through the tease, if only because relaxing in Tel Aviv's unusually pollution-free daylight was a luxury often pined for and frequently missed. It was simply too nicely crisp a winter morning to swap...without decent reason... brilliant, soul-energizing sunshine for the dull fluorescents under which moles basked while playing shadow games for which few inviolable rules were written.

"Zvi?!" Blumberg rasped anxiously, as if fearful of losing his last, tenuous link to the outside world. *"You still there?!"*

"As opposed to California, maybe?"

"Why an American target?"

"Likely because Newsweek reported U.S. intelligence as providing the fingerman cross-hairing the quarry," the Mossad officer recited. "A senior CIA operative made Biermann as he waded ashore at La Spezia, Italy, posing as a fisherman. Sir Spook trailed Biermann through Milan to Zurich, and finally to Mannheim. GSG 9 stepped in and took down the ANS neo-Nazi in Dortmund, while also notching their belts with eight of the running dog's skinhead comrades in arms."

"ANS Manifesto 743 states unequivocally that Biermann's killing was a preplanned assassination."

"They always do; those broadsides are printed long in advance, the same way big-city dailies write and file obits today for usage tomorrow."

"Actually, I've got to admit the ANS makes a pretty good case for their side of what happened."

"No doubt you would."

"So you still think it was retribution?" Blumberg pressed.

Still?

The loaded adverb added only a grain of starch to Zvi's spine, nowhere near enough to shift primary focus from French-curve lines delineating the harden/loosen passage of particularly well-sculpted high-heeled calves...and the cock-throb salesgirl to which they were so artfully connected.

"Payback? Sure!" Zvi lectured. "Revenge is still the

universal currency of the terrorist underworld. One side does the other and then gets done in return. We're supposed to be better at it than they are, so we specialize in two-for-one sales, and usually come out on top."

"Watch out, they don't soon start calling you Wrong-Way Corrigan," Blumberg chuckled smugly. "You're far astray."

"On ANS and IRA?"

"You getting static on your phone?" Blumberg asked rhetorically. "That's what I said, that's what I meant."

Game called on account of horseshit, Zvi thought, voice hardening as he shook loose a cigarette, lit up, and asked: "What've you got?"

"Not over the phone."

"This is a secure line."

"What isn't these days?" Blumberg countered contemptuously. "I'm talking physical evidence. It's something you'll have to check out with your own two."

"See you in thirty."

"I'll be at lunch."

"Postpone it," Zvi grumbled, and then he clicked off.

Twenty minutes of corner-cutting driving put Zvi's Sunbeam V8 parked half-assed crooked in ParaCon Technology's tow-away zone. He walked rapidly across the lab's neatly yellow-striped parking lot while toting up the factors shoving science whizzes..."whitefish," he called them...down to power structure's subcellar. Their irritating smugness was the mile-thick fog perpetually choking Zvi like inversion-trapped smog...the superciliousness—or super-silliness—Blumberg's ilk wore like a cheap whore's toilet water.

As the laboratory door clicked shut, Zvi engaged conversational gears with: "So? I'm here, and we're well past hunky-dory pleasantries. Let's talk numismatics."

The Mossad man's meditative counterpart, however, was in no immediate rush to discuss business...and Zvi knew that forcing the issue would be counterproductive.

David Blumberg's penetrating sapphire eyes bordered on deep-Pacific blue. Rugged Norseman's face was bisected by a fish-fin nose. Electrostatic hairstyle and wildly unkempt ash-blonde beard cried out futilely for barber's ministrations. The stocky, stained-smock science analyst wore his usual "cologne" – the acrid, metallic reek of stale Canola oil that had fried one too many hot-plate greaseburgers.

Blumberg rarely took leave of the three-room cluster lab that the headquarters nicknamed "The Hermitage." The science recluse had a shower installed, slept in a curtained alcove within leapfrog distance of test instruments and gauges, and left his workplace only for the Days of Awe, the 10 days of repentance between Rosh Hashanah and Yom Kippur.

"Those deutsche-mark coins," Blumberg said, blinking distractedly, as if slowly regaining consciousness on ascension from the melancholy depths of bottomless trance. "Calling cards the ANS left in LA, or so you thought."

"Still do," Zvi replied glibly, "since the more time going by without your coming clean, the longer you're withholding evidence that might convince me otherwise."

"That *will* convince you otherwise."

"We'll see."

"Sole and solitary?"

"Nope. In concert with co-conspirators," Zvi said, lighting a cigarette over Blumberg's hand-flurry protestations.

"Why do you always do that when you know I don't like it?!"

"As an inducement for you to start warbling the song you've been rehearsing for God knows how long before you called. The sooner you start hawking your wares, the sooner I'll be on my way."

The science expert unlocked a lab table drawer and pulled out a rubber mat to which six, one-deutsche-mark coins were loosely mounted, alternating heads and tails. He laid the mat carefully atop the laboratory counter.

"Zvi, these came from bunches scattered like an eight-kilometer wreath around the crater left when that truck got vaporized into molecular dust."

"With the money surviving an explosion damn near as hot as a nuclear furnace."

"Because it was specially prepped to," Blumberg commented knowledgeably, handing Zvi a thick-lensed magnifier with lightly tinted glass. "Check them out."

"I already did...as soon as they were airfreighted across."

"Consider humoring me, being as I'm your docent for the guided tour," Blumberg said good-naturedly. "Please repeat the exercise, as futile as you may think it to be."

Zvi took the magnifying glass and carefully examined the fronts and backs of several coins. "I see nothing out of the ordinary."

"Didn't think you would. Not yet, anyway."

Reaching around to the side of the lab counter, Blumberg killed the overhead fluorescents, then pulled over and flicked on a blue-bulbed lamp.

"Close-in optical examination showed only the usual tarnish and circulation scrapes coins like these pick up during forty-five-year drifts through national monetary systems. So there was no way to draw any conclusion other than the one stemming from such tempting bait."

"Ha-Konseptzia."

"Right. 'The Concept' we all swallowed like starving salmon."

All except Judith, Zvi remembered ruefully.

"It was Arno who thought to try magnafluxing," Blumberg said, remaining true to the investigative credo of always giving credit where credit was due. "I don't know why he thought of it, but that's Arno for you."

"Magna...who?"

"Magnafluxing...the magnetic-based technology used to scan metal for stress-related problems that can lead to killer failure."

Blumberg dragged over the lamp until the coins were bathed in circular, bluish-purple light.

"Like X-rays?" Zvi asked.

"Nope. Magnafluxing is nondestructive, noninvasive testing. Simply put, we film-coat what we're testing, run it through a box with a lot of wiring and electricity..."

"Thanks for the boil-down."

"...and find metal-fatigue indicators before they become real, live problems. That's what Arno suggested we do with the coins. Now take another look."

Zvi did...and immediately saw that on the mint-date side of the coin, blue highlighting raised into bold relief stress ripples angling across the letters "AR" in Deutsche Mark.

"Magnafluxing revealed what's been chemically enhanced here for your visual enlightenment: that the midcoin insides of the A and the R are infinitesimally wavy, the crest of each oscillation rising only a fraction of a millimicron higher than the respective trough, with only the slightest indentation impressed into the reverse side, on which push force was applied. The gent leaving these messages is no barnyard mechanic," Blumberg said respectfully. "He's better than good. He doesn't screwdriver-scrape messages on the surface. A grade-school microscope would have picked that up immediately. He puts it underneath. You've got to really excavate what's subsurface on the alleged monogram."

"So he was jerking us off?"

Blumberg's chaotically disheveled hair bobbed in humble concurrence.

"And you're telling me that he's telling us 'AR.'"

"Louder and clearer than a Texas longhorn at full bellow, according to said signature massaged into the money."

"How?"

"With digitized, metalworking equipment of leading-edge sophistication, probably coupled to sonic-application software."

"Like sound waves used to pound-crush kidney stones into tiny, passable grains," Zvi remarked.

"That was the pilot model. Now, rocket ahead twenty-five generations."

"Not exactly what I'd expect to find at the corner hardware store."

"Nor even in most machine shops," Blumberg noted, "being as a precision tool capable of turning out this kind of work starts at around $10.8 million American, and can't be shipped abroad without U.S. State Department and Pentagon export-license approval. We're talking missile work, aircraft manufacturer, the armaments industry generally...likely armored fighting vehicles specifically. This guy is a first-class, supremely skilled machinist, and whether or not he owns this particular piece of hardware, which I doubt highly, considering its size, price, and inherent portability problems, he definitely had access to the best."

"Had? Not has?"

"I said the guy was skilled, Zvi, not stupidly repetitive. You're not likely to see the same scamwork twice, no matter how proficient he is."

"What about the other coins?"

"We stopped 'fluxing after the first dozen," Blumberg said nonchalantly, mooching a cigarette from Zvi and firing up with an antique, World War I trench lighter.

"I didn't think you indulged."

Blumberg drew the smoke in deep, exhaled heartily, and replied, "Only when I get nervous. Zvi, we could have checked ten, twelve, or a hundred thousand. But why bother? The half dozen I have here are the same as all the rest."

"You're sure?" Zvi asked in eager grasp for straws.

Blumberg nodded sagely. "Believe me. So artfully done that they'll work in vending machines, entertainment turnstiles, peep shows, or the best coin-sorting machinery available at any branch of the Deutsche Verkehrs-Kredit-Bank. You name it, these coins will feed it with nary a jam."

"So even if he'd misplaced a bag or two, there would have been no chance of a bad feed tipping his hand early in the game."

"A guy like this doesn't misplace anything."

"You think he's that good?"

"After what you've seen and heard of TransPac and L.A.,

that couldn't have been a serious question. Anyway, I'm just sketching in some background. Foreground painting is your specialty."

"Cute."

"Cute's for baby pictures, Zvi. We're talking professional. First the ankh and now these coins," the scientific investigator noted dourly.

"So what you're telling me is..."

"Write off CIA vs. ANS, and the IRA connection," Blumberg affirmed, "which was a weak-sister theory to begin with. Forget everything but this: TransPac was Act I, and L.A. was Act II of another abu developing toward full manhood faster than the gourd growing up to shelter Jonah after his prophesying sashay through Nineveh."

"Any chance our doer will wither just as quickly?"

"It's gonna take more than some God-made superworm to make this perp eat dirt and die."

"In Palestinian service?"

"Whoa," Blumberg protested. *"You're asking me?!"*

"Any and all input would be seriously welcome."

"Could be that he's bankrolled by monies diverted from the $120 million the generous Saudis spoon-fed Hamas over the past four years. Maybe he's financed by the mullahs' $60 million kick-in. Heard anything much from the Libyans these days?" Blumberg asked. "After the decades I've put into this business, it's not hard to get a feel for what's coming down. And simple intuition tells me that the father of whatever the R stands for has got in his hip pocket a sensational player. I'm talking about a seasoned, one-man wrecking crew whose per-capita damage scores make a team of U.S. Navy SEALs look like newborn goslings."

"So Abu R gets added to the passenger manifest," Zvi muttered softly.

"You can't really expect me to believe he's not on the hit list already," Blumberg observed with a wry grin.

Zvi conceded the point. "In the company of, among others,

Abu al-Abbas, Abu Alam, Abu al-Rahim, Abu Bakr, Abu Daoud, Abu Hassan, Abu Ibrahim, Abu Iyad, Abu Khaled, Abu Moussa, Abu Muhammed, Abu Nidal, Abu Tayib, Abu Zaim, and so on, and so on...*ad nauseam."*

"Surely they don't all wield enough clout to run our boy."

"A few do, but nowhere near all."

"Though there's more than enough for some serious whittling."

"All targeted. If we get orders to take them down, we will."

"But not too hastily," Blumberg admonished.

"Heaven forbid that we should arbitrarily upset the cosmic balance."

"What the hell does that damned R stand for?" Blumberg brooded.

"Abu R." Zvi pondered the enigma momentarily. "We'll find out later," he said confidently. "We always do."

"We've got ah-boos coming out the wah-zoo," Blumberg cracked.

"Which is nothing new. How about the Wire Works?"

"We A-to-Z'd it through every Black Ops computer in the world."

"East and west?"

"Top to bottom, North Pole to South, ours and theirs. I made sure everyone got tapped."

"As an update to the ankh?"

Blumberg nodded patiently.

"And you heard nothing?"

"You would have been among the first to get word."

"But not the first?" Zvi inquired half-seriously.

"One way or the other, the Butcher is always the first to know."

"Sorry, I asked."

"Remorse counts for naught," Blumberg laughed.

Blumberg flicked on the overhead fluorescents and picked up the ringing phone. "Worried?" Blumberg asked while helloing the caller.

Zvi nodded as the science expert said, "You're not the only one. It's the Director's secretary, with your name on her lips."

"Why not the Butcher's?" Zvi groused in genuine disappointment.

"Because it's your turn in the barrel."

The Mossad officer took the receiver and reported on the linkage Blumberg described, then listened for a moment, nodded grimly, and hung up.

"So?" Blumberg asked.

"So it's none of your business," Zvi said lightly, his red ears telling Blumberg that the Mossad man's instructions were both harshly severe and brutally direct.

"Dispatch before dawn?" Blumberg asked idly.

Zvi pulled on his jacket and turned to go.

"Not even a hint?" Blumberg wheedled, but the Mossad officer said nothing on his way out because Blumberg's pecking-order perch was nowhere near "need-to-know."

CHAPTER 17
DUTCH TREAT

Those living on...working the coastline of...or vacationing along the banks of Sweden's Lake Siljan chuckled good-naturedly while hoisting beers in discussion of the scrawny, hermetic "Eric the Red."

Often the sole subject of boisterous campfire gossip, Eric the Red was fleece-complexioned and lanky, with rarely focusing bronze-brown eyes and rust-colored, pony-tailed hair. Self-barbered locks extended just past a belt made of reef-knotted, half-inch lanyard holding up pants roughly cut from storm-ripped canvas tarp. His upper-body wardrobe was whatever burlap bag happened to be available, though no expense was spared when purchasing custom-made deck shoes.

The muzzy mariner patrolled in perennial exile, giving other boaters an overly wide margin except when emergency calls crackled over the airwaves. Then, like a rough-weather police boat, the orange-hull, 52-foot Cheoy Lee motorsailer *Marta* was invariably first on scene...her rawboned captain's rendering of aid often making the difference between triumph and tragedy, life and death.

Most importantly, the Strange One of Siljan, kindred spirit to the vagaries of winds and tides, never for a moment forgot the crucial significance of honorable repayment of debt. Above all, he knew how to get in touch with the man to whom obligation was owed.

The boatman's christened name was Erik Skovde. Until 17 months prior to his retreat into lake-water quarantine, Skovde had served capably as chairman of the board and CEO of SVENSKA-VAXO, LTD. The firm's wide-spreading tendrils first tasted nutrients in a suburban Stockholm garage. Erik Skovde's gifted creativity, foresight, and genius for both electrical and mechanical engineering infused the backyard tinkerman's shop with strength enough to sprout into a medium-sized company whose eagerly sought products were trademarked under the name of MALMO MECHANICALS.

The better business got, the more inclined Skovde was to delegate commercial dealings to high-level "hivers," which freed the tall Swede to engage in humanitarian give-backs...the last of which came within a corpsman's stitch of turning him into an "ethnic cleansing" statistic.

Skovde was frontline managing an unofficial relief effort funneling flour, salt, grain, gauze pads, surgical tape, and ointments to starving, blast-wracked Muslims in Bosnia-Herzegovina. This particular December 9th was an eye-tearing 12 degrees with blowing snow when Serbian field artillery scored two direct hits on the Srebrenica schoolhouse serving as a first-aid station and food-distribution point. Detonating high explosive collapsed the building's roof. Structural fragments and brick meteorites swirled like razor blades in a vortex.

Skovde screamed under the searing, crush-flat pain torching his left side. Roaring flames pitched him through tornadoing darkness. When he finally cracked eyelids, it was to warmly restorative Grecian sunlight over the Aegean Sea, in a hospital bed on a breezy, shaded balcony overlooking the waterfront cafes of Poros, a short sail from Piraeus.

"Don't shift around too much," said the fat man tending him. "You're just crawling out of a five-day coma."

As little more than hyperactive brain in a deadweight body, Skovde could make out a few details of the bulky benefactor camouflaged as he was by cotton-puff veils of slowly receding unconsciousness.

"We managed to save your left leg," Skovde was told.

The Swede tried elbowing his shrapnel-pocked chest halfway up, but weakness-fueled trembling, and he was easily pushed supine by the seated caregiver.

"However," the mirage related, "it took some doing... in the form of highly skilled Armenian surgeons working nine hours, including the insertion of four stainless-steel pins ensuring reattachment of nearly severed limb."

"What is your name and why...?"

"My name is Jargoon."

"A gemstone?" Skovde croaked. "Surely you can do better than that."

"Jargoon Kastamonu. And precious jewels..."

"What kind other than valuable merit mention?"

"The reappearance of your sarcasm convinces me you are indeed emergent," Kastamonu judged behind the obscurity of billowing, aromatic smoke birthed by butane flicker-flame tip-licking a long, South American cigar. "Anyway, valuable rocks are part and parcel of my business interests. Now as to the why."

The stoutly built visitor parked his panatela then swung back...cradling a chipped bowl of zesty mutton broth held to Skovde's chapped lips.

"The why and wherefore, Swede, are as follows. You were helping Muslims, and Muslims do unto others.... Well, no sense exhausting you through repetition of what you already know."

"I was helping people."

"You Scandinavians and your infernal distinctions!" Kastamonu lectured sternly while wiping lukewarm soup dribble from Skovde's chin. *"What utter pains in the ass you can be!* Anyway, that is a minor point, which I am fully prepared to concede...but only because you're forty percent dead, though steadily improving. Be that as it may, there remained unanswered a far more pressing question: What should be done with a man such as yourself, grievously wounded in an outhouse district of the world so contemptibly lacking in medical facilities that innocents are condemned to die from wooden splinters turned gangrenous?"

"Others have..."

Kastamonu waved off Skovde's half-gasp protest.

"Street-corner do-gooders, you mean? Circumstances

blow away such tambourine-bangers like two-ply ass-wipe in gale-force winds. But someone such as yourself? A real man slogging knee-deep through great personal risk instead of writing tax-deductible checks from thousands of kilometers away?"

"How did I get...?"

"My time with you has drawn to its inevitable close," Kastamonu sighed, "more because I am famished than because you are drowsy. However, I want you to rest assured that you will be well cared for by others whose manners are far more refined than my own. When you have recuperated sufficiently, you will be flown home. I have already personally seen to the arrangements."

Turning sapped Skovde's ebbing strength, and he could only wheeze and lean back in fluffed-up pillows. Still, the indirect sun felt good on his skin.

"One day I shall repay you," Skovde vowed.

"To the contrary. It is *I* who has repaid *you*. Mister, you have already done enough for my people, who are more in need of others' help...and general assistance from the rest of an uncaring world."

"And if I were to insist on further thanking you for saving my life? You yourself said it was something of value."

"Did I now?" Kastamonu queried, pausing in the bedroom's doorway where he stood radiantly backlit in wisp-rim light ghosting randomly orbital around Skovde's near-coma exhaustion. "Forgive the laughter, my friend, but you really must have been dreaming. Anyway, should the occasion arise, perhaps one day you can save mine."

"How will I...?"

"In the highly unlikely event that something comes to your attention...some fact, rumor, half-truth, or aspersion concerning a limp-along humanitarian named Kastamonu, you may get word to me as follows. Broadcast in the clear on 1600 kilocycles, the word 'KOMODO.'"

"The dragon."

"Yes. Make this transmission at zero-one hundred hours

on the first morning, then at zero-seven hundred hours the following day."

"The reciprocal."

"Exactly. On the third day, broadcast at zero-three hundred hours."

"And zero-nine hundred the morning after."

"You catch on quickly."

"It's in my nature."

"Undoubtedly, your fatigue will preclude remembrance of these details."

"Don't make book on it," Skovde whispered hoarsely.

"I speculate only on intrinsically valuable commodities... never on anything as mercurially undependable as human nature."

"I see."

"Perhaps yes, perhaps no. Regardless, signal no more than I've described," Kastamonu cautioned. "We monitor continuously and will be in touch three days after your fourth transmission."

"And if this matter should be too important to wait that long?" Skovde inquired, as sleep's tenacious grip pulled him back and darkward.

"My friend," Kastamonu called to unhearing ears. "In the nearly sixty years I have lived to eke out a commendable living in this world, nothing has ever been that important."

And then Skovde's guest was gone.

When the emaciated Swede limped off Sabena Flight 2488 in Stockholm six weeks later, things at home had changed...and not necessarily for the better, though SVENSKA-VAXO LTD was still breaking speed records like the well-oiled, express locomotive it was. The problem was Skovde himself. After lengthy, clucking-tongue examinations, six specialists wrote up verbose variations on the same theme: combat neurosis; battle fatigue; shell shock; *psychopathia martialis;* post-traumatic stress syndrome. The patient's favorite phrase was "extreme concussive dissociation."

During one of his increasingly sporadic moments of lucidity, Skovde knew it would be better for shareholders' equity and corporate good health if he voluntarily relinquished the reins of power. The board felt likewise.

And though his five-room suite at the headquarters building's 55th floor was only infrequently used, access to SVENSKA-VAXO LTD's enormous intelligence network/data bank remained the Swede's favorite and daily accessed link to the outside world. Originally created to counter industrial espionage, information in its four-story data bank was wired back and forth between head-office transceivers and the Beeldsnijder-designed, trawler-rigged motorsailer in which Skovde circumnavigated Lake Siljan.

And then one whitecapped day, while on a time-killing, finger-tapping dance through gray-line datum, the debt-burdened Swede came across a vague reference to a foreign-intelligence operation that spun him around and forced an uncompromising stare down the shattered-mind byways of fade-in/fade-out past. After authorizing five slush-fund payments totaling 60,000 British pounds sterling, more compelling factors came to startlingly distasteful light...first served up on a computer screen, then radio-faxed directly to the 52-foot craft sea-anchored in Siljan's middle. With disheartening confirmation assured, Skovde wheeled his boat chair over to the trawler's powerful shortwave radio and broadcast: "KOMODO."

Kastamonu bit like a ravenous mako shark. Following Skovde's reciprocal zero-seven hundred hours transmission, timetable plus longitude/latitude instructions, all tightly wrapped in a weighted-oilskin packet, were tossed onto Marta's foredeck by a passing four-outboard speedboat, which quickly vanished in rain-laced lakeshore fog.

And so Erik Skovde—in bright-yellow slicker, hip boots, and heavy-wool, cable-knit sweater—departed Lake Siljan, sailed down the Dal River, and headed south through the Gulf of Bothnia. Nighttime found his wide-beamed, bath-tubby vessel moored in craggy, secluded inlets...a pattern he reversed upon reaching the broader, more open expanses of the Baltic and North Seas.

Pea-soup English Channel clime gave way to shirt-sleeve wave-work farther south. Skovde kept 50 nautical miles offshore... semicircling the Bay of Biscay...coasting closer to picturesque Spain and cheery Portugal...and lastly tacking in through the Strait of Gibraltar to the Mediterranean's final destination: Libya's Gulf of Sidra. Immediately upon penetration to within 25 miles of fortified shoreline, *Marta* was sniffed at briefly by five converging guided-missile attack boats that just as quickly turned stern-to and sped off like misbehaving dogs tugged back by angry masters.

Per preplanned route, Skovde sailed nonchalantly south until he hove-to halfway between Misratah and Benghazi... perpendicular to *Sur'ah.* The Swede's once and present host's 116-foot, knife-bow pleasure yacht, appropriately named *Speed* for the qualities she so ably embodied, drifted in tranquil, wave-lapped splendor one-half mile away in haze and glistening spray... the sleek, narrowly triangular wedge poised like a waterborne arrowhead primed for unleashing.

The Mulder-designed, high-speed craft had been constructed by Norship International in Norway's Ulstein-Eikefjord yards. Though tipping the scales at an athletic 125 tons, *Sur'ah* cleaved the sea like an Aronow powerboat on steroids... easily attaining 63.5 knots and comfortably cruising at 50... thanks to patented, water-planing hull enhancements and nearly 11,000 horsepower generated by a Combined Diesel And Gas—CODAG—propulsion system linking two diesels and one gas turbine for afterburner performance.

Internally, *Sur'ah's* bridge was more spaceship than seacraft, with dual radar screens sweeping out to 150 miles, paired computer-readout monitors on the yacht's internal systems, and extensive instrumentation. Below-deck areas featured a pasha-class saloon, 13-course breakfast bar, sit-down dining for 20, resplendent owner's stateroom, two posh double-bedded cabins, one twin-bedded cabin, and crew's quarters forward. The plushly carpeted Art-Line interior leaned heavily toward white leather, chrome, black-lacquered paneling, recessed lighting, and burnished mahogany woodwork.

But none of the boat's glamorous appointments was currently of interest to Jargoon Kastamonu...three-language muttering under his breath while impatiently pacing *Sur'ah's* heavily armored command/control section. A crewcut, headphoned crewman in a tan jumpsuit perspired nervously while eavesdropping on Skovde's boat, which had dropped anchor 14 minutes previously.

"What the devil's he up to now?" Kastamonu grumbled.

"Finished showering about eight minutes ago," the sailor stuttered, as trembling fingers adjusted the mixing board's gain. "Now he's blow-drying his hair."

Kastamonu stood a shoeless, six-feet-two. Of Turkish-Albanian ancestry, *Sur'ah's* chunky captain pendulumed between irascible and downright cross. Mocha eyes peered out from deep-set sockets beneath a widow's peak haircut to fuzz length around a knobbed head. A master gamesman forged in the kiln of a running heritage—drugs, guns, liquor, whatever could reasonably be expected to turn a worthwhile profit in cross-border trading—Kastamonu himself had been stone-wall legitimate for 30-plus years.

Despite yard-high reams of computer-generated innuendo, rampant speculation, and unsubstantiated implication, only two formal INTERPOL charges had ever been leveled against the wily Kastamonu...the last one more than five years ago...with neither one sticking. It was well nigh impossible to nail the portly Middle Eastern "gentleman" enjoying fiscal fruits attendant with sole proprietorship of Amsterdam's best-known and most highly respected diamond-cutting operation.

Much to the soundman's silent sigh of relief, Kastamonu abruptly departed the insulated listening post and grumped up the ladder toward the afterdeck's blue marble table laid out with honeyed yogurt, *souvlakia,* seedless watermelon, cantaloupe, pressed dates, and mineral water. Through high-powered

Swarovski binoculars, a marginally restless, feet-up Kastamonu watched Erik Skovde lower *Marta's* stern-davit dinghy, climb in, cast off, and start rowing across the gently lapping water separating the monster yacht from the weathered North Sea trawler.

After what seemed to fretful Kastamonu like a constipated eternity, the Swede's rowboat was lashed tightly to sleek *Sur'ah's* white-fiberglass hull, but still Skovde delayed. Before boarding, he stood spread-legged in the bobbing launch and saluted crisply.

"Request permission to come aboard."

"Of course! Of course!" Kastamonu bellowed from over the upper railing, completely at a loss to understand his guest's persistence in following nautical formality to a nettling tee.

Swede and Turkish-Albanian clasped forearms briefly underneath the flying bridge's sunshade extension, then Kastamonu threw his considerable bulk down into a purple-cushion wicker chair and gestured for Skovde to follow suit. The yachtsman picked up a palm-sized remote controller, pressed the large, central button, and asked, "Retsina?"

"Glenlivet Single Malt."

Kastamonu thumb-jabbed coded entries, tossed the controller down on the fat-pillowed seat beside him, and said, "You're looking well...and very much rested and recovered, my good friend."

"I am not your friend, good or otherwise. I have come here to do you a service. I have come to repay a debt."

"So friend or no," Kastamonu said coolly. "How have you been anyway?"

"We'll talk after whiskey," Skovde replied dully, as if transocean passage-making had drained all of his wattage and he was seriously in need of more recharging than alcoholic refreshment alone would provide.

Drinks were delivered by a teenage girl wearing a scooped-out, second-skin bathing suit, French-curved to maximum advantage...a skimpy, hot-pink Speedo propping up, pushing out and exposing more deeply tanned flesh than was covered.

Skovde gawked at the girl's lushly feminine bounty as she daintily laid down the drinks tray, curtsied politely, and stood hands at sides awaiting further instructions.

Kastamonu unsealed each bottle of liquor and poured two stiff drinks before noticing the guest's attention riveted to the sweeping rise and fall of late-teen charms.

"Want her?" Kastamonu grinned lasciviously. "Don't bother answering; I can see that you do. Okay, she's yours. And," he continued with a sly wink, "she is a medically confirmed virgin. Doesn't speak a word of English. Break her in, why not? I've got three more stashed below, but she's the pick of the litter. The best...for my guest."

"No, thank you."

Finally managing to unstick his eyes from feminine perfection, Skovde picked up his drink, turned back to Kastamonu and toasted the host's health...in response to which the diamond magnate jerked his head sideways, and the girl padded off toward the bow. Then the Turkish-Albanian took two deep swigs of Greek wine and expanded upon his original offer.

"So," he asked, hands clasped over a large, well-fed stomach. "Would you like to choose from any of the others? I can have them here in an instant."

"Better we should get down to business," Skovde murmured, guzzling four fingers of whiskey and pouring himself another drink. Then he asked: "If you needed to spirit large-carat bundles of your precious commodity out of the Netherlands, how would you go about doing it?"

As a matter of fact, I presently have that need, Kastamonu thought, as he said: "The easiest way, of course, would be to commit a looting."

"And as for getting them through customs?"

"Frozen inside ice cubes chilling the coolers of middle-class travelers."

"And the fencing?"

"I never get that personal on the second date," Kastamonu replied suspiciously.

Eyeing his guest skeptically, the yachtsman helped himself to a double-mounded serving of honeyed yogurt, dropped in some chunked cantaloupe, then added: "Next optimum tactic would be a burglary of my own goods, of course. But you know as well as I that not even Europe's best-protected banks enjoy the twelve-tier protection covering my business."

"With all of your sound-detection and motion-sensing equipment, I imagine such a plot would be well nigh impossible."

"So it would have to be an inside job."

"Preparatory planning has already been done," Skovde said.

How could he possibly know that? Kastamonu wondered.

Misreading Kastamonu's expression, the Swede noted: "I'm not that intuitive to have known what you were thinking just a moment ago. Or perhaps the fact that you have been thinking of such an action for some time now. After all, what commercial operator has never had such thoughts?"

Will you please get to the point? Kastamonu wished silently.

"There isn't a well-established businessman who hasn't at one time or another pondered the pros and cons of ripping himself off," the Swede said. "So I am not surprised at your surprise that there was really no surprise."

At this point, not so much surprised as confused by double-talking hyperbabble, the Turkish-Albanian thought. *However, we must be patient until the clipper's bowsprit once more swings around on course.*

"As I said," Skovde mumbled, "the planning's already been done."

"How so?"

"It's called Operation Pegasus."

"Pegasus. Yeah, I know," Kastamonu said, playing for time while pouring himself a double shot of retsina. "The flying horse."

"You're the flying horse," Skovde declared, "and it's your wings that are barber-shop bound for clipping."

"And you know this how?" Jargoon asked irritably.

"Explain it to me. I want to hear it all."

From the inside pocket of a brass-buttoned naval blazer, Skovde removed a grayish-white folder. He palm-balanced it momentarily, then put the paperwork down on the rectangular fantail table...rotating it so that Kastamonu could read the title-page writing on the plastic-sheathed report. The Swede next extracted a sterling-silver pointer, yanked its bullet-shaped nose to full extension, eased back in his chair, and tapped the rod's tip on the folder's face.

"Operation Pegasus is the name of the plan."

"So you said!" Kastamonu snapped, leaning forward and squinting to read fine print at the bottom of the folder. "I see the word 'Millwright.' What is the significance of that word?"

"Millwright is the code name of the man who constructed the maneuver."

"So what does this cocky bastard have to do to me?"

"Not cocky. Cockney."

"Their goddamned MI-6?!" Kastamonu bellowed, wincing from the excruciating pain of having been gored deep in his vitals. *"Their Secret Intelligence Service?!"*

Skovde nodded sagely. "SIS, yes. The Brits' foreign-espionage organization."

"And these letters and number here at the bottom-right corner. IDT-5? What about that?"

"The Millwright's department is one of five known IDTs."

"So will you feed me, please, without my having to pull it from you like pipe-wrapped roots?!"

"IDT-5 stands for "In Due Time Section-Department Number 5."

"Who is this Millwright, anyway? What does he do? *What is his stake in me?!"*

"He plots, he plans, he sets wheels, gears, and pinions into motion. Not today or tomorrow, but someday...hence the name: 'In Due Time.' In due time, SIS gets around to dealing with real or imagined threats, terrorist financiers and the like, and coffins them off to Jericho."

"Where?!"

"Their code name for purgatory."

"Dead?!"

"Fiscally or factually, yes."

"Just the British?"

"At present, yes. But SIS is, of course, linked to the whole of Western intelligence establishments arrayed against the East. And as for you, Jargoon Kastamonu...well, you popped up like a red-flagged tax return. Your time came up. Simple as that."

"Nothing is ever as simple as that. *What brought this about, and what concretely can I do?!"*

"The words 'random chance' answer your first question. And as for part two? Time is your ally. You're extremely fortunate this came to my attention early enough."

"Thank you, my friend."

"I am not..."

"Yes, yes! You've already made that abundantly clear!"

"As to what you can do? An elementary stratagem is perhaps your best bet."

"I am clearly not up to speed on this," Kastamonu sputtered nervously, momentarily taken aback by the enormity of the predicament's gnashing, prey-hungry teeth. "Give me more details."

"For appetizers, you should have known that sooner or later Western intelligence would get around to neutralizing, or at least attempting to cancel out, those whose interests run counter to its own plans for world order."

"Yes, of course, I had realized that," Kastamonu countered. "And how did you come upon this information?"

"IDT divisions process contingency plans like canned Spam. That is their job, and ultimately their Achilles' heel: All-case scenarios are proposed, thoroughly dissected, restructured, and charted, so that middle-level planners can cherry-pick and choose those best serving their ultimate purpose."

"This is quite some warehouse operation you are describing."

"It is only when intrigues float higher up the operational power grid—maturing from daydream conceptual to hard-core potential—that such write-ups are shoved under heavily cloaking shields of unbreakable encryption and catacombic security. But before then, there are so many conspiracies spilling out from bulging files under minimal, Level 1 protection that they are easily hacked into."

"And how is all of this to transpire?"

The Swede flipped to a grainy, passport-size photo on page two. "Here is the inside man. On page three, you will find the proposed timetable."

Kastamonu's eyes flared with hateful anger. *"I hired that camel-fucker personally!"* he raged, *"and only after the best of security checks!"*

"It would seem that SIS has proven itself quite a bit more adept at planting than you are at preventing."

"Clearly!" Kastamonu fumed, his voice heavy with vengeful aggrievement.

"And so when your number comes up," Skovde sighed, "this carefully orchestrated divestiture will fillet you two ways. First and foremost, the most precious jewels in your inventory will be lost."

"Many robberies are tried by those too stupid to know better," Kastamonu interrupted nervously with a dismissing wave of right hand. "Their success rate is less than one quarter of one percent. On top of that, I have ample insurance with Nederlandse ProTek, Greater Amsterdam Re-I and..."

"Lloyd's, of course," the Swede interjected. "You have it now; however, you won't have it then. Shortly before launching the raid on your hard assets, each insurance company's computer records will have been altered to show lapsed policies. Letters requesting payment of premium, posted via registered, return-receipt mail, will have been signed-for, though not acted upon."

"Signed for by whom?!"

"A fabricated straw man sending word to your former insurance companies that you are covered by other carriers.

Later, stories will be leaked that there was, in fact, no insurance at all...and that premiums went unpaid because you were, in truth, cooking the books and nearly bankrupt."

"Leaving me standing buck naked in the face of overwhelming loss."

"At which point, suspicion will be cast upon you, Jargoon Kastamonu, who might even wind up being arrested for planning the pillage in order to resell scam-swindle gems on the black market and thereby erase the financial difficulties of a suddenly struggling diamond operation."

"Money woes coming from where? *Stemming from what?!"*

"Page four, paragraph seven: bad plays on heating-oil options."

"Yet such inaction on coverage would have generated telephone calls!" Kastamonu blustered. "My insurers would not have simply rolled over and let that business lapse. It is very lucrative for them."

"And to whom would those follow-up calls have been directed?"

"I see," the multimillionaire murmured.

"Inquiries made to your chief operations manager, perhaps?"

"The SIS plant."

"Who would confirm that arrangements were made for insurance with other providers?"

"At which point, I would have been effectively wiped out." Kastamonu chugged directly from the retsina bottle and snarled, "I want to move on those rotten bastards!"

"More easily ached for than actually accomplished."

"There has to be a way!"

"One against many?"

"There has to be an answer!"

"Perhaps," Skovde acknowledged.

"Well?!" Kastamonu asked desperately.

"Move up the date."

"Move...?"

"Consider this. You've got the plans. The double-dealer knows the why and the wherefore, but has not yet been alarm-clocked, and so is not currently activated. Therefore, he stands ignorant of the specific when. So you, Jargoon Kastamonu..."

"Initiate the operation?"

"The job is done by the best strike team your money can recruit. That file is ammunition, giving you the wherewithal to lay blame directly on the doorstep of the SIS. Leak that dossier to the news media, and you're guaranteed to touch off an international incident."

"My insurers might even sue SIS for recovery!" Kastamonu cackled proudly, his grin brighter than a lustrous day's heralding sun.

"Very likely, once Operation Pegasus is glaringly unmasked as foreign meddling with the life of a well-respected Amsterdam businessman."

"The Dutch abhor such intruding trespass."

"And, as just desserts, you exterminate the mole undermining your foundation."

Kastamonu rubbed chin and cheek thoughtfully. "And this way, the robbery will be covered by insurance."

"Precisely. So you make out okay."

"Which is tantamount to having my moussaka..."

"And eating it too," the Swede broke in.

"And now back to we two. How then shall I repay you for this priceless service?"

"My debt has been canceled," Skovde said formally, jumping to his feet and stiffly extending his hand. "That is all that concerns me."

When the pickled carcass of Arne Franeker was found floating face down in the Herengracht with a blood-alcohol level of .29, Amsterdam detectives wrote up the drowned, dock-bumping unfortunate as just another jinxed tourist taking "the long swim" after bar-hopping through the door-to-door nightclubs and cabarets of the party-hearty Thorbeckeplein District.

But the radio-news announcement of Franeker's untimely demise cut short Cekal Fethiye's iron-pumping workout, made him skip showering, and goosed the 33-year-old Turk toward his next stop on a crowded agenda. For while Fethiye knew the late Dutchman was fond of stopping in at a taster bar here and there, an occasional tipple didn't add up to the kind of boozy overindulgence likely to terminate with a bloated body boat-hooked out of a brown-water canal.

The scion of well-to-do parents and heir to Turkey's largest international shipping concern, Fethiye had been easily recruited while majoring in International Business Administration at Oxford University. He saw his homeland's best interest as laying in the forging of stronger ties with the West. Fethiye fully comprehended that should militant Muslim fundamentalism topple home rule, both he and his parents would lose everything that his grandparents and great-grandparents broke their backs to achieve.

But Cekal Fethiye's rock-solid determination to balk at upcoming SIS instructions stemmed from more than the crisis of confidence guaranteed to flower when selling a fellow countryman down the river...no matter how dark and unremittingly dreary the portrait of Jargoon Kastamonu that Arne Franeker had been so fond of painting. Simply put, there were depths to which one just did not sink...unless dragged that far subsurface by cement boots.

Fethiye had long ago belched away all interest in working for the British. He had false passports under five identities, and in fact had transited in and out of Amsterdam, through America once, and past four Russian republic borders...on sightseeing travels during which all IDs worked flawlessly. And after lately becoming emotionally respectable, it just would not do to expose hazel-eyed Karin Hlohovec to the unavoidable risks of spousal secret agentry.

And what an extraordinarily fine woman she is, Fethiye reflected happily, his hoot-owl face and short-curl hair sweat-sheened by a hurried walk to an eagerly awaited rendezvous.

Learned in the ways of the world. Passionate. Liberated. Sensual. Physically aggressive...and extremely well built.

Spiritually stumble-bum exhausted from the puppet-dance sex acts of dissatisfying one-night stands, Fethiye bumped buttocks with Karin while browsing the Stedelijk Museum's *Nouveau Realisme* exhibition of Armand, Spoerri, and Tinguely. Shortly after first lunching with the incredibly beautiful woman from Mlada Boleslav, he used company facilities to check her vitals carefully...as was expected and instructed. No one working for Kastamonu Diamond House dared fondle anyone's privates before security clearances ranked "Green Gables"...and even employees themselves were subject to ongoing investigation.

And so shortly after falling desperately in love with Karin, Fethiye fully fathomed the endearing simplicity of choice: Either break his links to British intelligence or sever all ties to the woman he loved. And the virile Turk was not about to do the latter, considering how much pleasure achingly beautiful Karin daily lathered upon him...an up-and-comer whose position as chief operations manager of Kastamonu Diamond House veritably guaranteed the acquisition of any heart's desire.

Best of all, the timing couldn't be bull's-eye better. Fethiye had banked enough of Kastamonu salary, SIS payoffs, and family money...but most importantly, Karin would soon graduate summa cum laude from the Universiteit van Amsterdam, with an MA in theater arts clasped firmly in hand. At that time, scant weeks away, she would be more amenable to leaving.

Fourteen days then, Fethiye decided, waiting shoe-tap nervously on the Rijksmuseum's first floor—What a lover of art she is!—sweat-stink workout clothes deeply offending passersby while the Turk pretended to closely examine Dutch painting with Italian motifs: Asselijn, Berchem, Both, Dujardin-*Where the hell was she already?!*

One inch behind...and scaring his bladder nearly into dribbling...tiptoed Fethiye's delectably fragrant Karin, her sweet-smelling hands clasped over his expectant eyes...that magnificently curvaceous physique pressed hard against his sinew-wrapped spine.

"Guess whoooo?!" she giggled.

Fethiye whirled, shoved aside Karin's duffel-sized shoulder bag, embraced his main squeeze tightly, and calculated: *It will be several weeks before SIS replaces Franeker. First, they will plod carefully through lint-screen investigations: Suicide? Accident? Murder? They will not contact me again or threaten blackmail exposure for noncooperation until things have been thoroughly probed, scrutinized, and researched. Franeker had never been in touch more frequently than once every six weeks. It will take British Intelligence at least five to come door-knocking again. Karin will reach academic fruition in two. It will work, with at least 21 days to spare.*

"I have a surprise for you," Karin gurgled with an infectious grin.

"You know that I absolutely loathe surprises," Fethiye grumbled, turning Karin around and ass-slap propelling the short-fuse Czech love bomb out of the exhibit room and toward the nearest staircase. The Turk led the way down two steps at a time to find himself hyperventilating on street level.

"What's the rush?" Karin complained.

"This is going to be a very busy day," Fethiye panted.

"What are you telling me?" she pouted. "That have not reserved a time slot for your Karin?

"I only meant that..."

"Cekal, you promised!"

"Of course, I have set aside quality time for you!" Fethiye protested, carefully checking pedestrian traffic on Stadhouderskade because it was never too early to get and stay cautious. "Both late morning and all afternoon are yours."

"First we eat, yes? Then I shall show you my surprise."

"Whether I like it or not?" he stewed irritably.

"Correct! And then we shall visit the flower market on the Singel."

"It seems that you have our activities pretty well laid out," Fethiye mumbled, unobtrusively scanning vehicles and camera-toting tourists. *And what the hell am I looking for anyway?*

he speculated.

Karen broke loose from Fethiye's grip to flag down a fare-hunting taxi. She threw herself into the back seat, spread her sculpted, miniskirted legs wide open, and told the driver: "Korte Leidsedwarsstraat Twenty-two. *Five-alarm it!"*

Fethiye boarded close behind, barely managing to get the door closed as the tire-screeching cab sped off. *"Bistro Le Manchot?"*

"Its French cuisine will just about satisfy me completely. Since you refuse to allow me time enough for art-lust indulgence, you can at least fill my stomach with a top-notch midday meal."

"I have not been very hungry lately," he lamented.

"You may disallow me French painters, but you shall not deny me French food. And then perhaps," she giggled flirtatiously, leaning close to twist-spike her flickering tongue deep into his left ear. "Maybe some dabbling in the French arts, *cheri?* For that, you will be more than hungry. You will be ravenous. I promise you."

"You have expensive tastes."

"Just another reason why you love me so," she beamed.

Bistro Le Manchot was a shake-roof, one-story pseudo-chalet done up heavily with 1940's Paris flair: fresh-cut, window-boxed flowers; cedar shingles; highly polished woods, and the pervasive aroma of tulips in twilight. The tuxedoed, penguin-waddle *maitre d'* led arm-twined Turk and Czech to the businessman's reserved table diagonally across from the kitchen...a low-light corner from which he could quick-scan all entrances and guarantee a spry, self-preservation lunge through a close-at-hand window should death-sting bullets zing his way.

True to predictably lacking appetite, the preoccupied Fethiye pecked moodily through *poitrine de veau* and *pommes de terre*...while his girlfriend slurped *potage aux herbes* and nibbled heavily buttered bread. Over a desert of baby crepes and *café au lait,* Karin revealed her secret surprise.

"I have found an apartment!" she blurted out.

The darkly brooding scowl on Fethiye's face didn't

dampen Karin's rambling enthusiasm.

"We shall go there immediately after lunch, make love, and so inaugurate it properly."

Normally, I would jump at the chance to press my groin into hers...but an apartment?!

Amsterdam's perpetual housing shortage kept lodgings at a high-priced premium, but more than how Karin would pay for such a residence was the fact that possessing so precious a domicile would make his woman that much more disinclined to leave the city. And Fethiye wanted nothing anchoring them in place.

"And how will you come up with rent money for this apartment?" he asked.

"Actually, it's more condo than apartment."

"Damn!" Fethiye groused. "So now where is it?"

"The Fahbro Hotel..."

"That crumbling old dive off the alley halfway down Helmersstraat?!"

"Silence! I will tolerate no more naysaying from you. *Not a single syllable!"*

"They're about to demolish it!"

"Were about to," she corrected primly. "Plans changed."

"I see," he said sarcastically. "And how did you come to learn of this...this gold mine?"

"I found out from my Evocative Dramatics professor, whose cousin is the rental agent in charge."

"Ah, the inherent convenience of familial tout."

"It is already one-third remodeled. Those units are going remarkably fast."

"No doubt they have suckers lined up from here to Eindhoven."

"Brutal skeptic!"

"Where a day's wages are concerned, yes!"

"One-tracker!" she hissed.

"Agreed! So what will this do for us?"

"Let's go now! Once you see it, you will love it."

—

The taxi deposited them adjacent to double-line sawhorses blocking the Helmersstraat-turnoff construction that was associated, Karin explained, with converting the old Fahbro Hotel from a fleabag crash pad into an upscale condominium-apartment house. As the young lovers high-stepped over a rubble flanking a weed-strewn walkway leading to the structure's nearly caved-in main entrance, they were challenged by the foreman of a work crew forming up a new section of sidewalk next to an open manhole in the street.

"Hold on a goddamned minute!" Osso Buco roared, interposing his beer-gut bulk between the young couple and their obvious destination.

The fatty's enormous stomach spread like an oozy marshmallow through the gap line demarcating sagging jeans from a stained, shrunken T-shirt. Red-veined eyes angled 30 degrees off center in a face ravaged by at least six lives' worth of acne, some of which still actively festered.

"You can't go in there!" Buco stated emphatically.

"And why would that be?" Fethiye asked, anxious to get in, out, and home...where he could in/out with Karin.

"Contact lenses a little fogged today?" Buco challenged. "Any damn fool can see that this project is under substantial renovation and therefore not open to the general public. *How the hell did you access this section of street anyway?!"*

The rotund Buco stopped ranting only long enough to tip up a battered hard hat, scratch confusion off his liver-spotted pate, and glare up and down the blockaded alley.

"It's supposed to be completely sealed off. Goddamned Lars. I'll wager ten guilders he's drunk on the job again. *Hey, Lars!"*

"I got dragged around the barricades," Fethiye offered lamely.

"Whatever your alibi, you can't go in," Buco snorted, crossing stout arms over beefy chest, bulldog unwilling to give ground. "It's forbidden. I have specific instructions. There's been absolutely too much riffraff nosing around and about."

"Well!" Karin blazed indignantly. "We hardly qualify as street rubbish."

"Three street whores got the tip of my boot," Buco affirmed proudly. "Happened not fifteen minutes ago."

But blushing-red Karin, rummaging industriously in her nearly bottomless shoulder bag, finally dragged out a crinkled letter that she promptly and victoriously waved under the slimy Buco's nose.

What didn't she carry in there, Fethiye wondered idly.

"Here!" she crowed. *"See for yourself!* I have official permission in writing from Papendrecht Management, the designated sales agent for this property."

"Authorization?" the foreman asked dubiously, thumbs jamming into pockets while he backed off like Dracula confronting holy water and a crucifix. "Are you the new one, then? Number Thirty-Two?"

"Not only the new one!" Karin exclaimed proudly. *"The first one!"*

"Give me a moment to think about this," Buco said doubtfully, looking around in awkward tally of how many crewmen were working...and how many shovel-supported onlookers were already secretly gloating over his galling defeat.

"Just let this paper do your thinking for you!" Karin sneered in that snotty, guttersnipe tone Fethiye found particularly embarrassing.

"Okay then," Buco said gruffly, ignoring the work crew's snickering at the unsubtle shift in the balance of power. *"But be careful!"*

"Oh, we most certainly will," Karin laughed, turning and dragging Fethiye behind her.

"Or it will be my ass!" Buco shouted, but half his listeners were already out of hearing range and making attentive, mouse-step progress through the dilapidated, cross-boarded front entrance of the run-down, former flophouse.

It was an alertly watchful climb up three flights of

creakily protesting stairs, but after striding through the stout-oak doorway, Fethiye was forced to admit that the apartment, tiny though it was, would expand spatially once decorating was finalized. And the residence did have a requisite measure of native charm: a size-and-a-half bedroom, bathroom with stall shower; small sitting area looking out over a street perpetually under construction, and an alcove kitchen.

"Love me now!" Karin said from behind, pulling the sweatshirt top of Fethiye's exercise suit out of his pants and crisscross-grooving his back with skin-breaker fingernails. "Come," she urged. *"Oh, Cekal, I am so hot for you!"*

"What I think is that you're more excited for this apartment than you are for me."

"Well, wouldn't that fully suit your bill of particulars?" she asked brazenly. "To arrive at any hour, day or night, and have me perpetually hot for your elephant cock all the time?"

Karin, already statuesquely half-naked and nearly spilling from the confines of an amply filled-out push-up bra and black-silk panties, led her powerhouse hunk into the bedroom by his combustive hormones. But Fethiye's first sight of the love nest's threshold reined him up short.

"There's no mattress on the goddamned bed!" the Turk sputtered.

"That's coming at four p.m. this afternoon. Surely you don't want to wait that long before you come," she joked. "Look at the springs' span. *Mattress be damned!* These rings will support our weight."

"And this love mat came from where?"

"That unique design studio in Zaanstad."

"Starving Artists Unlimited."

"If you say so. The name escapes me now."

"And now we're encumbered with yet another disastrous Danish contraption," he grouched.

Karin prattled on while unhooking her brassiere, at which point Fethiye was powerless to do anything more than slump-sit on broad-ringed springs. His fiancée continued with her learned oral and manual ministrations until the last vestiges of pliant resistance melted like blowtorched Turkish taffy.

"My pants," he choked, enraptured by the pillowy flesh of Karin's incredible physical beauty.

"Shuck them," she ordered crisply. "The iron may not be fully cured yet, and I don't want your clothes getting stained." Then she kissed him hard while stroking his near-bursting manhood and throbbing testicles. "Mmmm, you *are* hung like a Brahman bull."

"I never tire of such accolades."

"Then let me restate my erotic position. You've got the biggest nuts of any man I've ever known."

"And how many have there been?"

"That is not your business," she whispered huskily. "Now off with your jockstrap, Tennis Balls. Don't be prudish, my darling."

"But the windows," he coughed in garbled protest.

"Being as we are three floors up and the glass is dust-streaked from roadwork below, you have nothing to worry about. Lie fully on the bed," she breathed earnestly, "and let me do you as only I can."

She began by kissing his hair...brow...tongue-stroking his eyes blissfully shut...

"Stretch into the star position, my potent stud horse," Karin cooed, and Fethiye obeyed...his large hands kneading her full breasts as gently probing fingers brought his woman's nipples hard and awake.

"Now tell me," she murmured in mid-neck nuzzle.

"The secret of life?"

"The feeling of naked springs pressed into the manly back."

"It is...good," he groaned, totally helpless under her tantalizing, seductive power.

Karin swung aerobic-animal thighs over and on, mounting up like a victory-starved jockey facing a win-or-else gallop. Astride Fethiye, with his turgidly pulsing glow-plug phallus fully inside her, Karin grind-rode slowly...vaginally clinching his tumescent maypole...ignoring kneecaps chafed by edges of wide-face springs.

Nail-rake fingers running up and down thickly muscled arms urged full extension...inching Fethiye's hands closer to the bed's tubular frame. Preliminary positioning achieved, Karin pelvic-thrust onward/rearward-onward/rearward-onward/rearward, and then breasts-to-chest forward...while reaching down for handcuffs stashed earlier.

Attunement to carnal motion and hot-breath pantings of thunderbolt lovemaking on bare metal masked the snick-clicks of Fethiye's wrists manacled to the inverted-U headboard. But he would not have cared less even had he noticed, for such spicy bondage had long been an integral part of the loving couple's well-seasoned, experiment-oriented sex life.

"Turn now!" Fethiye gasped, and Karin spun in spherical pivot, her sweetly rounded buttocks undulating rhythmically as she bent low to suck toe. This, too, matched patterned physical joining and today facilitated the cuffing of shivering ankles to the L-channel cross member. As the Turk's back flexed like a drawn hunting bow strained to archer's arm-strength limit, his near-manic thrusts nearly bucked love mate from steed...and Karin might have been so launched had she not already dismounted.

The earthquaking ejaculator gasped out spine-wrenching completion. Scalding jets of thick sperm spurted ceilingward, followed by creamily abundant semen coursing down the blue-veined shaft of his throbbing penis.

Thank God the hardest part is over, the aspiring actress thought bleakly, ears down nearly between her knees as she swallowed furiously to hold her half-digested lunch down where it belonged. For though she had not for a moment in 23 months ever forgotten the nature of her clothes-close Kastamonu Diamond House assignment, Fethiye's lover couldn't help feeling at least some affection for the man about to die.

And now, she urged silently, *BREATHE DEEPLY!*

When his need for air was greatest, reel-around Karin...

seated on the bed frame's edge and calmly measuring the moment...rudely pinched Fethiye's nose tightly shut. As his mouth opened wide to fill straining lungs with desperately needed oxygen, Karin pulled a balled sweat sock from the depths of a nearby shoulder bag and crammed it into the doomed man's mouth...carefully inserting it only far enough to muffle his screams but not so deep as to cut off his air.

Fethiye's pupils dilated in frigid realization of events terribly out of kilter and mushrooming horrifically wrong. While the spooked Turk snorted panicked breath through flared nostrils, Karin mechanically wrapped five windings of fireproof duct tape around recently kissed—now mashed flat—lips. Their eyes met briefly when she bent down to rip the adhesive with her teeth.

"This is all really too bad," she said sadly, stroking Fethiye's heaving flanks. "Why couldn't you have been content with everything that had gone right in your life? *Why?! WHY?!"*

For five, sniffle-tear minutes, Karin scrutinized her bound-and-gagged victim...but Fethiye could make no answer, and his ex was bone-dry on time.

Exhausted by the brief outburst which passed faster than a fall sun-shower, bleakly despondent Karin rose unsteadily and dressed slowly...facing away from Fethiye's frantically clinking fetters and muffled, baby-chick chreep-chreeping terror. Almost as an afterthought, she tossed both sets of handcuff keys into the room's far corner.

The coppers will need those eventually, she fretted, while gnawing her lower lip. Then the Czech woman sighed unhappily and continued on with the civilian counterintelligence operation. Choices were nonexistent; Jargoon Kastamonu's hooks were in deep enough to tap her DNA.

You did...or you died.

Karin swung open the fuse box behind the bedroom door and pushed a black button. The wall behind clamped-down Fethiye slid away as the frame to which he was manacled rose slowly vertical, suspending him upside down in an oven-enamel recess. White-button push closed the panel.

Next step was turning the rheostat control fully right. The dial's needle tip closed a transmitting circuit, broadcasting a signal energizing a red light in the under-street utility conduit... where a marginally interested Osso Buco threw a large, two-blade DPDT switch. A blue spark *clack* diverted from the underground line, the 600 volts needed to electrify the stove-element coils on which bruised-rib Fethiye struggled futilely head-down in the dark. Scrubber-filters would keep the stench fairly well confined.

Karin waited only long enough to imagine whiffing the first thread of broiling-flesh odor seeping out from not-quite-airtight seals. Just the thought of maybe hearing the crackle-drip of sizzling body fat was enough to get the performing artist in gear and moving.

Death alone would not suffice, Karin reflected somberly. *Bureau T policy was quite specific. It was not enough merely to kill traitors. A statement also had to be made.*

With a dejected shrug, she reached into her capacious shoulder bag and glanced at the SIS file titled "Operation Pegasus." Its delivery to Pieter Voorst of the Netherlands state radio, and perhaps a courtesy copy faxed to the socialist station VARA, would ignite an international megascandal of hell-raising proportions.

Before leaving the apartment, Karin took one last look at the weasel-trap door behind which the hapless Fethiye grilled. By the time she dawdled down to street level, Buco and the construction crew were gone.

While in a daring daylight heist just under four miles away, nine heavily armed robbers hit Kastamonu Diamond House for a take of $20 million in internally flawless, blue-white diamonds. The Turkish-Albanian reported the loss as $41.5 million, a claim that withstood skeptical adjusters' intense scrutiny, reimbursement for which was covered by policies bought through and still in force with Nederlandse ProTek, Greater Amsterdam Re-I, and Lloyd's of London.

And back in the only refurbished room of the rundown

and lately condemned shell of the Fahbro Hotel, the corpse of Cekal Fethiye cooked for three days before a power-company inspector, checking unusually high kilowatt usage, came upon Osso Buco's underground shunt and cut the cabling of the electric-line splice.

Two rat-gnaw days later, a spaced-out druggie scavenging in the crumbling, near-to-collapse Fahbro came upon the macabre, charred-carrion remains. He freaked out and ran screaming for 18 city blocks until tackled by plainclothes policemen. Another 72 hours expired before he remembered what he'd discovered and where it was hanging.

CHAPTER 18
ICE PACKS

Dieter ("Diki") Vauban didn't do lunch, didn't do drugs, and he never did Heathrow.

Tapped bountifully into the treasure-cave wealth of Old Age France, Diki traced *ancienne noblesse* ancestry back to time's first musty ticks in Celtic Gaul. There'd been only one closet skeleton along the way...an unfortunate detour dead-ending in gene-pool depletion. Chubby squaller Diki, the spoiled-brat offspring of a squire/secretary coupling, arrived 8.5 months later.

Vauban's *grand jete* life was in itself an achievement, considering that any motion first had to overcome the anchor-weight inertia of a back-bending, piss-off attitude. Dogs were the renegade Frenchman's passion, world-class schnauzers his *metier;* international travel his *raison d'etre.*

When Diki breezed into town, trumpeting, kennel clubs rolled out red carpets. Fawning women flocked to Vauban like honey badgers in heat. Fang-and-claw competition for consort status was rooted deeply in bottom-line practicality: Bedded attendees' animals were guaranteed first sperm from his.

Diki's 5′ 11″ frame carried 185 chiseled pounds with the lithe fluidity of a trapeze acrobat. Toast-brown hair was pruned Caesar-cut short; anything longer than one inch invariably "got in the way." Black-bead, falcon-flick eyes pinioned weaklings targeted for ruthlessly quick exploitation. On or off elite European sports courts, Vauban was an opponent never taken lightly...nor a man to be trifled with.

Diki's tightly wedded relationships with eight underground-resistance organizations gobbled up 93 percent of his time. The Frenchman was gambling that gusher-flow investments of time and money would enable him to slough off dictated imperatives that required proof of additional commitment before he would be permitted to run his own paramilitary maneuvers.

In that regard, GIGN's raid on foppish poppa's villa... rather than an individual setback...had actually been a most fortuitous happenstance. Diki's father had been personally embarrassed; political fallout jolted the elder Vauban to his very marrow, which was payback aplenty...considering the old man now had more tails than a zoo full of monkeys. Moreover, the young upper-cruster had taken no loss; confiscated cash had been other people's money, and the leak was traced to a Bulgarian tipster later liquidated in Crete. More importantly, the busted operation's grand scope...as reported with lip-smacking relish in the right wing's scandal-sniffing press...blessed the silent architect with merit enough to command attention from underground gangsters guiding tactical programs executed by the 6th of March Group.

In keeping with his enviably affluent financial station, personal resources in excess of $867 million, Diki's methodically organized, long-distance travel arrangements were orchestrated by virtuosos in the employ of Dobra/Ringgit/Kwanza, PLC. Next stop: RAF Smollett Heath.

After the saber-rattling USSR fractured into a quarrelsome basket of bickering republics, the long-expected cutbacks of the U.S. Air Force in Europe began. British coffers withered; the island nation's staff and support were pared back to one-ninth their former glory. RAF Smollett Heath was placed on the world real estate market by a perpetually cash-poor English government, where it was snatched up by the aggressive Moeder-Strenz Partnership, a consortium running tax-proof deals from six square miles of financial complex in Basel-Stadt, Switzerland.

Though Smollett Heath's original borders had neither welcomed nor encouraged casual tourists' offhand interest, its forbidding perimeters were landscaped to boost environmental hostility. Slash-and-burn change quickly denuded the English countryside. Now surrounded by peat bogs, quicksand, and snake-filled moors, and accessible only by Carlyle-Addison's private road and aerial freighters, the former Royal Air Force facility twinkled as a select private airport catering strictly to moneyed sophisticates.

Wholly owned intercontinental Boeings dropped in for avgas and truffles. McDonnel Douglases tanked up and flew off. A340 Airbuses refueled and refit. Hustling ground crews aimed visitors' planes toward final destinations, launching them with crisply snapped, white-glove salutes.

And I am almost there, Vauban thought from the recesses of a deeply upholstered Rolls-Royce Corniche IV comfort.

Diki's favorite flier loomed on rain-drenched tarmac just beyond the fluorescent-lit hangar. Twinkling rainwater sheeted off the drooped snoot of a highly waxed, meticulously restored Lockheed L.1649 Starliner. Its opulently furnished interior was a *carte blanche* creation of Neoteric Designs, Madrid...with four food stations, two tended bars, baronial oak furniture, and thickly plush Andalusian carpeting. The ultimate expression of triple-tail, Constellation-design philosophy, "Power Trippe" was Diki's hands-down choice for "skips across the pond."

Further advantage lay in the majestic Starliner's easy accommodation by the runways and maintenance facilities of New York's centrally located LaGuardia Airport. Immediately after American landfall, entry was finessed through the VIP Customs' Processing Center operated by the U.S. Customs Service, which billed Moeder-Strenz at an agreed-upon 27.5 percent premium. Kennedy Airport, located painfully distant from the potently vibrant Manhattan heartbeat, was too inconvenient for those demanding the immediate gratification of world-class finery.

All that later; first things first, Diki groused silently...gazing longingly through the wide rear door of Smollett Heath Customs to where his curvaceous mount's beckoning engines murmured at low RPMs.

Before boarding the elegantly sculpted conveyance, however, Vauban faced the badgering of dignity-robbing "fondling." British Customs agents, having conserved time by waving the celebrity's retinue through, now applied saved minutes to impede both Diki's passage and that of 16 canine champions, ensuring top billing at breeder's cup competitions stretching from Mobile to Malibu.

Genetically prime schnauzers passed with agonizing slowness under agents' hand-held scanning devices, one brushed-aluminum travel cage at a time. Chief Inspector John "Irish Johnny" McNeil swung his hand-held electronic checker over napping dogs' necks as if dowsing for water...edging aside ruby-crusted collars while doing so. The laser-beaming device bleep-swapped codes with programmable chips permanently nestled under animal skin. More to postpone procedural windup than as an added safeguard, Chief Inspector McNeil checked each tranquilized furball for ticks, fleas, and recently healed incisions but found nothing worth writing home about.

"Everything in order?!" Diki rasped, jaw-twitching impatient with Chief Inspector McNeil's sluggish plod toward the conclusion of anal-retentive procedures.

"I hear that a GAAT advisory's been posted," the Irishman noted dryly.

"Then maybe you'd better lock up your mother," Vauban smirked.

"Mind your manners, guv," McNeil replied coolly while bending to his work...Vauban's surliness having given license to further brake forward progress. "Here I am trying to help, and you're giving me sass."

"So file a grievance with the union."

"Don't have one."

"Tough darts."

"Bad attitude makes my arthritis flare up, don't you know," McNeil countered, "and Pesthead Dieter won't get through any faster, no matter how obnoxious he is...rule being rules, after all." *Something about this son-of-a-bitching frog stinks to high heaven,* McNeil mused, *but there's nothing I can do about it now.*

After marching stoically through a lashing downpour, Diki

double-timed up the ramp steps. Then the Frenchman ducked under an evergreen-scented overhang, the cabin attendant closed the door, and "Power Trippe" was buttoned up tight.

Diki snarled irritable "hellos" while making his way aft. Then, leaning back comfortably in the brocaded master's chair at the cabin's rear center, the Contemptuous Sovereign surveyed his lavishly appointed domain. Vauban gazed through panoramic side windows as Captain Dennis throttled up…and the elegant Starliner eased right, accessed Taxiway 4, and rolled toward Runway 35L.

"Takeoff in seventy-five seconds," First Officer Eaton crackled cheerfully, which was as expected. Liftoff invariably occurred within two minutes of pressurization because delays were unheard of at Smollett Heath.

As the growling Starliner broke ground and swan-soared smoothly up through 14,000 feet on an effortless climb to the assigned trans-Atlantic cruising altitude, Diki took dimmed-lamp stock of the bimbos and toadies comprising his self-indulgent troupe. There was the requisite number of high-breasted females... *Elle*-fashion queens whose bra sizes significantly exceeded their IQs...escorted by men of bisexual persuasion.

Most importantly, he thought, *they are completely under my heel. And as far as The Movement? Well...control over that, too, will come in time.*

Diki's sexually charged coterie, recruited fresh for each new excursion, was a clique of hard-core orgy animals who invariably melded fluidly, all having been bred from similar parasitic bloodlines. Dominion over such jellyfish increased the closer the feeding time came.

Every now and then, however, an odd fish broke the surface. Tonight's coelacanth was a vaguely unnerving, Danish-looking stud whose thistly aura hampered even-tempered meshing with party-hearty groupies. Diki's practiced analysis catalogued the misfit's physicals as being a shade too misshapen for smooth socializing.

Droning engines, single-malt whiskey, and designer drugs

took their inevitable toll, and one by one, Diki's pet leeches nodded out...then lapsed into near-comatose slumber on leather couches, velour divans, and tiger-hide love seats. When the last pale-pink fluorescent winked out, Diki almost faded too, but a wind shift generated by an intrusive arrival snapped the Frenchman alert to a shadowy presence levering up a nearby recliner's footrest.

"Don't turn on the light," the ghost ordered curtly.

"You're the Dane," Vauban whispered.

"Vic," the man breathed.

"Victor with a 'c' or Viktor with a 'k'?"

"Neither," was the hoarse, half-chuckled reply. "It's in the initials."

"Vee-eye-cee?"

"Da-da. As in vanilla ice cream."

"Plain..."

"Faceless and anonymous. Your report card carries all A's so far."

"If you are with The Movement," Diki stalled, "you can confirm that by..."

However, Vic wasn't inclined to play password games. "Were I not who I purport to be, you would have been popped weeks ago."

"String-along could be part of the scheme."

"The inner workings of which you have no way of knowing. Simply continue on as imperiously as you have," Diki was told.

"All of which is well within my nature."

"Which is why you were chosen."

"I am someone you can depend on," Diki vowed.

"Had that not been the case, you would not now be midway up the mountain."

"There is more I wish to do," the Frenchman offered earnestly.

"Perhaps later. For now, just keep band-leading this minstrel show," Vic ordered. "Make sure you reach all your stops no more than 25 minutes on either side of the originally scheduled ETA."

"Will you be flying further west with me?"

"Air travel gives me the vapors," Vic joked. "You will go on alone."

And then the agent jacked down his chair and was gone... leaving a fuming Diki Vauban lambasting himself for lacking the balls to force the revelation of the emissary's face. Such a transgression, however, would not have even scratched the steely authority backing Vic's brawny confidence...nor reduced the ozone odor of lingering menace convincing Diki it would not have been wise to eyeball an ID.

La Guardia's "Barker's Bivouac" was a stinkpit miniwarehouse run by Transco-Uniformity under contract to the U.S. Customs Service. The drafty, holding-tank operation boarded imported wildlife ranging from white mice to African elephants. After off-loading from cargo planes or oceangoing freighters, "guests" were held pending transshipment to interim medical facilities where they were checked for any diseases they might have contracted between lockup and landing.

"It's gonna be a busy night," Willy Nathans wheezed to Billy Friar.

The obese, gravy-stained security guards were loose-boot relaxing over a game of five-card draw. Poker hands were dealt on a rickety table centered inside a patched building constructed of stacked Quonset huts. Corrugated walls were ripe with the reek of fouled, wall-to-wall cages dripping watered-down disinfectant. Twenty wire-mesh boxes corkscrewed lazily at the end of kinked wire dangling from cross-hatched, rusted-iron rafters, atop which cooing pigeons strutted with aggressive, neck-bob abandon.

The nearest crapper was a two-year-old Johnny-Spot portable flanked by industrial-waste drums 150 feet north and 200 feet east. The toilet's distant location meant nothing to Willy or Billy, since the odds were four-to-one against its working. And with the wind-chill factor at 5° F, it was too cold outside for real men to do anything but hold their water.

"So what's sprouting in the cabbage patch?" Billy asked Willy, while stuffing a lumpy, undercooked cheeseburger into a raisin-eye, greasy-crease face that looked like a punched flat beach ball.

"A hundred and fifty triple-cased four-leggers swooping in on a Chiang Mai DC-8," replied Willy, whose fleshy features carried the crookedly glazed expression of a lobotomized baboon.

"From where?"

"Bangkok."

"Fucking Bangkok?!" Billy bitched. *"One fucking fifty?!"*

"Three to a crate," Willy muttered ruefully. "Fifty fucking cases," he added, noisily chomping a cheek-filling bite of deep-fried fish fillet.

"Not Royal Thai Airlines?"

"No-say, doe-say," hairy-nose Willy replied. He loudly broke wind and brushed crumbs off his strained-seam shirt to cloak the reclamation of two spades edging out of the deck's bottom. "Those skinks wouldn't dirty a dolly with pooch trash."

"Christ," Billy huffed disgustedly. "You'd think we got enough bow-wows here for testing."

"Well," Willy pontificated. "It's not like we're talking inky-dinky numbers. It's also the uniqueness of the strain."

"So what are you telling me?" Billy asked, snarl-belching out the foam of a warm-beer chugalug. "That they're bred for goddamned beauty?"

"Nope," Willy responded with the lofty expertise garnered through overseeing previous Far Eastern shipments. "Physically, they're A-one...except they're bred for shrunken legs."

"Who?!"

"Makes them less likely to run off when getting jabbed with needles and goosed with juice."

"Mutant dogs?!" Billy gasped, nearly throwing his cards down in awestruck disbelief. *"Jesus H. Christ!"* he bellowed indignantly. *"What if they fucking breed?!"*

"Not much chance of that."

"The last goddamn thing this United States of America needs is another load of fucking mutant dogs," Billy bellyached.

"Their legs..."

"Yeah?" Billy asked, pulling in vain to an inside straight.

"Too stunted to hold them up, so there's no way in hell they'd even get close to going AWOL," Willy opined pompously, this particular night being the 37th shift during which he'd prepped for the same drill.

Willy-Billy duty was building-block simple: Stay awake and occasionally rattle locks to ensure that if any tranquilized dogs woke up prematurely, no "foamers" would try crawling toward freedom.

Also on the Watch Bulletin's RON roster was the champion-schnauzer shipment of the Frenchman Diki Vauban. "Hoity-toities" always got marginally better quarters, i.e., burlap-mat pens whose bottoms were elevated two inches off the chilly cement floor

"Fed chitchat has it the GAAT may be planning a visit," Willy said.

"FBI?" Billy asked.

"Well, it wasn't the goddamned CIA."

"Says who?"

"NYPD faxed word to Morty downtown."

"You telling me just to scare me out of my cheese sticks or what?"

"God's honest truth," Willy averred, right hand held high in half-sloshed, boy-scout entreaty.

"Nuts!" Billy scoffed. "We get spooned the same bullshit every fucking time a load's inbound from Chinkytown."

"Orders are to look out just in case," Willy mumbled.

"So this makes what? Notice number four-hundred and thirteen?"

Willy's eyes flared wide in gaped amazement. But before bestowing *idiot savant* status on Billy, the fast-shuffler leaned right and glanced at the clipboard jammed into a caved-in sack of off-brand dog meal. "Right on the money," he said respectfully.

"I peeked when you were checking the weather," Billy confessed to the card cheat. "So nothing's new, then."

"Same old, same old," his partner sighed complacently.

GAAT—or the Group Against Animal Testing—was a loosely knit confederation of sexist, machete-wielding madmen whose misguided lights blazed hottest during dispensation of brutally quick euthanasia. Vehemently opposed to chimps, dogs or cats suffering medical testing's indignity and unceasing pain, GAAT's self-professed mission lies in hacking laboratory animals to death.

Aside from four hit-and-runs, the band's most spectacular triumph was a raid in which 145 dogs were decapitated six hours after entering U.S. Customs Quarantine at Stapleton International Airport. Establishment reaction was swift and sure. Lightning-quick counterstrikes yielded 11 arrests. Coffin-tight indictments followed. Seven more members were collared within three weeks of the attack. Nineteen fiends remained at large.

For 13 months, GAAT's overactive public-relations *apparatchiks* had been pumping out increasingly strident warnings of upcoming chaos. But time's passage, coupled with documented inaction, bolstered blase contempt, and so GAAT signals were given the same credibility bestowed upon other fringe hysterics. The group's "Calls To Alarm" were spiked for filing in drawers holding "Maybes" that were quickly forgotten.

Diki Vauban's Starliner flexed smoothly down through snow-laden cumulonimbus shrouding La Guardia's outer marker. Landing was magic-carpet soft, as befitting a supremely capable Captain Dennis commanding a flight crew with a combined 250,000 flying hours under its collective belt.

After splashing off the puddled taxiway, the silver Lockheed gently dipped as brakes locked near the floodlit approach to VIP Customs' Processing. Passengers, travel luggage, and animal cargo were conveyed out for inspection by the carefully watchful eyes of U.S. Customs officers, paying special attention to dogs' implanted chips. Custody of the snoozing schnauzers was then lateraled to Transcon-Uniformity's Willy Nathans and Billy Friar, who ferried them via a tractored luggage cart to the stenchy, double-high Quonset mercifully two city blocks downwind of U.S.-government civilization.

Seventy minutes later, Chiang Mai Flight 581M greased in on a three-point-slick landing. Its drugged-canine cargo was duly processed through Customs/Freight/46-C, then ferried to Transcon-Uniformity storage. Willy and Billy continued dealing no-limit poker during the wind-down of a 10-hour shift, each man breaking even because Willy's heavy boozing counterbalanced the dirty dealing he'd done.

Pudgy chunks, Willy and Billy signed off as their dimwit replacements signed in, and the porkers parted ways. Each was fast asleep in equally rundown East Village apartments when GAAT commandos, under the cover of a howling blizzard, invaded Transcon-Uniformity's Shed A-44 at 3 a.m.

After pepper-gassing and binding two soiled-pants guards, GAAT beheaders slaughtered Diki Vauban's prized breeding stock. Head-lopping was surgically precise; disembowelment was affectionately patient. Not so much as a whimper was heard from the sedated dogs that GAAT troopers released from "all earthly misery." The savage butchery was a textbook demonstration of carefully orchestrated barbarity, but the regimented killing was 100 percent effective, and each dog died quickly.

Horror-stricken eyewitnesses to hellish antics later narrated every detail to note-jotting investigators. One guard alleged that the dark-haired "Major Cutter" knelt to pray, while the second reported the satanic perp as rooting around in entrails spilling from the gashed-open bellies of Diki Vauban's gutted schnauzers.

Shortly after 7:49 a.m., a plain-featured man of vaguely Norwegian extraction weaved through the slushy mayhem of midtown Manhattan's pedestrian traffic. Vic's destination was Keizner's Diamond Exchange. He was six minutes distant from a sit-down meeting scheduled 12 days previously. In the steel attaché case manacled to Vic's right wrist were plastic baggies stuffed with $15 million in internally flawless, blue-white diamonds...only a portion of the precious stones whose most recent residence had been the vaults of Amsterdam's prestigious Kastamonu Diamond House.

After gems' "liberation," packaging for rectal transit and passage through U.S. Customs, the "ice" had been recovered from the slashed-open intestines of Diki Vauban's axed-dead schnauzers, whose guts...commingling with mongrel viscera on the industrial flooring of a malodorous doggie hotel...had already been splashed photographically across Page 1 of *The New York Post.*

As important as hard goods on hand were *Cabala*-based codes stair-step stacked inside Vic's frontal lobe. UHF verification would guarantee this shipment as a "kosher" swap between Israel's Orthodox Jews and New York City's Orthodox Jews. Rocks would then be changed into millions of untraceable cash.

The broad-shouldered toteman could only speculate on vague details governing the payment's future course. Best guess was the money's being bulk-wired to Bank Leumi, Tel Aviv. Once there, it would likely be halved for consignment through the Netherlands. After quartering, $1.25 million "pucks" would be slap-shot to banks in Rome, Florence, Naples, and Milan. Following further dilution as deemed appropriate, portions would trickle back through North American savings and loans. Small-denomination withdrawals and lump-sum recombination would come next...financing the "direct actions" of Tangiers planners whose blueprints were verbal-only orders chattered in the rat-bite world of back-alley covenants.

As Vic was buzzed in through Keizner's hot-wired, titanium security door, he knew that messenger's duties would soon be over...just as surely as others' waiting would begin.

And as for Diki "Dickhead" Vauban, the operative thought while *"shaloming"* his way down to a basement bunker guarded by bearded, Uzi-armed hulks, *well, the nervy prick had value to "The Movement," although Frenchy had no clue as to whose transfer had been accomplished...where the money was going...and who was really masterminding the marionettes.*

And then Vic sat down to enjoy warm Jewish hospitality and "a glass of tea" as diamond buying's preordained procedures got fully underway.

CHAPTER 19
RISING SHINER

Christening's ceremony was a 500-milliliter guzzlement of tea-warm, *Gusano Rojo* mescal. Shattered Mexican glass sent Switchover slipping down oaken-trusswork ways. Foghorn toots and fireboats' sprays celebrated the commencement of his jouncing journey toward murderous midnight rendezvous.

Mr. Egg-To-Be-Orby emulated Christ on a humming, thermion-rich crucifix. Bomber's last temptation was the rolling of a booze-pickled worm over tongue and between gums, wooly-brained, counting the moments remaining before melting resistance allowed biting the booster and sparking ignition of a kick-ass, E-ticket ride through comet-streaked infinity.

Airy-fairy bookkeeping tallied 18 hours soulfully invested in nearly insensate dangle. Da Vinci Man was drug-drift suspended as a saggy-skin bag of barely connected body parts. Jaybird naked, he flopped, stretched spine disjointed against square channels, metalworked artistically from 100 percent pure, lovingly caressed copper. Chafing wrists were aluminum braceleted; flittering fingers stroked strum-de-dum chords on the catgut strings of envisioned violas.

Three concentric copper rings rotated around Orby's pulsating, sweat-stained rood, each turning at 11 gyroscopic RPMs. Precisely timed whirl ensured da Vinci Man's full absorption of magnificently robust amperage, every whack of which was mandatory for nightwork looming ahead.

Ring One: Power-cable wires curlicuing down from ceiling pass-throughs...and plugged directly into outer ring's axial nib... had dutifully ferried meager input from solar panels jammed edge-crunch tight on the workshop's roof.

Ring Two: Gently moisturizing Orby from two thousand weeping pinholes were misting-fog jets of needle-valve vapor, warmly guaranteeing pores' full openness and ensuring total absorption of incoming EMUs.

Ring Three: Innermost circle's core was Rocky Mountain iron wrapped with lustrous, ruby-glow copper wire, thirstily sucking up 880 vigorously potent DC volts.

The electromotive force required for the upcoming operation had been carefully computed over 11 weeks of slide-rule numbers-crunching. Voluminous mathematical and physics formulas had been triple-checked on two dozen engineering calculators used once and discarded. Error's pesky margin had been shaved to a peach-fuzz insignificant +/- 0.0011%.

Spread-eagled into a live-wire pinwheel, Orby gurgled contentedly. Battered cerebral sextants jingled crazily. Erratic circumnavigation bobsled-bumped through rainbowed Xanadu haze. Foaming narcotics frothed in blood vessels, bubbling like liquid-filled Christmas tree ornaments. Opiated moonshine dripped in intravenously.

Swishing vibrations from slowly rotating circles of concentric copper shivered Orby's timbers. The psycho killer slumped deep-sea relaxed, as if mast-napping aboard a tea-trade clipper, knifing aquamarine ocean. He grinned to the imagined snap of curving, full-bellied sails...and groaning rigging yanked taut by the whiplash gusts of horse-latitude tradewinds.

Zonked, nearly comatose and drooling, Head Man chuckled nonsensically in whirligig ascension through whizzing, cotton-ball muddle: feet up; buttered popcorn within easy reach; straw hat cocked back crookedly; drunkenly tapped-in to river-flow, rum-laced Cokes; binocular-scanning froth-licked beaches for unicorn-ethereal Jamie, the torched child who'd never be espied in full-flowered womanhood.

Oblivious to time-march reality...slack-jawed limp in the purple glow of sunlamp ceiling...tone-deaf yodeling to Jimi Hendrix riff-blast resonating in stereo headphones...Orby's flesh soaked up toasty ions osmosing through the glistening sheen of uniquely conductive, zinc-chromium sunscreen.

At 9 p.m., timered flash units fired sequentially around the circumference of the stuffy workshop. White-light bursts activated photoelectric cells, closing shunt circuits that permitted AA batteries' juice to energize tiny servomotors. Alcohol's flow was terminated.

Thirty minutes later, flash guns fired again...opening valves permitting venous entry of whisk-awake rouser. The invigorating cocktail was a fructose-based solution of cranberry juice, caffeine, brown sugar, finely pestled Bombay crank, and Detroit's finest methamphetamine.

Lancing through arteries and veins at terminal velocity, the turbocharging concoction flogged Orby's tendons. Nerves twitched; muscles fluttered; respiration soared; pulse pounded; overrevving heart hammered crazily.

Every gleaming beacon in the mutating upper story crackled hotly lavender, fueled by brain-girdling arc lightning, electrocuting eagerly receptive neurons.

Rolling thunder kettle-drummed Orby's ears.

Limbs jerked.

Organs spasmed.

Howitzered from deep sedation's enslaving depths... apogee-flowering from cannonball compression to swan-dive extension...Orby shrieked starched-ligament awake at precisely 9:35 p.m. on December 31st...and then he bit the worm, opened his eyes, and saw God.

CHAPTER 20
...AND A HAPPY NEW YEAR

Bundled up a burly five layers deep in dogged self-defense against subzero cold, Sergeant Arthur Peabody Nichols, horseman *sui generis* at least in his own mind if not in anyone else's, sat imperiously astride his Peterbilt like a gate-guarding Prussian *Uhlan* in NYPD blue.

A nose restructured by a lead pipe swung in vicious anger, bisecting his slightly jowly, vase-shaped face. Nichols's waxed, handlebar mustache added a dash of theatrical flair to an otherwise stoically impassive mien. Taupe, kestrel eyes ran a square-X surveillance pattern across his field of view. Peaked, bat-sensitive ears formed an aural BMEWS Line, proficiently screening the unremitting chaff of general street commotion from the occasional, terrified scream of distress. Sergeant Arthur Peabody Nichols prided himself on the fact that nothing got past his audiovisual early warning system.

Nichols's sleek, muscle-rippled black stallion had been named only after several weeks of careful consideration. The sergeant was of the personal though hotly contested opinion that, pound for pound, this prime example of magnificent horseflesh was more than a match for any 18-wheeler ever seen during his 16-some-odd years as a twice-decorated veteran of New York City's mounted Finest.

"No doubt about it, Peterbilt. This is definitely a triple-A evening: anarchists, atheists, and assholes," Nichols groused, his breath popping out puffball white.

Peterbilt snorted vapor streams, nodding twice in regal affirmation before giving an exclamatory shake of well-brushed mane.

"And maybe even the Antichrist in that crowd of Mongolian hooligans," Nichols mused, leaning forward to pat his steed's neck. "Goddamned New Year's Eve. Let me tell you, Peterbilt, I goddamned hate it."

Nichols's six-dial military chronograph told him the teeming mass of humanity in the "Cattle Pen" was about 22 minutes shy of the celebrated event broadcast globally. He knew for a surety that the street scum wringing out a strong-arm living along the borders of police barricades would be responsible for most of the violent crime...picking off stragglers like trap-door spiders, and vanishing just as fast. A goodly portion of the trauma they inflicted went unreported by virtue of the victims' shocked embarrassment at having been ripped off during the *soiree* of the year.

Amazingly enough, over 90 percent of those inside the party-hearty crowd were surprisingly well-behaved, mainly because quick escape was impossible, which kept the lid ratcheted down fairly tight on premeditated felonies. Aside from the camaraderie shared by those freezing their asses off for no earthly reason, Nichols could grasp that most of the barely ambulatory loonies afoot tonight were so brain-fried on designer drugs as to be half-insensate, if not outright catatonic.

"Okay, now what the fuck?!" Nichols rasped indignantly, briskly reining Peterbilt around to face down a blazing, rainbow-hued light show inching deliberately up Eighth Avenue with its left-turn signal on.

Both the motorhome and its accompanying trailer were gaily festooned with more revolving beacons and multicolored light bars than a fleet of tristate highway patrol cruisers at the funeral of a fallen officer. A dizzying oscillation of blue strobe lights outlined each vehicle's edges, reversing direction haphazardly like a garish Las Vegas billboard and threatening the mounted policeman with the onset of flicker vertigo.

"Not tonight, my man. Ain't no fucking way!" Nichols declared, slow-walking majestic Peterbilt over to the lumbering Airstream and its 6′ x 14′ foot kaleidoscopically decorated trailer.

Sixty-four parallel, etched-brass cylinders of various lengths extended up from the trailer's roof. Short puffs of smoke *oom-pah-pah'd* from the tubes, keeping perfect time with strident steam-organ music.

"MR. SMOOTH'S TRAVELING GROOVE/ REFRESHMENTS GALORE ARE WHAT'S IN STORE" was hand-painted in expansive, hot-purple cursive script under the driver's side window, the glitter-edged letters glimmering under the uneven pulses of quartz-halogen street light.

"Okay, hold it right there," Nichols commanded, leaning down and emphatically rapping the motorhome's chartreuse side twice with his nightstick. "That's as far as you go."

Underneath the deep, golden-brown burnish of Nichols's gloss-waxed saddle, Peterbilt sidestepped nervously, shoes clip-clopping arrhythmically on cold tar stress-cracked from the severity of the freeze. *Has to be the diesel fumes,* Nichols thought, unobtrusively blowing his nose into a gloved palm.

"And who might you be?" the policeman demanded gruffly, snatching up the sheaf of papers offered with timid respect by a slightly jaundiced driver dressed in a coonskin cap and fur-lined, crimson parka.

"Special request of City Hall," the meek, middle-aged plumpkin said amiably, forcing a gap-toothed smile through blowing cold. "I'm here to see that they have a ball."

"Sorry, buddy," Nichols said, shaking his head slowly and resolutely. "Try back on Memorial Day. There's a parade then, and you'll fit right in. But today's marching orders specify absolutely nothing about my letting through any special refreshment truck."

Nichols scrutinized the front and back of the wind-whipped paperwork under the beam of a five-cell flashlight. *Looked legit,* he thought, *but you couldn't go wrong by erring on the side of caution.*

"Head north on Eighth for another two blocks," Nichols offered, gesturing with the beam, "then go east or west. The Square's sealed off to vehicular traffic. You definitely can't come through here."

"It's really all there in black and white; special request of His Honor tonight," Mr. Smooth said, his shell-game eyes dancing with high-tension mirth. "He's having it tough this election year, and is out to garner some votes, I fear."

Nichols scanned the increasingly restive street before rechecking wind-riffled sheets of paperwork and wiping his nose on the back of his sleeve. Sixteen years on the force, the last two New Year's Eves spent on duty at the Madhouse at Midnight, and this was definitely a new twist. But then you had to figure that grimy machine politicians were just the kind of vote-hungry *desperadoes* likely to come up with exactly this type of pathetic, back-pocket stunt.

So all of this actually did make some sense in a bizarre, three-ring sort of way. Mayor Good-for-Naught's popularity spent so much of last month power-drilling itself to new, all-time lows that it must be halfway to Beijing by now. And this? Sure! Why not? And yet...

"I'll call this in, it being New Year's Eve and all," Nichols said, softening only fractionally, "but that's all the slack you're likely to be cut right now." He was only marginally able to control an increasingly agitated Peterbilt. "Damn bus stinks. When was the last time you had your emissions checked?" Nichols sneezed twice in rapid succession, then smacked the motorhome's door forcefully with his nightstick.

"Sir...?"

"Never mind," Nichols grumbled, turning slightly left, eyes zeroing in tight on the driver while hailing his higher-ups. Peterbilt lurched suddenly sideways, nervously breaking discipline in a desperate quest for much-needed breathing room.

But even as close and acutely observant as he was, Nichols couldn't see Mr. Smooth's left knee slam into and press down a large push button on the inside left wall of the motorhome's cab. The sharp movement came before Nichols could utter a word into the walkie-talkie clipped to a fur-collared riding coat. A small electronic jammer masquerading as an in-dash, compact-disc player immediately blended Nichols's transmission into gibberish blanketed by an intense blizzard of growling static.

"It's really quite legal," Mr. Smooth offered, dreamily nonchalant. "Okay to pass through? There's so little time, and there's so much to do."

"Hold your water," Nichols ordered, earnestly trying another call but getting only distorted *wee-yow-wee-yews* and catfight squeals for his trouble.

"Maybe later. Just stick it in Park for right now. I'll check you out," Nichols said, backing away slightly...thinking that perhaps his call was masked by the massive physical metallics of the motorhome and the juice it was generating to power its prismatic spectrum of spangling lights.

Mr. Smooth's ebon eyes, at first wide in respectfully polite appeasement, narrowed like a lizard's as his foot eased ever so gently off the motorhome's brake pedal. The vehicle inched forward incrementally, the slight movement going unnoticed by Nichols, who was walking Peterbilt slowly back along the full length of the vehicle as he studied decaled endorsements on the traveling circus.

The garish oddity of two-vehicle carnival demanded that Nichols carefully file the mental notes taken of the driver's features, which were extraordinarily bland but then no one was ever completely 100 percent plain vanilla and so Nichols came away with: White male; approximately 250 pounds—hard to tell underneath the parka, which looked as if it had been expertly tailored to camouflage excess poundage on a bulked-up frame; nose hooked slightly left below the bridge; four-haired mole over left eye, pinchfist lips pursed during uneven whistling under his breath.

Expectant onlookers gurgled around the motorhome/trailer combination, at times pressing eagerly against it as if to urge the pair on. One passerby bent over just long enough to ram a stainless-steel spike through the sidewall of the right rear outside tire, which immediately started hissing briskly.

As the image of an ever-cautious Nichols dwindled in the side-view mirror, Mr. Smooth casually unbelted himself, took off his coonskin cap, and massaged his bald head briskly with a callused right hand. Gnarled fingers moved circumferentially, first counterclockwise, then clockwise. After making 11 meticulous circles each way, he knocked a stony index knuckle once on the top of his head. Then he yanked open the top three snaps of his parka, fished around under his left armpit, and slowly drew out a purring, six-week-old kitten, which he nestled carefully inside the coonskin cap lying open on the console beside him.

With Nichols taking his time looking over the back end of the trailer and transmitting inquiries that had no chance of getting through, Mr. Smooth picked up a palm-size mike and broadcast his own high-volume entreaty to the impatient crowd compacted into an impenetrable wall of flesh just inside sawhorse barricades.

"You fellas and gals, will you please move that line?" he boomed. "I've come here with munchies, good spirits, and wine."

Merrily enthusiastic in anticipation of a free midnight snack, the crowd halved itself swiftly, then immediately closed up into a surging riptide of ebullient humanity measuring first two, seven, then 13 deep...and finally comprising a human doughnut more than 30 people thick around the vehicles' sides and rear as Mr. Smooth bade them: "Come in closer."

Yes!

PACK YOURSELVES IN TIGHTER!

The brusquely jostling tumult abruptly wedged Nichols farther away from the vehicles. Peterbilt circled in aimless confusion, seriously unbalanced by the fumes, which Nichols suddenly realized were subtly laced with RC-86, the military's latest riot-control agent. His bellowed protests were lost to the crowd's joyous hurrahs and the dingdong "Hip! Hip! Hurray!/ Food is on the way!" chant of Mr. Smooth on the motorhome's bass-thumping PA system.

Scratchy calliope music filled the Square as side panels creaked down haltingly on polished, stainless-steel cables, revealing generously stocked shelves loaded with beer, wine, eight kinds of chips in one-ounce bags, popcorn, salted and unsalted peanuts, crackers, 19 varieties of juice, and, most welcome of all, a wide-ranging assortment of hard-liquor miniatures.

Men and women at the geographic center of Times Square gravitated toward the victuals like lint to static electricity. Famished imbibers swarmed in the style of army ants until they were standing in impatient, belly-growling clamor more than 75 deep, merged into a tightly packed barrier that prevented Nichols and his snuffling horse from closing on the vehicles.

The sergeant tried his radio again, this time getting through as clearly as if dispatch were beaming an unobstructed signal from just down Eighth.

"No. Absolutely not," Lieutenant Beeker huffed with double his usual noseful of acerbic, bureaucratic snot.

The lieutenant was clearly blissed out with the gleeful realization that a subordinate's screwup would pay off royally in the kind of delectably enjoyable ass-reaming he was only too happy to deliver-anytime, anyplace.

"And you may rest assured, Sergeant Major-Horse's-Ass, that we've checked all the way up to the office lickspittles who are this evening fully arrayed in fawning attendance of His Honor the Mayor himself. Absolutely no, repeat NO—capital N period...capital O period—NO vehicles have been approved for entry into the Pen proper tonight."

"Okay, I'll get him out of there," Nichols sighed, his annoyance clearly evident as he spurred a sickly, stubborn Peterbilt forward through the jostling, freebie-hungry crowd.

"More to the point," Beeker crackled back, *"is why the hell you let him get past you in the first place!"*

Peterbilt was hard-pressed to drive his gallant chest and shoulders west through an increasingly turbulent crowd unwilling to give ground for any interruption, especially police interference. Every door on the motorhome swung completely open to casual trespass as glowing merrymakers stoked the feeding frenzy while helping themselves by the armload.

"And all the condemned ate a hearty meal," Mr. Smooth tittered gleefully as he slid off the plush captain's chair and stoop-walked down three steps and out through the front passenger-side door. "When you get up to heaven, *then* we'll see how you feel."

He turned his body sideways, sliding politely past two rapping revelers. Next inside were two full-breasted Dallas Cowboys cheerleaders and their well-hung, New York Jets escort, who closed and latched the sleeping area's privacy panel, eagerly stripping down for action. Mr. First String's pants were down around his ankles when the trio was rudely interrupted by a strung-out murderer who bulled through the flimsy partition and viciously stabbed the football player twice in the groin with a rusty trench knife. The two-fisted killer wasted no time in savagely beating both screaming cheerleaders into bloodied silence, after which he stole their purses, gold chains, and rings... and then, almost as an afterthought, he castrated the quarterback and performed two very sloppy, double-radical mastectomies.

"The ball moved!" someone outside shouted.

"Bullshit!" a second party-goer retorted.

Leading first with his left shoulder and then with his right, Mr. Smooth apologized profusely, excused himself submissively, and wasted no time angling self-effacingly upstream through the oncoming surge of ravenous citizens still flocking in toward the motorhome, all fully intent on scarfing down free food long ago slurped up by voraciously insatiable night-feeders.

Mr. Smooth pulled the mewling kitten out of his coonskin cap, quickly wrung the animal's neck, then dropped its body precisely 11 steps later and exactly 111 feet away from the vehicle. He glanced back through the milling crowd, still partying potently on its feet. Boisterous street pirates nearby took swaggering bets on whose robber-bait Rolex would register the exact moment that old year would foal new.

Twelve minutes to midnight...and a handful of those closest to the motorhome whiffed leaking gasoline as timer-controlled spigots drained the main tank. Others were too cockeyed drunk to notice the acrid odor, but no one remained oblivious to skyrockets suddenly roaring upward from the trailer's steam tubes. The missiles soared aloft to various altitudes, though none higher than 550 feet. Glistening sparkle arced across the star-holed veil of purple-black sky. There they exploded with muffled *whumps,* spreading fiery streamers to every point of the compass, with no comet tail extending past the actual physical boundaries of the milling mob pent up in the Square below.

To the *crump-crump* accompaniment of faraway thunder, each carefully constructed warhead coughed out multiple, cast-iron meteors, most of which plummeted earthward to carpet bomb the edges of the crowd. The balance spiraled down slowly underneath triple olive-drab parachutes.

Torrential, high-velocity metal balls dented car roofs, smashed windshields, and pierced heads. An incensed Rastafarian stooped down to retrieve the smoking sphere that had just cracked open his best friend's brainpan. He eyed the ball a moment too long before deciding to fling it away. The orb exploded in his face, the incendiary blast blowing off both hands, burning all the skin off his skull, and setting fire to his dreadlocks.

A high-tech quartz detonator ticked time methodically to ensure that the motorhome self-destructed at precisely 11 minutes to midnight, in a blast meticulously engineered to turn the center of Times Square into so blood-doused an *abattoir* that the sensationalist press would cover the story for three weeks straight.

First to erupt were two 15-gallon body-panel tanks, the outside walls of which had been carefully and lovingly seeded with .36-inch diameter steel balls. Held lightly in place by a thin coating of epoxy that melted immediately in the fiery blast, the 000 buckshot scythed out to slice people open like murderously efficient, point-blank grapeshot.

Six backyard-barbecue propane tanks, three on each rear quarter of the motorhome, launched next...shattering limbs as they rocketed horizontally through the crowd, their fiery tails torching anything flammable. The ground-skimming antipersonnel devices tumbled wildly before erupting to maim those far enough away to have survived a 50-foot-diameter fireball of gasoline, naphtha, and benzene that immediately crisped the ground-zero remains of those eviscerated by the initial explosions.

The trailer, which had been knocked end over tumbling end backward from the blasted motorhome, crashed down on its roof, crunching its brass tubes flat. The violent gyrations activated an acid-through-metal tilt switch with a 65-second delay. Individual eruptions at each of its three exposed sides spewed out thousands of high-velocity, .25-caliber steel darts and cast-iron pellets, shotgunning dazed victims downrange from those who had been vaporized in the initial blasts.

Four hundred and eighty-seven celebrants were killed outright in the first series of explosions; another 129 lay scattered in the pretzel twists of convulsive, spasming torment...dying of bone-charring burns, succumbing to multiple gunshot wounds, perishing helter-skelter from the concussive death of aerial mining, the deadly fruit of which still banged down heavily to smash limbs while clanking and rolling through screams of unfathomable horror...severing and shredding in oddly spaced intervals as delayed-action fuses ticked down to zero.

The first six patrolmen inside the charnel house, as well as four paramedics and one battalion fire chief, were killed by time-delay blasts: legs blown off at the hips, stomachs ripped open, bloody eye sockets hemorrhaging like running sores...all courtesy of dwarf fireballs spitting malicious metal in striking resemblance to blast-borne spores of deadly, man-killing milkweeds.

Word raced at light speed from epicenter to perimeter, instantly alerting recently arrived Emergency Services personnel. Ambulances, fire trucks, and police cars skewed to crooked, brake-burning halts. Trauma medics and disaster-relief crews crouched behind flimsy cover to avoid trampling by a terror-crazed human deluge—the rampaging mob of panic-stricken survivors desperately seeking escape from the bloody sluice of grisly carnage.

Police Captain D'Artagnon Jones jammed a handkerchief under his uniform hat where a ricocheting 10-penny nail had gouged out a three-inch gash still bleeding profusely under the soaked pressure bandage he had to grit his teeth to hold in place.

"There are others worse off in there," he said, jerking an

impatient elbow upward at a nervously hovering paramedic. *"See to them first, goddammit!"*

"Fuck no!" she bristled. "You can hear it for yourself. That there's a goddamned combat zone. I ain't going in there. It for damn sure ain't over yet."

"Commissioner!" Jones seethed impatiently into his microphone, ducking involuntarily as three light-plastic ball mines, recently dragged over by small, windblown parachutes, exploded nearby in rapid succession. *"Sir! There are more arms and legs flying around in there than at the goddamned Battle of the Marne, sir!"*

He impatiently dropped his mike hand for a moment, trying hard to squelch the squawk of party sounds broadcast from the upstate-mansion ballroom where the commissioner was playing unabashed toady to the mayor and the governor. At first softly muttering, "Fucking asshole politician, as if I didn't know that already," Jones radioed back: "Believe me, sir, I understand completely. *But being as I've already lost six men in this here fucking war zone, I ain't about to send anyone else into that slaughterhouse until the bomb squad tells me it's fucking secured!"*

Jones clicked off at the sight of a spectral Sergeant Arthur Peabody Nichols dragging his left leg while limping out through curlicue whisps of frosty ground fog and soot-gray bomb smoke, his face blackened by flash burns, naked except for lacerated boots and shreds of trousers stuck to his legs by dead Peterbilt's blood, staggering slowly away in shell-shocked stupor and streaming-tear grief.

CHAPTER 21
POLESTAR

Each passing week of festering identity crisis found Danny Mahlouf less in need of material things in general and timepieces in particular, having long ago traded his mint-condition Bucherer with alarm chimes for a block of tarry, potent hashish...not so much to garnish the window dressing of current persona—he dared not risk the impairment that came with smoking the drug—but because he was inexorably divesting himself of worldly possessions and his past dependence on them.

He blinked awake in the darkness well before the *muezzin's* first hourly call to daily prayer. The clockwork good-morning "Yes, you're still alive" ache behind his eyes had given him all the wake-up nudge he needed, rousing him at half past four on a mist-jotted, central Amman morning. Danny had been averaging 30 minutes less sleep each day of this week. Soon he wouldn't be getting any...which really didn't matter because his prospects were nil and his future uncertain at best, and so lack of sleep would soon be of no more concern to him than eating, bodily functions, or sex.

Not that Danny had ever in his life had trouble "getting any." His Lebanese good looks and "immigrant chromosome" Persian-blue eyes placed him in a stand-alone contrast to those around him. Danny's athletic physique, coupled with the added fillip of prodigious sexual equipment, assured him a steady parade of women more than eager to share his bed while he played their erogenous strings *fortissimo*. His superb genetic inheritance, remarkable physical stamina, and astonishing potency comprised impeccable credentials for the current assignment.

Once known by former classmates at the University of

Florence as the "Adonis of the Adriatic," Danny died in a boating accident off the rocky coast of Sicily shortly after skillfully compromising the university's chancellor by working through the doddering old man's much younger and sexually susceptible wife. He resurfaced after some budget plastic surgery, a little electrolysis, and a few quick injections of collagen, segueing smoothly into the Middle East mainstream as Danny Mahlouf, starving Egyptian artist. His current patron was the regally evanescent Jahneen al-Birquafi...wife of Hassam al-Birquafi, the chief economist of the Royal Bank of Jordan.

Danny had brought Jahneen along very slowly, which was standard operating procedure. Overfertilization burned them up; too little attention and they withered on the vine. Sometimes they bore fruit; often they remained barren. Some took longer; others never panned out at all. Most recently, things had worked out very well in Italy, and so Danny's record was aces so far... but each assignment could go either way, and you were only as good as your last score.

True to form, Danny would soldier on stolidly either until Jahneen blossomed or until his services were more urgently needed elsewhere, in which case he would vanish like yesterday's sunset and materialize as a new man, perhaps no more than a country away or perhaps in another time zone halfway around the world.

Mother's scrimpy budget permitted only one other like him, but that competitor was now recuperating under an assumed name in a South African hospital—never to walk again without a limp—due to serious injuries inflicted in Johannesburg by a crowbar-wielding husband who wasn't as "ex" as everyone thought him to be.

So in Danny's case, it forever remained a question of placing circumstances on the platform scale of operational necessity and then allocating the limited resource he represented to wherever such application would do the most good in the fewest number of days.

Danny painted the impersonal shiftlessness of his

precarious existence with the broadly gray brush strokes of considerable morbidity. He slipped with frightening ease into the somber black enveloping his general preoccupation like a shroud of impending doom...all the while convincing himself that he would be less prone to self-abusive thought if only he had roots and were not a sprig of human tumbleweed blown hither and yon by the vagaries of bedroom espionage.

A self-avowed night-sider, Danny always managed to drive those thoughts away by one in the morning through the simple expedient of tapping paint-stained fingernails emphatically on the tarnished iron of the sagging headboard. He marked time while verbalizing admonishments, gulping in place of sleeping pills; drugs would dull the senses relied upon to ensure himself another day, however unfulfilling any particular 24-hour period might be.

Tick-tick-tick-fingertip on the metal – not now. Don't think about that now.

All well and good while dozing fitfully, but his mental machinery dished out bad thoughts long before breakfast...when his eyes first opened, when he was not awake enough to be in control...and so was at the mercy of bombinating wheelworks which had proven themselves to comprise a pitiless opponent. Danny had simply been "under" too long; the rough-and-tumble pillory of inexorable circumstance had worn him down to where he was thinner than tracing paper and curling at the edges.

Four-forty-five.

Danny snatched a brown, two-inch roach from under the tattered bedspread cloaking his naked body. He drew the pregnant female out, clinically observing its feverishly wiggling legs and antennae. He held the loathsome bug up close for a brief, side-to-side examination before abruptly squashing it flat between thumb and forefinger.

I need about six months in the Presidential Suite of the New York Hilton. Failing that, it is quite unlikely I shall ever make it back.

Jahneen would be arriving any minute. He didn't care enough to ask exactly what pretext she used as a smokescreen for their twice-a-week tryst; she, on the other hand, never volunteered details of her subterfuge. Not that it hadn't been good the first few times. Jahneen was lushly sensual in a late 60s sort of way, personifying the sexual ideals men cherished before standing idly by while their women dieted themselves halfway through anorexia's house of horrors.

On the downside, Jahneen was first and foremost starved for the thickness with which Danny so virily expressed her frustrated longings. She needed little more than potently urgent insertion and so embodied a strikingly paradoxical carnality: at once exotic, gorgeous, and opulently built, but with a sexual imagination inversely proportional to enrapturing physical charms. Danny had, of late, been hard pressed to keep mass in motion. Hoary relationships were best broken off sooner rather than later, and today promised to be as good a day as any.

The stairwell cat's piercing *Ree-Oww!* brought him back current with the immediate environment. Reflexes clicked into full alert, his basic instinct for survival now of primary concern. Danny's maudlin musings were quickly suppressed, his offhand ponderings dumped unceremoniously into Baggage Storage, all thanks to the invisible trip wire serving as his first line of defense.

One of Danny's cats lived with him in the peeling-paint shoe box that only a truly destitute unfortunate would call an apartment; the other cat lived in a tiny tape recorder hidden behind the small icebox in the kitchen, where roaches multiplied with ferocious abandon. Each night before going to bed, he changed the 26 or so recordings he made in his lead-lined cedar chest, the one place he was assured complete privacy from whatever listening devices might be pointed his way from windows across the street.

The sound effect was actuated when a pinpoint infrared beam was broken at the foot of the outside stairs leading only to his apartment. The "cat" pawing garbage under the steps would mew loudly and boldly enough to be easily heard from anywhere in Danny's rooms. The fake feline fooled Danny's real cat, an Abyssinian with one gray eye and one blue, which grew restlessly agitated while mewling in heated response, thus ensuring that Danny would be up one way or the other.

Eyes flicking around randomly and wary, Danny slid his Para-Ordnance P14-45 semiautomatic out from under the adjacent pillow. There was just no getting around the genuine worth of heavy-caliber stopping power. Fourteen rounds of Winchester .45 ACP 230-grain Black Talon hollow points ensured sufficiently authoritative gunfire to muster a convincing argument in whatever situation he might become embroiled.

The combat-customized gun was never more than a quick snatch away, safety off and ready to fire. A seamless swing onto the target, a gentle caress of hair trigger, and Danny's pocket artillery piece could be counted on to decimate any civilian opposition he was likely to come across. When confronting body armor, Danny shot for the face. He was casually flip about his extraordinary talent for popping both eyes even in treacherous, low-light conditions and at ranges well in excess of 30 yards.

Danny's pistolwork perfectly mirrored the fluidity of Hollywood's Old West gunslingers. His life demanded that his draw be no slower than light speed...his shooting no less than bull's-eye perfect every time.

In 25 seconds, he would hear the distinctive sound at Step 17, his clue that it was indeed Jahneen climbing the stairs in anticipation of ascension to the altar of his bed. Bad Guys would hug the wall, ever mindful of stairs always creaking in the middle but not at either end, in which case the silence of their approach would betray them.

Cree-akk!

Even with the first test seemingly passed, Danny's pistol still lay across his stomach, its barrel aimed between his feet and directly at the door's centerline. Test two was the flimsy lock, the inside of which he kept lightly dusted with talc-fine grit, and which now fought back against the grating pressure of roughly ground key, the third tooth of which was a fraction of a millimeter too short.

As expected, Jahneen was having trouble gaining entry...

the energetic rasp of key jiggling in recalcitrant lock becoming more loudly intense. Whereas no assassin would have pressed on so aggressively, she was becoming more urgent in direct proportion to rising frustration...feverishly insistent while striving to gain access to his sex. Then success, her perfume wafting fragrantly forward as she tiptoed inside and eased the door closed. Jahneen slipped the two bolts—top and bottom—as he had once instructed her to do. She was a fast study; very little bore repeating.

He smoothly slid the firearm into a cracked-leather pouch hanging from the pitted, tarnished bed frame and unholstered another, more potent weapon. Jahneen giggled while creeping into the warm depression left behind, her palm sliding over his stone-hard stomach, then lower toward his groin and the staff of pleasure now rising in full exercise of its own mind, oblivious to the little head's so-so attitude about the circumstances in which he was enmeshed.

Danny leaned through the dewy musk of a sweet-smelling aura. His mouth closed over Jahneen's, their tongues snaking tightly around each other, knotting then uncoiling like erotic serpents in rapt exploration of spiritual incandescence. He rolled smoothly left, right hand filling to overflowing with large breasts, its stiff nipple burgeoning with the warmth surging up from the epicenter of her ardor and spreading outward through chest walls. Lust stoked her brain fully aboil with the unbridled desire of long-repressed thirst about to be prodigally slaked.

Danny rose fluidly up on one elbow, the sheet tenting over his back as she wriggled under him, their lips still locked together in that first unbroken, deeply questing kiss. She glided beneath, legs opening and slightly raised, he kneeling before her as if in covetous worship, lovingly reaching down and gently probing the bejeweled forest adorning the base-camp mound betwixt lithesome thighs.

Jahneen greedily grabbed for his potent, throbbing manhood. She drew Danny closer, both hands tightly gripping the shaft of penis as if playing "choose-up-sides" with a baseball bat. All pretext at foreplay wantonly forgotten, she aligned her loins to devour him whole. Jahneen thoughtfully positioned hands on tightly clenched buttocks, dug nails into flesh, and pulled him hard into her, opening herself up roughly with the sheer girth of brawny virility, grunting against her lover in wide-eyed, slavish abandon.

Danny stroked Jahneen as a konzertmeister would a Stradivarius, evoking from her soul a passionate orchestration of fiery fulfillment. He moved directly against her at first, pressing his ramrod density firmly in and out, then slightly side to side and next in full rotation, his juice-laden organs swaying up and back in gentle nudge against the plushly warm flesh of quivering inner thighs.

Jahneen's fingernails scraped randomly, crisscrossed red jags along the full length of Danny's well-muscled back. She wrapped arms around his neck, palms over elbows, drawing him in deeper, sucking his tongue far down her throat, sighing in pleasure as the ridged stoutness of his powerful midriff pressed earnestly dominant into her softly yielding femininity.

Jahneen's breathing became a violently rasping gurgle of ragged, gulped gasps as Danny rolled her over and pulled her down firmly on top of him. He thrust narrow hips up off the bed in a precisely supercharged rhythm, driving his throbbing muscularity deep into the nether reaches of grasping rapture. His hands roamed up and down her sides, fingers at first playing piano on her ribs, then reaching eagerly up to full, free-swinging breasts. Jahneen's hands clasped hard over Danny's, pulling his palms deeply into pliant, scalding flesh. She growled deliriously while fully ingesting cosmic lightning, immediately bursting forth to backlight her in the sparkling supernova of ecstatic completion.

Jahneen's back arched stiffly, spine locking rigid as she bent backward like a hunter's bow strained to its absolute limit. Danny thrust the edge of right hand into her mouth. She bit down aggressively, jerking from side to side like a tomcat savaging a mouse...then roared gutturally, a lioness in urgent heat, her innards a sultry, lusty friction rubbing tight against tempered-steel maleness.

Jahneen yanked him tightly and further up to the hilt inside her, finally eliciting the response she craved: a massively spewing eruption propelling jets of sweet fluid high up into her juddering belly. Danny's potent deluge gushed powerfully as it spread mightily through her loins, his roaring spray of male completion going everywhere inside Jahneen as he pumped her full of everything he was and all that he would ever be in every incarnation he might blessedly enjoy.

The voluminous discharge filled Jahneen to overflowing. Her pelvis drove down hard as she drained Danny dry of every drop of superheated essence. Then their rhythm slowed, became slightly disrupted, and then totally disjointed before finally disappearing altogether as she rolled gently off him, gulped air, and waited for their breathing to normalize.

Danny's last thoughts as he lay there were that it had not been that bad after all. Quite the contrary; it had been very, very good. So good, in fact, that he was of a mind that something had unequivocally and unalterably changed between them. Just what that might possibly be, other than a clearly unmistakable escalation in the vigor of connection, he was unable to discern with even the slightest degree of certainty...but pondering it was the best prelude to the deepest sleep he had ever known.

In a comforting snuggle psychically reminiscent of womb-warmth, they lay against each other like two perfectly matched spoons, their minds kayaking the uplifting white water of exquisite come-down, which led them...riverine...to intoxicating dreams and sea-deep peace.

Danny jerked abruptly awake to the crash of breaking glass and a muffled curse...Jahneen was in the kitchen near the crackle-spatter sizzle of frying bacon. He lay back like a smiling teenager, hands clasped behind his neck, chest rising and falling, deeply relishing the delectable refreshment of good rest...negatively depressing thoughts exiled too far afield for tracking even if he were inclined to pursue so defeatist an agenda, which he definitely was not. He tossed off the threadbare sheet, swung his legs over the edge of the bed, and padded naked to the kitchen, his feet slapping loudly on splinter-riddled floor.

For the first time in total memory, dangling coils of flypaper were not bespotted with wiggling black dots of tiny insects in *extremis.* Towel-wrapped Jahneen had coffee percolating on a two-burner propane stove, domesticity apparently having been elevated to a highly cherished ideal. Danny eyed his woman appreciatively while sitting down on an empty fruit crate flanking a door askew on concrete blocks—his poverty-stricken excuse for a post-post-modern kitchen set. Yes, Jahneen had gained some weight since they had last feasted so eagerly upon each other… and even if the increase was no more than a kilo here, a kilo there. Still, in all, she carried herself very well.

Jahneen turned from the frying pan only long enough to blow a long, sensuous kiss punctuated by a brief thrust of tongue tip at the corner of her mouth.

"Daniel," she said gaily, carefully turning the bacon, "you are the only man I've ever known who could walk into a room butt-naked and not be a laughingstock. Now, how about some juicy breakfast meat for my starving artist? Cooked well but not burned, Heaven forbid. As you like it."

"Dear, sweet Jahneen," Danny said, resting his chin in his palm and looking at his lover as if seeing her for the first time. "It is always beyond me how you can put your own self-interest second to my own when we are together."

"I have more than just this meal for you, as you shall find out soon enough," she said mischievously.

"You know that I absolutely abhor surprises."

"In this case, you will have to bear with me. First of all, you must keep your strength up, as I do so enjoy this."

"Obviously!"

"I meant the mothering, you silly boy. Here and there, now and then, never having had children, I can...." Jahneen broke off and carefully rewrapped the blue, monogrammed bath towel comprising the sum total of her overnight kit, avoiding Danny's eyes as she turned away impishly. "I'm sorry," she said, suddenly sniffling and wiping her nose with the back of her hand. "Forgive me! Tears of joy, my love, simply tears of joy," she said, turning back to face him again, Chiclet teeth shining radiantly out past sensually puffed lips. "This is supposed to be a good time. A happy time. I have so few of them."

Danny rose and took Jahneen in his arms. She sagged against him, clenching her fists as she laid her head on his chest.

"I get such strength from you, Daniel."

"But of course."

"Promise that you will never leave me," she pleaded, not daring to look at his face.

"I promise," he said.

"And you are my baby, Daniel. No?"

"Always," he whispered.

"And to you, I am more than..."

"Of course! I couldn't live without you," he said in mock anger, holding her at arm's length while pushing his thumb up under her chin and peering intently into the unplumbed blackness of shimmery eyes. *"Never!* Nor could my work, being that you are a most worthy and all-too-generous patron of my art. Although, in truth," he sighed, suddenly disheartened, "I must readily admit that these days there's not much future in patronage as benevolent as yours."

"Now really, Daniel," she sniffed, glad for the moment that he had changed the subject. *I will tell him. In time. Yes! Sooner than later!* "I absolutely will not tolerate such defeatist talk from you. Your work is excellent. You will be discovered by others as knowledgeable as myself. I know that. If not here, then somewhere else. And soon. Very soon. I can promise you that."

"I actually fear that my talent is much more physical than artistic."

"Nonsense! Look at your landscapes, your sunsets, your..."

"Wallpaper is all they're good for. Spray them with the right chemicals, and they'd make ideal fly traps."

Danny stood up abruptly as if looking for trouble and sure that he would have no trouble finding it. Then he spun on his heel and walked rapidly into the tiny inset of the bedroom, as Jahneen raced along in worried pursuit. It was childishly easy to find a landscape not entirely to his liking. He curled his toes, made a fist with his foot, and angrily kicked through a five-by-five, heavily daubed depiction of scrawny sea birds wheeling off wintry Northumberland shore in vain search of sustenance.

Jahneen recoiled, horrified at the destruction as Danny glanced around and quickly found his second and third targets, stomping them out of their frames and destroying them both.

"Daniel! No! Stop!"

"Trash! All trash!" he yelled, wiggling the ruined art loose from his foot, then squatting and viciously ripping canvas from frames. Bits of flaked paint and cloth fluttered around Jahneen's black tresses like tormented confetti launched by a demented artist gone finally and unalterably mad.

She knelt down, spun Danny around, slapped his face side to side, then gripped his shoulders tightly and shook him brutally until his neck almost cracked under the strain.

"Stop it!" Jahneen screamed, teeth bared, eyes livid. *"Stop it, you little prick!* How dare you ruin fine art? You would destroy all of this? You self-centered bastard. *I won't stand for it!"*

She plopped down on the floor, suddenly exhausted by the effort, then took both of his hands in hers and pressed his fingers to her breast.

"Oh, Daniel," she cried. *"I'm sorry!* You must forgive me," she pleaded. "But I had to do it," she bubbled, suddenly brightening. "I had to stop you because...all right, enough about art for the moment. I can see that it upsets you. Fine," she smiled. "Listen to me, babbling on about you when I still haven't told you about me. Yes, there is good news. For you and for me. Yours first. I'm sorry. I do seem to be getting so much more easily confused these days."

"Good news? What better news could there be than your unqualified faith in me as an artist? Why, what happened here has proven..."

"Better than that," she gulped. "Much better. Well, there hasn't exactly been time to tell you, considering our agenda just passed, and thank goodness for that, I might add."

"Jahneen..."

"About the opening. Don't interrupt me, lest I forget again. The opening I arranged for you!"

"Opening?"

"Yes, my about-to-be-discovered artist. Fawzi says that his gallery is yours for the asking. And you thought that I was the only one who believed in you? *Fool!* Daniel, we have two weeks to gather up your work and make you more presentable."

"Well, you may as well just cancel it," Danny said, astounded not only that her feelings for him transcended his sexual prowess to encompass unvarnished faith in his work, but also totally amazed by the fact that Fawzi the Finicky had actually bought a slice of the masquerade. "I'm through, I tell you. I don't feel it here...in here," he said, driving a fist hard into his chest.

And it would definitely not do to be overly exposed to too many prying eyes, especially while in the company of Jahneen al-Birquafi.

Feeling more than just the walls closing in on him, Danny said, "I have to get away."

"An artistic crisis of identity, perhaps?" she said, drawing back and eyeing him skeptically.

"Call it what you will. This city holds nothing for me. My time here is up. I have to move on."

"I have thought of that, too. Believe me, if that is what it takes, then that is what we shall do," she said, nodding her head once in emphatic punctuation.

We?

"Jahneen, there is absolutely nothing more that I can do here. I am stifled; dulled out."

"On the verge of your first opening, and you talk this way? *Unbelievable!*"

"The decision has already been made."

"Without consulting me?! Of all the insufferably arrogant

things you could have done... *Shame on you!"*

"So be it."

"Others have struggled longer than you," Jahneen lectured sternly.

"No doubt that's true, and with far lesser emotional results. After all, they weren't blessed with a patron as loving and warmly giving as yourself."

"Perhaps a change of pace," she offered, hungry for Danny's assent. "A change of scene? *Yes!* That would do it, I know. It would work wonders for both of us."

"On a pauper's pay?" Danny snorted in disbelief. *"Hardly!* The trouble is," he said, walking over and sitting down on the edge of the bed, "even if I could get away, I wouldn't know where to go...what to do."

"The heel of the Italian boot. We could get lost there."

Again, that damnable we.

"No."

"Then somewhere else. Look, we can do it together. We must do it together." Jahneen knelt at the bedside and took Danny's hands in hers. "We will do it together. I have to leave my husband. I can no longer live with him. But the most important is..."

"Go on."

"I'm pregnant."

"Pregnant!"

"Yes, pregnant. *With your son!"* she beamed. "It will be a son. I know it will be a son. A strong, healthy, strapping son. You have given me a child, something that miserable excuse of a husband could never do. All those years of trying and he could never...not that he cared enough to try seriously after the first two years, but Daniel..."

"And it is mine, this child?"

"Don't go cold on me, you fuck!" she hissed, glaring up at him with clenched fists. *"Whose else would it be?!"* she blazed, punching him hard in the stomach. *"Do you take me for the village slut?!"* Then softly: "Oh, Daniel. *Forgive me!* I didn't mean...it will

work," she said, kissing his knee, then laying her cheek there.

"And live on what?" he asked patiently, outwardly calm while both inner selves sparred into open revolt. Emotionally, Danny, wanting to sup heavily on Jahneen's appealing rationale, now beckoned him toward the safe port he had squandered so much time craving. Practical Danny telling him to stay the course, to keep on track, not to confuse the job with personal considerations, because if she ever found out, as she most assuredly would one day, she would cut out his heart without so much as a by-your-leave and ram it down his throat before he was brain-dead.

With each half of the schizoid personality weaker than the whole, neither could fully carry the day, and so the internal conflict raged unabated. Morocco would be nice at just about any time of year. He had connections there.

God bless Jahneen; it just might work at that! No, it won't! It would never work!

We can't eat oil paint," Danny noted solemnly, "which I can hardly afford as it is."

"I can get us money. A lot of money. I have that all worked out."

"You're always getting me money."

"Don't become so suddenly proud; it doesn't suit you."

"All right, then. Tell me how?"

"Not until you make love to me again," she said lightly. She stood in front of him, the towel pooling at her feet. Danny leaned forward and laid his ear on her stomach.

"This will have to end," he murmured. "A failed artist. And now an unemployed father? I want to make a difference in this world. Certainly, I am not doing that now."

"Social work, Danny. In our newly adopted country."

"Which would be?"

"Wherever you would be the most comfortable," she said, again sitting down at his feet.

"Sweden?" Danny asked anxiously, truly wanting to believe.

"Yes, that is doable," Jahneen chirped.

"You make it sound so simple."

"That's because it is!"

"Do you have a passport?"

"Of course! Daniel, please don't take me for a complete idiot. Give me credit for having at least a teacup's worth of intelligence."

"Ah, but there's not enough time...and I do not have enough energy...to right even one quarter of all the world's wrongs."

"Of course, we could stay here, and you could find employment with my husband," she said snidely, "and we could pretend to be one big, happy family. Al-Birquafi," she scoffed, "the greatest money-launderer of the Middle East. He keeps four sets of books, you know. One for the king, one for the Iranians, one for the House of Saud, and one for himself."

Bear fruit, my lovely, Practical Danny thought, having won the immediate battle but not the wider war...seeing as how Jahneen seemed imminently ready to burst quite productively into bloom.

He pulled her up and sat her down beside him on the bed. She took his hands tentatively in hers and placed 20 spread fingers on her stomach, pulling them into the warm softness sheltering new life stirring within.

"I simply cannot bring myself to discuss your husband at a time like this," Danny lied. "It is bad enough that I have made love many times to the wife of another man. And you yourself really know nothing of me."

"I know that you are lovable, sweet, and kind," Jahneen whispered urgently, head bobbing forward as if she were pecking words at him. "I know that you have given me what no one has ever been able to give me before. Love...and a reason for living. I know that I love you, just as I know that you will come to love me, in time, even if you do not love me now as deeply as I love you. I promise that I will not be sloppy pregnant or disgusting pregnant. I will be a credit to you always. I will do my best to make you happy. I will stay radiant for you, my Daniel."

"No! I'm sorry," he said, emphatically shaking his head. "There is no way that this would ever work."

"I will get away with you or without you. I have it all planned. Besides, my husband has many, many problems, some of which are absolutely insoluble, not the least of which is that he talks in his sleep," Jahneen murmured. "That, I can assure you, will catch up to him one day, more likely sooner than later, and I don't want to be around when it does. Not only for my sake but for the sake of our unborn child. Personally, have you ever known anyone who would keep four sets of books?"

"I could see two, perhaps."

"But four, Daniel?"

"You are talking to an artist, my sweet, not to a high financier."

"Oh, and he does get high, believe you me," Jahneen chuckled. "That's another reason why I love you; you make me laugh so easily. And do you know when he talks the loudest? Right after he exits my bedroom. After spending most of the night with his little whore, he comes home wanting me. Can you believe that?! Why only then, and practically no other time?"

"Because he knows about us," Danny said simply, "and that is his method of taking revenge on you...his way of getting even."

"Impossible!" she snorted. *"No one knows about us except us!"*

"Jahneen, you are so much the child in so many ways. There are those who make it their business to know, and from them there are no secrets," Danny said solemnly. "And never any escape."

"I am always much too careful, my Daniel. I leave at different times. I vary my route on each visit."

She shook her head emphatically, clearly upset...even while thinking he might be right, and trying desperately to drive away the awful consequences her mind was particularly adept at conjuring up.

"I have the answer!" he said, finger-snapping his way

buoyant as if hurdling the single impediment so clearly responsible for generating the foggy gloom beclouding every waking moment. "Without a doubt, what you have told me is proof positive of how highly your husband regards you, the majestic esteem in which he holds you. After his escapade, it is to you that he returns every time. Don't you see? He always comes home to you because all other women pale in comparison."

"Spare me your dime-store psychology!" she spat. "Stop now before you disgust me further."

"I only meant that he probably only talks to that other woman you accuse of being his whore."

"So could he not talk to me?"

"There is not another woman alive who could match the incredible bounty of your beauteous charms," Danny said, evading her question for the moment as sensory alarm bells clanged in response to something more newsworthy than extramarital discord twisting slowly in passion's breezes. "And from what you tell me..."

"He comes into my room stinking, literally reeking of that bitch, and then he practically rapes me before going back into his own bedroom. I pretend to be asleep when he returns home in the early hours, but that has never stopped him. Truthfully," she said with a wry smile, "there have been times when I was still wet with your love."

"No doubt he thought the moisture was only your excitement and nothing else."

"Whatever the reason, believe me when I say that he takes great pleasure in humping up against me at that time—but at no other."

Gently now. Always prompt; never pressure.

"While he rambles on and on, you say?"

"No sooner is he back in his room snoring, but that happens."

"And he speaks of?" Danny asked innocently.

"About his latest assignment," she huffed, "which purports to be the biggest fiscal machination of his miserly life up until this date. A real bounty, considering the percentage he extracts for such services. He is right now preparing to handle a five-million-dollar payoff for a massive direct action."

You mean a terrorist atrocity, Danny thought glumly, as he said: "The Middle East is full to the brim with cabals and conspiracies, plans and schemes."

"This is far different. This payment is for the one who blew up that American airliner."

The one?

"Daniel," she said, tearing her gaze off intricately patterned, cracked-plaster walls and watching him intently, "do I appear to you as a doltish simpleton living her entire life perpetually in the dark...without so much as a flashlight-beam of hope to light her way? I apologize to you sincerely if I have conveyed so mistaken an impression. On more than one occasion, I have gained access to my husband's offices. I perfected the art of strongbox rifling while my husband was freshening up with hour-long, perfumed baths before his trips to his little whore," Jahneen said proudly. "And lo and behold, I came across some very interesting papers. I have listened carefully to what he said between snores. I have listened intently for what no one dared utter in polite Jordanian society. The little fool thinks he is making a difference by handling a payoff for this upcoming action. Do you remember those said to be behind the bombing of that airliner?"

Said to be?

"El-Fahd el-Aswad?" he offered.

"The same! He is their banker. For years, he and Gadhafi have been closer than toes scrunched together in an undersized boot."

"Since?"

"Dating back to the time of that raid on the OPEC oil ministers."

"The Carlos caper."

"Yes, that's the one."

"In the seventies, I think."

"Yes, whenever," she said impatiently, punctuating her

story with rapid hand movements as he listened raptly. while cautioning himself to: *Hint. Do not hasten.*

"And now those foul fellows," Jahneen said, "are planning to work through this overseas agent of theirs for another incident. That airliner? It was his letter of introduction."

His letter?

"I have since learned that the bombing was a calling card, if you will. His way of introducing himself."

His way?

"Now they will pay him off...

Pay him off?

"...for another, even larger operation on a much grander scale. It will take place at the exact dead center of the United States. Right in the heartland, as it were, or so I have learned indirectly from sources who have proved themselves to be quite reliable."

"This man, he is..."

"And there I go again," Jahneen laughed in high embarrassment, "running off at the mouth as if plagued by verbal diarrhea. So like a woman! That is what you are thinking, are you not? You don't have to say it; I know that is exactly what is right now on your mind."

"It's just that I am curious that this one man, as you say... working alone? It is hard to believe!"

"I will tell you what I believe," she whispered impishly, "seeing as how you are now more interested in what I have said than in me personally. Dear Daniel, if I didn't know you better, I would be forced to conclude that you are trying to pump me."

Careful not to do so too abruptly, he looked up from his hands and directly at her face.

"So are you?" she asked, brilliant eyes demanding an answer.

"Did you say...?"

"Pumping me," she repeated, suddenly nervously suspicious that she might have said too much to someone who, in all practical reality, might even be an agent of her husband, so well connected was the pig.

"I have every intention of pumping you in a most sensual way," Danny said, knowing that only the rashly adventurous pressed on when shields rose.

"Inside the U.S.," Jahneen said, inclining her head coyly while eyeing him melodramatically...not fully convinced of the honorableness of his intentions. "He goes by the name of Cue Ball."

"Cue what?!" Danny laughed.

"This man."

One man?

"I found a cryptic notation buried as a half-hidden accounting footnote in one of my husband's books," Jahneen continued. "A CB was listed as the president, chairman of the board, and chief financial officer of Black Cat Fireworks, out of Macau."

"So?" Danny asked, barely managing to stifle a chuckle.

"You'd better humor me, Danny, I'm warning you!"

"Okay, okay," he apologized. "So?"

"'So?' you ask. *'So?!'* Daniel, does it not strike you as odd that there is only one person doing a three-part job for a company no one has ever heard of?"

"Which, of course, you know for a fact."

"I made some discreet inquiries...in my own special way."

"Not all that unusual," he said casually. "Many offshore companies are nothing more than tiny import-export offices. Fronts, if you will. You have a mail drop, a desk, and a chair. Sometimes there isn't even a telephone in the room."

"Really, Daniel!" Jahneen gasped, striving to keep her exasperation in check. "Must I spell everything out for you?"

"I will readily admit that I am not a quick study for anything that even remotely comes close to what you have mentioned."

"You really do need a real woman to take care of you!" she snapped, clearly drained dry of patience.

"But this CB?" he asked gently, leading her back around to the critically important juncture.

"Cue Ball. That's what I got between snores. Actually, al-Birquafi the donkey brayed, 'You can always depend on Cue Ball to clear the table.'"

"And?"

"That's it."

"That's it?!"

"Yes," she sighed deeply, as if returning from seance-trance...and again looking at Daniel strangely, as if not trusting him 100 percent. "What more do you need?"

"Certainly more than that before I would take stock in so wild a fiction. Now, as for that other matter, I cannot afford to leave the country," he said finally. "You will have...you must have the baby here. I will disappear. Your husband will accept it, and you. Believe me."

"And why should I? What could you possibly know of such things?" Her eyes flared angrily. "He would sooner see me dead than pregnant in his villa, with a child he will have guessed could not possibly be his own. And as for the money, I know how we can get it."

"Not from your husband, I pray. It would not do to take from him his wife and the money with which to make good our escape," Danny laughed, sliding deeper in love because...wonder of wonders...Jahneen, rather than being just a cushiony snippet of Arab fluff, was showing herself to be a surprisingly accomplished woman with a solidly workable plan in mind.

"I have photographed his records extensively," she said proudly, defiantly. "I will sell them to the Israelis."

"Just like that?" he scoffed.

"Of course, just like that!" The Jews are always drooling for anything even faintly resembling what I have to sell."

"No! It is far too dangerous!"

"I have it all worked out."

"Nonsense! You'd be shot in a minute!"

"Not if I do it through Canada, as I plan to. I have family there; they can be trusted. You may rest assured that my husband is not the only Jordanian with connections. I also have a second uncle in Larnaca. He will..."

"Have you said anything about this to anyone yet?"

"No, not yet but..."

"Then don't!" Danny rasped emphatically. *"I absolutely forbid it!"*

"We'll talk more about this some other time," she said, suddenly tired of conversation and glancing anxiously around the room like a flight-weary sparrow in search of a branch on which to alight.

I will get this to Yousef later, Danny thought. *But for now...*

Danny drew Jahneen close. His strong hands moved south from her shoulders as she lay back on the bed, head inclined upward. Their mouths met, his manhood stirring and rising most potently, fired as it was with the passion pumping through arteries and surging through veins.

Jahneen reached for her love, desirous of satisfying the need bearing witness from the very depths of twinned spiritual marrow. Danny's roving hands eagerly explored the hourglass contours of Jahneen's voluptuous body as if for the first time... as they returned once more to worship ardently at the shrine of passionate union.

Ethereal satisfaction's rising tide crested over and past them both, tossing them about crazily like fragmented cork on tempestuous ocean...before finally depositing them winded and spent on love's far-distant shore...caressed by the foaming burble of gentle surf that muffled the meow of the cat at the foot of the stairs...and kept Danny from noticing the ominous silence at Step 17.

CHAPTER 22
BANKER'S HOURS

Hassam al-Birquafi, chief economist of the Royal Bank of Jordan and the personal financial advisor of His Majesty the King, loathed the cold, perpetually shifting crosswinds strumming the high wire he regularly, albeit unwillingly, traversed...the fragile, shoe-width cable bridging ruling-class debauchery to the merciless morality of the Muslim Army of God.

Behind him soared skyscraping peaks, lushly fruitful with prized personal possessions amassed during his 46 game-running years of life. Far ahead loomed mist-shrouded hinterlands, whose cloud-wrapped mesas were ripely fertile with all he still desired. Spread darkly in between...lying in avaricious wait far below... was the grossly misshapen, rock-toothed maw of the Valley of Death.

Al-Birquafi detested everything about the supporting role forced upon him by virtue of financial cunning. A bulge-eyed, frog-faced man given to overactive sweat glands and sebaceous eruptions, the banker long ago learned to fully appreciate the finer things in life...those tokens, toys, trollops and titles greedily raked in with madcap, craven grasp.

Massive personal fortunes had been garnered through determined exercise of superlative fiscal dexterity...a singular talent more than compensating for the curse of oily repugnance wreathing the banker like the acrid backwash stench of rancid musk. Such megabuck resources came in especially handy when the financier felt driven to satisfy rapacious sexual appetites. While al-Birquafi was a miserable failure at charmingly seducing physically attractive members of either gender, he had no trouble purchasing their amorous presence for however long it took to indulge his wide-ranging spectrum of depraved, prurient interests.

But his facile knowledge of negotiable instruments was a two-edged sword. Having comfortably ensconced him in the palatial surroundings befitting a man of multi-Keogh means, specialized proficiency also guaranteed no-choice recruitment by an organization for whom refusal was a fatally inappropriate response.

Dear friends and social-circle relations regarded with awe and wonderment his veiled allusions to fluid machinery especially designed for scrubbing dirty money clean. Among the myriad hangers-on peopling the whirligig swirl of business/ sexual universe, al-Birquafi was jokingly referred to as the Laundryman, though the trickster himself never ventured anywhere close to touching even slightly tainted currency. In the swirling fog, wheels-within-wheels underground governed by religious fundamentalism's rigid, iron-fisted rule, however, Hassam al-Birquafi was dossiered Koolooniyaa (Aftershave).

The heavy perfumes and unsubtle colognes upon which the portly al-Birquafi depended to camouflage the often-overpowering stink of sour-milk body odor were eschewed by his paramilitary counterparts. To a man, they preferred *eau de* cordite absorbed in earthy conjunction with half-lives eked out in firefight twilights of spiritual war.

Whatever bubbles their beer, al-Birquafi mused dispiritedly, gritting his teeth in response to yet another welt-raising conk in the head.

This moonless witching hour, the banged-around banker was masquerading in the threadbare coarseness of shabby workingman's garb worn during shanghaied passage to, attendance at, and return from irregularly scheduled meetings called and conducted under the velvet quilt of murky overcast. Verbally delivered call-code matched prearranged signaling arrangements, and so he went...in the company of others, proud to have surrendered all freedom of choice.

Al-Birquafi received no more than 10 minutes' advance

warning. The secular moneyman assumed, with a healthy dose of smug self-assurance, that no other invitee knew more than he. From the door knock on, he was under constant, six-guard surveillance. At that moment of summons, he was unceremoniously strip-searched for any sign of skin-flap surgery under which might nestle either homing devices or subminiature, flesh-tone microphones. The Jordanian paymaster had only enough time to don costume clothes, void bowels and bladder, and then place his shaky destiny in hands less trustworthy than his own.

Osmosing easily through password-porous Lebanese martial-law curfew, the rug-covered al-Birquafi was "trunked" blindfolded to the conference minus identification and all personal jewelry, especially wristwatch. The rear compartment of the bump-journey Peugeot was daubed liberally with the afterbirth of ewe and the excrement of wild donkey, as much to confuse Damascene sniffing dogs as well as to confound sharp-nosed agents, single through triple, who might be lurking in one-lane streets overcrossing the fortified chambers for which he was currently bound.

A wee-hour journey would not be compromised by a snout-tickling al-Birquafi emitting odors detectable 90 yards away.

Cramped, backache ride soon shifted the cashkeeper's mental focus to topics other than his pungency, which itself was now so unrecognizably alien as to be unworthy of further nasal attention. Clutched chest close was a small suitcase containing $5,000,000 in British currency and untraceable bearer bonds. White-knuckled grip verified inseparable linkage of cash to courier's life: Should he lose or otherwise fail to give a good accounting of the former, the latter would be summarily forfeit.

Tangle-twist routes contained nine times the number of abrupt, directional variances needed to confuse even the most highly skilled turn-counter. Best guess upon slow, muffled-brakes deceleration was that the pitch-dark passage had consumed roughly 40 minutes. After skewing hard to an abrupt stop inside a musty garage, the bullet-dinged car stood barely visible in the yellow haze of steamy oil lamps...before disappearing behind the composite armor of an electric-track door sliding down silently on thickly greased gear channels.

Shouldering upward at the click-pop cue, al-Birquafi threw off piled Persian-rug remnants and scrambled clumsily out of the feces-smeared luggage compartment. Ramaadee, the driver, offered just enough harsh, yanked-arm assistance to hoist the passenger and case clear of the deck lid and bumper. Then both were dropped like sacked spuds.

The Palestinian's nightwork jeans, windbreaker, track shoes, and brimless hat were all blacker than the wearer's sorely embittered disposition. His features half-matched a harshly weathered coconut. Left side: Round, brown, and hard, with one hyperactive gray eye doing the work of two. Right side: Lopsided hair tufts bordering scabrous, reddish-pink dappling distorted what remained of his face, which...along with three-quarters of his scalp...had been third-degree burned by Israeli napalm's annihilation of a 200-strong PLO staging area.

When "Yessir!" Arafat's militancy got moldy, Ramaadee joined Hamas. But convinced that disfiguring wounds would prevent his rising higher in the organization than four-wheel ferryman, the Palestinian lobbied for no greater responsibility... and received none in return. Totally absent from his acidly resentful mood was even a smidgen of solicitousness attaching any importance to, or indicating any care about, the banker's personal comfort.

"The case does not enter the room," brawny Zahab grumbled.

The Hamas guard was a robust Samson post of a man standing nearly doorway high. Cerebral compression caused by a Doberman-shaped skull too small for human brains ignited frequent near-migraines that booted his hair-trigger temper crazily across the slender bandwidth separating surly from sociopathic. And while heavily armed with an AKM assault rifle, three fragmentation grenades, two holstered pistols, and a regimental Gurkha Kukri MK3 knife, Zahab's five-specialty martial-arts mastery would make quick, bone-snapping work of Ramaadee and al-Birquafi both at once, should either fail to pass security muster.

"I have seen Zahab at work," Ramaadee cooed softly, his warning words whistling through gap-stained teeth. "You would be wise not to annoy him."

"This case?" al-Birquafi inquired sternly.

"I see no other," Zahab fumed irritably between rapidly reddening ears.

"It carries requested cargo," the banker replied testily. And then drawing strength from the millstone of awesome fiscal responsibility curving his hubristic spine into weakling stoop, the money broker added: "We are inseparable, this old valise and I."

"As inseparable as your head from your neck?" Ramaadee inquired with a cocky sneer.

Ignoring the taunt, al-Birquafi told Zahab, "This case goes nowhere without me."

"Though one day it most certainly will," Ramaadee predicted between noisy, slurpy chews on a cheroot-shaped spike of spicy beef jerky, "the day your usefulness to The Movement is ended."

"Which would be when?" al-Birquafi asked the Palestinian's sewn-shut eye socket.

"Impossible to say specifically."

"And yet you speak like a man who marks calendars long in advance of need."

"Perhaps such inked notation has long since dried," Ramaadee murmured sagely, "in the journals of directors pacing overlooks much higher than, while still in observance of, those smut-strewn balconies upon which dairy cows such as yourself carouse so obscenely."

"And then who would handle nimble-witted financial planning?" al-Birquafi sniffed condescendingly. "Simple-minded errand boys such as yourself?"

The pudgy Jordanian knew himself to be on solidly secure

ground...because with heavy money bolstering his side of the confrontational equation, he could get away with heckling either Hamas jackass, whether such provocation took place in the fundamentalist, web-weave underground of Beirut or anywhere else in the world.

"Use this sack," Ramaadee said menacingly, pulling a blanched-canvas carryall from under the automobile's spare tire and clattering jack.

Al-Birquafi gushed heavy sweat freely as his sudden squint took in the barely visible outlets of eight tarnished-metal tubes, two under each lip of the car trunk. It didn't take an advanced mechanical-engineering degree to figure that the piping hookup turned the auto's rear end into a crudely effective gas chamber.

Forcing his mind away from thinking how close Ramaadee's finger might have been to triggering the gas-passing apparatus, al-Birquafi laughed nervously as he chirped: "I carry more money than you have bag."

Anything to play more against less, he thought...fully amenable to sharing details because the weight of payment, however substantial, mattered little. Unlike himself, these body-blockers were neither gain-motivated nor greed-driven. What in less-devoted soldiers would spur instant armed robbery and whoring, the prospect of sybaritic flight made no impression on either Ramaadee or Zahab.

But neither Muslim loyalist's satchel was entirely devoid of tricks. Ramaadee quickly jabbed the freezing muzzle of a Star Model 30M 9mm semiautomatic into the banker's right temple while ordering Zahab to "poke" the suitcase. No Johnny-come-lately to protective procedures, however, the guard had already unpocketed a needle-point implement and was fully prepared to perforate.

Watching as the open case teetered atop stacked ration crates, al-Birquafi wavered in mutely amazed scrutiny of a sullen fanatic so infused with zealotry as to be totally unmoved by the sight of $5,000,000 in untraceable bonds and bills. Zahab's interest lay only in diligently pushing his battery-powered prober into, around, and through each stack of neatly banded legal tender.

"You realize, of course," Ramaadee chuckled amiably, "that if the tool's handle glows amber, you are a dead man."

"There is no explosive material to detect," al-Birquafi said confidently. "I am a banker, not a bomber."

"Well, let us say, if only for the sake of argument, that you are wrong. That you have, in fact, been set up."

"Impossible!"

"Stranger things have happened in both your lifetime and mine."

"Agreed."

"So?"

"All right," al-Birquafi sighed. "For the sake of this wearying discussion."

"Then should that be your situation," Ramaadee said, "being unfortunately wrong, I mean, would you prefer to see it coming head-on or would you elect to lose your brains sideways through blown-out cheek and skull?"

"Ventilate my testicles first."

"That could be arranged, though aim might present peculiar problems, considering the ridiculously small size of your masculine endowment."

"And you know this how?"

"Your reputation precedes you."

"Assuming your marksmanship is somewhere near par, you could next give me one in each kneecap."

"Indeed, I have always admired the Provisional IRA's enforcement discipline."

"So you're okay with the plan as I have laid it out so far?"

"I could live with it," Ramaadee nodded agreeably.

"Next, wait twenty to thirty minutes while I writhe in agony and spill blood."

"Sounds good to me."

"Finally, finish the job with one aimed at the chin's bottom for travel upward through the soft palate." Death's hovering in greedy, 9mm expectation didn't diminish al-Birquafi's surety.

"Because it will not glow amber."

"These tools?" Ramaadee shrugged pleasantly, his rolling eye taking up the conversational slack for a Hamas guard too job-busy to suffer petty distraction. "Periodically...through old age, humidity, jimmy-rigged parts or because, Allah be praised, it just happens...sometimes such bargain-basement gadgets do give false readings."

"Bargain base...?"

"Are you still so sure of yourself, little man?"

"It will not glow amber."

"I admire your conviction in the face of the constant, electromechanical uncertainty touching everyone enjoying temporary residence in this constant state of war."

"It will not glow amber," al-Birquafi replied, *although God help me if other wiring powers up the death-warrant light.*

Taking infinitely meticulous care and extended time, because VIPs' longevity depended on the exactitude with which such ritual tasks were performed, Zahab closely eyeballed, fanned, and smelled each stack of foreign exchange. He punch-probed carefully and slowly through the Italian calfskin-leather case, taking careful measure of edges, flaps, and sides. The Muslim security man paid extra-special attention to scraped brass fittings because a few grams of C4 tucked under scored metal was more than enough explosive to dust up the conference room and the occupants he so carefully guarded.

Finally nodding disgruntled satisfaction, Zahab allowed al-Birquafi to retrieve his case and begin passage toward the descending, reinforced-concrete tunnel and a heavy-steel door beyond.

"What did I tell you?" the banker asked snidely.

"Trust must be earned freshly each day," Ramaadee replied nonchalantly. "I will be here waiting for you when your business is done."

"I am sure of that," al-Birquafi noted fretfully, already dreading the return trip in the putrid trunk of a rundown sedan... *God forbid the piping should start pumping on the way back.*

Then, venting depression with half-hearted sigh, he trotted down the sharply sloping ramp, swung open a finely balanced, metric-ton door, and entered the character-annealing kiln of domed, steel-shell conference chamber. Eye-searing fluorescent lighting stopped him short as the three-meter-thick panel closed slowly behind, its swing cushioned by liquid-filled shock absorbers. Though artillery shells, cluster bombs, and other heavy ordnance might pulverize neighborhood hovels above, ground-zero hits by 4,000-pounders would be neither heard nor felt "downstairs."

"Da' al-filoos alat-taawalah!" were the first, harsh words barked at the banker. "Put the money on the table!"

"Shukran ala muqaabalatak al-kareemah," al-Birquafi fired back. "Thank you for your very warm welcome."

"Tafadal. Anta ma' asdiqaa huna," said the bespectacled Dr. Haraj, recently arrived from Damascus to oversee distribution of certain ways and means...as well as the enterprises such resources would underwrite. "Please sit down, *yaa* Hassam. You are with friends here."

The Syrian's skewering, king-cobra eyes peered intently over wire-rim reading glasses whose downward slide was stopped by the flared nostrils of fleshy date nose. Russet complexion still carried the dust-mote scarring of preteen acne. Bristle-cut hair was lightly pomaded. In stark contrast to compatriots' dull, olive-drab combat fatigues and partisan headgear, Haraj sported a navy suit over a monogrammed, powder-blue shirt silk bisected by swirling, purple-orange abstracts down a loosely knotted tie. The ballsy display of a brilliant-diamond Alpha Tau Omega fraternity stickpin surprised al-Birquafi.

Definitely sniper bait, the finance capitalist conjectured, *but certainly in keeping with the pretentious conceit so endemic to the side Haraj represented today...although who knew about tomorrow?*

"Mumkin atakalam ingleezee?" al-Birquafi asked idly, plunking down ponderously into a loose-legged, canvas-back chair nowhere near as plush as seats occupied by those aligned against him. "May I speak English?"

Nodding disagreeably, as the banker knew they would, were Council hotshots glowering irately across the opposite side of an elliptic, cedarwood conference table in the temperature-controlled bunker. To have signaled anything other than peevish consent would be to risk appearing stupidly uncosmopolitan. Such an openly acknowledged shortcoming would restrict confessors to low-profile, localized theaters of military action...an operational expedience sure to rub blimpish psyches bloody raw, al-Birquafi knew, because four gamesters trying futilely to stare the banker down were already stressed out with the exertion of reining in rabidly ambitious egos.

In concord with long-established rules governing staggered-time marriages of convenience, the money manager would remain always a bridesmaid...never a bride, which meshed perfectly with fiscal realities as al-Birquafi loved to experience them. Complete and total extrication from the whole digestion-disturbing process, though an unattainable goal, would, of course, be ideal.

And then finger-snap time redirected observational awareness. The accountant's preoccupation with intestinal throbbing was squelched—and curious attentiveness stoked—by a just-noticed, left-end appendage to the esteemed Council of Seven. A casual, brief glance at the stranger mandated calculated movement of the money-laden case marginally backward and fractionally right...to account for the *ghareeb,* the newcomer promptly christened Freshman...who also required accommodation.

In keeping with inbred pins-and-needles anxiety, four attendees flinched visibly as the banker first snapped open one side of the case, then paused theatrically before popping the second hasp. Each snick-clack of rectangular, tarnished-brass fitting slapping scuffed base plate sparked eye-blink anxiety in the bravest of them all...the impact sounding as it did like a crude antipersonnel bomb's arming mechanism. But had suicidal assassination been al-Birquafi's goal, no conferee would have comprehended noise's deadly significance before a shrapnel-spewing, brassworks mine blasted bombastic chest cavities into cracked crocks of scarlet-syrup ooze.

Though what would be the good of giving up my own life, al-Birquafi tallied in true CPA fashion, *especially with more unemployed killers roaming free than there were jobs for filling?*

With the extra-catch asset of Freshman to consider, the financier enjoyed maximizing the obvious discomfort easily generated by the noisemaker fear. The nerve-grating sounds recharged some measure of power callously stripped away by the heaped-on indignities of a 1 a.m. summons, tattered rags of clothes, woolly blindfolds, and noxious, foul-reek ride.

While "head-pricing" each skittish chieftain, al-Birquafi's skin crawled in paranoid retreat from the fickle quirkiness inevitably broadcast by ranking militiamen of "liberation," "popular," "redemption," "rejection" and "resistance" fronts, three of whom felt it beneath their station to be grinding interpersonal gears in the same soundproof room. As he again checked Freshman, the moneyman touch-counted part one of his precious payload. He unceremoniously unloaded stacked English pounds and pushed them halfway across the table's width, taking great pains to ensure that the funds transfer stopped in the furniture's exact physical middle.

"Two and one-half million," the banker stated flatly.

"You talk as if you expect a receipt!" PFLP-GC snapped.

"Most certainly and in good time," al-Birquafi replied impassively.

"Do not forget who you are dealing with!" Eagles of Palestine growled.

"Would that I only could," the money broker complained.

Dr. Haraj reached out, took crisp, crook-armed control of evenly stacked British notes and passed the payoff line-left... into Freshman's eager possession. And though his eyes were only partially visible over warped-rim eyeglasses, with features half-cowled in a red-spiral *ghutrah,* there was no mistaking the twinkle of pure pleasure glinting brightly in pupils guarded by wrinkled skin aged during long years of nearly ceaseless desert travel.

"With our profound thanks, *Abu* Alam," Haraj intoned gravely, "for the direct actions carried out so capably...deep in the worm-infested bowels of the Great Satan."

Freshman = Abu Alam, al-Birquafi noted silently. *Superb!* Name-linked faces invariably upped the ante, general stakes, final bid, and banked Swiss francs.

"Thank you, oh my brother," the wizened Alam whispered respectfully, nearly losing complete control over the widening vainglory of his self-obsessed grin.

"And what of this next action spoken of?" al-Birquafi inquired innocently, while uncasing neatly stacked bearer bonds.

"Perhaps it would be good of you to enlighten me!" the Syrian huffed.

"Words common to us all pass repeatedly through the mouths of others with wigwag tongues considerably looser than your own, while I sit here ready to commit to the pipeline this $2.5 million balance of payment...the other half of which is already in the United States, or so I have been told."

Arab Revolutionary Brigades jumped up abruptly to deliver a tongue-lashing reply, but Chairman Haraj waved the guerrilla leader silent and seated.

"The details you seek lie safely buried in the province of others' responsibilities," the Syrian replied sternly.

"This money is my responsibility."

"Getting it here has fulfilled your responsibility."

"Totally?" the banker asked dubiously. "I don't think so."

"Do not overestimate your importance," Haraj warned solemnly.

Al-Birquafi's vibrant belly laugh was a 50-50 mixture of amusement and derision...though chef-like apportionment ensured that the latter did not too obviously outweigh the former.

"I regularly transit circles heavily populated by very influential people," the banker proclaimed in agitated, hand-waving defiance, "whom you...all of you...would do well to avoid the same hundred-kilometer distance you keep between yourselves and Israeli sharpshooters on perpetual safari for your hides. The persons with whom I am in touch would likely take great pleasure in reporting you to the police themselves."

"Most of whom live blissfully contented lives in the palms of our hands."

"Most, perhaps. But certainly not all," al-Birquafi retorted, skillfully fending off verbal intimidation with the same disdain that accomplished knights reserved for lesser jousters... invigorated as he was by the knowledge that where asset management was concerned, he maintained a uniquely singular persona: fiscal wizard without equal.

Which was why al-Birquafi had no doubt he would leave this underground assembly unhurried, to oversee business as usual...and return at some later date and time—however grudgingly—when duly and properly summoned. As surely as retaliation followed direct action, tonight's emissary-only work would segue into tomorrow's high-finance shenanigans—machinations capable of being administered only by someone of his phenomenal skill.

And now down to the next order of business, al-Birquafi thought, as calmly as humanly possible, considering his tendency toward glandular excitability. Because even though this particular addendum had been "walked through" many times before, there was always the chance of fallible gearworks sabotaging the chunky Jordanian's most lucrative sideline of all.

Removing the balance of legal tender had exposed, in the case's inside back wall, a tiny, leather-lined microswitch constructed of small basswood sticks capped by minimally metallic pinhead contacts. Al-Birquafi mentally plotted the obtuse-angle extension of his case's right-rear corner. All eight faces half a table distant were fully encompassed by the arc connecting outward lines of sight...with at least 36 inches to spare.

"Concerning future actions," Haraj noted dourly, as if teaching a pitifully slow learner, "there is nothing further in the way of specifics you need to ascertain from this meeting."

"Concerning an American avenue named after that

country's Keystone State?"

Haraj's eyes narrowed in barely constrained fury. "You were called upon only to deliver the money, Mr. Messenger, so that what must be done will be done."

You could always make book on a Syrian demeaning his counterpart's status, whether such belittling was deserved or not, al-Birquafi thought sourly, as he replied: "Make sure that you add to my job function the responsibility for seeing that remaining assets multiply geometrically, so that future actions can be financed just as easily as whatever this money mulches in your fields of thought tonight."

"Yes, there is that too," Haraj acknowledged reluctantly, edging back and away from tyrannical ascendancy over the lectern of high-handed arrogance.

But al-Birquafi heard nothing of the council leader's concession. Customary Hamas-laudings and anti-Zionist harangues signaling the meeting's pending conclusion were drowned out by a thumping heart sending blood pounding through throbbing eardrums as the banker concentrated solely on his right index finger pushed gently but firmly down on ancient calfskin masking the photographic—*SMILE!*—trigger.

Capping the end of an accurately positioned case leg was an aspheric fisheye lens set to hyperfocal distance and diaphragmed to f11. Behind "new-brew" Batch 77 Hasselblad glass lurked a specially modified 1/24,000th second, quartz-timed Compur shutter. At al-Birquafi's touch, the precision-engineered, auto-exposure marvel's inaudible snick permitted fluorescent light's wash over a 1.5-cm-diameter dot of supersensitive Kodak 7700ECT Night-Surveillance Film. And as had been promised heatedly long before gold bullion changed hands, and well-proven through 1,001 dry runs, no sound jeopardized the financier's life.

For what the West lacked in militant-fundamentalist resolve was counterbalanced by its lock on the late-minute technology of highly advanced engineering. And in the international marketplace where anything was available to one for whom price was never a consideration, Hassam al-Birquafi stood tall as a man of mammoth means.

Never one to let life-insurance opportunities pass by untapped, al-Birquafi maintained dynamic alliances through which small disks of high-resolution film were manipulated in top-secret Norwegian laboratories staffed by supremely skilled technicians...gifted men and women who daily advanced the frontiers of "push-processed photo enhancement." Other small circles of film, shot cleanly and later developed into remarkably clear 5x7 glossies, were salted away in safe-deposit boxes all over Europe, North America, and the Far East. Long-distance voyaging on the high seas of commercial finance served up bank-vault convenience in every port of call.

"And what of our unnamed colleague's itinerary?" the banker asked disinterestedly, snapping the case closed and sliding it off the table toward affectionate placement tight against his right leg, for now it was the financier's turn to smile congenially, especially at Freshman.

"We have only just received word," the Muslim Brotherhood offered.

"It has taken this long?!" the banker asked, seriously dismayed.

"Time enough so that his associates can bunker down before final transfer is made, perhaps to alert themselves if the vine withers."

"And when will this exchange take place?" al-Birquafi inquired.

"There is no need for you to know," hissed the leader of the Council of Seven.

"Ana moowaafiq," Pan Arab Command seconded angrily. "I agree."

"The locus of the action?" al-Birquafi pressed, as if the henchman's burgeoning temper tantrum were unworthy of notice.

But Dr. Haraj, calmly paternal now that the "dirty" business of money-handling was wrapped up, announced only that, "You have completed your part of this plan. It pleases me that you have done so well. Your actions meet with my complete approval, and word will be passed along accordingly. Now you may go. Your transportation will see you home."

"Five million dollars is a lot of hard currency not working for us fiscally," al-Birquafi protested mildly, relieved that attention's focus had been diverted back to monetary matters and away from the nuts and bolts of mass murder. "I must assure myself, and those from whom this largess springs, that such investment capital is put to good use."

"Assure yourself only of this," Haraj murmured, pulling a cocked FEG MBK-9HP semiautomatic from his shoulder holster and two-fist aiming it dead center at al-Birquafi's forehead. "Leave this minute without further query or objection, lest I put a bullet through your brains and leave your body here until all the flesh rots off it."

"Shukran ala istima' akum," al-Birquafi said, casually disdainful of a threat he knew was emptier than his multifunction valise. "Well, I think that's everything."

And then the banker, who had been in business long enough to distinguish empty boasts from genuine power plays, picked up his case, rose formally from his chair and without a word of farewell turned and pushed through the heavy-metal doorway to the upper-level anteroom where his monstrously scarred chauffeur...having pulled off a doubling-cube backgammon coup against the unpredictably violent Hamas guard...was on the verge of winning a month's wages.

"Done so soon?" Ramaadee asked in genuine disappointment, though clearly not expecting an answer.

Majaaneen Su'adaa, al-Birquafi thought to himself. *Happy fools.*

He clambered into the battered sedan's grease-rimmed trunk, assumed the fetal position, and made himself as comfortable as possible in the nose-prickling stink of tightly cramped quarters sloshing with puddles of recent urination. *Piss on you too,* he fumed silently. As mildewed carpet pads came down and lamplight dimmed, the banker reminded himself to whiff for errant exhaust gases.

Ramaadee, utterly disgusted at having been forced to abandon a blitzkrieg game, slammed the trunk lid shut and cursed himself blue while sliding behind the wheel. Then he angrily yanked his door shut, started the engine, and carefully backed the dented, rust-flecked Peugeot out of the grimy, back-alley garage.

In the rear compartment's disorientating darkness, al-Birquafi sniffed suspiciously for internal combustion's by-products while reviewing memory's minutes on the just-concluded meeting. The typically Middle Eastern wrap-up had each side coming away richer...the banker benefiting by coming out alive—plus. Because even while realizing the utter futility of accurately calculating the intrinsic value of one's own life, he knew that only a complete and utter nincompoop declined additional insurance coverage...especially when so much was regularly and readily available.

Al-Birquafi's abundant commodity, stockpiled for eventual retailing, was in greater demand than water in drought-ravaged Africa. And with so silo-busting an inventory, he was in no rush to transform hotly pursued assets into market-drenching gluts. Above all else, the fence-straddling capitalist knew the folly inherent in flooding a troubled world's intelligence community with too much too soon.

Men dying of thirst should be made to sip slowly, he thought happily.

As the road smoothed out, Hassam al-Birquafi, chief economist of the Royal Bank of Jordan and personal financial advisor of His Majesty the King, nodded off...then drifted contentedly off to a deep sleep aglimmer with the shimmering, REM-rich gleam of billion-dollar dreams.

CHAPTER 23

KOENIG

Zvi marched purposefully toward MATS Hangar 9 at the U.S. government's end of New York's John F. Kennedy Airport, eager to renew his worshipful love of American technology. Cavernous enough to swallow nose-kissing B-52 heavy bombers, the gray, guano-streaked structure instead housed the ever-burgeoning army of law-enforcement officers and investigative agents swelling the ranks of the JTTF: the Joint Terrorist Task Force.

"So, pilgrim. What brings you to my neck o' the woods?"

The question posed by Colonel Marc Westphall, Delta Force Intelligence, was accompanied by a strong-grip handshake equally matched by the Mossad officer, quick-stepping over ice-sheeted blacktop near the guard shack fronting RESTRICTED PARKING-Lot H14a.

Westphall was built like a bulldog barrel cactus: short, stocky, and oven-tempered mean. The colonel was dressed in no-name, cross-training shoes, faded jeans, a NYU sweatshirt, and an expertly tailored M-65 tactical field coat with hidden pockets in unexpected places. Cerulean eyes gave no quarter when whittling down pretenders to any throne, up to and including the commander in chief, which made Westphall an ulcerating embarrassment at White House briefings. Close-cropped white hair gave proud display to a pink furrow carved front to back atop his head...said memento gouged by British 30mm cannon fire sent the colonel's way during Gulf War operations behind enemy lines.

"Well, I just happened into the neighborhood," Zvi said, "and suddenly got antsy to check out your latest foray into research ergonomics."

"Bullshit!" Westphall barked.

"Would you believe that I'm thinking of putting down an earnest-money deposit on a duplex down the street?"

"You're up to no good," the colonel fired back, "and no amount of underarm deodorant is gonna gussy up that stink."

Unless full-court pressed, Zvi never confessed to anything more than casual basics. Motivational truths were wild cards in the high-stakes power play of interagency cooperation, where unnecessary disclosure equaled cardinal sin, and where one's hand was forever played peekaboo close to a bulletproof vest.

Three hours earlier on the snow-flurry Tuesday, Zvi was just wiping French fry grease off his fingers when a personal call came through on Orange Line 4. Standard operating procedure dictated parking Zvi's caller on a 10-second hold; the brief waiting period, coupled with the conversation, usually yielded ample time for a high-speed trace. But even though LanceBak hardware came online immediately, the caller broke contact before more than basic information was snared: Yaakov the Netmaster got only as far as nailing down an Upper West Side exchange.

Per Zvi's instructions, the call coming through 65 minutes later from the Lower East Side was punched through immediately. The electronically masked voice of an "old friend" strongly encouraged Zvi to: "Amble through New York JTTF between 1 and 6 p.m. You might find something interesting." And there the conversation abruptly ended. The Mossad officer knew Colonel Westphall would not have made so cryptic a call, but someone had...and there Zvi was.

Heavily armed Air Force MPs on hangar-perimeter patrol checked both visitors' IDs, then saluted smartly and opened the Hangar 9 PERSONNEL-ONLY door. Once inside, Zvi's mouth curved into a deep, ear-to-ear grin.

The hangar's enormous interior was honeycombed with cubicle PC workstations and halved into glassed-in working areas: smokers to the left, nonsmokers to the right. HQ's center featured a plastic-cased, minutely detailed sectional model of midtown Manhattan, constructed on a scale of 48 inches per city block. The tiniest perfections were guaranteed through heavy use of aerial-mapping photos snapped over the years by Ground Scan satellites, SR-71 Blackbirds, and F-117R reconnaissance overflights.

The three-dimensional slice of war-torn reality depicted the square encompassing 42nd Street to 46th Street, Eighth Avenue to the Avenue of the Americas...with Broadway meandering northwest to southeast. The tract's center was devoted to Times Square. Street-side construction displayed nightlife immediately preceding the devastating New Year's Eve explosion.

Bracketed to each glass wall was a laser-light projector. Every quarter hour, multiple beams combined centrally in the creation of a gruesome, three-dimensional hologram depicting the midnight terrorist attack, details of which had been reconstructed from carefully structured and cross-referenced interviews conducted with rescue workers and hundreds of maimed witnesses still screaming their way through nightmare reruns of mass murder.

Curious visitors could watch the motorhome's slow, lumbering progress up Eighth Avenue, trailer in tow; entry into the Cattle Pen; surging clusters of doomed victims pressing forward eagerly to slake cold-night hunger; near manic consumption of freely offered snacks and drinks...followed by a horrifically detailed holographic explosion: motorhome's disappearance inside slowly rising fireball; metal-toothed, buzz-saw shock wave racing outward; skewed and broken casualties blown into a panoply of grotesquely twisted pretzels; spherical bombs arcing down in overhead plunge to evaporate in fuzz-rimmed secondary detonations; blast-broken limbs launched upward like cyclone-tossed thatch...the scene made more hellishly disturbing by the graveyard silence shrouding re-created hell on earth. Surround-Sound headphones, however, were available for the stout of stomach.

Mounted on the hangar's back wall was an immense, ceiling-high image of corpse-strewn wasteland. The black-and-white photograph was divided into ID-numbered, yard-square plats, each representing 250 square feet of city-surface area. Keystroking a number into any one of the 750 PC workstations brought forth both CRT display and hard-copy printout of what forensic specialists recovered from that particular section of blood-drenched killing zone. Inventory ranged from crisped and shriveled body parts to pieces of motorhome or trailer to unidentified splashes of steaming organic matter long since cooled...all of which had been photographed, catalogued and finally hosed off or carted away to leased ex-Brooklyn Navy Yard buildings for reconstruction into life-size dioramas representing life immediately preceding forceful rearrangement by high explosive.

The hangar's inside air was a temperature-controlled 78 degrees. Zvi shrugged off his parka while nodding approvingly at steadily billowing, milk-hue clouds soaring roofward through large plastic collection tubes to where huge exhaust fans ingested stale cigarette smoke for excretion skyward.

"You've got one hell of a circulating system," he observed.

"The cornerstones of which are four 15,000-ton units," Westphall replied. "Plus, we had to file environmental impact statements with the EPA and state agencies. Everyone is fresh-air crazy these days."

"Believe me, that particular pain in the ass recognizes no national boundaries."

"I've got an up-front workstation reserved for you."

"Thanks."

"Yeah, right," Westphall chuckled. "Fair thanks will be your telling me what, if anything, you come up with."

"Any late developments?" Zvi asked.

"We originally keyed in on a signature indicating linkage between the blaster's handiwork and hangers-on from the August Second Movement."

"Iraqi agents commemorating their invasion of Kuwait?"

"At first glance."

"I thought you completely crushed and flushed that network."

"Me too," Westphall replied, "but you can never guarantee extermination down to the last roach. Even one left alive can lay a lot of troublesome eggs. Anyway, it got us thinking."

"So you figure Times Square was either revenge for Desert Storm or a signal of their willingness to again try digesting the emirate."

"Nope," Westphall said. "And here's why. First off, those camel-jockeys convinced themselves that standing up to us short-term was victory enough, even though they lost over 100,000 men, women and children doing it. Second, despite Fat Boy's bellowed threats, there was hardly any concerted terrorist activity during Desert Storm."

"As I recall, a total of six tourist offices got popped here and there."

"Yeah," Westphall admitted, "but nothing big time. And that lack of major action convinced us that terror groups can be held strongly in check...if their host countries, read that as our erstwhile coalition partners, damn well feel like it."

"As in Syria."

"Right. Also, we shredded the nest pretty good. What wasn't bagged through initial infiltration was neutralized after interrogations began."

"Geneva Convention procedures?"

"Oh sure," Westphall smirked. "Have you ever tried reading fine print during predawn strikes?"

"Why, Colonel," Zvi admonished, hands on hips in mock dismay. "Do I hear you correctly? Are you telling me your world-class Boy Scouts actually didn't play by the rules?"

Westphall laughed gruffly as they came up to Zvi's cubicle.

"Our hands weren't tied by protocol because we weren't at war with those scumballs. Not officially, anyway. On top of that, we barely had diplomatic relations with them. And as we closed up their shop, we found they were just about Saharan on gas and damn near running on fumes. Their D.C. embassy was long ago ground down to the nubbins; the consulate here had been padlocked and shuttered for some time."

"Ira Green?" Zvi asked.

Westphall shook his head. "Nope. Not IRA either, despite Provo hardware found fused into what was left of the motorhome frame. As powerful as they were, the explosions didn't completely obliterate bits of spot-weld holding bogus clues conveniently in place."

"Hocus-pocus," Zvi murmured.

"Yep," Westphall nodded. "The call sign of your Arab splinter group was on this trigger."

"AR showed up again?!"

"Bingo."

Westphall held open the self-closing door of Zvi's workstation cubicle.

"Your entry code is 1948."

"Cute."

"Figured you'd like it. Punch that in, then type in MAIN. INVT. And then enter five-two-four."

A split second later, the 36" screen was filled with a color illustration of a panel from the destroyed Airstream motorhome.

"Arrow-key your way in toward the center," Westphall said, "then hit Command Z, for zoom in."

As Zvi did, Westphall leaned over the Israeli's left shoulder to tap a gold fountain pen on the screen: "Right there, front and center. The A and R were removed from the logo. Making it 'blank-i-blank-stream.'"

"The blast didn't do that?"

"No; it happened before the big bang."

"Absolutely sure?"

"No question about it. Laboratory analysis provided confirmation beyond the shadow of any doubt," Westphall said. "Mounting holes behind the 'A' and 'R' were more than empty; they were whistle-clean. Those holes would have been filled with sheared-off positioning pins if the letters had been blasted off. Electron microscopes didn't pick up even a fragment of the shank. There was no glue, no nothing. More to the point, the panel itself had been sprayed with six, carefully overlapped coats of FireKill."

"Military-grade fireproofing?"

Westphall nodded. "The best currently available on the aftermarket. Also, the panel was clipped to the vehicle with non-OEM frangible mounts, thereby ensuring ejective departure from structure..."

"Meaning it got blasted well clear by shock wave," Zvi broke in, "before damage or incineration by secondary explosion or localized fire. Looks like our friend has quite the eye for detail."

"Oh, he's a regular rocket scientist, all right. What did you come up with based on the specifics wired your way?"

Zvi adjusted the image's contrast, then lit a cigarette. "Nothing," he said dispiritedly.

"Not even a blip?"

"Nope," Zvi replied honestly. He tipped his chair back, put his feet up, and made himself as comfortable as possible in the bare-bones circumstances. "We've got division-level tape drives bulging with data on a regular laundry list of abu's. I can safely say that nearly every one of my Semitic brethren is the father of someone or something. Every town square in every village, far and wide, has its own cause and an honored martyr to boot. IDF Intelligence, Shin Bet, and Mossad process it on a Level 2, As-Can basis."

"Can you pump up the priority?"

"Sure...right after our national-security ducks are lined up and quacking in size-place row."

"So what you're telling me is that you're doling out all we're likely to get."

"Believe me, Marc, you'll be immediately apprised of whatever we uncover," Zvi said quickly, anxious to prevent even trace fractures in a long-standing covert relationship. "But this may take a while. You've got to see it from our perspective."

"Talk to me."

"That code-name prefix shows up more often than Smith and Jones combined in your Manhattan telephone directory."

Westphall tamped Pirate's Cove tobacco into the bowl of

ornately carved, death's-head meerschaum...and fired up while staring hard at Zvi until convinced he was getting all candor due. Then the colonel said, "I'm too much of a gentleman to come right out and ask who rearranged your nose."

"Your discretion is very much appreciated," Zvi said, stubbing out his cigarette. "Although your curiosity, I most certainly could do without."

"One of theirs?" Westphall inquired.

"Are you kidding?!" Zvi replied sarcastically. "One of mine, of course."

"Ouch," Westphall murmured sympathetically.

"You don't know the half of it," Zvi remarked, uncomfortably reliving the dreamy, slow-motion impacts attendant with Colonel Yossi Gavron's pummeling rearrangement of facial topography. Still, in all, the incident had been nowhere near the unmitigated calamity it had originally promised to be.

The day before entering the ring, Zvi bet $1,000 that he'd at least go the distance. At the opening bell, he was a 13-1 underdog who wasn't figured to be standing at the end of Round Three. But Zvi confounded the odds-makers by staunchly refusing to kiss canvas. Thirty seconds into Round Five, public opinion was wholeheartedly in his corner. Halfway through Round Eight, a disbelieving crowd was on its feet, roaring enthusiastic approval of Zvi's eclectic, southpaw boxing style as the Mossad officer brutally worked Gavron's body and skillfully counterpunched his way through the remaining four rounds. At the fight's end, the bookie barely managed to cover the payout. Although painful, Zvi's "personal best" experience had been damn well worth it.

"Enjoy your computer time," Westphall said. "Dial nine for an outside line. Six for me. I'm on the floor for the next three hours. They'll page."

Then the door hissed shut, the overhead fan automatically upshifted into medium, and Zvi was alone with his terminal. He brought it out of the screen saver, accessed MAIN MENU, selected TIMES SQUARE OVERVIEW, and punched in #1. A millisecond later, Zvi was reading the manifest of post-blast objects carefully recovered, sifted, and cataloged. He checked his STRAC watch while barely managing to stifle a yawn. There was time aplenty for a leisurely stroll through mainframe data banks, seeing as he had nothing to do but casually surveil random comings and goings without too obviously waiting for Godot. After all, it was anyone's guess how long he had before the mysterious caller played "Reach Out and Touch."

No matter, he thought confidently. *I excel at waiting.*

But four bloodshot hours later, Zvi wasn't so sure. Scratchy throat and humming headache were all he had showing for his industrious, eye-ache exercises. Completely oblivious to the waning day, the letter-quality printer to Zvi's right soldiered on stolidly, spitting out printed manifests detailing each 250-square-foot segment accessed.

Welcome distraction finally materialized in the form of a 3:57 p.m. runner from FOODSTUFFS arriving under the escort of a burly USAF military policeman. Zvi looked toward the triple knock, put his computer to sleep, and beckoned the deliveryman inside. The MP stood just outside at parade rest, watching every move both guest and courier made.

And no doubt lip-reading, too, Zvi figured. "I didn't order anything," he told the spindly Jamaican.

"Courtesy ya Uncle Sam an' 'is management team," the stick-figure islander replied.

He was dressed in a striped, Roy G. Biv knee-length poncho, frayed overalls, engineer's boots, and a wide-brimmed calypso hat. The delicatessen boxman carefully positioned a cut-off cardboard tote on the desk's side extension shelf.

"Bettah open it, mon. Lemme know quickly now if she be ta ya likin'."

"I'm sure it will be."

"Sorry, chief," the Jamaican laughed, eyes rolling widely white behind spread fingers arcing like windshield wipers. "No can do. Me standin' orders be I wait 'til ya check 'er good. An' den I go. It's procedure written inta food-deliv'ry contrac', or so th' talkin' be. I don't obey, mon, I find meself job-hungry...an' wid a wife, tree kids, 'nother on da way." The Jamaican shrugged. "See it clear from me slippers, bruddah. I wait. No rush if ya be middle-groundin' somethin' or other."

"That's all right," Zvi said, unwrapping enough waxed paper to quickly check the late-afternoon snack. And then he reached for his wallet.

"Oh no," the Jamaican protested. "Bill's been seen ta. You an' th' othas roun' here be set up in guest territ'ry I be told, 'cordin' to th' contrac'."

"Even the tip?" Zvi asked.

"Even dat, mon, thankin' ya kindly an' all, tho' th' wife an' kids, ya see, wouldn't mind me bringin' home an extra handfulla change, or whatever ya be kind enough ta send me way, seein' as we ain't been too long gone from our beautiful island jewel-a homelan'."

The Jamaican accepted Zvi's $20 bill with effusive thanks, in exchange for which he handed the intelligence officer a yellow/white NCR-paper receipt.

"Fer ya expense account, mon, an' I be thankin' ya muchly."

The door closed, the fan kicked back up to medium, and vagrant thoughts were quickly booted toward a wild, downhill stumble by the ravenous targeting of deli food. Two healthy bites heavily damaged a delicious lox/cream cheese/kaiser-roll sandwich, the balance of which soon vanished in cheek-filling bites washed down by steaming black coffee.

It was while wiping his mouth on a crumpled-up napkin that Zvi glanced at the receipt's total of $2241 circled in brown ink. *Quite a substantial price for fish, bread, and drink,* he mused idly. Even if the decimal point had been in place, $22.41 was still arm-and-leg pricing for so little so voraciously consumed.

Padding his expense account was out of the question, regardless of what Kingston, Jamaica, suggested. There was no point in keeping the receipt because such double-booking shtick was frowned upon by compatriots half a world away.

None of which explained the missing decimal point.

Zvi might have been tired, but he wasn't comatose. Hope-laced curiosity cooked up enough instant stamina to block out fatigue as the workstation came back to electronic life and he punched in 2241. The new manifest appearing one second later detailed findings retrieved with archeological precision from a 250-square-foot area located 111 feet due east of blast's ground zero.

There were 127 blue-screen entries. Overanxious skip-scanning yielded back-to-back dry runs. Zvi rubbed his tired eyes with balled fists, geared down his reading speed, and forced separate, thoughtful enunciation of each syllable, starting again from: "ITEM ONE—High School Graduation Ring; De Witt Clinton; Class of '88. ITEM TWO—Brown Florsheim Imperial Dress Boot; 8-1/2D; No Zipper. ITEM THREE—Pinky Finger; Caucasian Male; 42 Years Old. ITEM FOUR..." and just over two-thirds through the manifest...to the entry whose slo-mo reading kicked him hard in the stomach.

Grinning like a breathless fool, Zvi carefully rechecked Item 86. Tired though he was, fatigue was still no excuse for rushing headlong into error. So the Mossad officer lit another cigarette and redid the drill. Then he highlighted Item 86 and hit Command S1/P. His terminal beeped twice as the screen flashed: "Line Item 86—Specifics Unavailable; Detailed Input Uncatalogued. See Day Watch Coordinator/Station 4." And so with hard-copy confirmation that what he'd seen wasn't a fairyland daydream, Zvi logged off his computer and strode earnestly toward the hangar's nerve center.

The Station 4 desk quickly hove into view as a 10-foot metal table bent concave under snaking Con Ed trunk cables, four 12-line phone consoles, a scatter of No. 2 pencils, overflowing ashtrays and papered disarray surrounded by man-size stacks of ledgers, reports, computer printouts and logs...all of which were more than enough to half-bury one seriously attractive woman.

"Be still, my foolish heart," Zvi whispered, too loudly for his own good.

B. Steele looked up indifferently and said, "Okay, cowboy, what's on your mind? Besides the obvious, that is."

"What does the 'B' stand for?"

"Bonnie. What's on your shopping list?"

"This manifest..."

"Plat number?"

"Twenty-two forty-one."

"Line item?"

"Eighty-six."

"Not fully catalogued yet," she said, her eyes still locked on his.

"You know that without looking?"

"Trust me," she stated flatly. "But I'll see what I can do."

"Running slow?" Zvi asked, eager to extend casual conversation.

"We catalog everything here," she replied coolly, "from melted hatpins to missing heads. *Todas las cosas. Comprende?* The whole nine yards. And we're not even halfway there yet."

"I didn't mean to..."

"Rush me?" she asked. "That's nothing new. Apology accepted," B. Steele said, looking down to cross-check logs while holding out her hand for Zvi's list. After circling Line Item 86 on Zvi's sheet, she returned his paper and then eyeballed the five-inch-thick spines of four obese ledgers before targeting the one she sought.

Unwilling to disconnect from long, red-painted fingernails sliding fully down one page and up the next, Zvi slouched in B. Steele's general direction, hoping for indefinite extension on page-flipping. At about the time he was fully fantasizing the delicious raking such nails could deliver, B. Steele highlighted an entry with a yellow Magic Marker.

"Gotcha!" she said triumphantly. "Right here. Plat number twenty-two forty-one. Line item eighty-six. It's a cat."

"I already know that from the monitor and printout. What kind of cat was it?"

Steele looked up slowly, carefully weighing Zvi's tilt toward seriousness or silliness. "You're a new kid on this block," she said. "Am I right or wrong?"

"What kind..."

"Right or wrong?" she pressed.

"Yeah."

"Thought so. Because you don't look at all familiar."

"The cat," Zvi said slowly, uncharacteristically patient because such interpersonal largess would bring extra loiter time to evaluate the thickness, texture, and sheen of B. Steele's shoulder-length, crow-black hair. No less alluring were the woman's burnt-almond eyes and cushion-plush lips, behind which glowed strontium-white teeth.

"What kind was it?" he asked again.

"Do I look like a veterinarian to you?"

"No."

"But you'd tell me if I did?"

"In a split second."

"Thanks."

"Look, I'm not implying that you're anything different than what you really are."

"Which is?" she asked.

"Someone whose assistance I humbly beseech."

"Thank you."

"But the breed of cat it was just might be in your ledger."

"Probably."

"Well, can you look?"

"It was a cat-cat," B. Steele said, hard-set stare taking the full measure of Zvi's mettle. "As in 'meow-meow.' I really hope you're following all of this."

"Hanging on to every word."

"How about bird-chaser, mouser, kitty, tabby, dog bait. What kind of cat was it?" she asked rhetorically. "Cat's a cat is all I've got to say."

Zvi laid his hands flat on the edge of B. Steele's desk and used downward isometric pressure to shunt off his precipitously rising blood pressure. "Did you happen to know that most cat associations in your country commonly recognize ten short-haired breeds and seven long-haired breeds of cat?"

"No doubt you can name them all."

"I will, if you'd like."

"Spare me."

"I really and truly need to know," he said, "what goddamned kind...of goddamned cat...it was."

Zvi's choice of adjective counted far less than rising voice, which was as loudly out of place as wet farts at High Mass. Roped in by incipient commotion, passersby halted casual strolls and swerved sharply in right-angle turns toward the research desk.

B. Steele spent 90 seconds scrutinizing Zvi and four newly arrived flankers, then carefully reexamined the Mossad officer for any hint of levity. Seeing only a half-glare stare evincing readiness to gnaw through sheet titanium, Day Watch Coordinator 4 figured that playing it straight made eminent sense.

Most likely, the asker's upstairs lights were flickering, but no one was laughing. So be it.

"Hang on a second," B. Steele murmured.

"I'm absolutely riveted to this spot," Zvi replied.

"I can well imagine. You don't strike me as a chain-puller who shoves off empty-handed."

"Take your time with this."

"You bet I will," B. Steele said, bending once more to her work.

"Accuracy or nothing."

"Appendix Forty-Three," she declared without looking up.

B. Steele's head bobbed quickly while checking desk ledgers. Then she half-turned and dove for one at the base of behind-back stacks...while Zvi gazed longingly at step-toned legs sweeping up from shiny black high heels toward mid-thigh hem of a dark-blue business suit.

"Gawking doesn't become you," B. Steele lectured sternly, face red with the exertion attendant with awkwardly hoisting the foot-thick ledger onto her book-strewn desk. After diligently working halfway through the massive volume, B. Steele announced, "Here it is."

"A Manx?"

The CIA woman's suddenly up-flicked eyes beaconed sullen annoyance. "If you already knew," she snapped irritably, "why the hell did you put me through the hoops finding it?"

Because I had to be sure, Zvi thought. "How did this unfortunate Manx meet its untimely end?"

"How did... *What?!*"

"What stopped its clock?"

B. Steele opened her mouth to speak, then burst out laughing...leaving Zvi awestruck, blind by the brilliant radiance of dental perfection.

"You are putting me on, right?!" she asked incredulously. "You just have to be cranking my rotor."

"No joke," Zvi said evenly. "I really need to know."

"Hey, come on!" B. Steele protested. "Look, a joke's a joke... and I can take one as well as the next guy. I'm a sport, too. I contribute to all BBB-approved charities. But all of this...is...just..."

And then B. Steele's locked-lip voice trailed off, silent as she frankly evaluated scowl lines engraved deep into the corners of the Israeli's osprey eyes and down-turned mouth.

"My...God!" she whispered. "You *are* serious."

"Very, very serious," Zvi said softly, his voice a barely audible rasp of opaque monotone.

B. Steele checked a sixth ledger and said, "Okay, fella. Got it right here. What did you say your name was?"

"I didn't," Zvi replied.

"Well?"

"Harry Truman."

B. Steele tightened up, and Zvi immediately regretted his flippancy.

"Okay, spook," she said, "Message received. Sorry about our prior misunderstanding," she said coldly, "but I thought you were running a game on me. I can't be faulted for that."

"Agreed," Zvi said.

"Footnote 771," B. Steele reported. "Manx kitten. Approximately six weeks old. Tagged with Hold Order TSBI-

4413, which is still in effect." She slammed the book shut and looked up. "So the body wasn't disposed of."

"That's good news," Zvi said.

"Figured you'd enjoy hearing it," B. Steele replied.

"Where was it taken?" Zvi asked tiredly, hoping B. Steele wouldn't short-stroke the details. Black coffee's initial, jump-start kick had trickled down to little more than an occasional twitch, and Zvi knew that sullen law-enforcement officers would take a decidedly dim view of him nosing up on chemical stimulants.

"Riverdale-West Animal Hospital."

"Look, B. Steele, I think we got off on the wrong foot."

"And ended there, too."

"How about dinner when your shift's done?"

"No."

"On me or 'halfsies'," Zvi insisted. "Whatever won't compromise your principles."

"Sorry," B. Steele said flatly. "Ball game's over. If there's nothing else you need from me, please give serious consideration to moving on."

"No second chances?"

"See this hardware?" B. Steele asked, waving her left-hand ring finger high enough for the weighty stone to mirror spectrum light.

"Not as brightly beautiful as your teeth," Zvi tried.

"It's not just for show."

"I had it pegged as shark repellent."

"Guys in your line always do."

"Just for dinner," Zvi said hopefully. "We could discuss the case."

"Yeah, sure."

"Honestly."

"Forgetting for the moment the impediment of secrecy oath, it doesn't take a gumshoe PhD to know you're not from this neighborhood," Steele replied. "That means you're not on my firm's A List. So at the very least, there'll be no entangling alliances, thank you very much."

"What was your first clue?"

B. Steele slid a mechanical pencil behind her right ear and leaned back, arms crossed over her chest. "Back when you used the words 'your country,'" she said smugly.

"Oops," Zvi said sheepishly.

"For damn sure," B. Steele replied casually.

"Well, I will admit to having gotten waylaid by your incredible beauty."

"That excuse holds about as much water as your bladder would if a blown cover got you shot full of holes."

"I think I'll back off gracefully now," Zvi said.

"Smart move, Boris."

Grateful that he was still at least partially under wraps, Zvi said: "You got a number?"

"Private and unpublished, because that claim has already been staked," B. Steele said. "But you score two points for trying harder."

"I meant for the animal hospital."

"Oh."

"Disappointed?"

"I'll survive. Got a pencil?"

Zvi fumbled in his pockets and came up empty.

"Never mind. I've got one," B. Steele said, and wrote down the digits. Zvi reached for the paper, but B. Steele held her end tight until she caught his eye. And then she said, "Another place...another time...and you'd have definite possibilities. A little abrasive, sure, but all things considered, I prefer starch to soft-gut soufflé. Maybe in the next lifetime."

"Thanks," Zvi said.

"Male ego assuaged?"

"'Twas never endangered to begin with."

"Go make your call," B. Steele said.

Figuring his cubicle's phone was wired straight to and through Delta Force headphones, Zvi used a newly installed pay telephone outside the men's room. Riverdale-West Animal Hospital's switchboard kept him parked on hold long enough for a prerecorded voice to request more money.

When the receptionist came back, Zvi identified himself as Colonel Westphall, telling them, "I need information about a cat sent your way after the Times Square bombing."

"Specifically?"

"Cause of death."

"Hang on," Zvi heard...and once again he was trapped on 50 cents worth of hold.

The call was finally routed to a technician who asked, "You the guy wanting to know about the cat?"

"Yeah."

"Okay. In confirmation of your query, I can report that, yes, a kitten was sent to us."

"A Manx?"

"That's the one. Remains are still on ice. Wanna swing by and see 'em?"

"No."

"Have 'em shipped anywhere?"

"No."

"You sure? Because we really could use the cooler space and..."

"Hold it!" Zvi shouted.

"Yeah, what?!"

"Don't give me every option on your menu. Just tell me how the goddamned cat was killed."

"My, my. We are touchy today."

"Spill it, for Christ's sake!"

"Its neck was wrung, okay?!"

"Dead before the blast?" Zvi asked hopefully.

"What do you think?"

"If I knew, I wouldn't be wasting your time!"

"The fur was singed, but the lungs were clear. No gases or fluids. Internal organs were intact. No sign of fire injury, trauma, outside objects cutting their way inside, shrapnel damage, nothing like that."

"How was it killed?" Zvi asked again.

"Look, General Whatever-Your-Name is. I just told you..."

"You haven't told me enough!" Zvi raged. *"This is a matter of national security!"*

"Gee, Mr. High and Mighty, I never would have guessed."

"So please concentrate and give me every detail of the specific sequence."

"Hang on a second."

"Don't take too long," Zvi said, anxiously searching for pocket change and finding none.

"I have to consult some notes."

"Hurry!"

"Up yours, General," Zvi heard, and then he was on hold again.

This time, the technician wasn't long in coming back. Zvi listened for 20 seconds, smiled grimly, then hung up and sauntered through the hangar toward his cubicle. B. Steele's chair was empty; a hand-lettered sign said: "Back in 10 minutes." Zvi briefly considered leaving a note, then thought better of it.

Ships in the night...

Zvi retrieved his parka to the accompaniment of silently shuffling ESP cards forming strangely wonderful combinations inside his head. On his way out, he paused to stare at the awful hologram replaying tragic history with maddening regularity. *How many other 3-D displays will have to be set up,* the Mossad officer thought, *before this bastard is finally run to ground?* Zvi wondered if a similar exhibit replayed in terrible detail the L.A. truck bombing. It worried him that he didn't know for sure.

Once outside the hangar, Zvi threw his parka wide open to refreshing chill, rising wind, and falling snow. He lit another cigarette, then just as quickly ground out the tasteless smoke on salt-flecked black ice.

Races are best run and most often won by getting one leg up, the Mossad man reflected somberly on his way across the recently sanded parking lot. After heating the car key with a cigarette lighter, he unlocked the Ford Crown Victoria, slid behind the wheel and fired up the engine. Defroster on high, Zvi waited for the windshield to clear.

He now had time...which, in the absence of easy answers and quick solutions, ranked as the most precious commodity of all. Zvi laughed while thinking back to the Kaiser roll, a nice touch of genius there. Appropriate "Thank you," in the form of a "birth congratulations" telegram, would soon be wired to Koenig, aka Johann Haeckel...the Mossad man's counterpart in Germany's foreign-intelligence service.

In the gritty, back-scratch murk of Black Door operations, such cherished friends were as hard to come by as they were good to have.

CHAPTER 24

THE CAT'S MEOW

Judith parked her borrowed Land Rover a block away from Haifa's Rambam Hospital, on a side street already submerged under seven inches of rain and blown-in seawater. Outer-bay overcast surged and eddied ominously, like black ink clouding an aquarium. She ignored the rain's threatened resumption while soccer-kicking pebbles along a 1.5-mile path leading to the tip of the Haifa Port breakwater. Clanking around in her waterproofed-canvas knapsack were a thermos of beef bouillon, half a pack of Camel Filters, one-quarter box of saltines, a portable radio/cassette player and three Michael Bolton tapes.

Disturbingly aggressive gulls wheeled and squawked annoyingly, but their diving feints couldn't hammer through the invisible, stone-solid armor Judith wore on her self-absorbed trudge down to land's end. Sonorously gurgling sea foam was a perfect acoustic perfume for the tailor's work at hand: reweaving threads ripped loose while dancing with death during the subterranean interrogation and her subsequent escape two weeks previously.

She sat down cross-legged on the uneven tip of the breakwater and frankly took stock. Cold, barbed needles busily jabbing heartward were thankfully physical and not emotional...a chill caused only by bleakly raw weather. The slight inclemency worming its way inside her down-filled, Rockies Rancher parka was quickly defeated by tongue-searing gulps of steaming broth.

All-weather binoculars brought into close view a sea-rescue operation underway dangerously far out on the storm-whipped whitecaps of Haifa Bay. An 85-foot motor yacht bobbed cork-like in dire straits, its rain-slick rails orangely bumptious with panicky, life-jacketed sightseers. The larger craft drifted powerless while an Israeli Navy tug backed in to fire tow lines to the stricken vessel's bow.

Two helicopters were actively involved in the mission. A red-and-white Aerospatiale AS-365 Dauphin on scene for maritime terrorist interdiction hung patiently overhead, its efforts coordinated with a circling Dabur fast-patrol boat because one never knew when a handful of hooligans in all-weather gear and a motorized dinghy would try to make their point with the business end of a rocket-propelled grenade. Also standing by, though farther westward so its rotor wash wouldn't compound the confusion of nip-and-tuck situation in an already-roiled sea, was a large Sikorsky CH-53 Yasur carrying an Aeromedical Evacuation Unit, just in case the large pleasure craft went bottom up before reaching the safety of the inner-harbor docks.

And then Judith noticed the impertinent presence of another, more telltale aircraft. Five hundred yards closer inshore, buzzing in hover like a curious carpenter bee, was Zvi's aerial taxi—a muddy, stripped-down Bell 212 chopper ready to carry him away when his intrusive business was through. Said unpleasantness would commence momentarily, Judith knew, because Zvi's robust personality always broadcast its commanding presence long before his actual arrival in audiovisual range.

Footsteps clattering unevenly on black, storm-smoothed stones told Judith that time-out was over. In defense against disturbance, she turned the cassette's selector from AM/FM to TAPE, pushed PLAY and turned the volume up to MAX on "Love Is A Wonderful Thing." Popcorn music it might very well be, but it gave considerable substance to thoughts of her Michael... and the happy-go-lucky orchestration somewhat salved raw psychological wounds still bleeding profusely despite her best efforts at pressure-bandaging.

Life as a tracking officer in the farthest rear echelon of never-ending war was one thing. It was quite another to be dropkicked over the front line, then tranquilized like a dumb jungle animal. Waking up as a helpless prisoner, breaking out, and then staying alive for the 48 hours it took to wend her way safely south from Juniyah and finally out through the unreliable Beirut Harbor pipeline had been more unnerving than Judith told the debriefing team.

It was only later that mental chaos shook her senseless. One didn't need a PhD in Personal Assessment to fully appreciate the utter dearth of inventory in the larder of her life. And so Judith had absolutely no qualms about reaching into her parka and pulling out the white business envelope she had been carrying for the past seven days, and which she now waggled over her right shoulder without turning around.

Even as he took the envelope, Zvi said curtly, "You know that I cannot accept this letter."

"I know nothing of the kind."

"Based on what's inside..."

"You could not know that until you have read what is inside."

"Our office talk left little doubt." Zvi rocked on his haunches on the cold unevenness of the jetty, the awkward posture more challenge than bother. "Besides, such a missile..."

"Missive," she corrected.

"No. 'Missile,' as in surface-to-surface weapon of war. In speaking with you, I would be terribly remiss were I not to choose my words very, very carefully. Such a missile would have to be presented in my office for it to have official weight, and since we are not now in my office...." Zvi shrugged. "So even though I am holding it physically, it is illogical for you to expect me to accept it officially."

Judith sipped soup, then recapped the thermos and laid it down carefully between them as a clear line of demarcation, as if she were separating groceries at a supermarket checkout.

"Your office is anywhere you can park your ass, even less comfortably than it is now, while taking great pleasure in manipulating weak-willed people to your personal and political gain."

Zvi thoughtfully tapped the envelope on the rocks, then

ripped it into pieces as small as his gloved hands could manage. He purposely threw the debris overhand toward the water, knowing that the wind would blow the torn scraps back in their faces.

"Judith, you are now witnessing proof positive of how much I think of you. For you, and only for you, snow has been brought down to sea level." When he saw his attempt at humor about to run hard aground, Zvi quickly changed tack. "Anyway, this resignation business is a very serious matter, and I cannot conduct serious matters out here in such miserably nasty weather."

"Environmental concerns never stopped you before. Since when did you become such a stickler for details?"

"Since I got a crucially important update on the New York bombing," Zvi said softly, the lowering of his voice those few critical octaves clearly signaling the inevitable shift from casual human relations to pressing business at hand.

Zvi cared little for her personal needs; that much Judith knew for a fact. Not that he wouldn't have liked to; he *couldn't...* for reasons going far beyond the normal rules regulating his service to the state. Zvi was simply incapable of giving much of himself, if anything at all. It was the way he had been brought up; it was just Zvi. Emotionally, he was astringency personified. Everyone got equally short shrift from Zvi; in that regard, he played favorites with no one. Judith often thought that Job would have been a better name for him—not the Biblical prophet...but trade, profession, business, calling, vocation, career, occupation, preoccupation, since he wore what he did like a second skin. Which was why Zvi was so damnably good at the intelligence work he performed for far less of a living than he truly merited.

Then Judith callously corked her outpouring of silent empathy and resumed her surveillance. Seamlessly and effortlessly, Zvi had almost gotten to her. That demanded watching.

She swept her binoculars over the choppy waves to where the tugboat had finally succeeded in getting two stern lines to the bow of the troubled pleasure cruiser. The yacht's grateful sailors quickly lashed ropes around tie-downs as small clouds of diesel smoke puffed from the tug's stack and the gray, broad-beamed vessel inched forward slightly to tighten the hawsers and start the tow.

"I am no longer interested," Judith said. She flicked saltines to spiraling gulls, luring them closer in the hope that their raucous chatter would drown Zvi out. "Not in you, your business, or your personal life. Not even in what you have found out. New York does not belong to us."

"You speak with such conviction."

"That is because I am sure."

"You are?"

Judith finally turned to face Zvi, looking at him as she would a burn victim, directly eye to eye to avoid distraction by the damage inflicted on his once-youthful face. Pressure-cooker aging had turned him into a chapped and flaking "old man" of 39 going on 65. Judith almost felt sorry for him, but stopped herself because if Zvi got wind of what she was thinking, he would shamelessly use it as a crowbar to gain an edge.

"Look," she said patiently, "nothing has been uncovered to indicate that the Times Square bombing was a hate crime directed against Jews, which has always been a prerequisite for our involvement, *sub rosa* or otherwise. Neither did TransPac 117 fit our bill, based on the particulars that have emerged. New York is an American city, and what happens there falls under the province of American law enforcement. This matter is not under our jurisdiction; it is under theirs."

"And Los Angeles?"

"The same," she replied, going back to watching the water. "What occurred there is part and parcel of an American problem. I do not work for them. And based upon what was in that letter, I no longer work for you."

"Well, I plan to tell you anyway." Zvi paused, picked up a flat stone, and skipped it across the water. "Whether you listen or not is your choice, of course."

"You know," Judith replied coolly, "I used to hate it when you strung things out. There was a time that I absolutely detested you for jerking me around like a toy poodle on your leash. But not anymore. Trust me when I say that you can wait as long as you want, but you may rest assured that I will be no more interested two hours, two days, or two months from now than I was before you arrived to interrupt my well-deserved peace and quiet. After all, I have not been hermetically removed from the gossip about New York. One does not have to be a master detective to know that something big is in the air. And yet did your phone ring with a call from me?"

"No," Zvi acknowledged.

"Have I shown even one iota of interest in any specifics?"

"Again, no."

"That in itself should tell you how much I care about all of this."

"Normally it would," Zvi admitted, "but what speaks volumes is that you must not have wanted this self-imposed isolation as much as you think. After all, I did know exactly where to find you."

Judith's grin was patently mirthless. "Old habits die hard. The protocols under which I used to work demanded that I check out properly. It was a mistake that I shall not repeat."

"Maybe...maybe not."

"Well, anyway, you are here. And you are too damned practical, go somewhere for nothing...to just waste a visit."

Judith's disappointment was so keenly expressed that Zvi was seriously worried, but only for a moment.

"You do know me well," he said.

"As well as anyone else has so far cared to."

"That is not entirely true."

Judith flashed a glance at the Colibri on her right wrist, blood pressure rising alarmingly when she saw how much jealously guarded personal time had already been wasted in preliminary fencing. But she defused the time bomb she had become, took a deep-breathing 10-count, and forced an uneasy calm upon herself.

"So say your piece," she sighed.

"So the doer was Gunther Prosh. So there; my piece has been said."

Zvi got up to leave, but not before Judith's left arm twined around his right leg and rooted him fast to the breakwater. She looked up anxiously, her body gone Himalaya cold, her head feeling as if it were creaking in crusted rotation on a spine of pure icicle.

"Catface?!"

"Yes," Zvi said noncommittally, while slowly sitting down and happily thinking: Bait taken!

"Absurd!" Judith retorted, quickly and nervously scanning her 360-degree vicinity the way she always did when that hated name fell on her ever-alert ears.

"He signed it, Judith."

"He couldn't have!"

"Still in all, he..."

"What you tell me is physically impossible, unless there is something critical to my personal safety that you are keeping from me. *Are you, Zvi?!"*

"That much of a self-serving bastard I'm not, in spite of what utter fabrications others may have woven. No, this comes out of the Joint Terrorist Task Force's files. A Manx was found. It was on their manifest, but they evidently hadn't had time to connect it...to get the meaning of it. But they will before too long. We can't sit on it forever because we have reciprocal sharing of intelligence. No doubt, one of our goody-goodies will tie that shoelace for them."

"The meaning, Zvi."

"Ah," he sighed theatrically. "Why waste words? You must have already figured it out."

"Sure, but I am fastidious when it comes to forensic confirmation. 'I wonder if' just doesn't cut it."

"The Manx cat...a six-week-old kitten actually..."

The word "kitten" straightened Judith's posture faster

than ice-cap water running down a naked, sun-baked back.

"...A—Its neck had been wrung," Zvi continued. "B—The twist was counterclockwise, and then backward. C—It was dead before the blast. D—You know what that means. On the surface, it would appear that Catface did the deed. Underneath it all, you know what you must do."

"Hit the brakes on this 'must do' business, okay?! Unless you are telling me something less than the absolute truth, there is absolutely no way Catface could have..."

"Exactly! Based on what we know, that's the yin and yang of this yes/no situation."

Zvi reached around behind Judith, swatted away two waddling gulls, and helped himself to half a dozen saltines. The first nibble of thin, salted wafer stung a day-old canker sore, immediately resurrecting bittersweet memories of his lost friend Tahsin Shamaal, recently found hanged in the living room of his Damascus home. Reportedly a suicide due to reasons of failing health, or so said the Baath Party newspapers. Pushing salt into his wounded lip forced away a more painful sadness. Having expressed enough personal grief in his own way, Zvi never hesitated when it was time to move on.

"Yes, Judith, Catface did it—indirectly; but no, he didn't do it directly. Don't you understand? This is the bomber's first mistake, and may very well represent our first break in the case. I am convinced of it."

"*Our* first break?"

"Yes."

"Zvi, I can understand your caring. After all, you are a self-confessed lifer...and so damned self-righteously proud of it...but I still cannot fathom why you think I should care one whit about any of it. After all, this is not our case. It was born and bred overseas, and that is where it belongs. What you should be doing is talking turkey to your strange bedfellows on the other side of the Atlantic."

Zvi reached around behind her and pushed the STOP/EJECT button on her cassette/radio. Just as quickly, Judith slammed the tape door shut, angrily mashed the PLAY button flat, and leaned right and in toward the music.

"I sense that you are fighting me on this, Judith."

"Shalom, Dick Tracy. It is good to see that you are finally receiving the message."

"Why?"

"By now, you should know exactly why. It was all in my report. And also in the letter, which you tore up so arrogantly, prick that you are. Not to worry, though. I have copies of both on my computer. First thing in the morning, you will have another one of each."

"On Shabbat? Judith, I am truly aghast."

"Zvi, please!"

"So it is true that you don't love me anymore?"

Judith gasped in astonishment. She glared indignantly at Zvi before lashing out viciously. *"How dare you?!* You should have your tongue ripped out by rabid hyenas for using that word. You sully its meaning as no other man ever could."

"It has many definitions, Youtka."

"None of which you are in the least familiar with! And don't call me Youtka anymore." Judith spun away. "I don't like it. You make it sound so..."

"What?"

Condescending; patronizing; cheap, she thought angrily. "Never mind what. Just don't call me by that name anymore. I don't have to give you reasons for everything I do. I don't work for you, remember?"

"Officially, you still do, because this resignation you speak of is still not official. Besides, what of this letter you mentioned? I see no letter."

"And even if I did, I do not have to lay out the chapter and verse of everything that is going on inside my head."

"Fair enough. I can accept that. May I have another saltine?"

"Why ask now? You didn't think to ask before."

"And some of your delicious broth?"

"Help yourself."

"This storm I can weather. What I really need is something to fight off your deep freeze."

"Zvi," Judith said impatiently, "being as I am on well-deserved medical leave, we should not even be talking about business at all. So if you have more to say, spit it out. You know," she said, barely stifling a laugh, "I could report you for this transgression. Medical Section would not approve. Imagine that?" she chuckled. "A stain on the great Zvi's illustrious record. The iconic Zvi—besmirched. It would be a small matter for me. Tale-bearing would cost me nothing, since my career is over."

"Only if you say so."

"As I have been saying all along: I do."

"'I do.' Hmmm. To me, that sounds like a wedding vow."

"Once again, because you have not been listening, I am telling you that I am finished."

"Are you afraid, Judith?"

"At times, more than you will ever know, but not about what you think."

"Being afraid is no sin. Only stupid people are unafraid, and they do not last long in our line of work."

"Zvi, your best mental mechanics can torque my lug nuts the week after next. I'll even pay to have it done myself after separation from service is completed. But for now, and just so this trip out will not have been such a total loss for you, what is so important that you have to worsen an already climatically miserable day?"

Zvi leapt eagerly for the opening.

"Judith, we know for a fact that Gunther Prosh couldn't have done it. *But Prosh may know who did!* He may have some idea who used his signature. The keys to the other bombings? Those signatures? We have connected them to groups, foreign groups, but never to people, never to individuals, never one as unique as the man whose name was put to the Times Square bombing."

Judith swept the sea with her binoculars. She gave no indication of having heard a word Zvi had said.

"Catface was always the odd man out in that regard. He always worked strictly alone. His support system was his own wits, which you more than matched before taking him down. But that, too, works to our advantage. Because Catface was so secretive in his operations, how would anyone know if he dropped out of sight? The answer is: they wouldn't...because until you came along, Catface was never really in sight to begin with."

"All of what you have said so far means very little."

Very little. Good, Zvi thought, prayerfully grateful that Judith had not said: "nothing."

"Don't you see?!" Zvi asked, urging Judith's understanding. "There is someone out there who used Catface's signature, in the hope of focusing blame and attention on Catface, and thereby diverting attention from himself and enjoying the attendant free rein. But this person had no reason to know that Catface had been out of circulation, that this recent quiet period had been more than just a normal hiatus from the business of mass murder."

"Catface has been out of play for a long time, Zvi. Black Leopard knew, thanks to Avraham Ya'rok. Someone else likely purchased that information. Others certainly know by now."

"But the one we want doesn't! That's our opening."

Judith scanned the decks of the listing yacht, still wallowing slightly but finally under safe tow. The Dauphin and the patrol boat moved away in tandem, expanding their circular reconnaissance seaward. The CH-53 shepherded the towed vessel from 300 feet up and 1,200 feet back from where merrymaking tourists danced with delight while gorging themselves on bagels, sweet rolls, and coffee. Zvi's chopper now hovered about 200 yards offshore and low over the water, like a sting-wagging wasp with its sights set on a tarantula.

Judith found herself almost wishing that the yacht would indeed capsize, so that all the idiots aboard, especially the captain, would be taught life's grim lesson about the stupidity of taking Mother Nature for granted.

"Are you listening?" Zvi asked, his query perilously close to little-boy whine. The rain was starting again, and he pulled the collar of his blue-black pea jacket tight around his neck. "This is important."

"Or you would not be here ruining my time off. Go on. You have perhaps forty-five seconds and maybe half an ear."

"At last, we have finally connected at least part of all that has happened to a person, and we know who that person is not. Which is not as important in its own way as knowing who that person is, I grant you. But it is not Catface, no matter what the signature was."

"Perhaps someone better than him."

"Hardly likely."

"Sounds like you might be running from the truth."

"Is that what you're running from?"

"What chases me is none of your concern," Judith shot back. "What matters is that a terrorist bomber or a Wild West gunslinger, no one stays on top forever. It looks as if Catface has been superseded."

"Judith, the blame for the other bombings? That, too, was probably bogus..."

"*Probably?!* Talk about a tremendous leap of faith."

"...and meticulously laid out so as to misdirect us as well. While everyone is looking for terrorist groups, they should have been laying out traps and snares for the lone wolf."

"Considering that he's not running with a pack, which is always more visible, he will be harder to isolate and neutralize."

"Initially, yes. But easier to profile in the singular."

"It will still take a very long time."

"Not with you working it."

"Which is very unlikely, but continue on so that we may get this unpleasantness behind us."

"Thank you."

Thank you? she thought. *He must really want this very badly to be so oddly polite. Such courtesy usually lay smothered by deep dust at the bottom of his interpersonal-skills inventory.*

"Okay," Zvi said, rubbing gloved hands together as if hopeful of generating additional warmth. "So now we have at least one kernel of hard intelligence. From behind all the smoke wafting past us, we can see the glimmer of at least one factual constant."

"You still have not told me why you're bound and determined to keep us waist-deep in this. It is not our problem. It is an American problem. Let them solve it. Give them what you know; they'll be able to figure out the rest."

"You think so?"

"Trust me, there are some brains in their barracks," Judith said, thinking again of Michael and how their shared tenderness was the sole curative for what ailed her. Only the soothing comfort of his all-encompassing warmth could fully expunge this current unpleasantness.

Marry him!

YES!

Please let him ask again! I will!

BUT HE WON'T!

But I would!

Zvi vaporized that rainbow bubble with, "It might mean giving them Catface. Would you agree to that?"

"Why even bother to ask?" she snapped, irritated by Zvi's clumsy probes. "What say would I have in the matter?"

"The question was: Would you agree to it? Could you rest easy if the transfer of Catface to American custody became part of the ultimate outcome?"

"You know that I never could."

"Which is why it is still at least partially our problem. We can narrow the field by probably eliminating those other groups. At least we know definitely that Catface did not do New York, because we have Catface and we know where that man has been for the past few years."

"*Man?* How dare you classify him in my presence? What you have is an animal!" Judith screamed, turning furiously on Zvi to better focus her unrestrained outrage. "In retrospect, I probably should have gunned him down in Frankfurt."

"Those were not your orders."

"Be that as it may, I was too weak-kneed morally to take direct action myself. But you?" Judith's brief laugh was heartily sardonic. "Ethical considerations don't keep you awake nights. You never should have brought him back alive. No one knew that we had him; no one would have known if he had been erased."

"We felt there was much to learn from him."

"The last I heard, all he has taught you was how to increase the size of our national debt."

"His incarceration doesn't cost all that much."

"Any price at all is too high to pay."

"We have our committee rules and bureaucratic procedures, Judith. We also have a court system..."

"Which has grown rusty with disuse in this case, Mr. Court System, so please spare me the sanctimonious lectures you are known to recite at the drop of a shekel."

"Preparing a proper case takes time."

"Not as much time as you have had him. How long have you held him in that little incognito cage of his...without bail and without formally charging him?"

"As you said yourself, he is an animal."

"Thank you!"

"Yet even still, we could not have simply murdered him," Zvi said, his tone almost wistfully respectful. "He is, after all, brilliant..."

"Zvi, you are beginning to nauseate me. The more repulsed I am, the less well I hear."

"We would know...

"We would know only that his reign of terror would never again be unleashed against our people!" Judith spat angrily. "What more would you have to...know?"

"This person in our custody...

"Bargaining chip, you mean."

"He may be the key to unlocking this for us. There is a very big chance, one which is critically important now." And then Zvi let her have it full in the face with: "Which is why you must go and talk to him."

"And risk getting caught up again in that mind trap?! No! Absolutely not! What you ask is completely out of the question."

"You have a duty to this nation."

"You know damn well what you can do with your duty!" Judith picked up a fistful of rocks and threw them hard into the sea, where they splashed in like a ragged burst of bullets. "Retirees as young as myself have no duty except to take care of themselves by finding a halfway decent day job and perhaps a reasonably dependable car. Being fortunate enough to have the latter, the former should not present much of a problem. I have not been in service with you long enough to warrant a pension. Therefore, my departure will represent even less of a drain on your precious budgetary resources than you first calculated."

"Since I never took your retirement seriously, I never ventured into that particular area of accounting."

"That I find hard to believe."

"Then at least do it for the sake of your heritage."

"Strike two, Zvi." Judith ran her fingers through wind-tousled hair. "What you mean is that I should do it for the sake of your selfishness. What do you plan to trade to the Americans? What is on the table that will be exchanged for what I might be able to extract from that beast."

"Judith, this request comes from farther up our chain of command."

"Well, that is hardly news," she scoffed. "When local appeals fail, it always falls to the mythical higher authority."

"In addition to all else I have said, you must clearly appreciate the fact that I am here as an emissary of the prime minister," Zvi said seriously, hunching lower in the teeth of moaning seaside wind. "He is worried, as am I, that this new menace may soon be turned against us...in ways that will cost us more than Catface ever did."

"You have no proof of that."

"If he has imitated Catface's signature, as we know he has, then he may very well soon imitate Catface's deeds."

"American security is just another way of saying 'sieve.'

Perhaps that is why they have fallen such an easy prey. You have no confirmation that he will go global and turn our way."

"Dare we wait until things explode in the faces of innocents?" Zvi asked pointedly. "I thought we'd had enough of that in Catface's last go-round. In any case, proof comes only after the fact, which for us means burying our dead, healing our wounded, and fitting children with artificial limbs. Surely you know how traumatic that can be."

"That was a very low blow," she spat contemptuously. "And from you of all people, the ramrod who is always telling me not to take this business personally."

"These unique circumstances demand that you make an exception to that usually inviolate rule. Judith, there is every likelihood that this unpleasantness will come home to roost in ways that will make you rue the day you turned your back on those needing you so desperately now."

Begging would be too strong a word for Zvi.

"It sounds as if you are pleading," she said.

"That's because I am!"

Zvi's acknowledgment only strengthened Judith's staunchness, making her head shake all the more defiantly. "You have others. Send in your real men," she sneered. "Let them try to muck their way through the quagmire of that maniac's mental maze."

"We've tried all kinds of feelers..."

"Medicinal as well as human, no doubt."

"Yes—both—and long enough to finally accept the fact that neither will ever work; however, Catface has told us on several occasions that he will talk to you, and you alone. Gleizer was right in that regard. There is none as good as you. We both know that."

"Stop stroking me, Zvi. I am not buying into your bullshit, no matter how fragrant the flattery with which you package it."

"Judith, there is something special about you and Catface..."

"Don't remind me of that, you bastard! I am out of it! Leave me

alone!"

"Now it is you who are asking the impossible."

"He gets to me, Zvi. You know it, and I know it, but worst of all, *he* knows it. I cannot risk being drawn in again."

"All of which sounds rather self-serving..."

"Because it is! And I am not ashamed to admit it. On the other hand, I will suffer no crisis of conscience since I will no longer be accepting your paychecks."

"Judith, only you can do this. After all, you managed it before."

"Which is why it would be insane for me to push my luck now! That is why I categorically refuse. And you cannot make me. What are you going to do, drum me out of the corps? That would play right into my hands, and you would become the manipulated, instead of the manipulator. I want out anyway," Judith said emphatically, her voice rising over the crash of waves against the breakwater rock. "You have no power over me."

The tide was coming in, the soup was gone, and vintage creeps used her knocking knees like hands on bongos, pounding home echoes of vast internal emptiness.

"Judith, in the depths of your heart you truly know why going one-on-one with Catface is something that you absolutely must do."

And I do know, damn Zvi to hell, she thought angrily. *I do know.*

Judith fought back tears while silently auditing the unique qualifications that made her the only candidate for this distasteful assignment. But damned if she'd give Zvi the satisfaction of seeing her cry. Two blinks stopped the tears, the slight residue of their fleeting existence barely noticeable only as the tracery of dried salt, indistinguishable from the windblown spray of increasingly turbulent sea.

"As long as he remained alive, you must have known it might come to this someday," Zvi said, kneeling next to Judith and squeezing her shoulder.

"The hell I did!" she shouted, shrugging him off violently

though not entirely convincingly. *"Zvi, please!* Don't you think that I have had enough?" she asked, immediately, while deeply regretting the poor choice of words that had just thrown her fate into his eagerly scheming hands. After so successfully winding her up, there was no question about which way she'd go when released.

Zvi grinned contentedly behind Judith's back, thankful that she couldn't see his self-satisfied smile. *Done deed,* he thought happily. Then, efficiently businesslike once more, he stood up, pulled out his two-way radio, and fired off a quick message. Even before he finished speaking, the helicopter that had been hovering perfectly motionless offshore started moving rapidly forward, whipping up foam and sand as it came toward them.

"Check in with Optics on your way over," Zvi said, ducking an onrushing landing skid with a muffled curse. "Our illustrious Mister Marcus has something you'll need to take with you."

"Clean out your ears the next time you shower. Didn't you hear me? *I said no! I am not going!"*

"You're going," Zvi said confidently, "and that's that. Arrangements have already been made."

"They can be canceled," she said hopefully, knowing there was little chance of it.

"They won't be," Zvi replied evenly.

He reached into his shirt pocket, pulled out a pack of cigarettes, and leaned away from the chopper's rotor wash as he lit two and passed one over. Judith took a drag, coughed out the tasteless smoke, then tossed the cigarette down the breakwater where it lay smoking only for a moment before an incoming wave killed it. Saltwater splashed them both, making Zvi shiver in spite of himself.

"Surf's up," he said.

"No need to remind me," Judith whispered morosely.

She stood up slowly, dusted the seat of her damp jeans, and gazed out across the harbor. With the yacht now safely lashed tight to the dockside, the babysitting CH-53 turned south for home. Judith sadly watched the big helicopter vanish in low-hanging scud, as if hidden in the vast recesses of *chuff-chuffing* olive-drab aircraft were answers that might unhook her, although there was no way of telling for sure.

Zvi put on goggles and handed Judith a pair. She pulled the strap down the back of her neck but left the eyepieces riding high above her forehead.

"You want a ride back in?"

Judith shook her head. "I need to be alone for a while."

"Don't be too long," Zvi said, brazenly self-confident now that he was convinced Judith was aimed in the right direction. "If it's any consolation..."

"Somehow I doubt that it will be."

"...remember that this is a one-shot deal. We won't be able to keep the Manx link quiet forever. It's bound to leak out sooner or later, and then chances are we'll lose him anyway. So either way, you'll be out of it after this."

"Sure."

Zvi walked rapidly toward his transportation. "Oh, and report directly back to me when you're through," he shouted over his shoulder before crouch-walking under the rotors of the Bell 212 just landed. "Absolutely no one else."

"Not even Gleizer?" she shouted innocently, knowing it would ignite his explosively overreactive temper.

"Especially not Gleizer!" Zvi blazed, straightening up and waving an angry fist perilously close to scything the main rotor. "Don't even think about giving that S.O.B. the time of day. If he tries to contact you, you are permanently unavailable...to him and to everyone except me. I don't want any repeats of what happened."

At first laughing at the rise she had gotten out of Zvi, Judith became deadly serious once more. "But you said that you got Avraham. You did, didn't you?"

"Yeah!" Zvi shouted curtly, legs dangling from the helicopter's open doorway, "We nailed the bastard all right, but you can never be sure there's not another termite tunnel in the

woodwork ready to pop out anywhere."

"What about Gleizer?"

"It wasn't TransPac he was interested in. Gleizer was just using you as a flare pot to smoke out Avraham. Because he knew that you two had a history. Other than that, he's clean as a brand-new agora."

In spite of what she'd been through, Judith wondered which one—the Turncoat or the Butcher—had presented the greater danger. Rationally, she knew that the former had put her in greater peril, but that didn't make the latter any less of a man to be reckoned with.

Zvi was calling to her again. "Look, you're more than welcome to come along with me. We can send someone to pick up your vehicle later."

"No thanks," she said, whirling the goggles over her head like David's sling before flinging them into the sea as a last act of defiance.

"Shame on you for wasting such hard-won government assets," Zvi chided loudly, but his voice was completely flat, lacking either the faintest dusting of humor or the slightest trace of halfhearted discipline.

Judith immediately turned her back on Zvi's takeoff, but he watched her during ascension and departure...until the fiercely independent woman upon whom he was depending so heavily shrank to an anonymous pellet no larger than the variegated stones lining the long, angled arm of the Haifa Port breakwater.

Briefings. Classes. Rehearsals. Drill, drill, drill...train, train, train... then do it again until the novel became ingrained second nature.

Mitzi in Optics directed Judith to Building 4, Room E-2 at the Krakauer Institute. After a credentials check, she was given a single-use plastic card permitting elevator access to Subbasement 5. At the east end of SCUD-proof, cinder-block corridor, at a post manned by an armed sentry and a bored sergeant, Judith underwent the obligatory palm print/fingerprint laser scan, then impatiently pushed her way through two swinging doors and into an exact replica of the room her compatriots laughingly called "The Scratching Post."

Judith had seen Catface's prison cell only once, before the terrorist himself had been brought in, so as to be reassured that once confined there her nemesis would never make good on his sworn promise to track her down and share with her his bragged-about expertise in Far Eastern lovemaking.

But this room was different, smelling as it did of carnations, gardenias, lilacs, and 14 other species of hydroponic flowers growing in brightly colored tanks along walls with picture windows opening out onto surprisingly in-depth murals of rolling Kansas prairie. The beige, low-key laboratory ran like clockwork under the intense, bespectacled and unchallenged authority of Mister Marcus, who was as proudly sloppy as the R&D facility was stickpin neat.

A flimsy-limbed bean pole capped by horn-rimmed glasses and an unruly mop of bunny-brown hair, Mister Marcus held despotic sway in a badly wrinkled, white laboratory coat, patched Guess jeans, "Beach Boys Forever" T-shirt, and *huaraches.* Mister Marcus, as he insisted on being called (the "Mister" having to be spelled out in memos, else no response would be forthcoming), wasted no time unleashing the harangue he liked to think of as personal training.

"Right! Let's get on with it, shall we? The cell in which Catface is housed is one hundred square meters. Just like this one."

"An exact duplicate."

"Precisely," Mister Marcus said. "One third of Catface's box is demarcated by lengthwise bars separating his living space from the rest of the room. That leaves two-thirds of one hundred square meters in which you can get yourself into very serious trouble unless you follow my instructions precisely to the letter."

"I understand."

"Highly unlikely," Mister Marcus sniffed with pompous disdain. "To continue, Catface is an inveterate pacer, which means he roams incessantly from dawn to dusk, stopping only for less than four hours' sleep a night." Almost as an afterthought, Mister Marcus added: "When receiving religious counsel, he stops midway down the length of the bars."

"In the middle?"

"Precisely in the middle."

"Wait a minute!"

"Yes, what, what?!" Mister Marcus huffed impatiently.

"Did you say religious counsel?!"

"To save his eternal soul," Mister Marcus murmured, blue eyes gazing upward under a deeply furrowed brow.

"You allow him civilian visitors?!"

"Not me personally. However, visitation rights cannot be denied, being as he is a man in search of his God."

"Yeah, that I believe," Judith huffed.

"It would be against all of our moral and ethical strictures to deny such a quest."

"I see."

"No, you don't, not really," Mister Marcus remarked, skirting Judith's sarcasm. "He promised that he would talk honestly and openly with us about certain matters past and present if we permitted him to, as he put it, 'seeketh after the Lord.'"

"And has he?"

"Episcopalian, Protestant and Shaker teachings gave way to Old World Christian," Mister Marcus rambled, "although he flirted with Greek and Russian Orthodoxy, Islam, Christian Science, Anglicanism and Augustana Evangelical Lutheran, as well as fire-and-brimstone Southern Baptist. It's a real *melange* of religious persuasion."

"And you bit on that?"

"I certainly did not!" Mister Marcus exclaimed with self-righteous indignation. *"Oh, no!* No, no, no. It wasn't my decision, but that of others willing to trade the innocuous for critically important information."

"Nothing about Catface is innocuous. He is always 'on.'"

"Agreed! But now back on track with me, if you would be

so kind. After outfitting here, you must be prepared to enter his room with your eyes closed..."

"With my eyes closed?"

"Yes. *And please don't interrupt!* You will have to walk precisely fifty meters, still with your eyes closed. Next will be a ninety-degree turn to your right, immediately followed by an advance of no more than twenty-five meters in the direction you have turned. All of this must be done casually and comfortably."

"As if my eyes were open."

"Right."

"But they will not be."

"Right again. They will not be open. In the beginning of the exercise, they will be closed."

"Closed."

"Precisely. *Closed!* Now stop playing Pol Parrot and let me continue. *Yes?!*"

"Go on."

"You must keep your eyes closed until you ask him your one specific question. Then, and only then, are you to open your eyes and look directly into his. Catface is precisely fifteen centimeters taller than you, which means that from the distance at which you stop, you must raise your eyes precisely seven degrees from perfectly straight and level. You must train yourself to do that. Train, train, train. Drill, drill, drill. Train and drill; drill and train. Again and again and again. And then repeat it again. Over and over, as many times as necessary, until all of your movements are measured and precisely right."

"And why must my eyes be closed?"

"Because of these," Mister Marcus said, handing her a clear plastic case holding what looked like a pair of stylish, slightly tinted Serengeti Drivers.

"Sunglasses?"

"As far removed from common, drugstore sunglasses as an American Corvette is from a Lada Priora. Our specialists precisely rearranged the molecular structure of common Saran Wrap, rewarding us with a most interesting effect."

Judith's fumbling with the case's clasp triggered frantic, hand-waving yells of: *"No!* Don't open it yet. First of all, go sit down at that table in the far corner, which has been bolted to the floor for reasons you will understand at some point this afternoon, if we can only get on with this," Mister Marcus huffed. "Now then. Once safely seated, and after some practice, you will put on the glasses while still keeping your eyes closed. And heed this advice: Before opening your eyes, make sure that you're tightly holding the edges of the table. Now, let's not take all day with this. *Go on!* Don't keep me in suspense. *Go over there and sit down!"*

Mister Marcus fidgeted impatiently until Judith was seated in the metal folding chair on the far side of a small bridge table.

"Now, even before you put on those glasses, I want you to memorize my position across the room here. Rehearsal first. See where my face is? Good. Now close your eyes."

Judith obeyed.

"Now open them. Were you looking directly at my face?"

Judith nodded.

"On the first try?" the restless scientist asked skeptically.

"Yes, I..."

"I find that very hard to believe."

"There is just..."

"Are you lying to Mister Marcus? You are, aren't you?"

Judith shook her head.

"Mister Marcus does not like people who lie in order to speed up the process."

"Uh...let me try it a few times. Just to be sure."

"I love catching a fibber."

Mister Marcus coughed a laugh into a bitten-knuckle fist, then waited in sandal-tapping impatience until Judith went through eight dry runs.

"Ready, Mister Marcus."

"Good. Now I shall test you. Keeping your head in that position and remembering precisely where I am, close your eyes. *Now open! Close! Open! Close! Open!* Did you see my face first each time?"

"Yes."

"Good. Now lock your head rigidly in position. And without moving your head even in the slightest, close your eyes, keep them closed, and put on the glasses. Then hold on." After Judith had done so, Mr. Marcus said, "Ready? Now open your eyes."

Judith was immediately thankful for the advice about hanging on tight. Even so, she shied back involuntarily as her instructor's zoomed-in face blew up to movie-screen size. More importantly, having followed his directions carefully, she was focused in so tightly that she saw more than his face. She saw...

"That's right!" Mister Marcus shouted gleefully. "My eyes. *Superb!* You do catch on fast, which is good...very good. Now back to my eyes. Remain focused on them. See how they change? Tell me precisely what you see from across the room?"

"I can see that..."

"Note how the pupils narrow as I incline my face slightly up toward the light?" Mister Marcus interrupted. "That is what you will be looking for. Pupil movement. You will know at once if your subject is worth bothering with further. If pupillary diameter doesn't change, you will know that he is a dry well, which will save you from wasting time trying to dig information out of him." After pulling each earlobe once as if to jog his memory, Mister Marcus said, "Thine eyes do bring all thy mysteries to light; all truth is told, hiding nothing from my sight."

"Ancient proverb?"

"Nah," Mister Marcus laughed behind an exaggerated wink. "Made it up myself. Just for you."

"I'm flattered."

"As well you should be."

"These lenses. Are they..."

"Extremely fragile, as you may well imagine. *No!"* Mister Marcus screamed. "Don't ever touch them. It's the warmth of human skin, you see, and its attendant surface oil. The plastic film is so thin that it turns liquid under the slightest touch. We're working overtime on a hardening agent, but no luck so far.

"Now practice, Judith," he said emphatically. "Practice without the glasses and with your eyes closed. Practice until you can casually walk into this room with your eyes shut. Practice until you can also turn to your right and stop precisely halfway to the bars...still safely out of his reach and with your legs slightly apart, toes pointed outward just a bit. I will have my assistant come in to measure your stride. We will arrive at an average in order to simplify your calculations."

"You seem to have seen to everything."

"'Seen' to everything. *Excellent!*" Mister Marcus applauded approvingly. "I so thoroughly enjoy good wordplay. Actually, there is one further subject I should touch on briefly, and that is the matter of RTFs: real-time factors. There will be some real-time factors that are impossible to elucidate fully here because this is an antiseptic training ground. Just be aware that they exist..."

"Real-time factors?"

"...and be on guard against them," Mister Marcus said. "Be of clear mind, of true heart, and—most importantly of all—stay on your toes! The less you see, the more you will have to depend on hearing and your sense of smell. Touch, of course, is out of the question. Incidentally, I might remind you that the loss of one sense is compensated for by increased strength of the others."

"I was quite aware of that."

"No doubt you were. Unfortunately, such compensation only occurs over a period of time, which you will have precious little of."

"That is why the practice..."

"Yes, of course, that is why the practice." Mister Marcus pushed on with his lecture. "Now, then. When the time comes, ask your question, open your eyes, and watch him carefully. You will have perhaps one shot at that. Afterward, I suspect that you, like our other testers, will become extremely dizzy. You run the very real risk of falling over, actually kissing concrete, as it were, because your perspective will be so skewed that it will take all of your self-discipline not to jump back immediately. That is why you absolutely must make a point of standing precisely with your legs apart, toes pointed outward just a bit, and with one foot slightly behind the other in order to increase your fore-and-aft stability."

"Toes pointed outward just a bit, and..."

"And that is also why you must practice so that you can achieve success on the first try, which very likely will be your only try because a person of Catface's antsy suspicion and intellectual prowess is unlikely to long remain under a microscope even as creative as this."

Damn your obeisance to that animal's intelligence, Judith seethed silently.

"Now over to the door with you, and practice!" Mister Marcus urged emphatically, slamming right fist into left palm as if marking the cadence of martial music. "Practice-practice-practice. Again and again and again. *Practice, practice, practice!"*

Makes perfect, Judith thought.

To Be Continued…

The story continues…

Alan L. Weinstein was born in the Bronx, New York, and attended De Witt Clinton High School, graduating in 1964. After high school, he attended The American University in Washington, D.C., where he earned a bachelor's degree in journalism and a master's degree in communication. After relocating to Phoenix, Arizona, Alan became a corporate publications specialist, while continuing to write on the side. In addition to "The Manx Dossier," he has authored a semi-autobiographical novel, two screenplays, and one novella. From time to time, Alan dabbles in creative photography, often shooting expired slide film (and having it cross-processed) using classic cameras from the 60s and 70s, which he calls "old iron." Alan drives a 23-year-old Toyota Tacoma Prerunner, and is fond of saying, "If it ain't broke, why sell it?" Other pastimes include watching YouTube videos and staying abreast of current events in the hopes of cobbling up another conspiratorial work akin to what he's already written.

www.ingramcontent.com/pod-product-compliance
Lightning Source LLC
LaVergne TN
LVHW090548110826
845146LV00001B/64

* 9 7 9 8 8 9 1 2 6 5 2 5 7 *